5.6/5.0

P9-ECX-479

DISCARD

The
JEDERA
Adventure

LLOYD ALEXANDER

PUFFIN BOOKS

PUFFIN BOOKS
Published by the Penguin Group
Penguin Putnam Books for Young Readers,
345 Hudson Street, New York, New York 10014, U.S.A.
Penguin Books Ltd, 27 Wrights Lane, London W8 5TZ, England
Penguin Books Australia Ltd, Ringwood, Victoria, Australia
Penguin Books Canada Ltd, 10 Alcorn Avenue, Toronto, Ontario, Canada M4V 3B2
Penguin Books (N.Z.) Ltd, 182-190 Wairau Road, Auckland 10, New Zealand

Penguin Books Ltd, Registered Offices: Harmondsworth, Middlesex, England

First published in the United States of America by E. P. Dutton,
a division of Penguin Books USA Inc., 1989
Published by Puffin Books,
a division of Penguin Putnam Books for Young Readers, 2001

1 3 5 7 9 10 8 6 4 2

THE LIBRARY OF CONGRESS HAS CATALOGED THE E. P. DUTTON EDITION AS FOLLOWS:
Alexander, Lloyd.
The Jedera adventure / by Lloyd Alexander.—1st ed.
p.   cm.
Summary: The further adventures of Vesper Holly and her faithful guardian Brinnie
as they travel to the remote country of Jedera where they brave many dangers
trying to return a valuable book borrowed many years ago by Vesper's father.
ISBN 0-525-44481-5
[1. Adventure and adventurers—Fiction. 2. Deserts—Fiction.
3. Middle East—Fiction.] I. Title.
PZ7.A3774Je 1989 [Fic]—dc19 88-38865 CIP AC

Puffin Books ISBN 0-14-131238-6

Printed in the United States of America

for all fond traveling companions

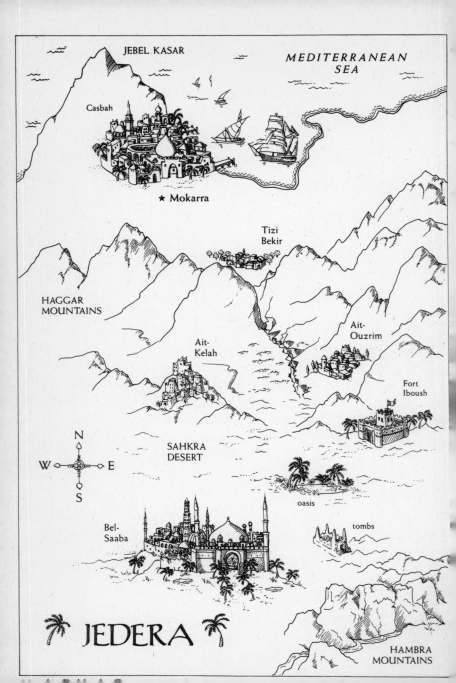

1

Miss Vesper Holly believes in keeping promises. Sometimes I wish she did not.

"Brinnie, what if somebody borrows a book and forgets to give it back?"

When Vesper asks one question, she usually has a few others in mind. But I had spent all a spring afternoon in 1874 floundering through a swamp of mildewed travel notes, and I welcomed the interruption.

"Dear girl, it must be returned, no matter what the circumstances. It is a sacred obligation."

"I think so, too," said Vesper. "What happened is, I came across this library book and—well, it's overdue."

"Better late than never," I said. "Overdue? How long?"

"A while," said Vesper. "Fifteen years."

"But—but that is unconscionable! Inexcusable, beyond explanation!"

"Father borrowed it."

That was explanation enough. The late Dr. Benjamin

Rittenhouse Holly, my old friend and traveling companion, a brilliant scholar, a fearless adventurer, tended to ignore trivial details. This included overdue library books.

Vesper now produced the object in question. It was a treatise on the curative powers of medicinal herbs, an exquisite little volume handwritten on vellum in ancient Arabic calligraphy. Its age might be eight hundred years; its value, incalculable.

"Do you realize who wrote this?" I could hardly believe my eyes. "The greatest physician of his day. Ibn-Sina—'Avicenna,' as we call him. A work from his own hand. Priceless!"

"Beautiful." Vesper carefully turned the pages, their margins filled with brightly colored, interlaced patterns. "A real treasure. But I don't suppose we should keep it."

"Certainly not. That would be dishonorable, worse than thievery. As your father's executor," I said, "I take the responsibility for returning it. I shall do so immediately."

"I hoped you would," said Vesper.

"You have my word," I assured her, and went on to suggest that a mere letter of apology would hardly suffice. Embarrassing though it might be after fifteen years of tardiness, I proposed handing such a valuable item personally to the director.

"I should be there, too," said Vesper.

"So you shall. That would be only fitting and proper. We must do so without further delay. Perhaps this very afternoon. The volume no doubt came from some special collection at the Library Company of Philadelphia or the University of Pennsylvania."

"Not exactly."

"Where, then?" I could think of no other institutions apart from Philadelphia's that could boast of possessing such a bibliographic gem. Surely not Harvard.

"Bel-Saaba," said Vesper.

I nearly sprang out of my chair and my skin. "Good heavens, you cannot mean—"

"The Bel-Saaba library," said Vesper. "In Jedera. You must know about it."

What scholar did not? For centuries, the city of Bel-Saaba had been one of North Africa's commercial and cultural centers. Its library was world renowned, a repository for every kind of lore and learning, of ancient texts on mathematics, medicine, astronomy, physics.

Indeed, I knew of Bel-Saaba. But why, I asked, did Vesper suppose the book had come from there?

"I found this between the pages."

She handed me a small sheet of parchment. With her astonishing gift for languages, Vesper is more fluent in Arabic than I am, but I could follow the brief text easily enough. It was a copy of a receipt, dated 1859, specifying the volume's origin and promising—under all manner of solemn vows—to return it; the signature, unmistakably Holly's.

"As you said, Brinnie, it's a sacred obligation. No way around it, we have to go."

I reminded her that Bel-Saaba, at the southernmost border of Jedera, lay beyond a notoriously rugged mountain range and across a disagreeable stretch of desert.

"It is a bit out of the way," admitted Vesper, "but I don't see any other choice."

"The postal service?" It was a feeble suggestion, but the best I could muster. "If we mailed it? Carefully wrapped."

"I doubt that there's local delivery," replied Vesper. "And you did say it should be handed over personally. It can't be all that hard. There must be trade routes. Caravan trails. Plenty of camels."

"Too many." I have had some experience with camels. For contrariness and foul temper, and a disgusting habit of expectorating, the creature is surpassed only by a Philadelphia banker.

Vesper shrugged. For a girl of eighteen, she can assume an air of bland innocence that a riverboat gambler, a rug merchant, or a horse trader would spend a lifetime perfecting.

"Whatever you think best. Still, you did give your word."

"Dear girl," I protested, "that was before I had any notion—"

"It's all right. I understand. A person can't always keep a promise. Not even my dear old Brinnie."

Vesper can be utterly diabolical when she chooses. But at that moment a rescuing angel came into the library: my wife, Mary, summoning us to tea.

I turned to her in joyous hope. Mary had taken over the smooth running of the household a few years previously, when Vesper moved us lock, stock, and barrel—including my beehives and unfinished history of the Etruscans—into her Strafford mansion. Mary and I, Professor Brinton Garrett, were Vesper's guardians. Mary would agree that we could not permit her to undertake the hardship, even danger, of such an enterprise. I quickly explained the circumstances.

Mary frowned and shook her head. "I do not approve of this kind of journey merely for the sake of a book by Ibn-what's-his-name."

I breathed a sigh of relief.

"However," Mary went on, "though I wish you had not, you did make a promise."

"Dear Mary," I exclaimed, "are you, of all people, saying Vesper and I should go camel riding into a howling desert?"

"No. I am only saying, dear Brinnie, that you and I have always believed it our solemn duty to keep promises."

Vesper had already embroiled me in earthquakes, rebellions, and attacks by ferocious hounds; she had saved my life on numerous occasions—after causing me to risk it in the first place. Now she proposed a foolhardy errand in some camel-infested corner of the world.

"When do we start?" I said.

2

Vesper, needless to say, lost no time embarking for Jedera. After a fairly smooth and rapid crossing, we docked in the capital, Mokarra, pink-walled under the granite shadow of Jebel Kasar, and began making the rounds of shipping offices and tourist agencies. My thought was to attach ourselves, for comfort and safety, to a large trading caravan led by an experienced guide.

We first encountered a hard-bitten cameleer in a battered crimson fez. Before Vesper could begin explaining our purpose, he assured us we had luckily come to the right place.

"Here you see the finest guide in all Jedera," he declared. "The prince—no, the king of caravans. I plead for the honor of serving you."

He did, in fact, look willing to transport his grandmother to the moon if the price was right.

"Yes, well," said Vesper, "we want to go—"

"It makes no difference," he broke in. "Wherever you choose, beautiful *anisah*. We can depart this instant for any corner of the world." He laid his hands on his chest and bowed. "I stand ready. My camels paw the ground in impatience. Only name your destination."

"We'd like to go to Bel-Saaba," said Vesper.

He abruptly straightened.

"Shall I waste my time with fools and maniacs?" He waved his arms at us. "Go! Out! Out! You have no dealings with me." He turned away, muttering something uncomplimentary about crazy *roumis,* as the Jederans termed any foreigners.

"I don't think he's much interested," observed Vesper.

We continued on our rounds, meeting with similar reactions, and I began to wonder if this was one library book that would be permanently overdue. At last, we did turn up a caravan leader willing to let us join him. He was expecting a freighter to arrive with a cargo of goods for transport direct to Bel-Saaba.

Vesper, delighted, asked when the ship was due in port. The caravan leader shrugged. He could not be certain. Perhaps within the next two days. Or three. Or four. Who could speak for the winds and tides?

With this, we had to be content. But now, at least assured of transportation, Vesper wished to turn the delay to advantage by sightseeing. We had found accommodations in a *serai,* a sort of inn, or public lodging house, and quite excellent they were: airy chambers, with our own private courtyard and surrounding garden, a sparkling little fountain, a pomegranate tree.

From this quiet haven, we set off across the public square. Vesper has a taste for commotion, and it was more than satisfied. For myself, I expected to go deaf at any moment. In addition to vendors hawking spicy kabobs, candied rose leaves, and steaming pilaf, drummers pounded away, flute players shrilled, street singers gargled and warbled, and everyone else seemed to be shouting and haggling at the top of their voices. Vesper loved it.

"Brinnie, what's over there?"

She led me into a loose ring of onlookers. What had caught her eye seemed to be a heap of whirling rags—until I realized it had arms and legs, and feet where its head should have been.

Dancing on his hands, spinning like a top, turning somersaults in mid-air, this street performer held Vesper's fascinated attention. She laughed gleefully and tossed down some coins, which he somehow snatched up with his flexible, and grimy, toes. Then, quitting his acrobatics, he squatted cross-legged, popped the coins into his mouth, and an instant later produced them from his nose.

"I want to learn that trick," said Vesper.

But now the fellow began a different performance: borrowing small objects from his audience and tossing them into the air, where they suddenly vanished only to reappear from unlikely areas of his anatomy.

We observed his antics for a while. Vesper, I thought, could spend her time in ways more uplifting than watching a vagabond's sleight of hand. I drew her aside, suggesting a tour of the French colonial administration buildings. Vesper reluctantly started to follow me. A moment later, she halted and turned back at the sound of bloodcurdling yells.

3

Two of the onlookers had seized the fellow by his legs and were vigorously bouncing him up and down. Despite his yelping and struggling, the pair kept on as if determined to take him apart piece by piece.

"That's not part of the act," said Vesper.

She pushed through the knot of bystanders. By now, the vagabond was in danger of a serious beating, for a couple more members of his audience had joined in.

"Let him up!" Vesper cried. "Are you trying to kill him?"

That appeared to be their goal. They might have had good reason, but Vesper did not wait for any explanation. She collared one of the assailants and flung him aside. The other, startled by her unexpected onslaught, loosened his grip. The vagabond collapsed in a heap.

Vesper has a forceful personality in any circumstances. In addition, the sudden arrival of a green-eyed, marmalade-haired *roumi,* impeccably garbed in elegant travel costume, left the audience dumbstruck for a few seconds, after which, they began shouting at her all at once, shaking their fists at the performer and making other gestures of disapproval.

The best I could gather from their racket was that "Maleesh," as they called him, was the thieving offspring of a diseased camel. He had borrowed a ring from one of the bystanders, caused it to vanish—but neglected to make it reappear.

The object of this accusation had meanwhile climbed to his feet. If the Jederans employed scarecrows, he would have qualified as a distinguished member of that profession. He appeared to be young, hardly past his middle twenties. Thus, it was all the more remarkable that he should have become so bedraggled in so few years. Yet, as he addressed Vesper, he did manage to convey a certain tattered dignity.

"That is a lie, *anisah,*" Maleesh declared. "The veritable grandfather of lies. My fingers slipped. The ring fell. I lost it."

Some disagreement followed his protest, and I feared they would start belaboring him again. However, in every corner of the world, the offer of cash has a soothing effect. Vesper, from her purse, gave handsome amounts to the plaintiff and his witnesses. It amounted to straightforward bribery and was immediately effective. The bystanders drifted away.

All but one. A tall, hooded figure cloaked in a burnoose lingered a moment. Perhaps it was my imagination, but he seemed about to approach us. Then, as if thinking better of it, he turned aside and strode into the crowd.

Maleesh, meantime, had thrown himself at Vesper's feet and flung his arms around her ankles.

"*Anisah,* you have saved my life! Daughter of the sun and moon! Oasis of my dismal existence! Angel from the seventh paradise!"

"I wouldn't go all that far," said Vesper.

We were not in the situation or posture for a formal introduction. Vesper, nevertheless, made one. Maleesh transferred his embrace from her ankles to mine.

"Bahrini el-Garra!" he cried, attempting to pronounce my name. "My gratitude, *sidi,* is eternal!"

The fellow was a barnacle with legs. The only thing that made him release his grip on me was Vesper presenting him with a handful of coins.

"May the heavens guide your footsteps," exclaimed Maleesh. "I call down the smile of the universe upon you."

Feeling this was ample thanks, I turned away and drew Vesper along with me. I was proud of her generous, compassionate conduct befitting a true daughter of Philadelphia and treated her to a glass of mint tea.

As we relaxed on the terrace of a refreshment shop, I could have sworn the burnoose-clad figure loitered nearby. I gave it no further thought, for the racket in the square had begun making my head ache, muddling any serious speculation. When Vesper suggested visiting the casbah, I welcomed the chance. This most ancient part of Mokarra supposedly contained the thieves' quarter. Thievery being a stealthy occupation, I hoped the casbah would at least be quiet.

It was not. Troops of urchins raced yelling and whooping through the maze of narrow streets and winding flights of stone steps. Women laughed and gossiped from doorways or open windows. In the local *souk,* or open-air market, hucksters tried to outdo each other in praising their fruits and vegetables.

There was much to capture our attention, but Vesper must have eyes in the back of her head.

"Brinnie," she murmured, "we're being followed."

I had not noticed. But now I turned to glance back, half expecting to see the man in the burnoose. Instead, I glimpsed Maleesh, stalking along some paces behind us.

"He's been on our heels for at least ten minutes."

The fellow was not only a barnacle, he was a leech. Clearly, he saw Vesper as a source of further wealth. I turned on my heel and went to confront him.

"My good sir," I said firmly, "this kind lady has already saved your life. She has also given you money, which you may or may not have deserved. Be satisfied. Charity has its limits."

"I am not a beggar, Sidi Bahrini," replied Maleesh, drawing himself erect. "Have I asked for alms?"

Vesper had come to join me. Maleesh turned to her.

"*Anisah,* you have done all good things for me. You have bound my destiny to yours with a golden chain."

If that were so, I told him, I suggested unlinking the connection and requested him to cease following us.

"I cannot do that. Our fates are joined. So it is written."

He made this pronouncement with such solemn intensity that Vesper could not help grinning at him.

"I don't remember reading that anywhere, Maleesh. Where is it written?"

"Why, *anisah,* it is written in the stars." He gestured upward in the direction of those celestial bodies, though he seemed, instead, to be pointing at a clothesline of multicolored laundry slung between opposite windows.

"I am your servant, your slave," he declared. "So it must be. I am yours to command."

His services, I replied, were not required. Our command was for him to depart. We wished to see no more of him.

"I am still your slave," answered Maleesh. "If my presence burdens you, then I obey your wishes. So be it."

"No—wait a minute," Vesper put in.

By then, however, Maleesh had disappeared around the corner. Vesper hurried after him, but the vagabond must have nipped into one of the alleys and lost himself in the shadows. He had taken my command literally.

"I wanted to ask him how he did that coin trick," said Vesper.

She insisted on searching the adjoining streets, but we saw not a trace of him.

We returned to our lodgings after that. Next morning, we went to the square. Vesper had two objectives: one, to seek news of the vessel carrying cargo for Bel-Saaba; the other, to find Maleesh.

What we found was a disaster.

No sooner had we started for the waterfront than we were caught up in a stream of Mokarrans shouting and racing toward the harbor. Clouds of evil-smelling smoke were rising from the port.

We could not help ourselves, we were borne along in the crowd, pressed and jostled to the dockside. A freighter had caught fire and was blazing out of control.

The vessels moored nearby were hurriedly casting

loose. A couple of feluccas, equipped with oars as well as sail, were rowing seaward; a trim, ocean-going yacht had already given a wide berth to the flaming ship.

The fire must have broken out in the midst of off-loading the cargo. Longshoremen frantically rolled barrels as far out of danger as possible or heaved those beginning to burn into the water, the ship's crew lending a hand. Over all hung a peculiar, stifling reek.

"Kerosene?" Vesper wrinkled her nose.

I had no chance to comment. The onlookers swept her away from me. For a moment, I lost sight of her and forced my way through the crowd, calling her name.

Finally, near the landing stage, I caught a glimpse of her and cried out in alarm. Vesper was struggling in the clutches of two burly sailors.

CHAPTER
❧ 4 ❧

"Brinnie, come on! Hurry!"

Vesper had sighted me; the dear girl's voice rang bravely above the tumult. Shouting encouragement, urging her not to despair, I fought through the crowd, heaving aside the curiosity seekers blocking my way, to fling myself on one of the sailors. I gripped the ruffian in the ninja death lock. The effect would have been devastating had the wretch's neck not been so short and his shoulders so heavily muscled. He grunted in surprise at the ferocity of my attack but shrugged himself loose.

Vesper has always been able to give a good account of herself, even against such powerful odds. Now, to my bewilderment, she was making no attempt at defense or any effort to escape the sailors' clutches. On the contrary, she actually seemed to be trying her best to embrace both of them at the same time.

I had stretched out my arms to renew my assault, only to find my hands caught and pumped up and down, one by each sailor.

"Look who's here," cried Vesper.

I blinked in disbelief at their smoke-blackened features, unable for the life of me to tell one from the other. Their moon-round faces, fringes of grizzled hair, and freckled domes were identical.

"Smiler and Slider." Vesper beamed at them. "Here, of all places, can you imagine?"

I could not. We had last seen the twins—how many thousand miles away?—in El Dorado, working Blazer O'Hara's riverboat. I was doubly astonished. Literally.

"Miss Vesper has it right." Smiler—or Slider—finally released my hand, and his brother did likewise. "Here, of all places."

"And here we'll have to stay," added Slider—or Smiler. "We're aground, sir. Beached, in a manner of speaking."

"Burnt out is the fact of it," added Slider.

"That's their ship," said Vesper. "Or, it used to be."

Our attention had been so caught up by this happy, though startling, reunion with the twins that I had momentarily forgotten the flaming vessel. By this time, there was little of it to remember. Although the crew, I gathered, had escaped unharmed, the freighter had burned to the waterline. Smiler and Slider shaded their pale blue eyes, both gazing with equal dismay at the charred hulk.

"*Our* ship, too," said Vesper. "The one we've been waiting for. The cargo—those barrels are going to Bel-Saaba."

"What's left of them," said Smiler. "That's correct, sir, as I told Miss Vesper. As for when they'll go, there's no guessing. By the time they're inspected and inventoried and claimed for insurance— Slider knows more of the ins and outs of such business than I do."

"Yes, and the captain is likely to be charged with endangering the port," said Slider. "Not to mention all the foreign red tape, a kind you don't find in the States. So, it can stretch out a good long while."

"We'll get along though," said Smiler. "It's times like this when we're all the more grateful to be twins. We keep each other the best of company, and that's a consolation when you're lost in a distant clime."

"You aren't lost," said Vesper. "You're found. First thing, you'll come with us."

Vesper led the twins from the stench and smoke of the port to the calm of the little courtyard. We sat comfortably by the fountain while Vesper asked for news of El Dorado and why Smiler and Slider had left that Central American republic. "Nothing wrong, is there?"

"Far from it," said Smiler. "We're all thriving and prospering. That's the only trouble."

"Old Blazer's retired," Slider added, "and so's the *Libertador*; the boat's past repair. But that Frenchy, de Rochefort—changed his name from Alain to Allano, he's that fond of the Chirican Indians—he fixed up that villain Helvitius's yacht for the river trade. Thanks to you, miss, things have never been better for the tribe. And for him, since he and Suncha tied the wedding knot."

"Slider and I trained a crew of Chiricans for engineers and pilots," continued Smiler. "They turned out better than us. What it came down to was, we hadn't much to do. It's restless-making. So, to occupy our time, as you might say, we took a berth on that freighter."

"And here we are, as you see us," said Slider.

"And Acharro?" asked Vesper. "He's well? He's still chief?"

"Every bit of one," replied Smiler. "He talks of you a lot, Miss Vesper. I'd go so far as to say—"

"Yes, well," broke in Vesper, as her cheeks flushed a little—or perhaps it was the afternoon light, "I think of him, too. But what I'm thinking right now is that we couldn't have run into you at a better time."

She explained our reason for coming to Jedera and her determination to reach Bel-Saaba. "If you'd like to go there with us—"

Here, I reminded her that it could be a long while before we went anywhere. The caravan would be indefinitely, even permanently, delayed.

"That's why I'm glad we ran into you. Why wait to join a caravan? We could have our own.

"If the twins agree," she added, "that's four of us. Safe enough to suit you, Brinnie. And I can certainly read a map."

Anxious though I was to finish my noble duty, to me the scheme was impractical. Vesper, I admitted, could make her way through any ordinary howling wilderness. But the Haggar Mountains, let alone the desert crossing, would be too much even for her remarkable abilities. Furthermore, assembling the necessary pack animals, provisions, tents, and other equipment would present a formidable task.

"That's where you come in," she replied. "Dear old Brinnie, you know you're a genius at organizing things. You'll find all we need in the bazaar. Camels, too, I'd suppose."

Purchasing camels, I protested, was a highly specialized skill. In any case, the twins had not been given the opportunity to express their own views.

"If I can speak for Slider—" Smiler began.

"As you certainly can," put in Slider, clasping his twin warmly by the hand. "We're always of the same mind. Yes, we'll be glad to oblige. We've never had any dealings with camels, outside a zoo, but they can't be crankier than the old *Libertador.*"

" 'Ships of the desert,' as they're called," said Smiler, "and ships is what we know. Square-rigged or four-legged, it should be one and the same."

"Settled, then," declared Vesper. "Brinnie can start tomorrow."

The twins had ceased paying attention. They suddenly leaned their heads together and exchanged a few whispered words.

As Vesper watched, puzzled, the twins stood and stretched, announcing that they felt the simultaneous need to retire to their sleeping quarters.

Slider strolled off in one direction, Smiler in another. The day's happenings had, I feared, been too much of a strain on their minds. Their decision to go along with Vesper's proposal would have been proof enough that they had temporarily taken leave of their senses. I was all the more convinced when they started racing from opposite directions to meet at the pomegranate tree and begin furiously shaking it.

What tumbled out was not a pomegranate.

❧ 5 ❧

Vesper jumped to her feet. "Maleesh!"

The twins, meantime, had laid hold of the vagabond and hauled him before us.

"Do you know him, miss?" said Smiler. "We're sorry. We thought it was an intruder."

"It is," I remarked.

"I have only obeyed Sidi Bahrini's command," said Maleesh, with more aplomb than might be expected from someone who had just been shaken out of a tree. "I did not wish to trouble you with my presence. It is not my fault that these twin moons of the heavens turned their gaze on the pomegranates of my hiding place. But they did well. For now I can do you a service: to warn you that your plan is ill-starred. The worst misfortunes will come from it. So it is written, and so it is."

"So it has been eavesdropped on," I said.

"Let him tell us what he means," Vesper said. "Misfortunes? Why? What's wrong with our plan?"

"First, do not assemble your caravan here," said Maleesh. "Why travel heavy-laden at the start? No, you should go lightly and easily to the gateway of the Haggar, Tizi Bekir. There, you shall buy all you need for the rest of the journey."

Vesper pondered for a moment. "That makes good sense. It's a fine suggestion, Maleesh. Thank you."

"But then, *anisah,* most important: Do not cross the Haggar and the Sahkra desert without a guide. You must have one who knows the turnings and twistings of the trail, who can speak the language of your camels, and who will guard you with his life."

"You're right." Vesper smiled. "You wouldn't, by luck, know such a guide?"

"Not by luck, by destiny," Maleesh corrected. "It is myself. I was born in the Haggar. I know every stone, every grain of desert sand. Did I not tell you our fortunes are linked? I shall be your guide and protector."

Being led through rough country by a street magician whose only demonstrated abilities were dancing on his hands and pulling coins from his nose did not inspire confidence. Vesper, however, had been studying Maleesh with that penetrating glance of hers. Finally, she nodded.

"If you really know the way—all right, we'll give you a try. But," she went on, as Maleesh seemed ready to fling himself around her ankles, "we'll take one step at a time. First, go with Brinnie and buy what we need for a start. We'll see about the rest in Tizi Bekir."

"Lo, it is written in the stars!" cried Maleesh.

I preferred it to be written in soap and water. Before anything else, Maleesh would have to take a bath.

I would be less than honest if I did not admit to occasions when my judgment might have been overhasty and when Vesper's insight proved clearer than my own. Maleesh was such an example. By the time he finished soaking and scrubbing himself, and exchanged his rags for some of my spare garments, he actually attained a modest level of respectability.

If this were not miracle enough, I must give him further credit. In choosing horses for us to ride and pack mules to carry our baggage, as we would not yet need camels, he showed himself to be an excellent, hardheaded bargainer. Since our present supply of clothing would serve us for the time being, he purchased only some burnooses, and those long, hooded robes proved to be as comfortable and practical as any garment in the world.

Thus, leaving the next morning to head south for Tizi Bekir, we indeed traveled lightly and quickly. We passed through a wide countryside of orchards and vineyards and soon came into a sparse, gritty landscape with only the rare stretch of greenery.

Vesper was thoroughly delighted by the efficiency of our little caravan. In this regard, Maleesh further astonished me. From the outset, he took charge of every detail. He chose the most suitable places to halt and organized our campsite, rationed out the water, built cook fires, served our food, and stood watch over us while we slept.

Though Smiler and Slider were not lacking in Yankee ingenuity, Maleesh taught them any number of special tricks in packing and unpacking our supplies, harnessing our animals, and giving the Jederan equivalents of *giddyup* and *whoa*. The twins willingly accepted his authority in such matters and quite happily and comfortably put themselves under his orders.

"We've done our share of traveling," said Smiler, with heartfelt admiration, "but we haven't met a fellow better at his job than Mr. Maleesh. We're glad to have him aboard."

For sailors, the twins proved unexpectedly skillful at riding and handling their mounts, which made Vesper wonder about their previous occupations.

"Why, we've turned our hand to all manner of things," replied Slider in answer to her inquiry on that subject. "Horses, among others."

"And would still be doing so," put in Smiler, "if there hadn't been that unhappy misunderstanding. A judicial disagreement, as you might say. We haven't been in the States since then."

"We get a touch homesick now and again," said Slider, "but we always cheer each other up. That's the blessing of being twins."

Otherwise, the pair chose to remain vague about their previous employments. Maleesh had equally little to say about his own past.

"My village is Ait-Kelah, deep in the Haggar," Maleesh told her. "My tribe, the Beni-Hareet."

"Why didn't you stay?" Vesper asked.

Maleesh ruefully shook his head. "I believed, *anisah,* that my fortune lay not in some narrow village but a great city. And so I went to Mokarra. Woe unto me! I found no fortune, only the scrapings of a bare living, small tricks for even smaller pittances." Then he brightened. "Until now. Lo, *anisah,* it is written. You and I shall prosper together."

"I hope you're right," said Vesper. She pressed him for no further details—except instruction in his coin trick. She and Maleesh practiced at every halt, and she quickly grew adept. What a Philadelphian might have thought of her squatting in the dust, producing coins from her nose, I did not wish to imagine. Fortunately, we met none along the way.

Tizi Bekir—the town bore the same name as the mountain pass—must have been more than a thousand years old. And looked it. The black, jagged heights of the Haggar rose abruptly behind it, but the town itself was as flat as a pancake and considerably drier. It had a jostling, lawless atmosphere not unlike some of our notorious Western frontier settlements, only without the presence of a sheriff to keep order.

Here, Maleesh told us, we would buy the camels we needed. For riding as well as carrying our equipment, he assured us the creatures would be reliable on the most difficult mountain trails as well as in the desert.

Maleesh picked out lodgings in what he judged to be the best *serai,* and he and the twins set about unpacking our gear. Vesper was impatient to see what livestock was available, and so, while Maleesh arranged our temporary living quarters, she and I went off on our own.

"Maleesh will find us when he's done," said Vesper. "We can have a little look around in the meantime."

There was no shortage of camel dealers. At the first place we stopped, however, the animals were clearly in poor condition. We pressed on through the crowd. Vesper halted at a line of ill-tempered beasts tethered in the shade of a canvas awning.

"These look better than the others, certainly," Vesper

said, nimbly avoiding being nipped or kicked. "But— Brinnie, I just don't know. Maleesh is the expert. We'd better wait for him. He can tell if they're fit to carry us to Bel-Saaba."

Just then, from the tail of my eye, I glimpsed what seemed a tall figure I had seen before: the hooded man in Mokarra. This time it was surely not my imagination. Before I could mention this peculiar coincidence to Vesper, the camel trader sidled up to us.

"You are going to Bel-Saaba?"

The proprietor was a heavyset, sharp-eyed fellow with a red fez cocked on the side of his gleaming bald head. Naming himself as Bou-Makari, he took us by the arm and addressed us in low, confidential tones.

"Have my ears deceived me? Truly, is it your intention to go on such a journey? Do you understand the difficulty of your enterprise?"

The first difficulty of our enterprise, I replied, was finding reliable transportation. As Philadelphians, we had little experience in evaluating camels.

"So distant from your home and you choose to go still farther?" Bou-Makari shook his head in wonder and admiration. "You are courageous, you and the lovely *anisah*. The Haggar, the Sahkra, can swallow up lone travelers without a trace."

"We'll manage," said Vesper. "Now, about these camels—"

"Worthless!" Bou-Makari snorted and waved a scornful hand. "It is not in my heart to deceive you. They will not serve your purpose. No, no, even if you begged me, I would not sell you such inferior merchandise.

"I have better stock," he went on, motioning for us to

follow him. "Of such excellence I do not offer them to any common buyers—*pfah,* what do they know of quality! Only for your sake, *anisah,* would I part with a few."

He went rattling on, praising his livestock, declaring that he treasured them as his own children, all the while leading us around the corner and a little way from the bazaar.

"Lazy limbs of a five-legged donkey!"

Bou-Makari addressed this comment to a pair of scruffy young men leaning against the wall of a large *serai* and toying with harness leathers.

"Goods to show," he declared. "The best, you understand."

His assistants fell in after us as we entered a crowded eating room. Bou-Makari indicated that we should pass through it and make our way to the courtyard. We followed him down a covered walkway.

"Odd place for camels," Vesper muttered from the side of her mouth. "All of a sudden, I don't like this. What's he up to?"

"He would hardly attempt to rob us," I assured her. "Not in broad daylight."

"Forget the camels, Brinnie. Let's get out."

Vesper was about to turn around, but her instinct served us too late.

Her words hardly left her lips before Bou-Makari's colleagues sprang upon us from behind. At the same time, the camel trader wheeled and blocked us with his burly arms.

Vesper does not have the temperament to let herself be mauled without raising objections. She kicked furiously in all directions; one of the hirelings yelped in pain, but, despite her efforts, harness leathers were lashed around our wrists. We were hauled roughly along the passageway, down a flight of steps, and flung headlong into a lightless, vile-smelling chamber. The door was slammed and bolted behind us.

"Dear girl," I gasped, "we are not being robbed; we are being kidnapped!"

Vesper wasted no breath in reply, but immediately set about trying to untie my bonds. I attempted to do the same for her. Useless. The knots held fast.

Finally, exhausted, we gave up, and I sank down on the stone floor. The chamber was pitch dark, but Vesper located the door and, from there, inched her way along the walls. No doubt she hoped to find some other exit or even some discarded object that might serve us. Except for the odor, our cell held nothing.

"We have to think of how to get out of here," Vesper said. "The only trouble is, it's impossible."

"Then we have no hope!" I cried. If Vesper admitted defeat, we were surely lost.

"No," said Vesper. "Sooner or later, they'll have to do something with us. Give us food or water. They've kidnapped us, but they can't intend to starve us to death. But they're the ones who'll have to open that door. When they do— Well, I don't know yet. We'll wait and see.

"Don't forget, Brinnie, Bou-Makari thinks we're alone. He doesn't know about Maleesh and the twins. They must be looking for us this very moment."

I could not share her optimism. Though she urged me to rest and conserve my strength, I was unable to follow her advice. My wrists ached, and my heart even more. Vesper stretched out beside me, silent. How long we remained thus, I did not know, for I had lost all track of time.

Indeed, I had lost all hope as well. Vesper had been correct, but only to a limited extent. Eventually, our captors did come for us. If Vesper had contemplated escape at that instant, she had no chance to do so. We were quickly and efficiently dragged from our cellar chamber, hustled up the steps, and shoved into an open courtyard.

"At least we're outdoors again," Vesper whispered. "That's an improvement."

The sun blinded me for a moment. We had, I calculated, suffered a night of captivity, and it was now midmorning. Vesper glanced around in surprise.

"What's all this?" she murmured. "Who are they?"

Some dozen or more men stood about in the courtyard, all of them very richly dressed. I would have guessed them to be merchants or travelers of substance, indeed, of large wealth, judging from the rings on their fingers and the gems in their turbans. My heart rose.

"Gentlemen!" I burst out. "Help us! We are Philadelphians, abducted, held against our will!"

"I don't think they care about that," muttered Vesper.

To my horror, they observed us impassively. Not one of them lifted a finger on our behalf. The disgusting Bou-Makari clapped his hands and urged them to draw closer.

"See for yourselves," he called out. "I spoke truth when I invited you here. Can there be finer merchandise? But only one of you will be rich enough to afford it. Who shall it be?"

Vesper turned to me. "Brinnie, we're not being kidnapped. We're being sold."

"I wonder," Vesper mused, "what's the going price for a *roumi* slave in Tizi Bekir?"

"Sell us?" I burst out. "Impossible! It is against the law!"

As indeed it was. The French had forbidden that abominable trade years before our late lamented President Lincoln had emancipated slaves from their bondage in our freedom-loving Union. To find the vilest of human transactions in a land governed by a republic whose proud motto was Liberty, Equality, Fraternity—no, this went beyond belief.

Nevertheless, Bou-Makari's assistants had hauled out a wooden bench and forced us to mount it. The disgusting camel trader continued to encourage the onlookers.

"Open wide your purses!" he cried. "Be generous in what you offer for this emerald-eyed gazelle, this fairest flower in the garden of beauty. The other one I give you free of charge."

"This is outrageous!" I flung at him. "Intolerable!"

"Brinnie, be quiet," Vesper suggested. "Make a fuss and they'll gag you. Just don't do anything. When we see what we have to deal with, we'll deal with it."

Vesper said no more, but held her head high, her glance unwavering. I tried to follow her example even when a couple of Bou-Makari's customers strolled over to inspect us.

"The maiden alone is worth a thousand gold pieces," remarked one of them, looking Vesper up and down and hardly giving me a moment's observation.

"A thousand?" retorted his bejeweled and ostentatiously dressed companion. "My first bid will be twice that!"

The nauseating Bou-Makari, smelling his fortune already made, broke in.

"Patience, my masters. You shall each have your chance. Let us now begin in proper fashion."

Bou-Makari signaled that the auction was ready to start.

"I offer the first bid."

The voice from the back of the crowd rose no louder than a tone of quiet conversation, but all in the courtyard—including Bou-Makari—fell instantly silent. Bowing deeply, the would-be bidders drew aside, leaving him a clear path.

The individual producing this effect stood a full head taller than any in the courtyard. He walked toward us—rather, he padded like a tiger, with noiseless, loose-limbed strides. Glancing neither left nor right, he paid no attention whatever to the respectful salaams. He seemed used to this kind of reception and took it for granted.

At his side hung a straight, two-edged sword, and slung over his shoulder, a long-barreled musket. A dagger in a leather sheath was bound to his left forearm. In brief, he was a walking arsenal. Yet, even without this array of weapons, he would have been a commanding figure.

"Brinnie," Vesper whispered, "he's blue!"

Blue indeed he was. Stained by the indigo pigments used to dye his belted tunic and trousers, his skin had absorbed their coloration, so that even his hands were blue. His face likewise, as much as could be seen of it; for he wore his blue turban with an end of it veiling most of his features. But it was this veil, more than his complexion, that set him so strikingly apart, as if it hid some unfathomable mystery. I confess that my blood ran a little cold—not only with fear but fascination.

Vesper must have sensed his magnetic force, too. Whoever or whatever he was, she could not take her eyes off him. Nor could anyone else in the courtyard.

For many long moments, he stood silent, his arms folded. He appeared accustomed to looking out across great distances; even when he fixed a searching gaze on Vesper, it was both intense and remote. And altogether inscrutable.

Bou-Makari, meantime, was smiling and salaaming and practically knocking his head in the dust.

The blue stranger gave an almost imperceptible nod. "May I be permitted to name the first price?"

Bou-Makari murmured that it would be an honor.

The man reached into the leather sack at his belt. And brought out one copper coin.

Bou-Makari choked a little.

Our would-be purchaser swung around to face the

crowd. He held up the coin for all to see. His hands were long and slender, surprisingly delicate. They also looked capable of doing highly disagreeable things to people, if necessary.

"This much I offer. Who offers more?"

Dead silence. The blue man waited patiently, eyes going from one face to another. No one moved a muscle, let alone raised the bid.

"Nothing higher? Speak now, once for all."

Bou-Makari's smile had frozen into a yellowish grin as the blue man continued, "What, among all you masters of riches, possessors of treasure, will none bid more than my humble copper coin?" He turned to Bou-Makari. "My price stands, then."

Bou-Makari began opening and closing his mouth in a fishlike manner. Beads of sweat covered his face.

"You seem ill at ease with our bargain." The blue man turned his glance from Bou-Makari to the silent onlookers. "Have I not observed the rule of the marketplace? Does one of you disagree? If so, come forward. Let us discuss the matter."

No one took up his invitation. I could hardly blame them.

"So be it. Judged and accepted by all," the blue man said quietly. "Bring them now to me."

Bou-Makari gave a few stifled wheezes. Whether choking from rage or fear, he was not a happy man. He managed to nod in feeble agreement and gestured to his henchmen, who fell all over themselves in their haste to help us down from the bench.

The blue man tossed his coin into the dust at Bou-Makari's feet and motioned for us to follow him. The crowd fell back to let us pass. Bou-Makari looked daggers, but made no attempt to stop us. Vesper cast him a pleasant smile.

Our owner—as, in the technical sense, he was—led us a little distance away. Satisfied that we were well out of Bou-Makari's reach, Vesper stopped in her tracks.

"You bought us," she said, "but we aren't for sale."

She went on to introduce us, explaining our purpose and the treachery that had put us in the camel dealer's clutches.

"I am An-Jalil," replied our purchaser, his blue veil hiding his expression. "An-Jalil es-Siba."

"I'm sure you'll understand," said Vesper. "In my country, we don't buy and sell people."

"But you are in *my* country," replied An-Jalil. "Yes, the French have outlawed slavery. Yet there are some who disobey our masters. In many ways."

"My good sir," I put in, "we shall gladly reimburse you for your expenses, plus any inconvenience—"

An-Jalil's eyes blazed. "You offer me payment?"

"Forgive Brinnie," Vesper said. "It's nothing against you personally, but—"

The blue man snatched out his dagger so quickly I never saw his hand move, and heard only the terrible hiss of the blade.

CHAPTER

7

What a blessing that it was over quickly, before Vesper so much as blinked. Usually, the dear girl is remarkably nimble, but, in this case, her least movement might have spoiled An-Jalil's aim—with disastrous results. The keen blade merely whispered through the tough leather without even grazing her skin. I shut my eyes and held my breath while he sliced through my own bonds in a single—fortunately accurate—stroke.

"Take your freedom, *anisah.*" An-Jalil sheathed his dagger. He bowed slightly and swept a hand from his heart to his lips and brow.

"Thank you." Vesper gave him her most gracious smile.

"Do not thank me for returning what was already yours," An-Jalil replied. "I make no claim upon you or your companion. Did you believe I would have done so against your will?"

"We didn't mean to offend you," said Vesper, rubbing

her wrists. "It's just that we don't want to be owned. Not by anybody."

"You speak only truth, *anisah.* 'Even the slenderest chains weigh heavy.' So it is written."

" 'I thought myself free until I contemplated the eagle,' " returned Vesper, finishing the quotation. Naturally, she recognized those lines by ar-Ramadi, the illustrious twelfth-century Moorish poet.

An-Jalil's eyes glinted; with surprise or pleasure, I could not judge. Afraid he might launch more verses, I suggested it was unwise to linger in the vicinity.

"Sir," I said, "you have been our benefactor, no doubt at some risk to yourself. But we, too, are still at risk."

"That's right," said Vesper. "Bou-Makari wasn't overjoyed having his merchandise sold off at a bargain price. He'll try to get even."

"He will not trouble you," An-Jalil said.

Given that assurance, Vesper was in no hurry to return to our *serai.* I was. Our narrow escape had left me unnerved. Also, something teased the back of my mind, but I was too muddled to make sense of it.

"My dear sir, we must be on our way," I told him. "I do not know how to express our gratitude. With all respect, if there is any service we might render to you, we shall gladly do what we can."

"Be of service to yourselves," An-Jalil said. "You spoke of journeying to Bel-Saaba? Go not. I warn you against it."

"We won't turn back after we've come this far," said Vesper. "Why? What can you tell us?"

Before An-Jalil could reply, joyful shouts rose from the

top of the street. Maleesh, waving his arms, pelted toward us. Beside him ran Smiler and Slider. A little distance behind marched a detachment of French troops: Foreign Legionnaires in blue coats and white trousers. White cloth havelocks were fitted on their caps to shade their necks from the sun. They carried bayonetted rifles at the ready.

Vesper hurried to meet the twins and Maleesh.

"Safe and sound, are you?" Smiler beamed with delight and relief. "We've been hunting for you since yesterday. You might say we turned the place upside down, in all senses of the word."

"We did a good bit of turning," added Smiler, "and a fair amount of shaking where it seemed called for. But it's Mr. Maleesh who deserves the credit."

Maleesh grinned proudly. "While these twin gazelles of the mountains sought you by strength of their arms, I discovered what had befallen you. By this"—he tapped his ear—"which heard gossip in the bazaar. And this"—he touched his mouth—"to ask a question here and there. I learned of slaves offered only to the richest buyers. One was a chalice of burnished gold set with emeralds and pearls. The other—forgive me, Sidi Bahrini—an old crock. I knew it must be you."

"I was sure you'd find us sooner or later," Vesper said. "Twins, you must have done quite a job of shaking and turning. Maleesh, that was clever of you. Now, here's someone I'd like you to meet."

She turned to present An-Jalil.

He was gone. Our blue benefactor had vanished.

"But—where did he go?" Vesper's face fell. "We hardly thanked him properly."

By now, the French officer had approached us. Saluting, he introduced himself as Colonel Marelle. His men, he explained, had arrived in Tizi Bekir that morning. Maleesh had urged him to form a rescue party.

"It would seem, mademoiselle, that our services were not required."

Colonel Marelle, heavyset, with a sun-blackened face and a scrubby, pepper-and-salt mustache, had the hard-bitten air expected in one of his profession. But he gave Vesper a smile that was half humorous, half ironic. "Alas, the Legion is deprived of the honor of rescuing—how says one in English?—the damsel in distress."

Vesper thanked him nonetheless. I suggested that Colonel Marelle could at least have the honor of arresting the treacherous camel dealer and clapping him in irons immediately.

"I shall do so, of course," Marelle replied, "if you and Mademoiselle Holly insist."

We certainly did insist, I told him. Such an outrage could not go unpunished. Marelle raised a hand.

"Allow me to explain our situation. Come, let us take first a little refreshment. Mademoiselle Holly, you have denied me a rescue. Do not deny me the pleasure of your company."

Vesper gladly accepted. Marelle dismissed his men, and we walked back to the bazaar. Seeing us in safe hands, Maleesh and the twins headed for our quarters, while the colonel led us to a table in one of the open-fronted eating houses. Having nearly been auctioned off as a slave a short while before only put a finer edge on the dear girl's excellent appetite. While she absorbed melon slices and ripe figs, Marelle began:

"We do all possible to stamp out this abominable traffic." He had taken off his cap, revealing gray hair shaven almost to the bone, and leaned back in his chair. "Yet, it persists to some extent in these backlands. Sooner or later, we shall do away with it completely. For the moment, it is the better part of wisdom to look the other way.

"We are few in Jedera. The tribes outnumber us. If they ever cease to squabble among themselves and join together, they will drive us into the sea. Yet, La France desperately requires money. I am not proud to say this, but Jedera is our milk cow—who must be milked very delicately or she will kick the bucket."

"Kick over the bucket," Vesper gently corrected. "Kick the bucket means 'to die.'"

"It comes to the same. So it is my first duty to avoid trouble and not to stir it up or seek it out. It is a practical policy. For myself, I would prefer it if the French were not here at all. But I am an officer. Above all, an officer of the Legion. I command. Also, I obey."

This attitude struck me as unusual. Most of the colonials I had met during my travels set the natives an example of European civilization by brutalizing them. Marelle, as Vesper drew him out a little more, was not usual.

She soon learned that he had been born in Mokarra of a Jederan mother and French father, that he was fluent in all the tribal dialects, and that his devotion to Jedera was as fierce as his devotion to his beloved Legion. He was the sort of fellow who should be a governor-general and seldom is.

When Colonel Marelle finished his account of himself, Vesper told him all that had happened to us. After she described our benefactor, the colonel appeared greatly impressed.

"You have had the rare privilege of meeting a Tawarik, the most ancient and unyielding of all the tribes. Depending on the season, they tent in the Haggar, but prefer to roam the desert. From what you say of him, he was an *eggali,* the noblest caste of knightly warriors."

"His name," said Vesper, "was An-Jalil es-Siba."

Marelle's eyebrows went halfway up his forehead. "An *eggali*? The *amenokal* himself! The veritable chieftain of the Tawarik! Do you understand the word *es-Siba*? It means 'the unsubmitting.' He is well named."

"You know him?" asked Vesper.

"By reputation. I have never seen him. Until now, we have chosen to avoid each other. How do you say it? An agreement between gentlemen. But, recently, I have reports that he hopes to rally the tribes against us. Not only in the mountains but the towns. It is rumored that he was, not long ago, in Mokarra."

"So he was!" I exclaimed. Suddenly it came clear to me. Though without the burnoose, An-Jalil had the same stride, the same bearing. When I told this to Vesper, she gave a perplexed frown.

"Do you think he was following us? Why should he? Was it only a coincidence?"

"I cannot guess his purpose regarding you, mademoiselle," put in the colonel. "As far as it concerns us, he could pose the greatest threat to our authority. Thus, it is my sworn duty to arrest him if possible, shoot him if necessary.

"And yet"—Marelle smiled regretfully—"for myself, I

wish I might meet him face-to-face, man-to-man. He is a worthy opponent, a most gallant enemy."

"For us, he was a gallant friend," said Vesper. "Do you know why he warned us against Bel-Saaba?"

Marelle shook his head. "I have no information. But I have advice. When es-Siba gives a warning, heed it."

Vesper, I could tell from a certain look in her eyes, had no intention of doing so. She let Marelle's comment pass and took up another subject. During his conversation, the colonel had spoken of leading his men to Fort Iboush. Vesper, offhandedly, questioned him about it.

"It is a small fortress," Marelle replied. "We keep a garrison there only as a matter of principle. A question of showing the flag. It is at the edge of the Sahkra. We do not patrol beyond it."

"It's on the way to Bel-Saaba, isn't it?" Vesper asked innocently.

"More or less. Fort Iboush is a little to the east of the pass. As one reaches the desert—" Marelle broke off and gave Vesper a sidelong glance. "Ah, mademoiselle, you try clever tactics on an old soldier. Logic tells me you wish to accompany us. Your charm tells me you intend to persuade me. *Non,* I cannot allow it."

"I should have known I couldn't outmaneuver a Legionnaire." Vesper shrugged. "Too bad. If you can't, you can't. Just for the sake of argument, though, you'll admit we'd be safer traveling with you."

"Unquestionably. Two things, however, make it impossible." Marelle held up one finger. "First, we must be en route within the hour. You are not prepared. You have not sufficient animals or equipment." He raised another finger. "Second, you could not keep up with my troops. You have never seen the Legion on the march? If forced, we go as fast as cavalry; in bad terrain, faster. It is a matter of pride with us."

Vesper, in her turn, raised a finger.

"Point one, suppose Brinnie could get all our equipment together before you leave." She added another finger. "Point two, suppose we could keep up the pace."

"You suppose a great deal," said Marelle.

"Point three," Vesper went on, "suppose we didn't insist on arresting Bou-Makari and just called the matter closed. It seems to me I showed more fingers than you did."

Colonel Marelle laughed in spite of himself. "Mademoiselle Holly, I expected you to assault me with charm. Instead, you wish to conquer by arithmetic. *Très bien,* I challenge you. Meet my conditions and you shall accompany us."

Vesper was correct to the extent that Marelle's troops would be a safe escort. For myself, I would have settled for the arrest of Bou-Makari. With the best will in the world, I could not assemble all we needed in so short a time.

But before any further discussion could take place, we were interrupted by Maleesh dashing up to our table.

"Anisah!" he shouted. "Come and see! Six camels are standing at our gate. With harness, saddles, everything! Chests of clothing, boxes of food, skins of water!"

"Whose are they?" Vesper jumped to her feet. "Can we buy them right now?"

"They are yours!" cried Maleesh. "A gift from the

heavens! No, not the heavens. The boys who brought them said they came from Bou-Makari."

"Take it all back," I ordered, in spite of Vesper's jubilant cry. "We accept nothing from that scoundrel. How does he have the gall to send us a gift? Return everything to him immediately."

"But that cannot be done," replied Maleesh. "I am told that Bou-Makari is gone. Where, it is not known. He is not expected in Tizi Bekir again."

Vesper grinned at Colonel Marelle and held up two fingers.

"*Voilà,*" she said. "Point one. And point three."

CHAPTER

8

Regarding Vesper's point two, Colonel Marelle could have flatly refused to let us go with him. He was, perhaps, too much the gallant Frenchman to break his agreement, though surely he was as astonished as I by the miraculous arrival of supplies and transport. More likely, the hard-bitten Legionnaire had simply found himself outflanked and hopelessly bamboozled by the dear girl—as had others before him.

The camels, in any case, were excellent, probably Bou-Makari's private stock. I suspected that An-Jalil had something to do with their sudden appearance, but I wondered what sort of persuasion he had exercised.

"Don't look a gift camel in the mouth," said Vesper.

While Smiler and Slider packed our belongings, Maleesh took charge of the animals. Our horses and mules, he assured us, would be well suited to the mountain trails. He advised us to ride the horses, keeping the mules and camels for pack beasts.

Maleesh again proved remarkably competent and efficient. From Bou-Makari's bales of clothing, he picked out sturdy garb for Vesper and me: tunics and trousers, tough-soled but comfortable boots. Under his leadership, harnesses were buckled, boxes and chests roped, and loads balanced with amazing speed.

Thanks to him, we stood ready to depart a good fifteen minutes before Marelle's troops put themselves in marching order. The colonel, astride a stocky, deep-chested horse, gave Vesper an admiring salute.

"Mademoiselle Holly, you have my felicitations and compliments. For the moment."

We left the town and almost immediately found ourselves engaged in the first ascents of Tizi Bekir and an abrupt change of landscape. The caravan route itself was fairly smooth, after a thousand or so years of traffic, but the slopes rising on either side of us were bleakly depressing, bare except for scattered clumps of stunted vegetation. Towering above us, the black crags of the Haggar, grim and looking hard as iron, were streaked with dazzling white snow.

As we wended our way, Vesper's thoughts turned to An-Jalil. "I'm sorry I didn't see more of him. I understand why he disappeared when Colonel Marelle showed up. For the rest, it puzzles me."

It puzzled me, as well. A blue-tinted individual who goes around armed to the teeth and quoting twelfth-century poetry is not easy to comprehend. Yet, I admit I shared Vesper's fascination with him.

Caught up in the intriguing subject of An-Jalil, Vesper only now realized that Marelle's Legionnaires had outdistanced us. Maleesh hurried back to instill some enthusiasm in our camels. We put our mounts into a brisk trot in order to catch up.

Colonel Marelle, riding back and forth along the column, flashed a hard grin.

"Recall to yourself point two," he called. "Keep pace."

He wheeled his horse about. I assured Vesper that the colonel, having taken us this far, would not leave us in the lurch.

Next thing we knew, in spite of their heavy packs, the detachment broke into double-quick time, with Marelle still grinning and waving at us to follow.

We urged our horses to a faster pace, but it was all we could do to keep the gap between our caravan and the Legion column from widening. Maleesh, Smiler, and Slider rode up to us to learn the cause of the sudden speed.

"Marelle's sticking to his bargain," said Vesper. "I'll do the same."

There was a gleam in her eyes, but I did not grasp the full significance of her remark until she sprang down from the saddle.

"They're going on foot," said Vesper. "So will I."

She strode quickly to join the rear of the column.

"The *anisah* marches?" exclaimed Maleesh. "Then must I stay by her side."

Dismounting, he ran to overtake Vesper. The twins looked at each other.

"I don't see as how we can let those Frenchies outdo us," declared Smiler.

"I don't see as how we can let Miss Vesper take them on without, you might say, our moral support," replied Slider.

The pair nodded identically, jumped from their mounts and, keeping exact step with each other, trotted after the Legionnaires.

Though tempted to follow, I suppressed that impulse. True, a point of honor and possibly the reputation of Philadelphia were at stake. On the other hand, our untended pack animals had begun wandering off the trail. Someone had to herd the unruly beasts into line.

By the time I came in sight of Marelle and his troops, the Legionnaires had mercifully halted. In the midst of them stood Vesper, slightly flushed but scarcely winded, laughing and joking, a Legionnaire's cap and havelock perched on her head.

Marelle, mopping his brow, came up to greet me.

"I have not played fair with Mademoiselle Holly," he confessed. "What you saw was our famous forced-march pace. We do it only in dire emergency, but here I could not resist a little test of her resolution. Which she passed with full marks."

"Too bad you weren't along, Brinnie," Vesper said. "Wonderful exercise."

From then on, we proceeded at a comfortably normal speed. At many points, though, we seemed to be heading back toward Tizi Bekir. This was because the increasing steepness of the mountains made straight progress impossible, so we followed long switchbacks and looping trails.

Vesper chose to continue on foot with the Legionnaires, who had adopted her as something of a mascot. The twins, feeling that they had sufficiently upheld American honor, stayed on horseback. Maleesh, however, marched at Vesper's side and showed an endurance equal to hers.

Thus we continued for several days, tenting wherever we found level ground, often sleeping under the enormous stars, our burnooses wrapped around us.

As for provisions, Colonel Marelle insisted that we share the Legion's rations and save our own against future need.

A thoughtful gesture, but eventually disastrous. For me, in any case.

One evening my helping of tinned beef was of dubious taste and color. By the next morning, chills convulsed me and I could barely speak.

"Brinnie, you've gone all green." Vesper put a hand on my forehead. Her face turned grave.

Colonel Marelle arrived with his medical orderly, who glumly shook his head. I dimly gathered that my condition required more treatment than the Legion could provide.

By then, I was past caring.

9

After conferring briefly with Colonel Marelle, Vesper came to kneel beside me. "We're taking you to a doctor."

In my fevered condition, I murmured that we had no appointment.

"Maleesh says we should turn off the trail and find a village," Vesper said. "We're going to do that."

"There will surely be a *tabib*," put in Maleesh, "wise in all ways of medicine."

"Here's a place just above us, in this upland valley." Vesper studied the colonel's map and traced a route with her finger. "It's very close. We can carry you easily and have you there in no time."

For all their desolation, these reaches of the Haggar held populations larger than one might expect. The key, of course, was water. A stream of any size always had a village nearby, with sheep and goats grazing in the little stretches of meadowland.

"That's it, then," declared Vesper. "We'll go to—what's it called? 'Ait-Ouzrim'?"

"No, no!" cried Maleesh. "Choose another, not Ait-Ouzrim. Anywhere, *anisah,* anywhere but there!"

"What's wrong?" asked Vesper. "It's the closest. Aren't the villagers friendly?"

"Very friendly," Maleesh replied. "They welcome all travelers. It is the tribal law of hospitality. Yes, they will feed and house you as honored guests."

"Well, if there's no danger—"

"No danger to you," said Maleesh. "To me. Woe unto your servant! Ait-Ouzrim is the village of the Beni-Brahim."

"Beni whatever," said Vesper, "as long as they have a doctor."

"You do not understand, *anisah.* I am a Beni-Hareet. The Beni-Brahim have fought my tribe for centuries, in hatred passed down from generation to generation. You they will honor, feast, give cushions to sit upon, anoint you with fragrant oils. Me—they will chop into small pieces. Sheik Addi, their leader, will kill me on sight."

"I see what you mean," said Vesper. "All right, you can go with Colonel Marelle and meet us later. Or stay in the hills for a while."

Maleesh brightened at this. Then he hesitated and finally shook his head. "Our fortunes are linked. So it is written. So it must be. I have sworn to stay by your side. Whatever befalls me, my spirit will look down upon you from the stars and guide you on your path."

"Hold on a minute before you start looking down from the stars," Vesper said. "This Sheik Addi—he knows you're a Beni-Hareet?"

"No, he has never laid eyes on me," said Maleesh. "The Beni-Hareet and the Beni-Brahim have hardly seen each other—only at shooting distance, over their rifle sights."

"Well, then, you don't have to let on. If anyone asks who you are, you're just my servant, you came with us from Mokarra. That's the truth—in a way."

Maleesh rubbed his jaw for a while, then nodded. "So be it. If you say I am your servant from Mokarra, none should question further."

Colonel Marelle agreed with Vesper's plan, and promised to wait on the trail until he had word we were safe in Ait-Ouzrim. The twins fabricated a stretcher from some of our tent canvas and hoisted me onto it while Maleesh put our caravan in order. Vesper said a grateful farewell to the colonel, and we set out for the village.

Sighting us well before our arrival, a number of villagers swarmed out to welcome us and lead us to a little square in the midst of flat-roofed, white-plaster houses.

Vesper, wasting no time on formalities, immediately asked for a *tabib* to help us. Fortunately, that professional gentleman happened to be in the crowd. He stepped forward and listened carefully as Vesper explained my misfortune.

Except for the turban and striped caftan, the *tabib* had the same air of stern yet noble dedication as our illustrious clinician, Dr. Samuel Gross. He poked and prodded, squinted down my throat and up my nose, all the while muttering to himself as incomprehensibly as our finest Philadelphia specialists. Finally, he pronounced a solemn prognosis.

"I cannot cure him."

Vesper cried out in dismay, but the *tabib* continued.

"No, I cannot cure him. Nor do I need to. He must cure himself, as he will surely do."

He went on to explain that my illness was rarely fatal. I required rest, sparse diet, and herbal infusions he would provide. Time, he assured us, was my best medicine.

By now, Sheik Addi himself had arrived. That is, he rolled up, for he was almost as wide as he was tall, plump-cheeked, with a turban twice the size of his head. His eyes lit up at sight of Vesper, while he greeted us in a voice like a bull calf.

As soon as Vesper told him our situation, he herded us all into his residence, a large house bursting with children of assorted sizes. While his three wives hurried to welcome us, Sheik Addi bawled for his eldest daughter, Jenna, to tend me. Smiler and Slider hauled me to a chamber, which Jenna set about arranging as a sick room.

Vesper took my hand. "Dear old Brinnie, you'll be good as new. The *tabib* says so. And I say so."

Vesper watched over and cared for me night and day. As did Jenna. A bright-eyed, handsome young woman with crimson cords tied in her shining black hair, she had natural skill as a nurse and healer. Thanks to her ministrations, and Vesper's, I gradually improved. Though unable to travel, by week's end I was up to taking short walks around the village. No longer confined to my sick room, I was welcomed into Sheik Addi's family life: as loud and boisterous as the sheik himself, with his offspring clamoring and Addi hugging or swatting them, depending on his mood.

Vesper quickly became their favorite, telling them sto-

53

ries to which they listened wide-eyed. Sheik Addi was equally fascinated. One tale he liked especially dealt with the hero Paw el-Revere galloping on his camel to warn the sleeping Bou-Stoni tribe of enemy attack.

As for Smiler and Slider, they were viewed as objects of wonder. Twins being rare among the Beni-Brahim, they could not set foot outdoors without a crowd gathering.

Maleesh, however, outshone them. He had become as popular as Vesper among the villagers. Now confident he would not be chopped into bits, he basked in his reputation as a worldly-wise visitor from the capital. He strolled around Ait-Ouzrim, striking up conversations, drawing worshipful glances, holding forth in a respectful circle of his sworn, but unwitting, enemies. I give him credit: The fellow did have a way about him.

"He could get himself elected sheik," Vesper observed, "if they didn't have one already."

His popularity, however, did not extend to Jenna. With us, she was smiling, quick-witted, with a charming, silvery laugh. Yet I saw clearly that she and Maleesh had taken an instant dislike to each other. Jenna, indeed, went out of her way to demonstrate her low opinion of him; once, she even smacked him on the ear. Maleesh, in turn, behaved with utmost impudence. Instead of avoiding her, he sought her out with the express purpose of squabbling.

Most irritating for him, she refused to be impressed by his tricks—unlike Sheik Addi, who, along with the rest of his children, enjoyed them so much that he demanded Maleesh perform each evening.

Maleesh, I must admit, was at the top of his form. He danced on his hands more spectacularly than in Mokarra and turned incredible cartwheels and somersaults. His conjuring had never been so brilliantly mystifying. One evening, he presented his disappearing coin trick—with added improvements—finally tossing the copper piece high into the air, where it vanished.

The children cheered and clapped their hands, Sheik Addi's wives gasped in amazement, and Sheik Addi himself outdid all of them, stamping his feet, roaring approval, demanding more. Jenna remained unimpressed.

"The coin did not vanish," she said archly. "You did not throw it in the air, but only made it seem so."

"Are you also a magician, little *anisah*?" Maleesh bristled. "Tell me, then, where it is."

"In your sleeve," retorted Jenna. "One does not need to be a magician to know that."

Maleesh snorted a denial. Jenna, nevertheless, kept at him, daring him to prove his claim. Maleesh, growing more and more vexed, finally gave a cry of exasperation and pushed both sleeves up to his shoulders.

Jenna gasped. Sheik Addi's eyes bulged and his plump cheeks went purple. Maleesh himself stared around, horrified at what he had thoughtlessly revealed.

On his forearm was a brightly colored, intricately designed tattoo.

"Beni-Hareet!" Sheik Addi jumped to his feet, no longer roaring with delight but rage. "The tribal mark of the Beni-Hareet!"

Maleesh clapped his hands to his head, cursing himself for being goaded into such carelessness. Jenna covered her face and rocked back and forth. The children stared, puzzled by the whole affair.

"Guards! Here!" Sheik Addi spat and shook a fist at

Maleesh. As his men raced in answer to his call, Addi pulled a dagger from the sash around his waist.

"Vile swine of a Beni-Hareet!" he bellowed. "Kill him! Strike him down! No! Let me at him first!"

10

"No! You can't!" Vesper had jumped to her feet as quickly as Sheik Addi to set herself squarely in front of him. Smiler and Slider planted themselves on either side of her, and I, despite my weakened condition, stumbled to join them.

Sheik Addi only responded with a growl of rage. Brandishing his dagger, he prepared to carve his way through Vesper and all the rest of us to get at the terrified Maleesh. Addi's guards hesitated, uncertain what to do.

"We're all guests in your village, in your home, under your roof," cried Vesper. "Break the law of hospitality? Harm one of us and you'll be disgraced forever."

It was a delicate moment. Vesper, hands on hips, boldly facing the infuriated sheik, had no intention of giving ground, and Addi, eyes blazing, hulked forward until he was practically nose to nose with her. His wives tipped the balance in our favor. They flung themselves on him and pulled him back.

"The *anisah* speaks truth!" one of them shouted.

"Hospitality is sacred. Shame yourself, you shame us with you."

Jenna added her voice to the protest while the children, alarmed by such behavior from their elders, cried and screamed. All this kept Addi from carrying out his purpose then and there but did nothing to soothe him.

"The law does not shield this maggot!" he bellowed. "Hospitality? No! Not for one of the Beni-Hareet!"

"Not a member in good standing," Maleesh piped up from behind his screen of legs.

"Worm!" Addi waved his dagger. "You were born a Beni-Hareet; you die as one."

"Wait a minute, Addi," put in Vesper. "You admit the law applies to us?"

"I have no quarrel with you," Sheik Addi flung back. "Only with this mange-ridden goat, this polluter of the oasis of my life, this blight on the fig tree of my generosity."

"We're under your protection, then," said Vesper.

"So I have spoken. So it is."

"All right, if we're under your protection, Maleesh is under ours. That means he's under yours, too," Vesper went on. "Things equal to the same thing are equal to each other. It's one of Euclid's unbreakable laws."

"Who is this Euclid?" retorted Addi. "He means nothing to me."

"I'll put it another way," said Vesper. "You wouldn't destroy our property, would you? Of course not. I don't mean that we own Maleesh. But we hired him. So, you could say we own his time. You can't separate his time from him, can you? If his time is our property, Maleesh is our property, too."

Addi's wives and Jenna murmured approval of Vesper's lucid exposition. Addi scowled, chewed his lips, pulled off his turban, flung it to the ground, and stamped on it. Of more immediate interest to us, he put his dagger—reluctantly—back into his sash.

"Your property? So be it. He is no more than a saddle blanket, a camel's nose bag. Let him stay with the rest of your animals." Addi spun around to his wives. "Out! Out! All of you!"

Maleesh hastily obeyed. The women bundled up the smallest children and shooed the others from the room. His face turning a variety of colors, Addi stamped after them, kicking at the cushions on the floor as he stormed out. Jenna stayed behind.

"What have I done?" She threw herself into Vesper's arms. "I did not mean to put him in danger."

"For heaven's sake, then, why did you prod him like that? Why did you want to spoil his trick?"

"Not to spoil it. To make it better. I knew the coin would not be in his sleeve. He is too clever for that. I only wished to make him show it was not there, as some might have thought, so his trick would be all the more astonishing."

"He'll be fine," Vesper assured her. "Don't feel bad. You meant well. Besides, he's only a Beni-Hareet."

"We women have no quarrel with the Beni-Hareet. Our men keep it alive, not us."

"Oh?" said Vesper. "Well, they've been keeping it alive a good long time."

"Beyond memory," said Jenna. "No one is even sure who began it. There was, long ago, an upland pasture. The Beni-Hareet claimed it as their own. The Beni-Brahim claimed their grandsires owned it centuries before. The Beni-Hareet then claimed their great-grandsires held it first, and the Beni-Brahim swore their great-great-grand-sires were first to graze their flocks there."

"And no one knows who it belonged to?"

"It belonged to both," said Jenna. "The Beni-Brahim and the Beni-Hareet descend from two brothers of the same father. The tribes were cousins to one another. Now they are mortal enemies.

"Do you believe we women worry about great-great-grandsires?" Jenna went on. "Year upon year, the village mothers see their sons' blood shed without reason. The pasture is long since fallow and useless. The men fight over what is dead and gone. Our concern is for the living."

"At least you don't have to grieve over Maleesh," Vesper said. "He's safe now. We'll leave as soon as we can."

The sooner the better, was my opinion. Smiler and Slider immediately offered to build an improved stretcher, or a horse litter. Vesper shook her head.

"Brinnie, you're in no condition to be moved on a stretcher or any other way. We'll go when you quit looking so green around the gills. The Beni-Brahim will get used to having a Beni-Hareet in their village."

Vesper was a little too optimistic. While she and the twins lost none of their popularity during the following days, it was not so with Maleesh. Word had spread. At this point, the wretched fellow could not have been elected dogcatcher.

Worse yet, Sheik Addi took Vesper at her exact words.

If Maleesh was property, he had no reason to eat. "Does a saddle need food?" Addi demanded. "Does a piece of baggage need water?"

"You can't treat him worse than a mule or a camel," Vesper countered.

"So be it," Addi retorted. "He shall feed like a pack beast. Let him eat hay."

As things turned out, Addi's wives and Jenna saved their leftovers and sneaked them into the stable, which was now the residence of Maleesh. Our guide and protector did not venture to put his nose out of doors.

Sheik Addi treated us as usual. That is to say, some days he would sulk, pout, glare silently at Vesper; others, he would shower her with praise. The only consistent thing about him was his delight in Vesper's stories.

His eyes popped at her account of the great Ben-Jamin who summoned lightning from the heavens. He bellowed and slapped his knees over Samu el-Adams and the Bou-Stonis who painted their faces, put feathers in their hair, and cast boxes of mint tea into the harbor. Vesper told him of Ibn-Jeffer and Sheik el-Washington, of the mighty bell of Philad el-Phia, of Betsi ar-Ross stitching a banner from her caftan.

"I don't know if all those stories are good for him," Vesper remarked to me. "Addi only likes the parts with fighting. He doesn't pay much attention to the rest."

Our host, nevertheless, called for more and more, refusing to let an evening pass without a tale. To avoid sending Addi into a tantrum, Vesper indulged him, with some reluctance. By now, I felt well enough to travel, and Vesper was impatient for us to be on our way. Each time she mentioned that we were ready to leave, Addi waved away the idea, his eyes glinted dangerously, and he demanded still another story.

"I'll have to think of something he won't like at all," Vesper told me. "Something boring. The banking system? Fertilizer production?"

Finally, she simply announced our firm decision. We would leave the next day.

"Is that how you repay my hospitality?" Addi shouted. "You scorn my generosity! You fling my kindness in my face!"

"Addi, we're not scorning or flinging anything," Vesper patiently replied. "We're grateful to you. We just can't stay any longer."

"The others may depart," cried Addi. "Not you. No, I do not allow it. You remain until I give permission."

"That won't do," Vesper said. "We're going, all of us. If you force your hospitality on us, we might as well be prisoners."

Sheik Addi chewed on that for a while. Then a sly look crept over his face. "So be it. Go, if you wish."

"We'll start packing now," said Vesper.

"The Beni-Hareet stays here. Once you set foot beyond Ait-Ouzrim, that worm will no longer be under your protection. I shall deal with him as he deserves."

"Hold on, Addi," Vesper returned. "We've already settled that. Maleesh goes with us. He's ours; you agreed he was."

"No," retorted Addi. "You tricked me. I am not bound by deceit."

"Tricked you?" said Vesper. "How?"

"I do not know. That is proof of your trickery."

Sheik Addi grinned triumphantly over his masterpiece of logic and hunkered down solidly on his cushion. "You go. The worm stays. And dies."

Vesper thought for a while, then shrugged. "If you say so, I won't argue with you. All right, we'll leave Maleesh behind."

Smiler and Slider gasped identically, glancing at Vesper in disbelief, as, indeed, I myself did.

"That is wisdom." Addi bobbed his head, smiling and licking his lips at what he had in store for the wretched Maleesh.

"We'd better get a good night's sleep." Vesper yawned. "Oh—I do have one more story for you."

"The Bou-Stoni massacre?" Added leaned forward eagerly. "I would hear that told again."

"A different story." Vesper crossed her legs, settled on her cushion, and began in the tones of a bazaar storyteller:

"Hear, O Sheik! A man had a friend who set out on a journey, leaving in the man's care a chest of belongings.

"But, once his friend had mounted his camel and departed, the man laid hands on the chest and broke it to pieces. He tore the goods it held and trampled them underfoot. He burned the splintered chest and cast the ashes to the wind.

"When his friend returned and asked for the chest, the man said, 'Lo, I have destroyed it and all it contained.' His friend asked, 'Why have you done this to what was mine?' To which the man replied, 'Because the chest was offensive in my sight. Therefore, I did with it as I chose.' "

Addi waited for Vesper to continue. She folded her hands. "That's all there is to it."

"What?" shouted Addi. "The traveler took no re-

venge on his false friend? The destroyer of the chest—
What man of honor would do such a vile deed? Monstrous! Unspeakable! That man is a wart on the nose of the universe! He should be cast out, his bones broken as he broke the chest! Can such a one truly exist?"

Vesper looked him squarely between the eyes. In the noble cadences of Second Samuel, Chapter Twelve, Verse Seven—the Authorized Version, of course—she declared:

" 'Thou art the man.' "

Addi jumped to his feet. "I? How dare you speak thus?"

"We're leaving our property behind," Vesper said. "Maleesh. You'll destroy him. Isn't a life, even a Beni-Hareet's, worth more than a chest? How are you different from the man in the tale? Hear your judgment from your own lips, O Sheik!"

Addi's plump cheeks went violet; he tore at his hair, pulled out his dagger, put it back again, clenched his fists and shook them in all directions. Vesper kept silent, while I feared he might come down with a fit.

"Go," he finally muttered in a choked voice. "Take the Beni-Hareet with you, to the depths of perdition. I will hear no more of that camel's nose bag, that flea, that descendant of cockroaches."

Vesper smiled at him. "I knew you'd be reasonable about it."

We left before the crack of dawn. The twins passed word to Maleesh, who had our gear already loaded. Ait-Ouzrim lay silent and deserted as we rode out. Maleesh, overjoyed at escaping with a whole skin, urged our camels to a faster pace.

With Ait-Ouzrim well behind us, Vesper ordered a

halt so that I could rest. Maleesh immediately set about hauling the roll of tenting down from the camel's back.

"We aren't going to camp yet," Vesper called. Maleesh paid no attention. She went over to him while he continued untying the ropes. "Maleesh, we don't need to pitch a tent now."

"*Anisah,* forgive me, but—" He unrolled the rest of the canvas.

Jenna scrambled out.

11

"I wish you'd talked to me first." Vesper held out her arms to Jenna. "You must have been half smothered in that canvas. And you, Maleesh, you should have told me ahead of time. I could have figured out something better."

So could I. Namely, seizing the idiot by the scruff of the neck and shaking him. If he had meant to take revenge by kidnapping a Beni-Brahim—an insane thing to do in the first place—he had compounded his rashness by abducting one who so despised him.

"My dear, dear Brinnie," Vesper said. "Jenna doesn't despise him. Don't you understand? I knew it from the start. They fell in love at first sight and had to do everything they could to make everyone think the opposite."

"That is truth, Sidi Bahrini." Maleesh looked half proud, half sheepish. "Forgive us, but no sooner did we set eyes on each other than I knew it was written: She is the flowering oasis of my heart, a fountain in the desert of my soul."

"And the pickle barrel of Addi's wrath," Vesper said. "When he realizes Jenna's missing, he has brains enough to put two and two together; easier, one and one."

Sheik Addi, I pointed out, would set after us with half Ait-Ouzrim. Had Maleesh given a passing thought to that? He and Jenna were gazing into each other's eyes. I doubted that they heard a word of what I said.

"We can be sure of what Addi's going to do," said Vesper. "The only question is: What are *we* going to do?"

"Have no fear." Maleesh disentangled himself from Jenna. "I have contemplated it carefully. We can keep on with all haste and hope to be safe in Bel-Saaba."

"And if Addi catches up with us before that?" returned Vesper. "He'll be on horseback, without baggage. He'll go faster than we can."

"I have thought of that, too," said Maleesh. "My second plan is this: We shall turn off the trail, hide, and wait for Sheik Addi and his followers to pass us by."

"Won't do," said Vesper. "If they don't see us ahead of them, they'll soon guess we're behind them. They'll comb the hills for us. Addi isn't the sort to give up easily."

"I have considered that, as well," replied Maleesh. "If it is our destiny, if it is written, they will find us."

Rather tartly I asked if he had considered what would happen after that? Romantic attachments, I have always observed, fog the mind and obscure sensible judgment.

"It is very simple, Sidi Bahrini," he said. "If Sheik Addi catches me, he will kill me for stealing his daughter. As for Jenna, he will only give her a beating and take her home."

"No," declared Jenna. "If he harms Maleesh, he must slay me first."

"Which is exactly what I won't let happen to either of you," said Vesper.

"We've had one or two brushes with unfriendly mobs," said Slider, as the twins had been listening to our conversation without appearing unduly upset by our plight. "I guess we can hold our own."

"We've had our little disagreements with highly aggravated Texans," added Smiler. "These Beni fellows can't be worse. We promise you, Miss Vesper, Slider and I will give a pretty fair account of ourselves."

"I know you will," said Vesper, "but that's what I want to avoid."

"I have one last plan," put in Maleesh. "Jenna and I have talked of it, but it is the least acceptable to me. Even so, I must speak it now. Our presence is your danger. We are the ones whom Sheik Addi seeks, not you."

"As long as you do not try to shield us," Jenna said, "my father will not harm you. He will bluster and rant, surely, but his vengeance is for us."

"In Jedera, I told you, *anisah,* that our destinies were bound together with a golden chain," added Maleesh. "So it was written, so it was. But now Jenna and I are bound with a stronger chain: the love in our hearts."

Maleesh dropped to his knees at Vesper's feet. "*Anisah,* I must ask you to break the link between you and me. I swore to be your servant and so I shall continue, if that is your will. Or, set me free of my word for the sake of my beloved.

"Jenna and I shall take leave of you here. We can hide more easily in the hills, only we two, and travel more quickly. We shall make our way to Mokarra. If we fail, if we should be captured, it will be our lives alone lost, not Sidi Bahrini's, not the twin moons'."

"Of course you're free." Vesper raised Maleesh to his feet. "I don't think your plan's all that good, but I haven't got a better one."

Jenna gratefully flung her arms around Vesper. Maleesh, looking resolute, embraced us and showered us with blessings. It was all very heartwarming, but, I pointed out to Vesper, the result was that we would now be in the middle of the Haggar without a guide.

Vesper did not find this distressing. "Do you still have Colonel Marelle's map?" she asked the twins.

"We do, miss," replied Slider.

"That's all we need," Vesper declared. "We can manage on our own."

Vesper insisted that Maleesh and Jenna take two horses and an ample share of provisions. We wasted no more time in extended farewells. The loving couple mounted and turned off the trail. Vesper watched as they disappeared into the uplands.

"Ait-Ouzrim isn't Verona," she said, "but Maleesh and Jenna make a good Romeo and Juliet."

I reminded her what happened to the star-crossed pair.

"That's only in the play," said Vesper.

As we set out again, Vesper turned unusually silent. She glanced back uneasily. I asked what was troubling her.

"I shouldn't have let Maleesh and Jenna go off by themselves," she finally answered. "They'd have been safer staying with us. Or would they? I just don't know if I did right or not."

I had never known her to be so uncertain. Her doubts made my own apprehensions worse, and I grew doubly nervous about our situation.

Indeed, the longer we continued on the trail the more I, too, wished Maleesh had remained. Without his organizing skill and his ability to hold our caravan together, our progress became slow and straggly. Dangerously so. Sheik Addi, I feared, would have no difficulty catching up with us. I found myself constantly listening for approaching hoofbeats.

Above all, I missed Maleesh because of the camels. In his absence, it became my duty to keep them in line and moving as rapidly as possible. He was more expert than I in dealing with the reluctant beasts. He had a way with them, much as he had with the villagers before his downfall. The creatures sensed an unfamiliar hand and turned rambunctious, trying to shake off their loads, so that I had to trot along on foot, giving each my personal attention.

The animal kingdom is untainted by the deliberate malice found so often in our human species. The camel is an exception. I soon grew convinced that our camels had conspired among themselves to make my life miserable. One spat on me while another tried to kick me. As the trail grew steeper and narrower, they reared and tossed their heads and constantly attempted to crowd me against the rocky wall rising to one side.

We had begun passing through the highest reaches of Tizi Bekir, where the trail fell sharply away as it followed the edge of a deep ravine. I had to goad the camel ahead of me to move forward while I pulled at the harness of the one behind.

As I did so, the beast lowered its long neck and gave me such a nip that, avoiding another attack, I sprang aside, stumbled, and lost my footing.

With the creature's gleeful snort ringing in my ears, I pitched headlong toward the ravine.

12

My exasperation at being so maliciously treated by the camel quickly gave way to concern for my life as I tumbled toward the bottom of the ravine, slipping and sliding, buffeted by outcroppings of sharp rocks. Clawing desperately at the side of the cliff, I finally halted my descent midway between the trail above and the dry riverbed below. I did not dare to move. Each time I sought a firmer handhold, the stones gave way, obliging me to cling there, frozen to the spot.

My persistent shouting had alerted Vesper to my difficulties. I glimpsed her, with Slider and Smiler, peering at me and distantly heard them encouraging me to hold on. I did so, having no better choice.

After a few moments, a rope fell dangling before me. Vesper called down, telling me to harness it under my arms. She soon realized I could not loosen my grip to follow her instructions, and, after several extremely long moments, she came scrambling to my side, well attached to the end of another cord.

"Brinnie, how did you—? No, never mind about that," she said, as I tried to offer an explanation. Suspended next to me, she deftly hitched me to the rope and, satisfied that the knots would hold, whistled through her teeth. The twins began hoisting me up.

My progress halted suddenly. For some agonizing instants, my heart sank. I feared something had gone amiss above us, with Vesper still in a highly precarious situation. Then I was drawn aloft even faster than before.

The twins took hold of my arms and heaved me onto the trail. I had no time to wonder how Smiler and Slider had been able to do this and still control the rope.

That same moment, I stared, astonished, at the blue-veiled face of An-Jalil.

Wasting no breath in greeting me, the noble Tawarik turned his attention and strength to hauling up Vesper. Her head and shoulders soon appeared over the edge of the cliff. At sight of him, she smiled warmly.

"I'm glad to see you, An-Jalil," she remarked, climbing to her feet and shrugging out of the rope harness. "Thank you—again."

"A bit of good luck Mr. An-Jalil happened along," said Smiler. "Slider and I had our hands full, getting the two of you back aboard and trying to keep the animals in order."

"Luck?" Vesper raised an eyebrow. "I suppose people do just happen to run into each other. Especially in the middle of the Haggar."

"Like a jinn, when needed I am there." Though An-Jalil's face was covered, I would have guessed he was smiling. Or perhaps not.

"That jinn seems to have been watching us ever since Mokarra," replied Vesper.

"I had certain business there. I was ready to leave the city when I saw you in the square, saving a poor vagabond's life. I saw courage and compassion shining like jewels. What woman is this? I wondered. Our paths matched; it pleased me to observe you. And so have I done."

"I'm glad," said Vesper. "We're in trouble with Sheik Addi. We sort of helped his daughter to elope. We need that jinn right now. Full time."

"So be it." An-Jalil nodded and indicated that we should mount and continue on our way, which I was happy to do, as I still listened uneasily for the sound of Addi's riders.

An-Jalil beckoned and his own camel obediently approached. If there is an aristocracy of these creatures, this one ranked among the noblest: Pure white, with slender legs and narrow body, it was a *mehari,* bred for speed.

"A racing camel?" Vesper gave an admiring cry.

"The swiftest of its kind. Will you ride with me, *anisah*?" An-Jalil made only the slightest gesture. The beast folded its legs gracefully—for a camel—and lowered itself to the ground. Vesper eagerly climbed aboard while An-Jalil inspected the rest of our caravan.

He was, I must say, even more skillful than Maleesh. Without so much as a word from him, the animals turned quite docile. An-Jalil assured me they would follow his own mount. My services as a camel driver were not required.

We made excellent progress. A little before sundown, An-Jalil signaled a halt where the trail widened, and he announced that we would pass the night here. Slider and

Smiler would have pitched our tents, but An-Jalil advised against it. Should we be obliged to move quickly, he did not want to abandon equipment we might need later.

"About that equipment and all the animals," said Vesper, "we were told they were a gift from Bou-Makari. I had to wonder if it was his own idea."

"My suggestion, which he wisely followed," said An-Jalil, "though I could have wished you had not used that gift to persist in your journey."

"That's something else I'd like to know," said Vesper. "Why did you warn us against Bel-Saaba?"

"Because there is a new *kahia,* a governor, in the city. Ziri el-Khouf, a man of ignorance and cruelty."

"All we want to do is give back a library book." said Vesper. "I'm sure he won't bother us on that account."

"He is a brutal man, and a dangerous one."

"We'll leave as soon as the book's safely where it belongs," said Vesper. "Besides," she added, "we'll have our jinn with us."

"Alas, no."

"But—I thought you were going to stay with us now."

"So I am," said An-Jalil, "but only to the city gates. There I shall await you."

"Not go in?" Vesper frowned. "Why? You know your way around there, which we don't."

"I am as much a stranger as you are," said An-Jalil. "The Tawarik have not set foot in Bel-Saaba for seven hundred years, nor shall we ever do so."

"I don't understand—"

An-Jalil motioned her to silence. He turned away,

head bent, listening. For a good long while he sat still, hardly breathing.

Then, in a flash, he was on his feet, holding his musket as easily as a pistol in one hand, his sword in the other.

13

Vesper followed as An-Jalil strode to the middle of the trail. By now, I clearly heard the galloping hoofbeats which the Tawarik detected sooner than even the keen-eared Vesper. The twins had jumped to their feet, and we hurried to make a stand against our pursuers.

An enormous full moon had risen, dazzlingly bright. An-Jalil made no attempt to conceal himself, only waited poised in clear view. While the sight of this blue warrior would have been enough to give any attacker second thoughts, the moonlight very likely saved the lives of the approaching riders. An-Jalil, muscles coiled like a tiger about to spring, could well have acted first and asked questions later, but Vesper called out and ran ahead.

"Maleesh! Jenna!" She embraced them as they dismounted. An-Jalil sheathed his sword and slung his musket over his shoulder. Arms folded, he silently contemplated this reunion from behind his blue veil.

"Well, sir," observed Slider, "it looks like the runaways have run back."

"We might all consider a little running," said Smiler. "That Mr. An-Jalil is some piece of work, ready to take on the whole pack of those Beni fellows. Straight out fearless. But Slider and I know a little about being outnumbered. Fearless don't answer; running does."

Whatever Vesper's opinion, at the moment she was overjoyed at the return of Maleesh and Jenna. For their part, the eloping couple looked more alarmed than delighted.

"We did not intend to rejoin you," Jenna said. "We believed you well ahead of us. We do not wish to endanger you but will keep on our separate way."

"No, you won't," returned Vesper. "I shouldn't have let you go in the first place. But—weren't you heading for Mokarra?"

"Yes," put in Maleesh. "We tried our best to avoid Sheik Addi and his band, but they saw and pursued us, forcing us south again."

Vesper turned to An-Jalil. "The tribes respect you. Take Maleesh and Jenna under your protection. Speak up for them. Sheik Addi will listen to you."

"I cannot," replied An-Jalil. "*Anisah,* understand this. It is a quarrel within families, between a father and his daughter, between a Beni-Brahim and a Beni-Hareet. To interfere would go against all custom. It would be dishonorable for me to side with one or the other in such a matter. Even if I could persuade Sheik Addi to let the couple go their way, I would be disgraced in the eyes of my own people by doing so."

"He speaks truth," Maleesh broke in, with a reverent salaam to An-Jalil. "He cannot help us, nor can you. So it is written."

"We'll see about that," said Vesper. "What we can do is get off this trail and find another. Let's have a look at Colonel Marelle's map."

Smiler produced it from his pocket. I struck a match while Vesper unfolded and studied the map closely. At last, she shook her head.

"Too bad. The only trail is the one we're on."

An-Jalil, having observed her in silence, now came and took the map from her hands.

"Have strangers drawn a picture of my homeland?" He tossed Marelle's chart to the ground. "The scribbles of a child. This shows nothing of the true Haggar. There is another trail. Only the Tawarik know it."

"Why didn't you say so right off?" returned Vesper. "We'll take that one, if you'll show us."

"The Tawarik alone have courage to follow it," An-Jalil said. "None other dares to venture there. The perils are great, *anisah*. To the body; even more, to the spirit."

"If it gets us out of here—" Vesper broke off and turned to Maleesh and Jenna. "I'm not the only one to decide. If you don't want to risk it, we'll think of something else. No matter what, I'm not leaving you two by yourselves again."

Maleesh and Jenna exchanged quick glances. Maleesh nodded. "Wherever you go, *anisah,* we shall be with you."

"So be it." An-Jalil threw back his head and gave a peculiar, vibrant call. Vesper was as puzzled as I, having no idea what the fellow was up to. A few moments later, I caught my breath in astonishment.

From the upper ledges and outcroppings, a dozen ghostly shapes sprang up, moving swiftly and noiselessly. Silver blue in the moonlight, garbed and veiled like An-

Jalil, the sight of them descending on us, leading their *meharis,* was impressive—and more than a little unnerving.

"For myself, I prefer solitude," said An-Jalil, "but my people would not have me journey unprotected. These are my close companions. They have watched over me as I have watched over you."

"Very wise of them not to let you travel alone," said Vesper, "and a good thing for us."

One by one, his warriors strode up and salaamed to their chieftain.

"Tashfin Ag Tashfin . . . Attia el-Hakk . . ." After An-Jalil presented each in turn to us, he drew apart to speak with them. Some moments later, he came back.

"I have explained your circumstances," he told Vesper. "They will go where I lead and where you wish. Our trail will take us from the Haggar a little west of Fort Iboush. There, the desert begins. We must cross a portion of it before we can again join the caravan route. We shall be well ahead of the Beni-Brahim. The path is swift for those who dare to follow it. My companions ask only to be certain the *anisah* understands the perils of her choice."

"I'll understand them better when I see them," replied Vesper.

"So be it." An-Jalil signaled to his companions. "*Anisah,* this I vow to you: Should you lose your life, it will be only if I lose mine."

I did not find much comfort in this chivalrous generosity.

Vesper smiled. "Better just make sure we all stay alive."

An-Jalil allowed us only a brief rest before setting out again. Once we started on the secret trail, Sheik Addi would not be able to follow us. The risk was his overtaking us before we reached it. To move faster and to be less heavily burdened, An-Jalil ordered us to discard about half our baggage. Also, at his instructions, we set loose our horses and mules, henceforth relying on our camels.

On the way, as if he had sniffed it out, An-Jalil halted at a shallow stream amid the rocks. We let our animals drink and filled our waterskins to the brim. At sunrise, we turned eastward and left the caravan route.

Vesper had expected our new path would take us higher among the crags. Instead, we struggled down through a rocky defile until it seemed we were at the very bottom of the Haggar; even then, the ground continued to fall sharply away. What would first appear to be a flat stretch of land strewn about with hunchbacked boulders and tall rock formations, standing alone like so many grotesque statues, often ended abruptly at the edge of a cliff.

"This must be what the moon's like," observed Vesper, scanning graveled terrain pockmarked with craters and shallow basins. The dear girl had exactly summed it up. Since, of course, it is impossible for mankind ever to set foot on that distant satellite, the Haggar is the closest equivalent, and equally desolate.

As for the perils to the body, of which An-Jalil had warned, they were what might be expected by anyone so foolish as to undertake such a journey: broken limbs, fatal falls, bruises, gashes, and all such usual inconveniences. Happily, we escaped them, thanks to An-Jalil and his companions. A stranger would never have survived, but the Tawarik could have made their way blindfolded.

Veiled as they were, it was impossible to guess the expressions on the faces of our blue guardians. I suspected they looked on the expedition as little more than a ramble in the country. They were big, rawboned warriors; the one called Tashfin stood even taller than An-Jalil. Many, in addition to their other weapons, carried barbed lances easily nine feet long and round leather shields slung at their backs. All in all, they made Colonel Marelle's Legionnaires look like a Sunday school class.

An-Jalil drove us mercilessly, taxing even Vesper's abundant vitality and stamina. The dear girl's face showed deep lines of strain, her features sunburnt and blistered, her skin cracked. Nevertheless, she set her jaw firmly, gritted her teeth, and never voiced a word of complaint. Nor, for that matter, did the twins.

"We've taken the occasional stroll through the Rockies," Slider remarked. "These Haggars are a little different, but we can't say they're much worse."

What was worse, however, were not the perils to the body but, as An-Jalil also had forewarned, the perils to the spirit. These we did not escape.

It would be fanciful to endow inanimate stones with a living personality. Yet, this lunar landscape seemed to exude an active malevolence. The sheer desolation bored into our brains and tore at our hearts. Often, during one of our brief halts, I would endeavor to nap for a few moments, only to be plagued by horrid nightmares, and would awaken crying aloud.

Vesper's eyes had taken on a glazed cast, but she fought with all her strength against the oppressiveness.

Only once did she come close to discouragement, as she turned her scorched face to me and, in a low voice, admitted, "Maybe we should have stayed in Philadelphia. You were right, Brinnie. We're going to a lot of trouble to return a library book."

Maleesh bore up as well as any of us and perhaps better. The one who suffered most was Jenna. Though she staunchly kept pace, from time to time she shuddered convulsively and her steps faltered. What sustained her were the fond ministrations of Maleesh and An-Jalil's assurances that we would soon come to the end of our ordeal.

By now, we had lost all track of time; for we did not always stop to sleep at nightfall, when the air turned bitter cold, but often continued in the icy moonlight. During the day, we stretched out for a few hours in the shade of some tormented rock formation, too exhausted to speak. The camels merely glanced at us with smug contempt.

On the morning of what An-Jalil expected to be our last full day on the trail, we set out along a rocky shelf, going on foot lest our camels lose their balance and plunge us into the ravine below.

Vesper had been keeping a sharp eye on Jenna, whose face had gone ashen, and whose gait had grown more and more unsteady. Before Vesper could reach her, the girl stumbled and sank to the ground.

14

An-Jalil motioned with his head. "See to her."

The gigantic Tashfin Ag Tashfin strode up, but Maleesh had already taken Jenna in his arms. The Tawarik chuckled at his efforts.

"Give over, little man. I can carry a burden twice that."

"No doubt," Maleesh grunted, "but she is no burden at all."

"Step back, Tashfin," An-Jalil ordered. "Let him do. If he can."

Maleesh, in fact, bore Jenna on his shoulders until we reached level ground and An-Jalil mercifully called a halt. Under the care of Vesper and Maleesh, Jenna revived. An-Jalil ordered an extra share of food and water for her.

Then he rounded on Maleesh.

"You did a foolish thing."

"I am not a wise man," replied Maleesh.

"Do you think you showed bravery?"

"No," replied Maleesh. "I am not a brave man."

"Why, then?" demanded An-Jalil.

Maleesh looked squarely at him. "It was my will to do so."

I would not have been surprised if An-Jalil had struck Maleesh for this impertinence, but the *amenokal* only turned a hard, measuring glance on him, then went to speak among his companions.

Later, An-Jalil called us all together. He announced that, by his calculations, we were at least a day ahead of Sheik Addi and his band; no question, we had safely outdistanced them. Once we reached the Sahkra, it would be only a matter of hours to Bel-Saaba. Therefore he allowed us an unexpected luxury: a full night's sleep.

Then he did something even more unexpected.

"Only among trusted friends," he said, his eyes going to each of us, "only among those we respect and love—"

He undid the portion of the turban covering his face.

"Then do we go unveiled."

He let the cloth fall aside.

An-Jalil had called himself a jinn, but I saw him as no unearthly spirit—unless the spirit of the desert itself. His cheeks and brow were pitted and grooved as if by countless sandstorms. Though his black beard was silver-shot, it gave no clue to his age. He could have been young; he could have been ancient. His mouth had the half smile of a dreamer; his eyes held the mystery of vast distances beyond any horizon. I also remembered how quick he was with a dagger.

Vesper went toward him. "For us," she said, "among those we respect and love—"

She embraced him, and we followed her example. An-Jalil's companions now put aside their blue face coverings and came to offer us their salaams. They were unnerving enough with their veils in place; without them, even more. All of them bore an assortment of scars; the huge Tashfin boasted a dozen. Attia el-Hakk had a set of teeth a wolf would have envied. Had it not been for the honor bestowed on us, I would have felt more comfortable if they had stayed masked.

Vesper, however, was soon laughing and talking among them as easily as she had done with the Legionnaires. Smiler and Slider came in for their share of admiration. The twins, indeed, seemed quite at home, as if they had been on familiar terms with this sort of rough company elsewhere. So, all in all, it was something of a festive occasion—if anything can be festive in the ghastly Haggar.

With Jenna well recovered and all of us in good spirits, we set off again at dawn the next day.

"Jenna and I shall be safe in Bel-Saaba," declared Maleesh. "Let Sheik Addi pursue us even into the city. There will be a thousand places we can hide past finding."

"Then what?" asked Vesper.

"Whatever is written," said Maleesh, "so it shall be."

It seemed to me that dancing on his hands and pulling coins from his nose was a poor profession for a married man. But I let that question go by. This was not the moment to discuss Maleesh's career opportunities.

By mid-morning, we passed through the shadows of a high-walled canyon. Emerging, the sudden flood of light nearly blinded us. Vesper shaded her eyes and scanned the barren expanse, the trembling horizon, the depthless blue of a frighteningly empty sky.

"My true home," said An-Jalil. "As el-Barak writes,

'The desert is the only purity, each grain of sand a burning truth.' Does it please you, *anisah?*"

"Yes," replied Vesper, "and compared with the Haggar, it looks downright cheerful."

I would not have applied that term. The terrain was gritty as well as hot enough to shrivel a salamander. However, we did move along with surprising speed. The course An-Jalil followed was more shale and gravel than deep sand, and he navigated skillfully between the dunes on either side of us.

We made such rapid progress that he treated us to a halt at the most miraculous phenomenon: an oasis, an island of green trees and shrubbery and tall grasses, with a diamond-clear pool of water. The camels drank; we filled our water bags, soaked our heads, and reveled in the sheer luxury of coolness.

Vesper leaned back against a palm tree, stretched out her long legs, and contemplated the surrounding expanse of sand. To all appearances, she might have been enjoying a relaxing day in Atlantic City. The dear girl, however, seldom loses the thread of a thought once it is in her mind, and now, with An-Jalil beside her on the soft grass, she returned to a question unanswered when their previous conversation had been interrupted.

"What were you telling me about Bel-Saaba?" she asked. "You said the Tawarik hadn't set foot in it for centuries. Is it forbidden to you?"

"We have forbidden it to ourselves," An-Jalil said. "Did you not know? The Tawarik founded Bel-Saaba, built the great library, planted gardens, raised fountains. It was to be a place of joy for body and mind, a happy city unmatched by any in Jedera. It thrived and prospered beyond imagination. We left it to its fate, swearing an oath from generation after generation never to return."

"I don't understand," said Vesper. "The city was thriving—so you left?"

"The blessing of prosperity brought the curse of greed," An-Jalil replied. "Bel-Saaba thrived too well. Those who came to dwell there cared little for the hopes of others and much for their own gain. Bel-Saaba grew rich—in selfishness. And blind to all but the garnering of wealth. In time, the fruit we had nurtured became rotten. We turned to the harsh purity of the desert."

"If the Tawarik governed the city," Vesper said, "couldn't they have done something about it?"

"Who can rule the passions? No law can order the spirit for good or ill. Our governors were honorable, but they failed. In those days, the office of *kahia* passed down through the eldest son of the eldest sister. After we departed, those who took power did so by force of arms, by treachery or bribery. Bel-Saaba flourished only in corruption."

I would have pointed out the difference between that shocking state of affairs and the unswerving honesty of Philadelphia's electoral processes, but Vesper interrupted.

"If it's a hereditary office," she said, "isn't there a descendant among the Tawarik today? Hasn't he ever wanted to go back, to be the *kahia* again?"

"An empty title," replied An-Jalil. "Yes, there is one among us to whom it belongs." He smiled ironically. "It is I."

15

"You're the hereditary governor of Bel-Saaba?" Vesper exclaimed. "If you wanted, you could claim your birthright—"

"Never," An-Jalil broke in. "Never shall I claim rule of a city my ancestors left to its fate. To break my vow would dishonor me."

"None of my business, of course," Vesper said, which usually means she is thinking of making it so. "It just seems to me there's more honor in trying to improve something than staying clear of it."

She would have gone on, but An-Jalil climbed to his feet and strode off, ordering his companions to remount. As we departed the oasis, his face was hard-set and remote. Vesper deemed it wise not to raise the subject again.

Soon after, we came in view of the city An-Jalil despised. For all his low opinion, Bel-Saaba was far from unattractive. It was, indeed, impressive. Set commandingly on a high plateau rising sharply from the desert floor, its walls, unlike the pink masonry of Mokarra, were golden. Or once had been. Now they were wind-ravaged and faded to a pale yellow. All around the city was the welcome sight of brilliant greenery. Thickets of palm and mimosa sprang up a little distance from the walls, along with a number of cuplike hollows, natural reservoirs of water set about with tall grass and shrubbery.

Vesper had expected An-Jalil to accompany us to Bel-Saaba's north gate, but he halted at the edge of one of the hollows. Not only had he vowed never to set foot in the city, he evidently also found it distasteful to draw closer.

His camel knelt and he dismounted. "Here, *anisah,* I take leave of you."

"But—you aren't just going to pack up and disappear?" Vesper replied. "I was hoping, after we returned the book—"

"When your task is done and you leave the city," said An-Jalil, "I will find you."

"I don't know how long we'll be," said Vesper. "We've come so far that I wouldn't want to miss a chance to look around the library."

"As you wish, but stay no longer than you must." He gave Vesper a courtly salaam. "Go in peace. Return in peace."

Ordinarily, Vesper could happily have spent several weeks exploring the fabulous library, and so could I. The warning tone in An-Jalil's voice took the edge off my appetite for extensive browsing. This apprehension grew stronger as Vesper, with Maleesh, Jenna, and the twins following, led our camels to the open gate.

There, two guardians halted us. A scruffy pair, in stained tunics and headcloths, their appearance as members of the local constabulary did not inspire great confidence. Also, instead of the muskets the Tawarik bore, they carried the latest model French rifles at their shoulders. I cannot claim they singled us out for special attention; they no doubt behaved disagreeably with all newcomers.

"We have business at the library," Vesper declared in answer to their gruff question.

One of them spat through his teeth. What he said made my heart plunge.

"Closed."

Vesper always takes an optimistic view. "You mean," she said, "it's closed for the day? When does it open again?"

The guard shook his head. "It does not."

"When they know what we're here for," said Vesper, "they'll want to open. It's important. We've come a long way—"

"Tell it to the *kahia.*"

"We will," declared Vesper. "How do we find him?"

"He finds you."

We could expect no more satisfaction from this oaf. My handing over a fistful of coins only bought the vague promise that our arrival would be made known. For an added sum, the fellow grudgingly pointed the way to what I hoped would be a decent *serai.*

The lodgings were almost comfortable, probably the best available, given the atmosphere of the city. Unlike Mokarra, here I sensed no exuberance. Crowds, yes, but by and large a glum, tight-lipped lot.

"Most of them look scared to death," observed Vesper, "and the rest as if they didn't want to be here in the first place. What's the trouble?"

"Let me go to the bazaar," Maleesh suggested while the twins saw to our camels and Jenna set about arranging our quarters. "A few tricks, a little talk here and there, and I can learn more in an hour than you could discover in a week."

"Do it," said Vesper. "Brinnie and I will take a walk around, too. I won't sit cooling my heels until the governor decides to find us."

This happened sooner than expected. My donation to the guard actually produced a result. Before we could set out on our own exploration, there arrived an officious fellow with all the overbearing arrogance of a junior bean-counter.

Satisfied that we were who we claimed to be, he declared that his master, the highly exalted Ziri el-Khouf, deigned to receive us. Giving no answer to Vesper's questions regarding the library and its closing, he led us a little way from the square—where Maleesh was doubtless pulling coins out of his nose and gossip from local tongues—to Bel-Saaba's equivalent of the town hall. The terraced gardens were ill-tended and weedy, but the building itself was still quite handsome, with its arcades of pointed arches and a watchtower at one end.

The functionary ushered us into a large, airy chamber lined with graceful columns. El-Khouf, squatting on a pile of cushions, glanced up and beckoned. In front of him was a tray of melon rinds and half-eaten fruits.

Vesper never makes the mistake of judging an individual by outward appearance, knowing that the roughest exterior may conceal a heart of gold. I have tried to do likewise. In this case, however, I suspected the *kahia*'s external and internal qualities were identical. He was heavyskulled, heavy-handed, with animal cunning glinting in his beady eyes. For a chief magistrate, he was not even neat in his apparel.

This unpleasant impression of el-Khouf was not what brought us up short.

Beside the *kahia,* a rancid smile dripping over his face, stood the loathsome camel trader, the scoundrel who had sought to auction us off in Tizi Bekir: Bou-Makari.

CHAPTER

16

Vesper is rarely at a loss for the appropriate comment. "Thanks for the camels," she said.

"Now you have brought them back to me." Bou-Makari smirked. "And yourselves, as well."

"No," said Vesper. "In fact, I thought the jinns got you."

Bou-Makari gave a nauseating laugh. "The Tawarik who cheated me had no stomach to slay an unarmed man. He forced me to compensate you and ordered me to leave Tizi Bekir. I gladly obliged, for I planned to do so in any case."

Bearing a trivial grudge is a flaw in one's character. Yet, the recollection of Bou-Makari offering to throw me in gratis at his auction still rankled.

"Villain!" I cried. "At last, you shall be brought to justice!" I turned to el-Khouf. "Sir, I have to inform you that this creature endeavored to sell us into slavery, against the laws of Jedera and the laws of humanity itself. I need not point out your duty as chief magistrate."

"This worm has already told me all that happened." El-Khouf glared at Bou-Makari. "The *roumis* do not concern you. Lay a finger on them and you shall pay with your head. Out! Obey your orders."

While the villainous camel trader stumbled over himself in his haste to depart, el-Khouf fixed an eye on Vesper.

"What do you want here?"

After Vesper detailed our errand, el-Khouf nodded curtly. "A valuable book, you say?" He reached out, rubbing his thumb against his fingers. "Give it here."

"I think not," said Vesper.

"How is this?" cried el-Khouf. "Bel-Saaba is in my charge. The book belongs to the city. I say what shall be done with it."

To prevent him from losing more of his skimpy supply of temper, I offered a further explanation. "Sir, Miss Holly simply means that it would be more fitting to put the volume into the hands of the library director. With receipts, documents, all in proper form; perhaps even some small official ceremony to mark the occasion."

El-Khouf cocked an eye at us. "Give it to Ahmad Baba?"

"Yes, if he's the director," said Vesper.

"He is Keeper of the Scrolls," el-Khouf replied. "What, you wish to meet him? So you shall. Now."

He climbed to his feet, kicking aside the melon rinds, and ordered us to follow him. He clapped his hands and a couple guards fell in behind us as he led us out of the chamber and down the arcade.

The library buildings—there were, in fact, several—rose from what had once been a beautifully landscaped terrace of gardens and walkways. Vesper paused a moment for the pleasure of contemplating the structures and their setting. Despite signs of long neglect, Bel-Saaba's fabled library remained one of the handsomest of its kind: long vistas of archways at ground level, balconies along its upper stories, a central dome, and slender minarets.

El-Khouf hustled us on, past the guards at the entry, to the largest area. Had this been our Library Company of Philadelphia, I would have called it "the main reading room," and it was fully as impressive as that honored institution. Except that there were no readers. El-Khouf showed as much respect as he would have for a storehouse of old newspapers.

"Better than I imagined," Vesper murmured, eyes brightening as she glanced around the spacious chamber illuminated by golden shafts of sunlight. A scent of ancient leather, parchments, and papyrus hung in the air. The floor of ornamental tiles glowed, as did the polished ranks of inlaid cabinets. High racks of pigeonholes, crammed with antique volumes, honeycombed the walls. It required no great stretch of the imagination to believe one could hear the whisperings of generations of scholars in the light breeze from the exterior arcade. The only jarring note was the presence of another pair of el-Khouf's guards, rifles at their shoulders.

"Why is the library closed?" Vesper's question went unanswered as el-Khouf ushered us through a Moorish courtyard and up a long flight of steps. Another guard moved aside as the *kahia* unbolted the door.

"Ahmad Baba!" shouted el-Khouf. "Up! Visitors!" He turned a cunning glance on Vesper. "You wished to see him. Go."

Leaving el-Khouf grinning at the doorway, Vesper hesitatingly entered what appeared to be a custodial or storage area. A couple of oil lamps provided the only glimmerings of light in a small chamber at the rear.

A fragile old man rose from a couch and came to peer at us. He wore a long white caftan and a cotton skullcap. He was gray-bearded and wrinkled, but his eyes were nevertheless sharp and quick. He regarded us calmly.

"Have I merited the pleasure of visitors?" he asked, with a tinge of wry humor. "Since I want nothing of you, logic tells me that you want something of me."

"Are you the Keeper of the Scrolls?" asked Vesper.

"I have been," he said. "Whether I still am is a metaphysical question I have not resolved."

This response puzzled me as much as the situation in which we found ourselves. Reserving her inquiries on that subject, Vesper politely introduced us.

Ahmad Baba cried out in astonishment. He put his hands on her shoulders and closely studied her features.

"Can this be so? The child of Ben-Jamin el-Holly! Yes, yes, I see the father's spirit in the daughter."

"What, you knew my father?"

"Indeed I did. And well remember him. Some of his monographs are preserved in this library." Ahmad Baba had grown quite animated, beaming at Vesper, shaking his head with pleasure and amazement. "I have read his brilliant works, but here Ben-Jamin el-Holly has created a true masterpiece of beauty—in this case, an opus of joint authorship with his beloved wife.

"A most excellent scholar," Ahmad Baba went on, "but perhaps a little absentminded. When I last saw him, I permitted him to borrow a book. What was it? Yes, a treatise on medicinal herbs. By Ibn-Sina. Handwritten on vellum, very nicely decorated—alas, I must add a small reproach to his honored memory. He did not bring it back."

"I know," said Vesper. "That's what we want to talk to you about."

"Discuss Ibn-Sina? You have come so far, to this unhappy place, on an errand of botany?" The aged Keeper of the Scrolls beckoned us into his alcove. "I am a little surprised that you are alive to do so. I would have expected el-Khouf to have put you to death without delay."

"Dr. Baba," I put in, giving him that title which he surely deserved, "the volume is long overdue, but death seems rather an extreme penalty."

"It has nothing to do with books," replied Ahmad Baba. "El-Khouf is quick to put to death any suspicious stranger, lest they threaten his mastery here. Why he permitted you to live, I do not know."

"We heard he was brutal," said Vesper. "I never thought he'd be that brutal."

"He is as ruthless toward the people of Bel-Saaba. They live in constant terror of him."

"That's dreadful," said Vesper. "Why do they put up with it? Why don't they get together and rebel? That's what I'd do."

"Alas, child, for that I blame myself."

Vesper frowned. "Why blame yourself for what el-Khouf does?"

"Because I am alive." Dr. Baba sighed ruefully. "Because I am his hostage. He imprisons me here to keep the people obedient to him."

"With all respect," I put in, "a better choice of hostage would be one in a position to fight against him, to rally the citizenry. Dr. Baba, forgive me, but—you? A peaceable scholar? You pose no threat to him."

"But I do," replied Ahmad Baba. "Allow me to be immodest, but I pose a very large threat. You see, I came here years ago to accept the honored duty of caring for this priceless collection and to pursue my own studies and meditations. The people of Bel-Saaba, I soon learned, were in sorry state. Many, both young and old, could neither read nor write. I took upon myself the duty of teaching them. Also, I possess a knowledge of medicine. Thus, I strove to enlighten their minds, to heal their bodies, to lift their hearts.

"I came to love these people, and they to love me. I was grateful for their affection. Now, I wish they had been less fond of me.

"El-Khouf, not long ago, was a mere commander of the city watchmen. I do not know how he armed himself and his ruffians, but he overthrew the old *kahia* and seized power. I was among those who raised their voices against him. The strongest of us—those best fitted to lead the struggle, as you suggested, Professor Garrett—were the first to be slain. Even then, the unrest continued.

"El-Khouf is a brute, but not an altogether stupid one. Instead of killing me and further enraging the people, he kept me alive. He knew their love for me, and knew they would do nothing to endanger my life."

Dr. Baba smiled bitterly. "As a philosopher, I should have a taste for such a perfect paradox. El-Khouf is the guarantor of my well-being, which is the last thing in the world I desire. And, much as he wishes to destroy me, he does not dare. For then he would have no further hold on the people. I cannot solve the dilemma."

"We can try to help," said Vesper, who had been listening sympathetically to Dr. Baba's unhappy account. "We have good friends with us. And some others close by."

The dear girl is always quick to put her courage and intelligence to the service of justice. Sometimes, I might wish her to be less hasty in doing so. But this case, the plight of Dr. Baba touched me to the quick.

"Sir," I said, "we shall do our utmost to put an end to your disgraceful captivity. I find it profoundly distasteful, I would even say intolerable, to see a man of learning, a fellow academic, so ill-used."

We should, I suggested to Vesper, quickly return to our lodgings and discover some appropriate means, preferably within the law, of assisting Dr. Baba. The old scholar called after me as I strode to the door. My mind, however, was made up. We could not permit this situation to continue.

The door was locked.

No amount of pounding, not even my sternest demands for our release, brought any result.

"I had a feeling," murmured Vesper, "it wasn't going to be that easy."

17

Vesper, chin cupped in her hand, stood watching my useless efforts.

"Give it up, Brinnie," she advised. "They won't answer."

"Dear girl," I exclaimed, "do you not understand? We are prisoners here!"

"I understand that very well," said Vesper. "What I don't understand is, why?"

The reason for our captivity struck me as unimportant. What we had to deal with was the immediate fact. We had been locked up by an insensitive brute who did not wish us well. We had been in worse situations, but a bolted door and subsequent deprivation of liberty has always disheartened me. Vesper, however, maintained her usual calm.

"If there's a way in," she said, "there's a way out. It's just a question of finding it."

Dr. Baba had joined us meantime. Once realizing that el-Khouf had imprisoned us, the old scholar was far more distressed by our plight than Vesper, and more concerned for us than for himself.

"I do not know el-Khouf's purposes, but I am certain your lives are in peril. Ah, child, I wish you and Professor Garrett had never come to Bel-Saaba."

"We had to," said Vesper. " 'A sacred obligation,' as Brinnie calls it. To give you this."

From her tunic, she produced the little volume which had been the source of all our grief. My satisfaction at keeping my word of honor was minimal.

Dr. Baba, however, was delighted. His eyes brightened as he took the treatise and lovingly examined it.

"Blessings upon you!" he exclaimed. "After all these years, it comes back safely!"

"The book may be safe," I commented, "but you are not, nor are we. We must find a means of escape for all of us."

"That could take some time," replied Vesper. "I haven't had much chance to look around. From what I've seen, though, we don't have many choices."

"I fear you have none at all," said Dr. Baba. "I myself have studied every possibility."

Vesper's eyes had gone to a narrow opening close to the ceiling of Dr. Baba's alcove. It was hardly more than an air vent, not large enough for any of us to squeeze through.

"What about that?" Vesper went to stand on tiptoe, studying the vent. "Can we knock down the masonry around it?"

"To no purpose," said Dr. Baba. "We are too high to jump down safely. We would have to climb upward and make our way across the rooftops of the library. I am a feeble old scholar, not an acrobat. If you have the strength, make the attempt. I shall stay behind."

"I don't want to leave you," Vesper said. "I'll have to figure out something better. Now—Dr. Baba, do they keep you here all the time? Never anywhere else?"

"From time to time," said the aged librarian, "I am allowed to walk a little on the front balcony. Thus, el-Khouf shows the people of Bel-Saaba that I am still alive. I am always closely guarded on those rare occasions."

"That's useful to know," said Vesper. "It might give us some kind of chance. But I'm still trying to understand what el-Khouf has against us. It's not just a matter of getting out," she added, "it's what to do afterwards. I'm hoping An-Jalil can help us, too."

"The chieftain of the Tawarik?" Dr. Baba raised his tufted eyebrows.

"Yes," Vesper said. "He's also the hereditary governor of Bel-Saaba. Centuries ago, the Tawarik used to govern here."

"I know their history," said Dr. Baba. "I cannot blame them for abandoning the city. They are a people of noble spirit and high ideals. By their lights, they were correct in choosing the desert and the mountains. Yet, I believe they were wrong in staying aloof for these hundreds of years.

"The people of Bel-Saaba have greatly changed during that time," Dr. Baba went on. "They have been victims of one harsh governor after another, downtrodden, brutalized. El-Khouf is merely the newest. For example, in the fourteenth century—"

Dr. Baba showed every sign of beginning a long discourse. As tactfully as possible, I suggested that events of five hundred years ago could scarcely help us now.

"Alas, they cannot, Professor Garrett," Dr. Baba agreed. "Forgive me if my thoughts wander. I only intended to say that the people of Bel-Saaba would gladly welcome the Tawarik. If el-Khouf were overthrown, I have no doubt they would hail the chieftain as their rightful governor."

"I don't think An-Jalil wants to be hailed," said Vesper. "He's sworn an oath never to return to Bel-Saaba."

"Nor will he," said Dr. Baba. "He would rather die than break a vow. Indeed, he and his Tawarik must be admired for that. And yet," he added, smiling wryly, "their idealism, their inflexible honor—these are qualities ill-matched to accept the frailties of ordinary mortals. Would the citizens of Bel-Saaba be truly happy under such a rule? Would the Tawarik be happy ruling them? I do not know. But how is it that you came to encounter the chieftain himself?"

No sooner had Vesper begun her account of our treatment by the nauseating camel trader than Ahmad Baba broke in with a cry of outrage.

"Bou-Makari?" The scholar's kindly expression changed, his eyes blazed. "He is a creature of el-Khouf. He aids him in the most despicable of commerce: the slave traffic.

"I spoke of the fourteenth century," Dr. Baba went on. "In those days, Bel-Saaba was the center of that ignoble trade. For generations, the sale of slaves, of wretched beings shipped to all corners of the world, was a source of wealth—for those who conducted the reprehensible business. Over time, the slave trade dwindled. The slavers turned their attention to the western coast. Many of these were your own countrymen. Bel-Saaba no longer gained wealth from the sale of human flesh.

"In recent months, however," added Dr. Baba, "I have heard rumors of the slave traffic beginning again, under el-Khouf and his hireling."

"So we were still merchandise as far as Bou-Makari was concerned." said Vesper. "But then why did el-Khouf tell Bou-Makari to keep his hands off us, we were none of his business?"

"I understand your plight no more than you do." Dr. Baba shook his head. "Whatever the reason, it bodes ill for you."

Vesper said no more, but I knew her penetrating intellect was continuing to seek the purpose of our captivity.

"I don't suppose there's a little something to eat?" she said.

Dr. Baba begged our pardon for not having offered us refreshment. He was, as he showed us, modestly but not uncomfortably provisioned with a charcoal brazier on which he could brew mint tea, a sack of fruits, and flaps of Jederan flatbread.

"El-Khouf does not wish me to starve," he explained. "At first, I refused nourishment, hoping that would hasten my demise. His guards fed me by force—most unpleasantly. And so I gave up that futile attempt. Come, take what you wish."

Vesper gratefully accepted the old scholar's invitation. I had neither heart nor stomach to do so. While the dear girl munched away, chatting with Dr. Baba as if neither of them had a care in the world, I sank into thoughts of my faraway Mary and the unfortunate consequences of making rash promises.

Night had fallen by this time, and the only illumination came from the guttering oil lamp. A breeze had risen, hissing and whistling through the vent.

In my state of gloom, my imagination seemed to give a voice to the draft.

"Anisah! Anisah!"

I hurried to the vent, for a voice indeed it was. Vesper and Dr. Baba followed me. I distinguished a pair of eyes and a nose—upside down.

"Maleesh!" Vesper gave a glad cry. "I was sure you'd find us. How did you know el-Khouf locked us up?"

"The whole city knows," whispered Maleesh. His reversed posture, I realized, resulted from his lying prone on the roof tiles and hanging head down. "El-Khouf had it cried throughout Bel-Saaba. Two spies of the French had been captured. Once I heard that, it was only a matter of reaching you. It took longer than I expected. The guards are everywhere."

"Are the twins and Jenna all right?" asked Vesper.

"Safe," replied Maleesh. "In the bazaar, I made friends with some of el-Khouf's enemies. The twin moons and my pearl of the universe have gone into hiding with them."

"You are a friend of this brave child and the professor?" Dr. Baba put in. "You must act quickly. Remove them from here. Their lives are in utmost danger."

"I shall inform the twin moons, *anisah,*" said Maleesh. "Whatever it requires, we shall discover a means to free you. I shall return in an hour, two at most."

"Get word to An-Jalil," Vesper began.

Maleesh, however, had disappeared and was, no doubt, making his way across the tiles. He had vanished in the nick of time before a handful of el-Khouf's henchmen came stamping into Dr. Baba's chambers. Their leader gruffly announced that his chief demanded our immediate presence.

Dr. Baba was brave despite his years. He had nothing to lose but his life, and would gladly have given it up then and there. As the guards laid hold of us, he tried to fling himself on them, daring them to shoot him. The ruffians merely guffawed at his feeble efforts. They locked him up again and marched us down the steps and through the courtyard. They hustled us to the residential wing of the building and there prodded us into an apartment far more sumptuous than the governor's business office.

The chamber was hung about with beaded curtains, rich carpets covered the floor, and the heavy, spicy fragrance of incense wafted from iron braziers. At one end of the room, a pair of serving women washed and perfumed the feet of the reclining occupant of a cushioned divan.

The feet did not belong to el-Khouf.

"Do partake of some fruit, Miss Holly and Professor Garrett. I recommend the figs. They are excellent," said Dr. Helvitius.

18

"We've had dinner," said Vesper.

The dear girl's face had gone pale; yet, apart from that momentary indication of shock, she stood undaunted, her glance unwavering. For my part, I confess it was all I could do to remain on my feet. My legs felt about to buckle under me, and they might well have done had it not been for Vesper's gentle but reassuring hand on my arm.

Villainy comes in a variety of degrees. Bou-Makari, for example, was an oily, treacherous, greedy creature but, no doubt, at heart a sniveling coward; the ham-fisted, thick-skulled el-Khouf, no more than a crude butcher. Despicable as they were, neither approached the towering villainy of Dr. Desmond Helvitius.

This monster, this self-styled connoisseur of art and music, this archfiend who arrogantly considered himself a member of the academic profession, surpassed that pair of common scoundrels in depth and height of undiluted infamy. No wickedness was beyond him, no maliciousness beneath him. Not long before, in the Grand Duchy of Drackenberg, he had sought to murder us, including my dear, gentle Mary, through the device of an exploding sausage. Even overlooking his previous attempts to destroy us with dynamite bombs, living burial, Gatling guns, and the cruelest of mental tortures, that lethal sausage alone put him, in my personal opinion, beyond the limits of human consideration.

"Pray reconsider, Miss Holly." Dr. Helvitius raised himself on an elbow and indicated the array of dates, oranges, figs, and pomegranates on the table beside him. He smiled cordially, revealing a set of powerful teeth. "It may be your last opportunity."

"You think so?" replied Vesper. Nevertheless, with a shrug, she accepted a handful of dates. The dear girl's analytical mind usually calculates and foresees every range of possibilities and the most unlikely turn of events. Now, she made a rare admission, "I can't say I expected to see you in Bel-Saaba."

"Surely you did not," replied Helvitius. "Yet, I expected to see you. And I am not disappointed."

He waved away the serving women who, during this exchange, had finished anointing his feet and had encased them in a pair of soft babouches. His large, muscular frame was draped in an embroidered silk shirt and voluminous pantaloons. A turban, ornamented with an egg-sized emerald, concealed his shock of white hair. He appeared much more at ease than at our last encounter, when he had made a hasty escape in a hot-air balloon.

Since then, Helvitius had obviously prospered, and prospered luxuriously. Whatever new villainy he had undertaken, he had done quite well for himself. The sight of him, smiling complacently, decked out like the Caliph of Baghdad, might cause one to question the justice of the world. Virtue, however, is its own shining reward. We, at least, could take justifiable pride in having fulfilled a sacred obligation despite our present misfortune. In pointing this out to him, I spared him none of my contempt.

"But, Professor Garrett," he replied, "you and Miss Holly both look in reasonably good condition, all things considered."

"No thanks to you," returned Vesper.

"On the contrary, it is thanks to me." Helvitius sat up on his divan. "You are alive; you have been kindly treated—compared with what el-Khouf wished to do with you. I was not here to welcome you personally, but I gave express orders that you were not to be harmed."

"You?" Vesper is seldom taken aback by events no matter how unexpected. At this, she startled and came as close to outright astonishment as I had ever seen. "You gave el-Khouf orders?"

"Naturally. He follows my instructions. As you may have observed, he is an individual of forceful actions but limited mental capacity. He is useful, in fact essential to me. His natural inclinations, however, must be curbed and properly directed."

"Oh, Brinnie," Vesper murmured in vexation and self-blame, "I should have known that lout wasn't doing all this without orders from someone else."

We both, no doubt, should have suspected. Whatever evil roamed the world, the probabilities were excellent that Helvitius had a finger in it. Even so, to imagine him in the distant reaches of Jedera stretched suspicion beyond normal limits. I urged the dear girl not to reproach herself.

Vesper faced Helvitius again. "Then I guess you're the one who told el-Khouf to denounce us as French spies. That's a lie and you know it."

"A convenient untruth," Helvitius corrected. "If the citizens of Bel-Saaba feel threatened by the French, they will pay less attention to their own situation. It was a happy opportunity."

"So now, I suppose you'll have us shot," said Vesper.

"Heavens no," replied Helvitius. "That would be a pointless waste of still another opportunity."

"Then what?" Vesper demanded.

"I intend to make good use of you," said Helvitius. "The world, Miss Holly, abounds in rich resources. It requires the eye of the imagination to recognize them.

"For example," he continued, "I first came to Bel-Saaba with an altogether different goal in mind—a goal, I should add, I am on the brink of achieving. At the same time, I found el-Khouf making energetic but disorganized attempts to establish a highly profitable enterprise."

"The slave trade," said Vesper. "Yes, that suits you."

"Have you stooped so low?" I burst out. "I thought that you had already overstepped every boundary of human decency. This infamous traffic surpasses all else."

"For which, in a sense, I thank Miss Holly," replied Helvitius. "You know my wealth is considerable, greater than you could possibly imagine. But Miss Holly's constant interference has, I confess, caused me significant financial damage. I merely wished to regain what she has made me lose. And so I shall, a thousandfold.

"The slave trade, regrettably, is illegal in many parts of the so-called civilized world. Yet, that is a blessing in disguise. The supply of slaves has decreased. Therefore the demand, and thus the price, have increased: a simple law of economics. Even in realms where slavery is accepted, or at least winked at by the authorities—Arabia, the Ottoman Empire, the Far East, to name only a few—it has become a most lucrative commerce.

"What my imagination allowed me to envision," Helvitius went on, in a tone of almost poetic fervor, "was a vast organization with its center in Bel-Saaba. An efficient, well-regulated network—which I can easily achieve through my close acquaintance with so many individuals in high places throughout the world—drawing its inventory from Ethiopians, Circassians, Turkomans, and other benighted peoples, to meet the demands of an eager market. In short, Miss Holly, adapting the same methods as your own barons of industry."

The audacity of this archvillain in subverting the honored practices of American enterprise to the basest of transactions shocked me as much as the slave trade itself. Then the implications of his vile scheme, as they pertained to us, struck me with such horror that my head reeled.

Vesper understood the significance immediately. "You won't shoot us. You'll sell us."

"I have not yet decided," Helvitius replied. "When Bou-Makari came to Bel-Saaba and reported his misadventure, I instantly realized—to my astonishment and delight—that you and Professor Garrett were making your way here, into my waiting hands. What to do with you? The possibilities are richly varied.

"Yes, Miss Holly, I might sell you. Or make a special

gift of you to an important gentleman in Constantinople. Or Damascus. Or farther. Or even," he added pleasantly, "keep you for myself. With Professor Garrett. Or without him."

"Monster!" I cried. "Miss Holly will choose death before such dishonor, and so will I. You shall neither sell nor separate us. I shall die before I permit it."

"That is yet another possibility. I must ponder it." He set his glance on Vesper. "Much will depend on Miss Holly and her degree of cooperation."

"I can tell you the degree," Vesper said. "Zero."

"You may be less hasty in your decision when you see what else I offer," said Helvitius.

"You needn't offer anything." Vesper made no attempt to conceal a yawn.

The dear girl, no doubt, was exhausted by this painful conversation with the abominable Helvitius. Past a certain point, even villainy grows tiresome. Then I recalled that Maleesh had promised to come to Dr. Baba's chamber within an hour or two. Surely he would have our rescue already in train. Vesper had understood that our time was too precious to waste in listening to Helvitius's threats.

"It's been a trying day," she added. "I haven't any more to say to you. You might as well lock us up again."

"So I shall." Helvitius gestured to his guards. "In due course. You are both leaving Bel-Saaba. You shall not return."

When civility, moral resolution, and all else fail, Vesper resorts to physical action. That failed as well. Despite our struggles, the guards overcame us and quickly bound us hand and foot. Vesper then employed her voice, not an altogether feeble weapon, in the vain hope that her shouts might somehow reach sympathetic ears. The only result was that gags were forced into our mouths.

At first, I hoped that Maleesh might eventually locate our new place of imprisonment. My heart sank when I realized we were being removed from Bel-Saaba then and there. Flung over the backs of horses, we clattered and jolted through empty streets. The city lay deserted, undoubtedly under strict curfew.

We emerged, as best I judged, not from the north gate but the south, and struck out across the countryside. We continued some uncomfortable while until our captors slowed their pace. My position made it difficult to see where they had brought us. Under the bright moon, I could only glimpse a long, low structure, white as dry bones. What once had been towers rose at either end, so eroded by wind and sand that they appeared to be skeleton fingers twisting skyward.

We were unloaded at a side entrance, roughly hauled through a honeycomb of passages and chambers, and at last shoved into a small stone cell. Our captors, at least, had the common decency to untie us and remove our gags before bolting the massive door upon us.

"Where is this?" Vesper lost no time surveying our sparse, even monastic, quarters. There was little to survey: no sleeping accommodations, no furniture, only thick walls of white stone; and, in one, a window barred by an iron grille.

"We're close to some foothills," Vesper pointed out as I came to peer through the grille. "If I've got my bearings right, they're south of Bel-Saaba. The Hambra Mountains?"

Topography, I suggested, did not immediately concern us.

"Not right now," said Vesper, "but it might be good to know, if we can find a way out."

My heart filled with admiration. Here, even in the most hopeless circumstances, the dear girl's thoughts had turned confidently toward eventual freedom. Though I applauded Vesper's indomitable spirit, I feared it would avail us nothing. Nor would the efforts of Maleesh. We were far beyond his attempts at rescue.

Vesper turned away from the window and sniffed the air. "Notice that smell, Brinnie?"

I could hardly fail to do so. I had been aware of it when we were conducted here; with other concerns in my mind, I had disregarded it.

"In Mokarra," Vesper murmured. "On the day of the fire. I smelled it there, too. The cargo for Bel-Saaba?"

Speculation was pointless. To me, the vile odor was merely an added discomfort, for our cell was bitter cold. Vesper, arms wrapped around her, paced back and forth while I sank down on the stone floor.

"Whatever Helvitius has in mind," she said at last, as if reading my thoughts, "he's not going to separate us."

"Dear girl," I groaned, "I could bear anything but that."

"He won't, Brinnie. That much, I'm sure of."

"How can you prevent him? We are in his power. And at his mercy, of which he has none at all."

"That's the only part I'm not sure about," said Vesper.

Nevertheless, her tone of resolution and Philadelphia dignity in the face of the most shameful prospects kept me from giving way to complete despair. Then, as if noxious odors were not enough, our unhappy state was further aggravated by sounds of rattling and clanking.

"Have they got some kind of factory here?" Vesper listened carefully awhile, but could find no reasonable interpretation.

The primary effect of this racket was to deprive us of sleep. Vesper usually dozes peacefully, whatever the circumstances. Now she remained as wakeful as I. All in all, we passed a miserable night. The morning promised to be worse, the sun turning our cell into an oven.

Vesper pricked up her ears as the bolts at our door were drawn. "Breakfast?"

"Good morning." Dr. Helvitius, flanked by his rifle-bearing ruffians, stood in the doorway. He had exchanged his turban and silken garments for a jacket and pair of riding breeches. A cloth cap sat jauntily atop his white hair. The scoundrel looked cheerful and well rested.

"I spoke to you of my original purpose in coming to Bel-Saaba," he said, as we were marched down one of the narrow corridors. "It is of far more importance, and profit, than even the wealth I shall derive from my enterprise with el-Khouf.

"As you shall see, Miss Holly, it is a work of profound significance. I do not exaggerate when I assure you I will change the entire course of history."

"I'm sorry for history," muttered Vesper.

We had, by now, left the honeycomb of chambers to emerge on a flat, sun-baked expanse surrounded by the eroded walls and towers I had glimpsed the night before.

"Long ago," said Helvitius, "this place held ancient tombs. It was, as well, a place of seclusion and meditation. It suits my requirements admirably."

He clapped his hands and a ragged crew of unhappy-looking wretches pulled away the canvas tenting draped over some large object.

Vesper caught her breath. I could only stare, not believing my eyes. What I saw convinced me that Helvitius had finally overstepped the limits of sanity.

"With this," he proudly declared, "I shall reshape the destinies of every nation on earth."

19

What stood before us was an impossibility. Over the centuries, intellects more powerful than that of Helvitius had vainly striven to comprehend this baffling mystery. Swedenborg, the learned scientist and theologian; the Englishmen, Stringfellow and Henson; and so many others—all had failed, even the great Leonardo da Vinci. But Helvitius, in his overweening arrogance, gestured grandly toward this insane conglomeration.

A long rectangle of oiled fabric, stretched upon a wooden frame, surmounted a wicker cage equipped with wheels. At the rear spread a fishtail contraption with fanlike blades attached. Wires, rods, and braces held the structure together. It was not only an impossibility; it was lunacy.

"A flying machine!" exclaimed Vesper.

Helvitius beamed with insufferable pride. "I knew that you, Miss Holly, would recognize the magnitude of my achievement."

One should not take pleasure in the failure of a fellow

scholar's efforts. In the case of Helvitius, however, it served him right. I confess to a measure of satisfaction as I addressed him.

"Sir," I said, "have you brought us here to display your useless apparatus? What you call an achievement violates every law not only of science but, as well, natural philosophy. You have wasted your ill-gotten fortune in a hopeless effort. Had nature, in her wisdom, intended us to fly, she would have endowed us with the means to do so."

Helvitius disregarded my irrefutable logic, beckoning Vesper to draw closer and examine this ungainly contrivance. To my astonishment, she seemed momentarily to have forgotten our desperate situation, thoroughly intrigued by the ridiculous mechanism.

"Observe the excellence of construction," said Helvitius. "The most skilled of Bel-Saaba's metalsmiths, jewelers, and cabinetmakers have fabricated it under my instruction."

Vesper is always practical. "Yes, but does it work?"

"It will," replied Helvitius, with bland confidence. "It must. I have devoted the most intense study to every aspect of its engineering and design. I have deeply pondered the works of Archimedes, Roger Bacon, and the latest researches by the Swiss Bernoulli. I have understood why others have failed, and, therefore, why I shall succeed.

"I have accomplished what no previous inventor has done. I have solved the problem of combining lightness of weight with the most powerful motive force."

Helvitius directed Vesper's attention to an array of pipes, tanks, and what appeared to be a combustion chamber. "A steam engine of my own design, Miss Holly. A steam engine the like of which has never been dreamed, let alone produced. It is the most compact, powerful, and efficient of its kind.

"Its components were machined to my specifications by a dozen different manufacturers throughout Europe, so that no individual could guess the full nature of its construction."

"Nicely made," Vesper admitted, herself an excellent student of engineering, among her other numerous abilities. "One question: What makes it go?"

"A volatile liquid from your own state of Pennsylvania," replied Helvitius. "A substance heretofore discarded as worthless, yet, in fact, the world's most remarkable fuel. For lack of a better term, I call it 'petrol.' It is fractioned from a type of naphtha."

"Of course!" exclaimed Vesper. "That's what I smelled here—and in Mokarra."

"No doubt you did," said Helvitius. "I was awaiting such a cargo. Unfortunately, much of it was destroyed by fire. It is only a temporary loss. Petrol is abundant and inexpensive. I shall replace my stock with a later shipment."

Vesper cast her eyes over the contrivance, nodding to herself as if she seriously considered it might have practical application. "Why here? Bel-Saaba isn't the most convenient place in the world."

"For my purposes, it is," replied Helvitius. "Its very remoteness guards my secrecy. But there is another reason, more important—indeed, vitally essential to my work. Bel-Saaba's library.

"Previous experimenters have followed the wrong path. They have not grasped the true nature of what I might call 'aerodynamics.' One genius alone understood it, but he had not the benefit of our modern materials and techniques to put it into practice, and so it remained only a theory, overlooked and long forgotten.

"That scientific genius, whose vision reached far ahead of his time, a Moorish Leonardo da Vinci, is Souliman Ibn-Salah. His works are housed in only one place: the Bel-Saaba library.

"The writings of Ibn-Salah are the key to all my efforts. From this ancient genius, I have gleaned the secret which no human being in our modern age has grasped: the secret of flight. You see it here embodied in this vehicle."

"Suppose you're wrong?" asked Vesper.

"Not I, Miss Holly. Ibn-Salah. If his theories are incorrect, then I must conclude that a flying machine is, in fact, impossible. However, I do not foresee that will be the case."

"You will have conducted a pointless experiment nevertheless," I put in. "Your device can have no practical application. As a means of transporting goods and passengers, it will be no more useful than a child's kite."

Helvitius gave me an arrogant glance. "Your imagination, Professor Garrett, unlike my own, is sadly limited and earthbound. Did I speak of passengers? Of transportation? No, sir, I did not. My flying machine will carry a different cargo."

Helvitius turned his eyes upward in an expression of dreamy pleasure. "What, then, will it carry? Bombs, Professor Garrett. Powerful explosive charges."

Vesper's face paled with horror as this monstrous madman continued, "Destruction will literally rain from the air. Cities, human habitations, bridges, railroads, whole armies in the field—none can escape. Every nation will beg to purchase my invention. They must. At any price. For I am the sole supplier, the sole possessor of the secret of its manufacture. If I sell a fleet of my machines to France, Germany must likewise buy them. So must Great Britain, and your own United States.

"Dare you tell me now, Miss Holly, that I exaggerated when I said my work would change the course of history? It will change the entire nature of warfare, an occupation which has constituted so much of our civilization."

Vesper said nothing for some moments; nor could I find words for any adequate response to this most diabolical of all his villainous schemes.

"Leave it to you to think of something like that," Vesper at last replied. "Still—how do you know it will work?"

"I do not know," said Helvitius. "My invention has yet to be tried aloft, and Ibn-Salah's theories demonstrated not in the pages of a book but in the skies."

"With any kind of luck," said Vesper, "you might break your neck."

Helvitius laughed in high good humor. "Do you think me so foolhardy? Surely, you have learned to know me better in the course of our acquaintance. No, no, the risks at this early stage are far too great. Endanger myself? Not in the least.

"You, Miss Holly, shall be the first to test my flying machine."

❧ 20 ❧

"Reptile! Miscreant!" Scarcely able to control my outrage, I shook a fist at the smiling fiend. "You are condemning her to death!"

"Steady on, Brinnie." Vesper laid a calming hand on mine as she replied to Helvitius, "What happens if I won't?"

Helvitius shrugged. "To me, it makes little difference. To you, a great deal. Until your opportune arrival, I had planned to instruct one of these mechanically skilled individuals"—he gestured at the workmen regarding us in unhappy silence—"in the operation of my aircraft. The controls could not be simpler. Even the most ignorant could master them. But you, Miss Holly, with your knowledge of physics, engineering, kinetics, would be better able to report any technical flaws in my design.

"If you are unwilling," he added, "I shall manage without your assistance. Before you make your final decision, I urge you to consider your alternatives. On the one hand, a life of involuntary servitude in some distant clime, far from Professor Garrett. On the other, I might allow you to remain here with me, to aid in my further research. You would find it a stimulating challenge. You might also wish to conduct your own scientific investigations. Professor Garrett would find the contents of the library sufficiently interesting to occupy his life—whose duration, of course, depends on your obedient behavior."

"A devil's bargain!" I cried. "Dear girl, pay no heed!"

Vesper, to my dismay, instead of rejecting this vile proposal out of hand, hesitated for some moments. Turning her attention to the flying machine, she said to Helvitius, "Before I decide one way or the other, I'd have to know how it works. You claim it's easy? I want to see that for myself."

Dr. Helvitius nodded, beckoning for us to approach the vehicle. He opened a hatchway in the framework. Vesper bent and crawled inside. There, with great interest, she examined the apparatus while Helvitius continued, "The controls are extremely delicate, but their manipulation is simplicity itself. The vertical rod directs the machine up or down. The pedals at your feet cause the craft to turn left or right. The small lever in front of you regulates the fuel supply and speed; the larger one, forward motion."

"It looks easy enough," said Vesper. "Let me make sure I've got it all straight. Now, what was it you told me? This stick? Oh, yes. It makes the machine go right or left."

"Not the stick, Miss Holly," Helvitius replied impatiently. "The pedals, as I have just this moment explained, control sideways motion."

"Which pedals?"

"The ones in the flooring," snapped Helvitius. "I advise you to pay closer attention."

"Oh, yes," Vesper said. "Now I see them."

She leaned down. A moment later, I heard the sound of ripping and the jangling of wires. Helvitius cried out angrily as Vesper crawled from the hatchway.

She held up a tangle of broken wires and shattered rods. Marvelous girl! With a few energetic tugs, she had destroyed what appeared to be the entire control mechanism.

"Is this what you meant?" she innocently inquired. "You're right, they're delicate."

The face of Helvitius tightened. "I take it, Miss Holly, that is your answer."

"No," said Vesper. "I'm still thinking it over. By the time you have all this repaired, I'll be ready to decide. It could take awhile, I guess, but we're in no hurry."

"Miss Holly," Helvitius said icily, "you have made a serious miscalculation."

If Vesper expected him to remand us to our cell, she had indeed miscalculated. Instead, Helvitius ordered horses to be brought. He mounted and, under the aimed rifles of the guards, we were compelled to do likewise.

"Dear girl," I whispered, as our cavalcade of guards, Helvitius leading, trotted from the courtyard, "your action was courageous. Alas, I fear it will only bring some new punishment."

"I knocked his flying machine out of kilter, anyway," said Vesper. Then she added, "I'm half sorry I did. Really, Brinnie, he'd put it together very nicely. Fascinating. I wish I'd seen more of that new engine, too."

Vesper left off as Helvitius turned his mount and came to ride next to us. Until now, I had assumed we would be taken to Bel-Saaba, there to face what further devilry the monster had in store. Once away from the eroded building, we headed not in the direction of the city but into the Hambra foothills.

"I salute your enterprise and daring, as I have come to know them so well," remarked Helvitius, "but now I give you fair warning. For your own sake, Miss Holly, give no thought to escape in these hills. As you see, my men carry the latest and most accurate rifles—which I myself obtained through, let us say, private channels. Believe me, neither you nor Professor Garrett would live long enough to enjoy even temporary freedom."

Helvitius pronounced this threat in a completely matter-of-fact tone and would, unquestionably, have carried it out in the same fashion. The prospect of being shot down in our tracks was enough to dampen Vesper's usual optimism. She lapsed into silence as we passed through the scrubby vegetation of an ascending trail.

Midday had passed before we ceased jogging upward and Helvitius led us over a relatively flat stretch to a peculiar construction created not by nature but the labor of human hands.

A long, steep slope had been cleared along a hillside. This roadway, or smooth track, swooped sharply downward, ending abruptly as it overlooked the countryside below.

Vesper gasped and clapped a hand over her mouth. Helvitius had swung from his saddle, calling out orders to a group of his enslaved laborers.

"I did miscalculate," Vesper murmured. "Brinnie, he's got another one."

A second flying machine! My heart sank as Vesper pointed to an identical craft moored with ropes at the upper end of the track.

"You should not be surprised." Helvitius came up to us and indicated that we should dismount. "What you saw before, Miss Holly, was an earlier model for purposes of study and demonstration. This newer one has been improved in many details. The system of control remains the same. You have already been instructed in its operation. I am resolved to launch my vehicle without delay.

"I shall spare you the painfulness of indecision and long-drawn-out shilly-shallying. Miss Holly, you will accept or decline this opportunity here and now. Immediately."

"If you put it that way," said Vesper, "then—yes, I'll do it."

"This is deliberate murder!" I burst out. "You give her no chance even to practice manipulating your infernal machine."

"I rely on Miss Holly's intelligence and ability," replied Helvitius. "She is resourceful, quick to learn, and these qualities will be enhanced by a strong motivation: Her life is at stake."

"So is your flying machine," said Vesper.

"I can always build another," said Helvitius. "You cannot do likewise."

"I insist on accompanying her," I declared. "You shall not allow her to face this peril alone."

"You insist?" returned Helvitius. "You are not in a

position to insist on anything. It is I who insist. Yes, Professor Garrett, you shall join her. You shall aid in her observations and make note of all significant details."

At that, he left us and went to converse with his laborers. Vesper took my arm and hurriedly whispered, "There's no other way, Brinnie. We have to take our chances." She hesitated a moment, then added, "One thing worries me, though."

"I share your apprehension," I said. "I, too, fear this monstrous apparatus will crash."

"No," said Vesper, "I'm worried that it won't. It might really fly. I'll have to make sure it doesn't."

"Don't you see, Brinnie? One way or another, he has to believe his machine's a failure. If he sees it really works, you know what he'll do. His slave trade's bad enough. But if every country in the world can drop bombs on each other—no, Brinnie, I won't let that happen."

"But we are risking our lives and may very well lose them."

"Not yours, Brinnie. No, your life's the one thing I won't risk. I didn't think Helvitius would make you come along. I'll talk him out of it."

"That you will not," I answered. "Whatever fate holds in store, I will share it. You cannot deny me. I will be with you."

"Dear old Brinnie," Vesper murmured. "I wouldn't want you anywhere else."

She said no more as Helvitius returned to hand us each a pair of close-fitting green spectacles and a cap equipped with a leather chin strap.

"You may find the air currents quite strong," he said,

while we donned those items. "Unlike a balloon, which sails at the mercy of the wind, my flying machine is susceptible to direction. It will go where you wish. If my calculations are correct, you should be able to remain aloft long enough to demonstrate its functions."

"And if your calculations aren't correct?" said Vesper.

"You shall discover that very quickly." Helvitius fixed a baleful eye on Vesper. "I understand your mental processes, Miss Holly. I suspect that even now you contemplate some manner of escape."

"Last thing in the world I was thinking about," said Vesper.

"How sensible," said Helvitius, "because escape is impossible. There is not enough fuel to carry you any great distance. And where, in any case, could you hide? The open desert? My men are watching below; you would be seen and recaptured easily. I, too, shall observe your every movement," he added, indicating a pair of binoculars slung over his shoulder.

Helvitius motioned for us to proceed to the upper end of the runway, where the flying machine awaited. I squeezed through the hatch and took up a cramped position at the back of the wheeled cage. Vesper climbed in after me. As she settled herself at the controls, Helvitius produced a large revolver which he pointed directly at her.

"None of your clever but ultimately futile tricks," he said coldly. "If I perceive one suspicious move on your part, I will shoot both of you instantly.

"Now, Miss Holly, I suggest you brace yourself securely. My machine, as yet, has insufficient power to lift itself from the ground. Hence, this runway will allow it to achieve maximum velocity before the moment of flight."

Helvitius paused, turning his eyes to the clouds. "As a classical scholar, I am naturally reminded of the myth of Daedalus and Icarus, with myself, of course, as Daedalus the artificer. And Icarus—Miss Holly, I sincerely hope you do not share the fate of that unfortunate youth. Do not fly, in the figurative sense, too close to the sun."

With a disgusting look of self-satisfaction at having made this unsettling allusion, Helvitius closed the hatchway. "Now, I can only wish you bon voyage."

"Bon voyage?" muttered Vesper. "Better say something like happy landings."

One of the artisans, meantime, had activated the powerful engine, which began roaring and chugging. The blades at the rear of our cage spun into motion as the crew unloosed the mooring lines.

On either side of the vehicle, the crew laid hold of the framework and pushed it down the slope, running along until the machine gained such speed that no longer could they keep up with it.

We shot over the brink. Suddenly free from the reassuring solidity of earth, we hung poised for an instant. The top of my head felt detached from the rest of me as the nose of the flying machine dipped, and the vehicle plunged downward.

"Hold on, Brinnie!" Vesper shouted above the roar of the engine. "Hold tight!"

My cry of terror seemed to hang in the air above us, along with my stomach. Vesper grasped the vertical rod and struggled to pull it toward her. We continued to plummet. The desert floor came closer at an alarming rate, until, at last, the flying machine righted itself. The wing above our enclosure shuddered as if it might rip apart under the strain. Then we swooped upward, soaring past the slopes of the Hambra. Helvitius, binoculars trained upon us, had become a tiny, insignificant figure.

I clapped my hands over my ears to shield them from the deafening whir of the blades and the racketing engine. I could scarcely catch my breath. Had human beings ever been propelled through the air at such speed? In defiance of nature's own inviolable laws? Despite the churning of my interior organs, the sensation was not altogether disagreeable.

Vesper glanced back at me, her face alight with sheer joy. "Brinnie, it's marvelous! What a shame to smash it!"

Maintaining her grip on the rod, she endeavored to operate the pedals. The flying machine gave a lurch and sheered off to starboard. The wires twanged, the wooden struts rattled as she trimmed the craft and set it straight again. The engine, meantime, had developed a sort of bronchial cough. With a sickening drop, the vehicle lost its former altitude.

"Helvitius got his calculations wrong," Vesper called back to me, "or he misunderstood Ibn-Salah. The machine isn't staying up. I won't have to crash on purpose," she added. "That's going to happen by itself. If I can catch the air currents, I'll try to fly it like a kite and think of an easy way to land."

Helvitius, for all his arrogance, had failed to defy nature. There was, at least, some small consolation in that. The engine, by now, had ceased functioning. A stench of overheated metal filled my nostrils. A geyser of steam spurted from the rear of our cabin.

We continued, nevertheless, to be airborne. Vesper's brilliant manipulation of the controls carried us in the direction of Bel-Saaba.

Vesper pointed downward. "What's burning?"

Indeed, a cloud of black smoke rose from what I could discern to be the library building. Vesper brought us farther down until we nearly skimmed the walls. The public square seethed with running figures.

"El-Khouf's guards! There—Brinnie, those people fighting in the street. They look like Addi's tribesmen!"

At that moment, a blast of heat scorched me. A backward glance told me that the fishtail assembly had caught fire.

"That's Sheik Addi himself!" exclaimed Vesper. "He's in trouble, too. The guards have him cornered.

"Hang on, Brinnie," she added. "If we have to crash, we'll do it in Bel-Saaba."

❧ 22 ❧

"No way to crash gently," Vesper called out. "I'll do what I can."

She pulled back on the guidance rod and kicked at the pedals on the flooring. The flying machine veered and dipped as Vesper fought with all her might to control this diabolical invention which, I had no doubt, would provide our final resting place. The aircraft tilted to one side then the other. We had, by now, cleared the city walls and were speeding toward the town hall at the breathtaking rate of what I judged to be some fifteen or even twenty miles an hour.

As the last remaining wires snapped, Vesper brought the yawing vehicle earthward, heading for the terraces and gardens. The ground heaved up to meet us.

Vesper kicked open the hatchway. "Jump! Now!"

She flung herself from the cage. I plunged after her, to go sprawling into a bank of shrubbery. Brave girl! Her presence of mind and calm courage had kept us from breaking our limbs and, very probably, our necks as well.

The flying machine continued on its course, skidding across the dry fountain basin while flames streaked from the fishtail. Moments later, it shattered against the trunk of a palm tree. The subsequent explosion sent blazing fragments of cloth, wood, and metal into the air.

Vesper disentangled herself from the bushes, tore off the spectacles and cap, and was running across the terrace by the time I collected my wits and stumbled to catch up with her. The immediate result of our arrival and the destruction of the flying machine was to flush out the nauseating Bou-Makari from behind the palm tree.

Whatever the events taking place in the city, the treacherous camel trader had apparently chosen to observe them from this vantage point. In view of the explosion and the debris raining down on him, the terrified Bou-Makari opted to leave the vicinity. Knees pumping, turban unwinding to stream behind him, he raced off as if the jinns themselves were at his heels.

Vesper's observations from aloft had been correct. Sheik Addi was indeed in Bel-Saaba and, at the moment, hard pressed by some of el-Khouf's guards. A further benefit of the exploding machine had been to send portions of the shattered wing spinning into the pack of ruffians besetting him. They scattered and fled, while Addi stared agape at the flaming wreckage.

"Addi!" Vesper ran up to him. "What are you doing here?"

The sheik popped his eyes at her. "We came to save you."

"We're saved already," Vesper replied. "Save the library."

The smoke which had first drawn her attention to the

city continued rising from the library building. Too bewildered to do otherwise, Sheik Addi obeyed Vesper's command, beckoning to some of the Beni-Brahim tribesmen close by, and set off across the terrace.

Vesper would have followed, but as she started up the flight of steps, Jenna ran from the arcade and seized her by the arm.

"Flee the city!" cried Jenna. "*Anisah,* make haste!"

"Where's Maleesh?" Vesper demanded. "Where are the twins?"

In reply, Jenna only continued urging Vesper to make her escape. "The north gate. Go, *anisah!* An-Jalil awaits you!"

"I'll go," said Vesper, "as soon as you tell me what's happening."

Any explanation could, in my opinion, be offered later. I took Vesper's arm and, despite her protest, pulled her away and rather forcibly directed her across the square.

We broke clear of a knot of townspeople armed with cudgels, eagerly joining the Beni-Brahim in confronting the guards.

Though Helvitius had armed el-Khouf's ruffians with the latest firearms, he had apparently given them inadequate instruction in their use. Most of their shots went wild, and, exhausting their supply of cartridges, they were compelled to employ their rifles as clubs. In the hand-to-hand melee, it was difficult to judge which side held the advantage.

The north gate stood open. We ran toward it. "There!" cried Vesper. "The Tawarik!"

That moment, a blow to the back of my head sent me

pitching to the ground. Half stunned, I staggered to my feet. What I saw caused me to shout in horror.

El-Khouf had gripped Vesper with one burly arm. With his other hand, he brandished a dagger.

"Stand away!" he ordered me. "I pass or the *roumi* dies."

"Villain!" I exclaimed. "As villainous as your master! If you dare to harm her—"

Vesper, for her part, kicked and struggled, striving to wrench herself away from el-Khouf's grasp. Little by little, her efforts brought her and her captor closer to the gate. There, I caught sight of the giant Tashfin, of Attia, and of An-Jalil himself.

"Help us!" called Vesper. "Here!"

An-Jalil understood her plight immediately. Eyes blazing above his blue veil, a terrifying war cry on his lips, he sprang through the gate, his vow shattered, the first Tawarik to set foot in Bel-Saaba for seven centuries.

Sword in hand, An-Jalil sped toward the *kahia.* "Coward! Do you hide behind a woman?"

El-Khouf bared his teeth. "Tawarik, let me pass."

"Stand against me first," declared An-Jalil. "Face me in single combat, if you dare." He raised his sword.

El-Khouf gave a scornful laugh at An-Jalil's weapon. He flung Vesper aside. Before she could regain her feet, he drew a revolver from his tunic. Vesper cried out as he fired.

An-Jalil pitched forward. The sword dropped from his hand. El-Khouf spun around and darted through the crowd. Tashfin, shouting with rage, set after him for a few paces; then, concerned more for his fallen leader, he turned back. An-Jalil's other warriors ran to help him. Vesper was there before them, kneeling at An-Jalil's side.

"Take me to the desert," he murmured. "There, it is a clean death."

❧ 23 ❧

"You aren't going to die in the desert or anywhere else." Vesper drew aside his veil and loosened the collar of his tunic. Under the blue stain, An-Jalil's face was mottled gray.

"We must obey him." Tashfin knelt beside her. The huge Tawarik's eyes brimmed. "Take him from this accursed city. He told me death awaited him if he set foot within, yet he did so. Now we shall do as he commands. So it is written."

"Not yet it isn't," Vesper declared, though as near to weeping as Tashfin. "The only place we'll take him is to a doctor."

An-Jalil's eyes had closed; his breathing came in shallow gasps. The warriors gathered around him, ready to follow their chieftain's last order. Although the fray continued on the far side of the square, the Tawarik had no heart to join it. Had things fallen out differently, there was no doubt in my mind that they would have made short work of el-Khouf's ruffians. It was questionable now whether we could even make good our own escape.

"Anisah!"

Maleesh had arrived. He cried out at the sight of the fallen An-Jalil.

"We need Dr. Baba. Right away," Vesper told him. "Where is he?"

Maleesh gestured toward the library. "Perhaps he is still there. I do not know. El-Khouf's men bar the way."

Though I saw nothing of el-Khouf himself, his guards indeed had taken a position along the arcade and showed every sign of preparing to attack the tribesmen. As I judged the situation, the Beni-Brahim stood an excellent chance of being defeated. The element of surprise might, at first, have worked in their favor, but the tide of battle was now rapidly turning against them.

"Tashfin," Vesper pleaded, "go help Sheik Addi and his people. They'll be killed if you don't."

The big Tawarik glanced up in the direction of the fighting. His eyes glittered with vengeance. He nodded curtly and sprang to his feet. He motioned to Attia el-Hakk and half a dozen of the others, who unslung their muskets and set off across the square.

Vesper ordered the remaining Tawarik to carry An-Jalil to a more sheltered spot near the wall. Maleesh, during this, had not ceased urging Vesper to flee the city. To me, it was excellent advice, which Vesper determinedly ignored.

The crash of the flying machine must have damaged my hearing and caused my ears to play tricks on me. I shook my head to clear it.

"What's that?" Vesper listened intently. Unless she suffered the same affliction as mine, the sound was not imaginary: bugles blowing the charge.

"The Legion!" cried Vesper.

The urgent, brassy notes grew louder. Within another moment, Colonel Marelle, saber out and flashing, galloped through the gates. Their cloth havelocks bright white in the sun, bayonets glinting, the Legionnaires streamed into Bel-Saaba. At the rear, mounted on a pair of racing camels, came Smiler and Slider.

"There!" Vesper pointed to the arcades. "Follow the Tawarik!"

Colonel Marelle, excellent officer that he was, understood the situation immediately.

"Mes enfants," he shouted, *"en avant!"*

With the banner of the Legion snapping in the breeze, his men raced after him, speeding to the relief of the embattled Beni-Brahim.

Without waiting for their camels to kneel, the twins jumped down and ran to Vesper. Their joy at our safety was cut short by the sight of An-Jalil.

Shouts of triumph rose from the direction of the town hall. The charge of bayonets in the hands of those grim-faced Legionnaires in the wake of the fierce Tawarik broke el-Khouf's men completely. Saving their own skins outweighed any loyalty to their vanished master. Flinging away their weapons, they took to their heels with such enthusiasm that even the Legion's famous quick pace could not overtake them.

"We did our best, Miss Vesper," Slider said. "Too late, it looks like."

"Seems that little shindy's over," Smiler added, in a tone of disappointment.

"Another's just starting," said Vesper, returning to An-Jalil. "We're going to win that one, too."

Vesper's optimism, I suspected, was more an attempt to raise her own spirits than a statement of fact. An-Jalil remained unconscious as his companions bore him through the jubilant crowd to the town hall and the chambers once occupied by el-Khouf.

Leaving his men in charge of his sergeant major, Colonel Marelle came to join us.

"I regret to see a gallant warrior in these painful circumstances," Marelle said. "As for you, Miss Holly, my men and I were glad for another opportunity to be of service. Thanks to Monsieur Sleedaire and Monsieur Smeelaire, who brought news of your captivity."

"Thanks more to Mr. Maleesh," put in Slider. "It was all his idea. We'd started thinking how to get Miss Vesper and the professor out of that library." He turned to Vesper. "After he went back and found you'd been taken off somewhere—unavailable for rescue, in a manner of speaking—he sent us to carry word to Mr. An-Jalil and borrow a pair of camels from him."

"Then he told us to ride hell-for-leather to Fort Iboush," said Smiler. "Which is what we did. You should have seen those Frenchies hustle. They got here in no time."

"It was Mr. Maleesh who told Doc Baba to set a smudge fire," added Slider. "If that sidewinder el-Khouf thought the old boy was in danger, he'd send his men to save him. Mr. Maleesh calculated how that would keep some of those guards too occupied to fight us."

"Maleesh planned the whole thing?" said Vesper. "What about the Beni-Brahim?"

"I don't rightly know," said Smiler. "That was Mr. Maleesh's own part in it. You'll have to ask him."

Though now apparent that Maleesh had masterminded a campaign that would have done credit to our gallant general and president, Ulysses Grant, he had not come to accept our grateful praise. He seemed, rather, to be making himself deliberately scarce.

Instead, it was Jenna who now hurried in with Dr. Baba.

"We came as soon as we learned what happened," said the aged scholar. "This young lady and I were tending the wounded. She has, by the way, proved to be a remarkable healer. Yes, yes, in time she could be a better one than I."

He and Jenna went quickly to examine An-Jalil. The old man turned away, shaking his head. "He may require more skill than the two of us possess."

Dr. Baba spoke hastily with Jenna, requesting her to fetch medicines. At his further instructions, Tashfin and Attia carried their unconscious leader into the adjoining chamber. Only Jenna, when she returned, was permitted to aid Dr. Baba. The grim Tawarik reluctantly waited in silence at the door. Vesper, despite her entreaties, was obliged to do likewise.

That night was as endless as any we had ever spent. From time to time, Jenna emerged to obtain materials from Dr. Baba's supply. When Vesper pressed her for word of An-Jalil, Jenna gave no answer.

In the course of our anxious waiting, Maleesh arrived with Sheik Addi. Seeing Vesper, Addi momentarily brightened, but he appeared in no mood for conversation.

Nor, for that matter, did Maleesh. When Vesper asked how he had managed to bring Sheik Addi and his band to our rescue, he was less than forthcoming.

"While the twin moons rode to Fort Iboush," he said tersely, "I set out to seek the Beni-Brahim. I found Sheik Addi almost at the city gates. I persuaded him to enter and help me find you."

"Then he's forgiven you!" exclaimed Vesper. "That's wonderful. Now, you and Jenna—"

Maleesh turned away, declining to say more.

Soon after dawn, Jenna and Dr. Baba stepped from the chamber. While Jenna ran to the arms of Maleesh, Dr. Baba approached us and the Tawarik.

"He will live." The old man smiled happily. "Yes, yes, he most assuredly will. Never have I seen one of such strength. Nor of such spirit.

"I feared I would be unable to treat his wound," he continued, "but I found the remedy. It was in the very book you returned to the library: Ibn-Sina's treatise on medicinal herbs. Without that, my child, your friend would not be alive at this moment—and asking to see you."

With a joyful cry, Vesper started up and would have gone into the chamber. Maleesh drew her back.

"*Anisah,*" he said quietly, "now that all is well, I must take my leave of you. You asked why Sheik Addi agreed to help? He wished to regain his daughter, and I alone knew where to find her. I promised to bring Jenna to him.

"And one thing more," Maleesh added. "In exchange for his aid, I offered him my life as forfeit. Now I must pay with it."

24

Learning that one's beloved has bargained away his life must always come as a shock. Though Maleesh had made a sublimely heroic gesture, Jenna did not see it in that light. She beat her fists on his chest.

"Fool! Idiot! What have you done? You told me nothing of this. To make such a pledge with never a word, never a thought for me, for us!"

"I gave you all my thoughts," replied Maleesh. "I said nothing, for I knew you would try to keep me from it. Pearl of my heart, you have blessed me with more happiness than I dreamed would ever come to me. That, I owe to you. But I owe the *anisah* a different debt. In Mokarra, she saved my life. She gave me kindness when I most needed it. This weighs heavy in the scales of the universe."

"It doesn't weigh in Bel-Saaba," declared Vesper. "Maleesh, you don't owe me anything. In the Haggar, I set you free of your vow, didn't I?"

"So I thought," Maleesh answered. "Then I understood that freedom was not yours to give nor mine to accept. *Anisah,* I once told you that a golden chain linked our lives. It cannot be broken by words; it still binds me. So it is written."

"So it's also written," declared Vesper, "that you're not keeping that bargain."

"He will!" Sheik Addi burst out. "He pledged his life. It is mine to take. My hand shall strike him down!"

Jenna's eyes blazed as she flung herself in front of Maleesh. "You shall have to kill me first."

"Keep out of this!" roared Addi. "I decide who I kill and who I do not."

"No, you don't," retorted Vesper. "You won't lay a finger on either of them. You have no right. You aren't in your village; you're in Bel-Saaba. You've got no authority here. As long as Maleesh and Jenna are in the city, they're under the rule of the governor."

"El-Khouf has fled," Addi flung back. "There is no *kahia.*"

"That," said Vesper, "is what you think."

Leaving the Tawarik to keep Addi at bay, Vesper strode into the chamber. Held in Tashfin's grip, the sheik had to content himself with hurling insults at Maleesh, unrepeatable but not lethal.

After some while, Vesper put her head out of the door and beckoned to Dr. Baba. Puzzled, the old scholar went to join her. Vesper emerged again and invited all of us to enter.

With cushions under his head, An-Jalil lay on a divan. Without the covering of a veil or turban, his mane of hair hung about his brow and shoulders. His features, despite the blue stain, were pallid. Still, for one who had been shot at point-blank range, he looked in pretty fair condition.

"An-Jalil knows the bargain Maleesh made," said Vesper. "I was right. Addi has no authority over anybody in Bel-Saaba. That belongs to An-Jalil. He's the rightful governor and always has been."

"No, *anisah.*" An-Jalil raised a hand. "For your sake, I broke my vow. For your sake, I would break it again, a thousand times over. But, as I have told you, there is one oath I shall not break. I shall not accept to govern here."

"I understand that," said Vesper. "There was something else we talked about."

"As I also told you," said An-Jalil, "when there is no successor by birth, it is the right and duty of the governor to name who will take his place. This I now do.

"I choose one who is brave enough to admit his fear, and wise enough to admit that he is foolish; who would risk his life for one he loves, yet give up life and love if he believes he must. If he accepts, I name: Maleesh."

Maleesh stood too dumbstruck to answer.

Sheik Addi did it for him.

"He accepts!" Addi jubilantly roared. "And I accept him! My son-in-law—the *kahia*!"

He flung his arms around the joyous couple in such an embrace that Maleesh was in danger of being squashed before he could even start his administration.

Colonel Marelle, observing all this, now approached An-Jalil and saluted stiffly.

"An-Jalil es-Siba, it is my painful duty to place you under arrest."

25

Colonel Marelle was either a man of incredible bravery or, what comes to much the same, a lunatic. Having made such an announcement, there was no way he would leave that room alive. Tashfin's dagger was already in his hand.

"Arrest me?" An-Jalil's eyes glinted. "Will you try your Legionnaires against my Tawarik?"

"I said it was my duty," replied Marelle. "I did not say I would carry it out. Why should I deprive myself of a gallant opponent? Another day, perhaps. Or perhaps not. Be warned. It may be different with those who someday will take my place. The times have changed. You, with your honor and chivalry, are not modern."

"Are you?" answered An-Jalil. "We are both only temporary. The desert and the mountains will outlive us. But a day must come when the French leave my land, as others before them have done."

"I do not speak as an officer of the Legion," said Marelle, "but as one who loves Jedera, and as one man to another. My friend, I hope you are right."

Dr. Baba, concerned that this was overtiring his patient, ushered all of us from the chamber and up to the balcony. At sight of their beloved benefactor, cheers burst from the waiting crowd below, and grew even louder when Dr. Baba presented Maleesh as the new governor.

"Maleesh is everything An-Jalil said he was," Vesper whispered to me. "Dr. Baba talked about frailties. Maleesh has enough of them, too, I daresay. He and Bel-Saaba are going to get along very nicely."

I agreed. After el-Khouf and so many other brutal governors, a fellow who could dance on his hands and pull coins from his nose would be a welcome change. It was fine for Bel-Saaba. It would, of course, never do for Philadelphia.

"An-Jalil made the perfect choice," Vesper added. "I'm glad I suggested it."

While An-Jalil continued to recover, Vesper and I at last had a chance to browse through the library. The workmen had, meantime, returned to the city. They reported that Helvitius had last been seen on a camel galloping across the desert.

"Too bad we didn't catch him," said Vesper. "Maybe he'll run into a sandstorm."

Though disappointed by the villain's escape, Vesper was more interested in the works of Ibn-Salah and reading his theories of flight for herself.

"Helvitius *did* misunderstand," she said, poring over the ancient volumes. "Yes—I can see how he miscalculated when he designed his flying machine. Ibn-Salah wasn't wrong; Helvitius was. Good thing these books are out of his reach. He won't come back to study them again. Besides, he's too arrogant to admit he made a mistake. He'll blame Ibn-Salah.

"Look here, Brinnie," she went on, "this diagram of how air flows over a curved surface—fascinating."

"Dear girl," I said, after urging Dr. Baba to lock up the precious volumes, "nature in her sublime wisdom has decreed that we shall not imitate the birds. A flying machine is impossible. As impossible as mankind ever setting foot on the moon."

"I wonder," said Vesper.

We remained in Bel-Saaba a few days more, until An-Jalil was well enough to leave the city. Colonel Marelle and his Legionnaires had already departed for Fort Iboush. Sheik Addi had grown even more overjoyed, envisioning his grandchildren and great-grandchildren, generation after generation of honored governors.

On our last morning, Jenna embraced us and the twins. *"Anisah,"* she said, "you have brought us life and happiness."

Maleesh echoed those sentiments and embraced us likewise, adding to Vesper, "Was I not right? The chain that links us is unbroken. So it is written, and so it is."

"Kahia Maleesh," replied Vesper, "you still have it backwards. First, it is. Then, so it will be written."

An-Jalil and his Tawarik escorted us back through the Haggar, this time following the longer but easier caravan trail. As a result, the journey was blessedly uneventful.

The Tawarik, however, would go no farther than Tizi Bekir.

"Here, *anisah,* we must part," said An-Jalil. "I long for my desert. I will be there as you voyage beyond the wide ocean." He touched his lips to his fingertips, which he gently pressed on Vesper's brow. "Salaam, *anisah.* Go in peace."

"And you," Vesper softly replied, returning his gesture. She smiled. "The spirit of the jinn flies where it wishes. Even to Philadelphia."

In Mokarra, we received unhappy news. The twins' ship had been burned past repair. There was no telling when Smiler and Slider could leave the country.

"We'll find another berth," said Smiler. "Don't worry. Slider and I can always manage."

"I'm sure you can," said Vesper. "But I've been thinking. You're clever with machinery. You could probably build a whole new sort of engine."

"No doubt of that," said Slider. "That's one of the things Smiler and I do best."

"Twins," said Vesper, "what would you think about coming to Philadelphia and staying with us?"

The offer of a trip to Philadelphia was one that could hardly be refused. Even so, Smiler and Slider glanced at each other uneasily.

"We'd be honored, Miss Vesper, as who wouldn't. But—we had that little misunderstanding with the law a few years back."

"No one's going to bother you now," said Vesper. "I'll see to it."

"Well, then," the twins replied simultaneously, "we couldn't ask better."

Fortunately, we had not long to wait for a vessel sailing to Philadelphia. The Tawarik had given us veils and tunics to replace our own garments and, for the sake of comfort, we wore them throughout the voyage. The veils especially offered excellent protection against wind and spray. However, the other passengers tended to give us a wide berth when they encountered us strolling the deck.

In Strafford, my dear Mary was delighted to make the acquaintance of Smiler and Slider, and welcomed them as happy additions to the household. She did show some dismay at our appearance.

"Poor child!" she exclaimed. "What's happened to you? And you, Brinnie! You've turned blue!"

"We'll explain later," said Vesper. "The main thing is, we returned the book."

"And quite properly so," said Mary. "You, my dear Brinnie, should feel especially edified at having done your duty."

"You'd have been proud of him," said Vesper. "If you'd seen him flying through the air—"

"What?" cried Mary. "Through the air? Brinnie!"

"He won't do it again," said Vesper, on her face a look of innocent sincerity which I knew all too well. "I promise he won't. Not for a while, anyhow."

CHRIST IN
Isaiah

F.B. MEYER

CHRIST IN Isaiah

F.B. MEYER

CLC ❖ PUBLICATIONS

Fort Washington, Pennsylvania 19034

Published by CLC ❖ Publications

U.S.A.
P.O. Box 1449, Fort Washington, PA 19034

GREAT BRITAIN
51 The Dean, Alresford, Hants. SO24 9BJ

AUSTRALIA
P.O. Box 419M, Manunda, QLD 4879

NEW ZEALAND
10 MacArthur Street, Feilding

ISBN 0-87508-770-1

The first American edition published in 1982 by
Christian Literature Crusade, Fort Washington, PA.

This printing 2001

Printed in the United States of America

CONTENTS

Most of the Scripture quotes herein are taken either from the King James Version or the 1881 Revised Version. However, the author sometimes uses his own paraphrases.

PREFACE

THE Exodus from Egypt is one of the most conspicuous landmarks of the past—not only because of its historical value, but because it inaugurated a religious movement which is the most important factor in our modern world.

The exodus from Babylon has never succeeded in arousing equal interest, largely because it was more gradual and uneventful. Yet it was a marvelous episode, and bore upon its face the evident interposition of Jehovah on behalf of his people. Its results, which culminated in the advent of the Servant of the Lord, were in the highest degree momentous.

The story of this exodus is anticipated in chapters 40 to 55 of the Book of Isaiah, which form the subject of this volume. But the story of the exodus itself is subsidiary and introductory to another theme, which soon absorbs our attention. Before us pass, in vivid outlines, the scenes by which our redemption was secured. The humiliation and suffering, sorrow and anguish of soul, substitution and death, exaltation and satisfaction of the Savior are portrayed with the minuteness and accuracy of a contemporary; and there is hardly a sentence from which we cannot begin and preach Jesus, as Philip did to the Ethiopian eunuch.

F.B. Meyer

1

"COMFORT YE, COMFORT YE"

(Isaiah 40:1)

"Ask God to give thee skill
In comfort's art;
That thou mayst consecrated be
And set apart
Into a life of sympathy.
For heavy is the weight of ill
In every heart;
And comforters are needed much
Of Christlike touch."

A. E. Hamilton

THINK it not strange, child of God, concerning the fiery trial that tries you, as though some strange thing had happened. Rather, rejoice—for it is a sure sign that you are on the right track. If, while traveling in unfamiliar country, I am informed that I must pass through a valley where the sun is hidden, or over a stony bit of road, to reach my desired abiding place—when I come to them, each moment of shadow or jolt of the vehicle tells me that I am on the right road. So when a child of God passes through affliction he should not be surprised.

In the case of the chosen people, who for nearly seventy years had been strangers in a strange land and had drunk the cup of bitterness to its dregs, there was an added weight to their sorrow—the conviction that their captivity in Babylon was the result of their own impenitence and transgression. This is the bitterest thought of all—to know that one's suffering *need not have been*. To know that it has resulted from indiscretion and inconsistency; that it is the harvest of one's own sowing; that the vulture which feeds on the vitals is a nestling of one's own rearing. Ah me, this is pain!

There *is* an inevitable retribution in life. The laws of the heart and home, of the soul and human life, cannot be violated with impunity. The sin may be forgiven; the fire of penalty may have been already changed into the fire of trial; the love of God may seem nearer and dearer than ever—but still there is the awful pressure of pain, the trembling heart, the failing of eyes and pining of soul, the refusal of the lip to sing the Lord's song. Surely, we ought not be surprised at the troubles that afflict us.

Look up. You are to be like the Son of God, who himself passed through the discipline of pain as a participator with the children of flesh and blood. If *he* needed to come to earth to learn obedience by the things that he suffered, surely *you* cannot escape! Could you be quite like him unless you are perfected by suffering? You must endure the file of the lapidary; the heat of the crucible; the bruising of the flail—not to win your heaven, but to destroy your unheavenliness. The glorified spirits who have gathered on the frontiers of the heavenly world to encourage you in your journey thither declare that the brilliance of their reward has been in proportion to the vehemence of their sorrows—allowing you also space and opportunity for the heroism of faith.

Look down. Do you think that the prince of hell was pleased when you forsook him for your new master, Christ? Certainly not! At the moment of your conversion your name was put on the proscribed list, and all the powers of darkness pledged themselves to obstruct your way. Remember how Satan hated Job; does he not hate you? He would vent on you the hatred he has for your Lord, if he might. There is, at least, that one case on record of hell being permitted to test a saint—within a defined limit.

Look around. You are still in the world that crucified your Lord, and it would do the same again if he were to return to it. It cannot love you. It will call you Beelzebub. It will cast you out of its synagogue. It will count it a religious act to slay you. In the world you shall have tribulations, but in the midst of them you can be of good cheer.

When the soul is in the period of its exile and bitter pain, it should do three things: Be on the lookout for comfort; store it up; and pass it on.

1. BE ON THE LOOKOUT FOR COMFORT.

(a) *It will come certainly.* Wherever the nettle grows, beside it grows the soothing dock-leaf; and wherever there is severe trial, there is, somewhere at hand, a sufficient store of comfort—even though our eyes, like Hagar's, are often restrained so that we cannot see it. But it is as sure as the faithfulness of God. "I never had," says Bunyan, writing of his twelve years imprisonment, "in all my life, so great an insight into the Word of God as now; insomuch that I have often said, Were it lawful, I could pray for greater trouble, for the greater comforts' sake." No, God cannot forget his child. He cannot leave us to suffer, unsuccored and alone. He *runs* to meet the prodigal, and he rides on a cherub and *flies* on the wings of the wind to the sinking disciple.

(b) *It will come proportionately.* Your Father holds a pair of scales. This one on the right is called *As*, and is for your afflictions; this one on the left is called *So*, and is for your comforts. And the beam is always kept level! The more your trial, the more your comfort. *As* the sufferings of Christ abound in us, *so* our consolation also abounds through Christ.

(c) *It will come divinely.* It is well, when meeting a friend
at the terminal, to know by what route to expect him,
lest he arrive on one platform while we await him on
another. It is equally important to know in what quarter
to look for comfort. Shall we look to the hills, the stable
and lofty things of earth? No—in vain is salvation looked
for from the multitude of the mountains. Shall we look
to man? No—for he cannot reach low enough into the
heart. Shall we look to angels? No—among the many
ministries that God entrusts to them, he seldom sends
them to comfort. Perhaps they are too strong, or they
have never suffered. To bind up a broken heart requires
a delicacy of touch which Gabriel has not. God reserves
to *himself* the prerogative of comfort. It is a divine art.
The choice name of the Son and the Spirit is *Paraclete*
(the Consoler or Comforter). Yours is the God of all comfort! It is when Israel is in the extremity of her anguish
that the Divine Voice sounds from heaven in strains of
music, "Comfort ye, comfort ye my people, saith your
God. Speak ye comfortably to Jerusalem." "I am he that
comforteth you." "As one whom his mother comforteth,
so will I comfort you."

(d) *It will come mediately.* What the prophet was as
the spokesman of Jehovah, uttering to the people in
human tones the inspirations that came to him from
God, so to us is the great Prophet whose shoe latchet
the noblest of the prophetic band was not worthy to
unloose; and our comfort is the sweeter because it
reaches us through him. In these words we hear the
Father calling to the Son, and saying, "Comfort ye, comfort ye my people." "Our comfort aboundeth *through
Christ*" (2 Cor. 1:5).

(e) *It will come variously.* Sometimes by the coming of
a beloved Titus. Or by a bouquet; a bunch of grapes; a
letter; a message; a card. Sometimes by a promise; or
the laying of an ice-cold cloth on our fevered brows.
Sometimes by God coming near. See in this chapter of

Isaiah the variety of considerations by which God would comfort the despondent soul. That their term of sorrow is nearly accomplished; that herald voices announce the leveling of difficulties and the approach of dawn; that the covenant stands sure; that the God of stars and worlds is the tender Shepherd, who will not overdrive his flock; that man at his strongest is but as the flower of the field, while God's Word is like the great mountains. There are many strings in the dulcimer of consolation.

In sore sorrow, it is not what a friend *says* but what he *is* that helps us. He comforts best who says least, but simply draws near, takes the sufferer's hand, and sits silent in his sympathy. This is God's method. "Thou drewest near in the day that I called upon thee; thou saidst, Fear not" (Lam. 3:57).

2. STORE UP COMFORT. This was the prophet's mission. He had to receive before he could impart. He had to be schooled himself before he could teach others.

The world is full of comfortless hearts. Orphan children are crying in the night. Rachels are weeping for their children. Strong men are crushed in the winepress of war, because their blood is the life of the world. Our God pities them all. But he cannot stay the progress of these awful years until the mystery of iniquity is finished. Still he pities, and he would assuage the anguish of the world through *you.* But before you are sufficient for this lofty ministry, you must be *trained.* And your training is costly in the extreme—for to render it perfect, you must pass through the same afflictions as are wringing countless hearts of tears and blood. Thus your own life becomes the hospital ward where you are taught the divine art of comfort. You are wounded that in the binding up of your wounds by the Great Physician you may learn how to render first aid to the wounded everywhere. Your limbs are broken that in the setting of them you may have a personal acquaintance with the anatomy and surgery of the heart.

Do you wonder why you are passing through some special season of sorrow? Wait till ten years have passed. I guarantee that in that time you will find some others—perhaps ten—afflicted as you are. You will tell them some day how you have suffered and have been comforted; then as the tale is unfolded, and the anodynes applied which once your God had wrapped around you, in the eager look and glistening eye, and in the gleam of hope that shall chase the shadow of despair from the soul, you shall know why you were afflicted—and you shall bless God for the discipline that stored your life with such a fund of experience and helpfulness.

Store up a careful memory of the way in which God comforts you. Watch narrowly how he does it. Keep a diary, if you will, and note down all the procedure of his skill. Ponder the length of each splint, the folds of each bandage, the effect of each anesthetic, tonic, or drug. This will bring a twofold blessing. It will divert your thoughts from your miseries to the outnumbering mercies, and it will take away that sense of useless and aimless existence which is often the sufferer's weariest trial.

3. PASS ON THE COMFORT YOU RECEIVE. At a railway station a kind-hearted man found a schoolboy crying, because he had not quite enough money to pay his fare home. Suddenly, he remembered how, years before, *he* had been in the same plight, but had been helped by an unknown friend, who enjoined him some day to pass the kindness on. Now he saw that the anticipated moment had arrived. He took the weeping boy aside, told him the story, paid his fare, and asked him, in his turn, to pass the kindness on. And as the train moved from the station, the lad cried cheerily, "I will pass it on, sir." So that act of wonderful love is being passed on through the world, nor will it stop till its ripples have circled the globe and met again.

"Go, and do thou likewise." "Speak ye comfortably to Jerusalem, and cry unto her." God comforts you, that you might comfort those who are in any trouble. You cannot miss them; they are not scarce. Your own sad past will make you quick to detect them, where others might miss them. If you find them not, seek them; the wounded heart goes alone to die. Sorrow shuns society. Get from the Man of Sorrows directions to where the sorrowing hide. He knows their haunts, from which they have cried to him. He has been there before you. And when you come to where they are, do for them as the Good Samaritan did for you, when he bound up your wounds, pouring in oil and wine. "Comfort ye, comfort ye my people, saith your God."

2

VOICES THAT SPEAK TO THE HEART

(Isaiah 40:2–11)

"The world were but a blank, a hollow sound,
If he that spake it were not speaking still;
If all the light, and all the shade around
Were aught but issues of Almighty will.

"Sweet girl, believe that every bird that sings,
And every flower that stars the elastic sod,
And every thought that happy summer brings
To thy pure spirit, is a word of God."

H. Coleridge

WHEN the heart is sad, and the years bring no relief, be sure to turn away from the fret of circumstance, the confused murmur of human life, the many voices that speak from the crowds around. Listen, rather, with ear intent, until your soul distinguishes those deeper voices that penetrate the barrier of sense from the land of the unseen—where God is, and life is at the full. There may be no shape or form, no speaker that can be recognized, no angel-messenger with radiant glory and wing of noiseless strength; but there will be voices— not one or two only, but sometimes, as in this marvelous paragraph, *four* at least—each the voice of God, but each with a different accent, a different tone.

The anonymity of the voices is unimportant. The multiplication table is anonymous, but it is not less true.

Some of the sweetest of the psalms, and the Epistle to
the Hebrews, are anonymous; but they carry their cre-
dentials on their face. Everywhere in their fabric is the
hallmark of inspiration. That these voices speak out of
the void, borne down the wind from eternity, while the
heralds themselves are veiled in twilight which is slowly
opening to dawn, argues nothing against their credibil-
ity and comfort. A strain is sweet, though we know not
the composer; a picture is noble, though we know not
the artist; a book is true and helpful, though no name
stands on the title page. The heart of man, made in the
image of God, recognizes instinctively the voices that
speak from God—even as a child, far from home in the
blackest night, would recognize instantly any of the
voices that it had been accustomed to hearing from its
cradle days.

This is one characteristic of the voices that reach us
from God: they speak "to the heart" (literal rendering of
"comfortably"). The phrase in the Hebrew is the ordinary expression for wooing, and describes the attitude
of the suppliant lover endeavoring to woo a maiden's
heart. Love can detect love. The heart knows its true
affinity. Many voices may speak to it, but it turns from
them all; it heeds them not . . . till one day the true
prince sounds on the horn the blast for which all was
waiting. The spell is broken and the sleeping maiden
awakes to welcome her true lover. So your heart will
recognize its Immortal Lover by this token. "I was asleep,
but my heart waked; it is the voice of my Beloved that
knocketh."

1. THE VOICE OF FORGIVENESS (v. 2). The first
need of the soul is forgiveness. It cannot endure suffering for long. And if that suffering, like that of the Jewish
exile, has been caused by its own follies and sins, it will
meekly bow beneath it, saying with Eli, under similar
circumstances, "It is the Lord; let him do what seemeth
good to him." But the awful sense of being unforgiven!

God's clouded face! The dark shadow on the heart! Neither sun nor star shining for many days! The oppressive weight of unforgiven sin! The question whether God's mercy may not be gone forever, and that he will be favorable no more! This bitterness of heart for sin is the first symptom of returning life. It does not justify, but it prepares the soul eagerly to seek and tenaciously to grasp God's method of righteousness. And before God can enter upon his great work of salvation, before he can clear away the debris and restore the ruined temple, before he can reproduce his image, it is needful to assure the penitent and believing soul that its "time of service" (R.V., margin) is accomplished, that its iniquity is pardoned, and that it has received at the Lord's hand double for all its sins.

In dealing with the question of sin and its results, let us always distinguish between its penal and natural consequences. The distinction comes out clearly in the case of drunkenness or criminal violence. Society steps in and inflicts the penalties of the fine, the prison, or the lash; but in addition to these, there is the aching head, the trembling hand, the shattered nervous system. So in respect to sin. Its violation of the holy law of God, its affront to the majesty of divine government, its personal injury to the Lawgiver—these could be atoned for only by the death of the Second Man, the Lord from heaven. He bore our sins in his own body on the tree—he put away sin by the sacrifice of himself. He was made sin, therefore our trespasses cannot be imputed to us; and God in him has reconciled the world unto himself.

But the natural consequences remain. David was forgiven, but the sword never left his house. The drunkard, the dissolute, the passionate may be pardoned, and yet have to reap as they sowed. The consequences of forgiven sin may be greatly sanctified, the Marah waters cured by the tree of the cross—yet they must be patiently and inevitably endured. It was thus that

Jerusalem was suffering when those dulcet notes reached her. She was loved with an everlasting love. Though the literal city was in ruins, and her sons in exile, yet to God they were Jerusalem stil—"Speak ye comfortably to *Jerusalem.*" But, nevertheless, the backsliding and rebellious people were doomed to serve their appointed time of captivity, and suffer the natural and inevitable results of apostasy. Hence the double comfort of this announcement: not only that all iniquity was pardoned but that warfare was ended, and that she had suffered double enough of natural punishment to serve the divine purpose of her sanctification.

You too have been suffering bitterly. Those early indiscretions and errors of your life have brought a terrible revenue of pain. You have passed many days over a path paved by burning cinders, and your feet are blistered. But God will not always be threshing you. The sword shall not devour forever. The billows of the sea shall pursue you to their limit, but not beyond. Your time of hard service as a conscript (literal rendering) has been completed, your iniquity pardoned; you have received double for all your sins. It has appeared to come from your foes, but it has been meted out by the Lord's hand—and he says, It is enough.

2. THE VOICE OF DELIVERANCE (vs. 3–5). Between Babylon and Palestine lay a great desert of more than thirty days journey. But the natural difficulties that seemed to make the idea of return chimerical were small compared with those that rose from other circumstances. The captives were held by as proud a monarchy as that which had refused to let their fathers go from the brickkilns of Egypt. Mountains arose in ranges between them and freedom, and valleys interposed their yawning gulfs. But when God arises to deliver his people who cry day and night unto him, mountains swing back as did the iron gate before Peter; valleys lift their hollows into level plains; crooked things become straight and

rough places smooth.

When Eastern monarchs travel through their dominions, they are preceded by couriers who require the towns through which they pass to repair the roads and highways. This is the purport of the herald voice, which rings out on the startled and trembling silence, "Prepare ye in the wilderness the way of the Lord, make straight in the desert a highway for our God"—and which foretells the leveling of obstacles even as a woman's hand may smooth creases out of linen, or a steamroller level the sand.

If you had ears to hear, you too could hear it. You are sitting solitary and desolate; the Lord's song has long been hushed on your tongue. The hand of the oppressor is heavy, and it seems useless to expect other deliverance than that of death. You have, like Job, courted and fondled the idea of dying. "Now should I have lain down and been quiet; I should have slept; then had I been at rest." But God has some better thing awaiting you in the near future when his glory is revealed. Dawn is at hand—and with dawn, deliverance.

It seems impossible. The tangle is so great, the obstacles so many, the hold of captivity so tenacious. There are, doubtless, smiling Italian landscapes; but the Alps stand as an impassible barrier, with inaccessible crags, and walls of ice, and yawning crevasses. Things are too crooked ever to be straightened in this world; too rough to admit of further progress, which is as impossible as that of sledges over hummocks of ice. But wait only upon God; let your expectation be from him! He will come with a strong arm. And as he leads you forth—as the angel led Peter—to your amazement insuperable obstacles shall disappear. Red Seas and Jordans shall yield pathways; mountains shall fill valleys; ropes shall be as tow in flame; and netted snares shall be like cobwebs, which a touch destroys.

3. THE VOICES OF DECAY AND IMMORTAL
STRENGTH (vs. 6–8). As man's soul is still, and becomes able to distinguish the voices that speak around
him in that eternal world to which he, not less than the
unseen speakers, belongs, it hears first and oftenest the
laments of the angels over the transience of human life
and glory. In this stillness, in which the taking of the
breath is hushed, the soul listens to their conversation
as they speak together: "Cry," says one watcher to another. "What shall I cry?" is the instant inquiry. "There
is," continues the first, "but one sentiment suggested
by the aspect of the world of men: All flesh is grass, and
all its beauty like the wild flowers of the meadowlands,
blasted by the breath of the east wind, or lying in swathes
beneath the reaper's scythe."

These words meet with a deep response in the heart
of each thoughtful man. "Man cometh forth like a flower,
and is cut down." "As for man, his days are as grass; as
a flower of the field, so he flourisheth." We have all seen
it. Our goodly sons, our sweet, fair girls, our little babes,
have faded beneath our gaze, and lie among the grass of
ordinary folk. Jerusalem had long been in exile; one by
one her heroes and defenders, her statesmen and prophets, had died in captivity. Her sons were now of a smaller
type. Nehemiahs in the place of Isaiahs; Ezras instead
of Jeremiahs; Zerubbabels for Hezekiahs. Where was
the Moses to lead this second exodus; the Joshua to
settle them in their land; the Solomon to build their
temple? There seemed no reply, save that given by the
sigh of the wind from the great Lone-land, and the edge
of Death's sharp reapinghook. Thus the deliverers and
champions of earlier days have passed away. Who now
shall succor?

But listen further to the voices of the heavenly watchers. The failure of man shall not frustrate the divine
purpose. Lover and friend may stand aloof, or be powerless to help. Ah, yes—the strong arm may be power-

less to fulfill its old promises. The prop of the family may have fallen; the breadwinner may be on his bed, unable to do anything to maintain wife and children. *But God will do as he has said.* He is independent of men and means. He can make ravens bring food. "The grass withereth, the flower fadeth; but the word of the Lord shall stand forever."

It is good to hear this angelic testimony to the permanence of the word of God. Of course we could not doubt it. By it were the heavens made, and all the host of them; and by it the wheel of natural revolution is ever kept in motion. And yet since our *all* depends on it, since it is the basis of our hope in the gospel, we may be forgiven for hailing gladly the confirmation of heavenly testimony that the word of God shall stand forever.

4. VOICES TO HERALD THE SHEPHERD-KING (vs. 9–11). The Authorized Version (K.J.V.) and the margin of the Revised Version are perhaps preferable to the Revised Version here. Zion, that gray fortress of Jerusalem, is bidden to climb the highest mountain within reach, and to lift up her voice in fearless strength, announcing to the cities of Judah lying around in ruins that God is on his way to restore them. "Say unto the cities, Behold your God! Behold the Lord God will come."

All eyes are turned to behold the entrance on the scene of the Lord God, especially as it has been announced that he will come as a Mighty One. But, lo, a Shepherd conducts his flock with leisurely steps across the desert sands, gathering the lambs with his arm, and carrying them in his bosom, and gently leading those who are with young. It is as when, in later centuries, the beloved apostle was taught to expect the Lion of the tribe of Judah, and, lo, in the midst of the throne stood a Lamb as it had been slain.

Do not be afraid of God. He has a shepherd's heart and skill. He will not overdrive. When he puts forth his own sheep he will certainly go before them, and they shall follow him. He will suit his pace to theirs. Words can never describe his tender considerateness. If the route lies over difficult and stony roads, it is because there is no other way of reaching the rich meadowlands beyond. When strength fails, he will carry you. When heavy demands are made, he will be gentleness itself. He is the Good Shepherd, who knows his sheep—even as the Father knows him.

These are the voices that speak to us from the Unseen. Happy is he who makes a daily parenthesis of silence in his heart, that he may hear them speak. It was a good habit for a devout servant of God to sit before the Lord for an unbroken period at the end of each day, that he might hear what God the Lord might speak. Ours be the cry of Samuel, "Speak, Lord, for thy servant heareth."

3

"WHY SAYEST THOU?"

(ISAIAH 40:12–31)

"Go, count the sands that form the earth,
The drops that make the mighty sea;
Go, count the stars of heavenly birth
And tell me what their numbers be;
And thou shalt know love's mystery."
T. C. UPHAM

IT is well in times when feeling is strong to say little, lest we speak unadvisedly with our lips, murmuring at our lot, or complaining against God—as though he had forgotten to be gracious, and had shut up his tender mercies in anger. Speech often aggravates sorrow. We say more than we mean; we drown in the torrent of our words the still small voice of the Holy Spirit whispering comfort. We speak as though we had not known or heard. It is wise, therefore, not to pass grief into words. Better let the troubled sea within rock itself to rest. "Why sayest thou, O Jacob, and speakest, O Israel?"

Was it a true thing these exiles said? They suggested that they had worn out the divine patience: that their way was no longer open to his view, and that their justice had ceased to be his concern. They were ready to admit that he had been the God of their *fathers*—but he had now withdrawn from his covenant relationship and would be favorable no more. That, they said, was the reason why they were allowed to languish year after year on the plains of Babylon. They spoke as though they had never known nor heard some of the most rudimentary facts about the nature and ways of God. "Hast thou not known? Hast thou not heard?"

In our dark hours we should revert to the considerations which have been familiar to us from childhood, but have of late ceased to exert a definite impression. It is remarkable what new meaning sorrow discovers in truths familiar as household words. It looks for the hundredth time into their abyss, and suddenly sees angels sitting. Let us recount some of these familiar facts; and perchance, as your troubled soul turns from men and things, from what depresses and what threatens, to the everlasting God, the Lord, the Creator, you will dare to believe that he has neither forgotten nor forsaken you; that he delights still in your way, which is leading through the tangled thicket into the sunlight; that he is weighing your case with infinite solicitude.

Nature has always been the resort of the suffering. Elijah went to Horeb; Christ to Olivet. And in these glowing paragraphs of Isaiah, which touch the high-water mark of sacred eloquence, we are led forth to stand in the curtained tent of Jehovah, to listen to the beat of the surf and watch the march of the stars.

A passage from the journal of a sad and lonely thinker, with singular beauty of language, tells of the effect of nature upon him. He is speaking of the month of April; and after alluding to the moist freshness of the grass, the fragrance of the flowers, the transparent shadows of the hills, the breath of the spring, he says:

There have been so many weeks and months when I thought myself an old man, but I have given myself up to the influence of my surroundings. I have felt the earth floating like a boat in the blue ocean of ether. On all sides stretched mysteries, marvels, and prodigies, without limit, without number, and without change. I kissed the hem of the garments of God, and gave him thanks for being Spirit, and being Life. Such moments are glimpses of the Divine; they make one conscious of eternity. They assure one that eternity itself is not too much for the study of the thoughts and works of the Eternal; they awake in us an adoring ecstasy, and the ardent humility of love.

The devout thought of these paragraphs of Scripture text passes in survey: First the *earth* gives testimony (12–20); then the *heavens* (21–26); and finally, the *experience of the children of God in all ages* (27–31).

1. THE TESTIMONY OF THE EARTH. It seems as though we are conducted to the shores of the Mediterranean, and stationed somewhere near the site of ancient Tyre. Before us spreads the Great Sea, as the Hebrews were in the habit of calling it. Far across the waters, calm and tranquil, or heaving in memory of recent storms, sea and sky blend in the circle of the horizon. Now remember, says the prophet, God's hands are so strong and great that all that ocean and all other oceans lie in them as a drop in a man's palm. His fingers are so wide in their reach that their measure when outstretched can compass the breadth of heaven. His arms are so strong that they can hold balances and scales in which the loftiest mountains and the multitudinous isles of the Archipelago lie as small dust might do on the brass scales of a merchant. And this God is our God forever and ever! He has taken not Israel only, but Jacob, into eternal union with himself. The Creator of the ends of the earth is our Father. Creation is only one of his *thoughts*; but you are his *son*, his *heir*, his *beloved*. See how full of care he is about lilies and birds, about the

delicate down on an insect's wing, and about the lichen traceries upon the stones. He cannot then fail you, nor forsake you!

Behind us lie the hills, and beyond them the mountains, and above them all Lebanon rears her snow-capped peaks like a bank of cumulus clouds built up in the sky. But all the wood on Lebanon, its cedars riven with tempest and rugged with age, would not be too much to lay on the altar of Jehovah. And if all its beasts could be collected and laid on the wood in sacrifice, and if Lebanon itself were the mighty altar of earth, there would be no extravagance in the vast burnt offering that would fill the vault of heaven with fire and smoke. So great is God that the greatest gifts of human self-denial, which have cost men most, are not too great. How preposterous, therefore, it is to liken him to any graven image or carving of wood! How needless to dread what men can do! How certain it is that he who spared not his own Son, but gave him to a greater altar and fiercer flame, will with him also freely give us all things!

All men may be in arms against you, encircling you with threats and plotting to swallow you up. But the nations are to him as a drop in a bucket, and are counted as the small dust on the balance. The isles are very little things in his esteem, and their inhabitants as grass-hoppers. You have no reason therefore to be afraid. When your enemies come upon you, they shall stumble and fall. The Lord is your Judge, your Lawgiver, and your King. He will save you.

2. THE TESTIMONY OF THE HEAVENS. The scene shifts to the heavens, and all that is therein. With a marvelous prevision of the earth's circuit around the sun, Jehovah is depicted as sitting on the circle of its orbit, and looking thence on the populations of the earth. From that distance the teeming multitudes of mighty Babylon would seem insignificant enough, and there would be no appreciable difference between the mon-

arch and the slave grinding at the mill. This is the anti-
dote for fear. Sit in the heavenlies. Do not look from
earth towards heaven, but from heaven towards earth.
Let God, not man, be the standpoint of vision.

But this is not all. To this inspired thinker, it seemed
as though the blue skies were curtains that God had
stretched out as a housewife would gauze (see the R.V.
margin), or as the fabric of a tent within which the pilgrim rests. If creation be God's tent, which he fills in all
its parts, how puny and pigmy are the greatest poten-
tates of earth. "He bringeth princes to nothing, and
maketh the judges of the earth as vanity." The child of
God need not be abashed before the greatest of earthly
rulers. Herod and Pontius Pilate, with the Gentiles, and
all the people of Israel, may be gathered together; but
they do whatsoever his hand and his counsel has foreordained to come to pass. They are but stubble withered by the blast.

And even this is not all. Day changes to night, and as
the twilight deepens, the stars come out in their numerous hosts; and suddenly, to the imagination of this
lofty soul, the vault of heaven seems a pastureland over
which a vast flock is following its shepherd, who calls
each by name. What a sublime conception: Jehovah,
the Shepherd of the stars, leading them through space;
conducting them with such care and might that none
falls out of rank, or is lacking. And will Jehovah do so
much for stars and naught for sons? Will he not have a
name for each? Will he not guide and guard each? Will
he not see to it that none are lacking, when he brings
his flock home at the end of the day? He who has kept
the stars full of light for millenniums, and sustained
them in their mighty rounds, will not do less for you,
his *child*. If you were reconciled to God by the death of
his Son, you will be surely saved by his life!

3. THE TESTIMONY OF THE SAINTS. Have you not
heard? Where have been your ears? This has not been

told in secret, nor whispered in the dark places of the earth. It has been a commonplace with every generation of God's people, that the Lord faints not, neither is weary. He never takes up a case to drop it. He never begins to build a character to leave it when it is half complete. He cannot be exhausted by the rebellion, backsliding, or fickleness of his children. Were this not so, heaven would have missed some of its noblest inhabitants. Jacob, David, Peter, and myriads more, are trophies of the unwearied pains which God takes with those whom he adopts into his family.

It is quite true that he may *seem* to forsake and to plunge the soul into needless trial; this, however, is no indication that he has tired of his charge, but only that he could not fulfill the highest blessedness of some soul he loved other than by sternest discipline. "There is no searching of his understanding."

There is another point on which all the saints are agreed, that neither weariness nor fainting are barriers to the forthputting of God's might. On the contrary, they possess an infinite attractiveness to his nature. We have seen a little weakling child draw to its cot some strong and burly man, the champion athlete of the countryside. Such a spell can weakness exert over might, and helplessness over helpfulness. It is the clear teaching of Scripture that the strong should bear the infirmities of the weak and not please themselves. Such is the law of God's existence. All that he is and has he holds in trust for us, and most for those who need most.

In point of fact, many of us are *too* strong, self-reliant and resourceful to get the best that God can do. Wait a little, till your strength begins to faint beneath the burdens and the noontide heat, till the energy that was your boast has slowly ebbed away and you are left without might. Then the Mighty One of Jacob will draw nigh to you, and impart both power and strength. Jacob must limp upon his thigh ere he can prevail with God and man.

They who *wait* on God *renew* their strength. It is new strength for each new duty and trial. As each fresh demand is made on them they receive some fresh baptism, some unrealized enduement. Ah, happy art, nearly forgotten in these busy days! Nothing, not even youthful genius and vigor, can be a substitute for this!

The gradation spoken of here (v. 31) is a remarkable one. At first sight it would appear that it should pass from walking to running, and from this to flying; but the order is reversed, as though it were easier to mount up with wings than to walk without fainting. And so, indeed it is! Any racehorse will start at full speed; but how few have staying power. The tyro in cycling will go at full pelt; but only the experienced rider can walk or stand. To pursue the common track of daily duty—not faltering nor growing weary—to do so when novelty has worn off, when the elasticity of youth has vanished, when the applause of the crowd has become dim and faint— this is the greatest achievement of the Christian life. For this, earthly and human strength will not avail. But God is all-sufficient. Never faint or weary himself, he is able to infuse such resistless energy into the soul that waits on him that, if it mounts, it shall be on *eagle* wing; if it runs, it will *not* weary; if it walks, it will *not* faint.

4

THE CONVOCATION OF THE NATIONS

(ISAIAH 41)

"Triumphant Faith!
Who from the distant earth looks up to heaven,
Seeing indivisibility suspending
Eternity from the breath of God.
Lo! with step erect
She walks o'er whirlpool waves and martyr fires,
And depths of darkness and chaotic voids."

E. TATHAM

THE imagery of this passage is superb. Jehovah is represented as summoning the earth, as far as the remote isles of the West, to determine once and forever who is the true God—whether he, or the idols and oracles of which there were myriads worshiped and believed in by every nation under heaven.

The test proposed is a very simple one. The gods of the nations were either to predict events in the near future or to show that they had had a clear understanding of the events of former days. "Set forth your case, saith the Lord; bring forth your strong reasons, saith the King of Jacob. Let them bring them forth, and declare unto us what shall happen: declare ye the former things, what they be, that we may consider them, and know the latter end of them; or show us things for to come" (vs. 21–22). On the other hand, the servant of

Jehovah was prepared both to show how fast-sealed
prophecies, committed to the custody of his race, had
been precisely verified in the event and to utter minute
predictions about Cyrus, "the one from the east" (v. 2),
which would be fulfilled before that generation had
passed away. Not, as in Elijah's case, would the appeal
be made to the descending flame, but to the meshing of
prophecy and historical fact.

Immediately there is a great commotion: the isles see
and fear, the ends of the earth tremble, they draw near
and come to the judgment seat. On the way thither each
bids the other take courage. There is an industrious
furbishing up of the dilapidated idols, and a manufac-
turing of new ones. The carpenter encourages the gold-
smith; and he that smooths with the hammer, him that
smites the anvil. They examine the soldering to see if it
will stand, and drive great nails to render the idols steadfast. The universal desire is to make a strong set of gods
who will be able to meet the divine challenge—much as
if a Roman Catholic priest were to regild and repaint
images of the saints on the time-worn altar of a fishing
hamlet in the hope of securing from them greater help
in quelling the winter storms.

History furnishes some interesting confirmations of
this contrast between the predictions of heathen oracles
and the clear prophecies of Old Testament scripture
which were so literally and minutely realized. For instance, Herodotus tells us that when Croesus heard of
the growing power of Cyrus, he was so alarmed for his
kingdom that he sent rich presents to the oracles at
Delphi, Dodona, and elsewhere, asking what would be
the outcome of his victorious march. That at Delphi gave
the ambiguous reply that "a great empire will be destroyed"—but whether the empire would be that of Cyrus
or that of Croesus was left unexplained. Thus, which-
ever way the event turned, the oracle could claim to
have predicted it. This is a fair illustration of the man-

ner in which the oracles answered the appeals made to them by men or nations when in the agony of fear. How striking a contrast the precise predictions of these pages, which give us the name of the conqueror; the quarter from which he would fall upon Babylon; his marvelous series of successes, that gave kings "as the dust to his sword, as the driven stubble to his bow"; his reverence towards God; his simplicity and integrity of purpose (verses 2, 3, 25; 45:1).

We are learning to lay increasing stress on prophecy. What miracles were to a former age, the predictions of the Bible are to this; and, unlike the miracles, the evidence of prophecy becomes stronger with every century that passes between its first utterance and its fulfillment. Probably there is an unrealized wealth of attestation lying in the ancient records of Egypt and Babylon which is on the eve of being made available against the attacks of infidelity.

How sad, on the other hand, it is to mark the trend of opinion, in quarters where we should least expect it, towards the muttering of oracles and the whispering of familiar spirits—the rehabilitation of that lying system which filled the world at the incarnation of Christ, but which Milton at least supposed had forever vanished before the rising beams of the Sun of Righteousness.

> *"So when the sun in bed,*
> *Curtained with cloudy red,*
> *   Pillows his chin upon an Orient wave,*
> *The flocking shadows pale*
> *Troop to the infernal jail,*
> *   Each fetter'd ghost slips to his several grave;*
> *And the yellow skirted fayes*
> *Fly after the night-steed, leaving their moon-loved*
> *   maze."*

Amid the excitement of this vast convocation, the idols
are dumb. We can almost see them borne into the arena
by their attendant priests, resplendent in gold and tinsel, flashing with jewels, bedizened in gorgeous apparel.
They are set in a row, their acolytes swing high the cen-
ser, the monotonous drawl of their votaries arises in
supplication. Silence is proclaimed, that they may have
an opportunity of pronouncing on the subject submit-
ted to them; but they are speechless. Jehovah pro-
nounces the verdict against which there can be no appeal: "Behold, ye are of nothing, and your work of naught:
an abomination is he that chooseth you" (v. 24). As Jehovah looks, there is no one. When he asks of them,
there is no counselor that can answer a word. "Behold,
they are all vanity; their works are nothing: their molten images are wind and confusion" (v. 29).

While this great cause is being decided, the people of
God are addressed in words of tender comfort, which
are as fresh and life-giving today as when first spoken
by lip or written by pen.

1. THE CIRCUMSTANCES IN WHICH GOD AD-
DRESSES HIS PEOPLE. They are poor and needy; they
seek water, and there is none; the heights are bare, and
the valleys verdureless; the track of their life lies through
the wilderness; they are surrounded by incensed enemies who strive with them; they are powerless as a
worm. It is among such that God has always found his
chosen. Not the wise and prudent, but the babes; not
the high and mighty, but the lowly and obscure; not the
king, but the shepherd lad; not Eli, but Samuel. He finds
them in their low estate, cast aside and disowned by the
world—and adopting them, he makes for himself a name
and a praise.

It is necessary that God should have room in which
to work: emptiness to receive him; weakness to be em-
powered by him. It is into the empty branch that the
vine sap pours; to the hollowed basin that the water

flows. The weakness of the child gives scope for the man's strength. The need of the countless multitudes that thronged Christ's earthly life gave him opportunity for the working of his miracles and the putting forth of his power. The lower the platform, the greater the proof of what God can be and do to those who trust him. Take heart, therefore, if you can see yourself in any of those that are summoned to your view by the roll call of want and weariness and sin. The prime blessedness of the kingdom of heaven is for the poor in spirit, the persecuted and the tempted, the wandering sheep and the famishing child.

2. THE ASSURANCES THAT HE MAKES TO THEM. No height, however bare, nor depth, however profound, can separate us from his love. He whispers, amid the gloom that has settled down upon the landscape of our life, "Fear thou not, for I am with thee" (v. 10). No enemies, however numerous or enraged, need dismay us; for he is still our God, bound to us by covenant relationship, able to throw reinforcements into the citadel of our heart, succoring us with horses and chariots of fire. Heart and flesh may fail; but he will strengthen. Difficulties may seem insurmountable; but he will help. The feet may be cut and bleeding with the desert march; but he will uphold with his strong right hand.

There is a striking passage in one of the psalms (Ps. 48) which expresses the pride of the patriotic Jew as to the glories of Jerusalem, the city of the great King, in which God had made himself known as a refuge. The kings of the nations, intent upon her destruction, assemble themselves and pass by her frowning battlements; but as they see the inviolable protection of God flung around them, they are dismayed, trembling takes hold of them, and they haste away. So, when strong enemies threaten the life, the purity, the well-being of God's elect, he flings around them so complete and inviolable a defense that foes become as nothing—as a thing of naught. And the beleaguered soul entrenched within its strong fortifications is reassured by the repeated refrain of Jehovah's voice, "Fear not; I will help thee" (v. 13).

And when God sets his hand to save any of his saints, he does not stop at this, but goes on to use the saved one for the blessing of others. Hence he not only comforts the few men of Israel with the assurance of his ready help—reiterating the words, as though never weary of repeating them—but he promises to make of them, worms though they be, a new sharp threshing instrument having teeth, which will thresh the mountains and beat them small, and make the hills as chaff (vs. 14–15). This prediction has been marvelously fulfilled in the history of the Jewish nation, which has exercised such a formative influence on the history of the world; and there is a similar experience awaiting all who will surrender themselves absolutely to the hands of God. In your own estimation you may be nothing more than a worm; yet if you will yield yourself absolutely to God, he will make you a new sharp threshing instrument having teeth.

Who is there that does not long to be renewed, to have a fresh baptism, a fresh beginning in work and energy of life? Who is there that does not wish to be delivered from the bluntless and obtuseness which comes from long use? Who is there that does not desire power to thresh the mountains of sin and evil, until they are dissipated like the heaps of chaff on the threshing floor before the evening breeze? Let such take to their comfort the assertion of Jehovah, *"I will make."* There is nothing that you cannot do, O worm of a man, if Jehovah, your Redeemer, the Holy One, takes you in hand.

3. THE DIVINE PROVISION FOR THEIR NEED. Life is not easy for any of us, if we regard the external conditions only. But as soon as we learn the divine secret, rivers flow over bare heights in magnificent cascades;

fountains arise in the rock-strewn sterile valleys; the wilderness becomes a pool, and the dry land springs; the plain is covered with noble trees, and the desert with the beautiful undergrowth of a forest glade (vs. 18–19).

To the ordinary eye it is probable that there would appear no difference. Still the tiny garret and the wasting illness; still the pining child, with its low moan of continued pain; still the monotony and lovelessness of a lonely, desolate life; still the straitened circumstances—still the deferred hope. But the eye of faith beholds a paradise of beauty, murmuring brooks filling the air with melody, leafy trees spreading their shade.

What makes the difference? What does faith see? How is she able to make such transformations?

(a) Faith is conscious that God is there, and that his presence is the complement of every need. To her eye common desert bushes burn with his shekinah.

(b) Faith recognizes the reality of an eternal choice, that God has entered into a covenant which cannot be dissolved, and that his love and fidelity are bound to finish the work he has commenced.

(c) Faith knows that there is a loving purpose running through every moment of trial, and that the Great Refiner has a meaning in every degree of heat to which the furnace is raised—and she anticipates the moment when she will see what God has foreseen all the time, and towards which he has been working.

(d) Faith realizes that others are learning from her experiences lessons which nothing else would teach them; and that glory is accruing to God in the highest, because men and angels see and know and consider and understand together that the hand of the Lord has done this, and the Holy One of Israel has created it (v. 20).

Some readers of these words may be wearily traversing the wilderness in their daily experience. They seek

water, and there is none; and their tongue fails for thirst.
But if only they would look up with the eyes of faith,
they would behold, as Hagar did, wells of water, and the
fertility of the Land of Beulah. Many pilgrims pass
through that land and see nothing like what Bunyan
describes—no sun shines for them; nor birds sing; nor
ravishing beauty charms the sense. These entrancing
delights are all around; but they are unseen, unknown—
while others find paradise in the unlikeliest surroundings. The difference between these experiences arises
from the presence or absence of the faith that takes

> " . . . *true measure*
> *Of its eternal treasure.* "

Therefore comfort your heart. Wait patiently. Let faith
have her way. Hope to the end for the grace to be brought
unto you. Ponder these things till, in your case also,
what seems only a desert to other eyes, to yours shall
be as the garden of the Lord.

5

"BEHOLD MY SERVANT"

(ISAIAH 42:1–7)

"He does not fail
For thy impatience, but stands by thee still;
Patient, unfaltering—till thou too shalt grow
Patient—and wouldst not miss the sharpness grown
To custom, which assures him at thy side."
                                        H. Hamilton King

WHEN our Lord took on himself the form of a servant, girded himself, and began to wash the feet of his disciples, it was no new office that he performed; for the life of God is ever one of service, of ministry. He rules all, because he serves all. Inasmuch as he is the highest, he must also be the lowliest, according to the everlasting order of the spiritual realm. The ministry of Jesus was therefore the revelation of the life that God had ever been living in the blue depths of heaven; and if once we can learn the principles of that life which filled hundreds and thousands of homes with blessing and joy during those marvelous years of earthly ministry, we shall have a model on which to form our own service to God and man. Our Lord's life and ministry revealed the ideal of service.

There is no doubt as to the applicability of this passage to our Lord. The Holy Spirit, by the evangelist Matthew, directly quotes this opening section of Isaiah 42 and refers it to Jesus, and says its meaning was filled to the brim by that matchless life which for a brief space cast its radiance on our world (Matt. 12:18–21). Oh that he who took upon him the form of a servant—who was among his disciples as one that served, and who proposes some day to wait on his wearied workers as they sit together at his table in his kingdom—oh that he would so incarnate himself in us that we, in our measure, may repeat those features of his earthly ministry. For these are dispositions which God can crown with the enduement of his Holy Spirit, and with which he can cooperate! "I have put my Spirit upon him," he declares. And, "I will hold thine hand."

They are rare qualities which Jehovah calls us to behold in the elect Servant in whom his soul delights: a divine modesty; a divine humility; a divine perseverance.

1. THE MODESTY OF THE BEST WORK. God is always at work in our world, leading the progress of suns, refreshing grass with dew, directing the flight of the morning beams, and even the glancing light of the firefly. And while lovingly compassing our path and our lying down, he is not too busy to determine the fall of a shell on the sand of the ocean bottom. But all his work is done so quietly, so unobtrusively, with such reticence as to his personal agency, that many affirm there is no God at all.

He spreads the breakfast table each morning for myriads living in wood and ocean, and in the homes of men as well; but he steals away before we catch sight of him to whom we owe all. We know that he has been at work; but he is gone without a sound, without a footmark, leaving only the evident touch of his hand.

Thus it was with the work of Christ. He put his hand on the mouths of those who blazoned abroad his fame. He repeatedly told the recipients of his bounty that they must not make him known. He stole away from the multitudes that filled the porches of Bethesda, and the healed paralytic knew not who had healed him. He lingered as long as he could in the highlands of Galilee, until his brethren remonstrated with him. He did not quarrel nor cry out, nor cause his voice to be heard in the street.

This quality is God's hallmark upon the best work. His highest artists do not inscribe their names upon their pictures, nor introduce their portraits among their groups. It is enough for them to have borne witness to the truth and beauty of the universe. They wish for nothing more than to reveal what they have seen in nature's holiest shrines, or in the transient gleams of beauty in the human face. To win a soul for God; to cleanse the scar of the leper; to make blind eyes see; to give back the dead to mother, sister, friend—this is recompense enough. To look up from the accomplished work into the face of God; to catch his answering smile; to receive the reward of the Father who is in secret—this is heaven, compared with which the praise of man is as valueless as his censure.

Are you conscious, fellow servant, that this is the temper of your soul, the quality of your work? For if not—if in your secret soul you seek the sweet voice of human adulation, if you are conscious of a wish to pass the results of your work into newspaper paragraph or the common talk of men—be sure that deterioration is fast corrupting your service, as rottenness the autumn fruit. It is high time that you should withdraw yourself to some lonely spot where the silt that darkens the crystal waters of your soul may drop away, and again they mirror nothing but the sky with its depths of blue, its hosts of stars. The only work that God approves, that is permanent and fruitful, that partakes of the nature of Christ, is that which neither seeks nor needs advertisement. The bird is content to sing; the flower to be beautiful; the child to unfold its nature to the eye of love; and the true worker to do the will of God.

2. THE HUMILITY OF THE BEST WORK. God's choicest dealings have been with shepherd boys taken freshly from their flocks; with youngest sons without repute; with maidens growing to mature beauty in the obscurity of some highland village. He has put down the mighty from their seat, and exalted the humble and meek. And so was it with our Lord. He passed by Herod's palace and chose Bethlehem and its manger bed. He refused the empires of the world, and took the way of the cross. He selected his apostles and disciples from the ranks of the poor. He revealed his choicest secrets to babes. He left the society of the Pharisee and scribe, and expended himself on bruised reeds and smoking flax, on dying thieves and fallen women, and on the peasantry of Galilee.

A reed! How typical it is of the broken heart crushed by the tread of unkindness and tyranny! There is no beauty in its russet plume. There is no strength in its slender stem. There is no attractiveness in the fever-breeding swamp where it grows. And if none would journey far in search of a reed, how much less of one that had been crushed by the boisterous frolic of the river horse, or by the tread of the peasant! So hearts get broken. Too fragile to resist the pressure of the mad rush of selfishness and the tread of unfeeling cruelty, without a sound they break, and thenceforth are cast aside as some useless thing, not worth a thought.

The smoking flax! How it smolders! How slowly the sparks follow one another along its fibers! How powerless it is to kindle the slightest gauze to a flame! So feebly does love burn in some hearts that only he who knows all things can know that love is there at all. So fitful, so irregular, so destitute of kindling power. Ah me! Reader, you and I have known hours when not the coals of juniper but the smoking flax has been the true picture of our love.

The superficial worker ignores these in rude haste. He passes them by to seek an object more commensurate with his powers. Give me, he cries, a sphere in which I may influence strong, noble, and heroic souls! Give me an arena where I may meet foemen worthy of my steel! Give me a task where my stores of knowledge may have adequate scope! And if these fail, he counts himself ill-used. "I will do naught, if I cannot do the best." Oh, foolish words! The best, the noblest, is to bend with a divine humility over those whom the world ignores, exercising a holy ingenuity, a sacred inventiveness; making of bruised reeds pipes of music or measuring rods for the New Jerusalem; fanning the spark of the smoking flax until that which had nearly died out in the heart of a Peter sets on fire three thousand souls within seven weeks of its threatened extinction.

This is also the test of true work. Where does it find you, fellow worker? Are you ambitious for a larger sphere; grudging the pains needed to explain the gospel to the ignorant, to cope with the constant relapses and backslidings of the weak, to combat the fears of the timorous and mistrustful, to adjust the perpetual disputes and quarrelings of new-made disciples; unable to suit your pace to the weakest and youngest of the flock? Beware! Your work is in danger of losing its noblest quality. The hue is passing off the summer fruit; the tender tone which God loves is fading from your picture; the grace of the day is dying. Before it is too late, get alone with God to learn that the noblest souls are sometimes found within bruised bodies, and the greatest work often emanates from the most inconspicuous sparks.

3. DIVINE PERSEVERANCE. Though our Lord is principally concerned with the bruised and the dimly burning wick, he is neither one nor the other (see R.V. margin). He is neither discouraged nor does he fail. In the primeval world, the successive platforms on which he wrought in the ascending scale of creation were per-

petually submerged by waves of chaos that swept them clear of his handiwork; but through all he persevered until the heavens and earth which now exist stood forth appareled in beauty that elicited from the lips of the Creator the verdict, "It is very good." Thus it shall be in the spiritual world. The centuries which have followed on Calvary's supreme sacrifice have witnessed alterations of chaos with cosmos; of disorder with order; of confusion with advancing civilization. In the eighth, ninth, and tenth centuries especially, it seemed as though the results of the tears and martyrdoms and witnessing of the earlier age were entirely lost. But the Master was never once discouraged, nor slacked his hand, but through good report and evil pursued his purpose.

This, again, is a quality of the best work. That which emanates from the flesh is full of passion, fury, and impulse. It attempts to deliver Israel by a spasm of force that lays an Egyptian dead in the sand; but it soon exhausts itself, and sinks back nerveless and spent. The renunciation of an enterprise undertaken in hot haste proves that it was assumed in the energy of the flesh, not given by the suggestion of the Spirit. Perseverance in the face of scorn and difficulty—in the teeth of pitiless criticism and obstinate hate, up the hill brow or across the trembling quag—is a proof that the task has been divinely given, and that the ardent soul is feeding its strength from the divine resources. If this perseverance is failing you, think whether your task is Heaven's or of your own choosing. If the latter, abandon it; but if indeed the former, then wait on the Lord till your strength is renewed, and you, too, shall neither be discouraged nor fail.

But qualities like these, however excellent, cannot avail—with us, at least—until there has been added *the enduement of the Holy Spirit.* "I will put my Spirit upon him." At the waters of baptism that promise was fulfilled; for as the Lord emerged from them, the heavens were opened, and the Spirit in a bodily shape descended upon him and abode. Then his mouth was opened, and his public ministry commenced. For thirty years he had been content with the obscure and contemplative life of Nazareth; now he stepped forth into the world, saying, "The Spirit of the Lord God is upon me, and he hath anointed me to preach."

What that scene was in the life of the Lord, Pentecost was for the Church. Then she was anointed for her divine mission among men: the unction of the Holy One rested upon her, to be continued and renewed as the centuries slowly passed. And what happened for the Church should take place in the history of each member of it. This anointing is for all, is to be received by faith, and is specially intended to equip us for work. Have you had your share? If not, are you not making a mistake in attempting God's work without it? Tarry till you are endued. Have you known it? Seek it on the threshold of each new enterprise. Be satisfied with nothing less than to be anointed with fresh oil.

And even this is not all. In the words "I will hold thine hand, and will keep thee" (v. 6), a suggestion is made of the cooperation of the Holy Spirit with every true servant of God. As we begin to speak, he falls on those who hear the word. As we witness to the death, resurrection and glory of Jesus, he witnesses also to the conscience and heart. When the voice from heaven speaks by our lips, the Holy Spirit says, Yes. Thus all the words of God through us receive the demonstration of the Holy Spirit, as though one were to demonstrate by experiments, optically, what a lecturer was expounding orally to the ear of his audience.

It is impossible too strongly to emphasize the necessity of relying in Christian work on the co-witness of the Spirit of God. It not only relieves the worker of undue and exhausting strain by dividing his responsibilities with his Divine Partner, but it reinforces him with immeasurable power. This is what the apostle means by "the communion of the Holy Spirit," which signifies the state of "having in common." Happy is he who has learned such community of aim and method with the Divine Spirit as to be able to derive the greatest possible assistance from his cooperation.

Such are the divine principles of service; and they need to be studied by each of us if we would hear God say of us, in our measure, "Behold my servant whom I uphold, my elect one in whom my soul delights!"

6

"YE ARE MY WITNESSES"

(ISAIAH 43:1–10)

"Out of that weak, unquiet drift,
  That comes but to depart,
To that pure heaven my spirit lift
  Where thou unchanging art!
Thy purpose of eternal good
  Let me but surely know!
On this I'll lean, let changing mood
  And feeling come or go!"
                              J. Campbell Sharp

THE magnificent concept with which chapter 41 opens underlies what we now are considering. We have still the vast convocation of the world, summoned to decide whether Jehovah or some idol god should henceforth be regarded as the supreme Deity. In the arena are the rows of helpless images, rich in paint and tinsel, but mute, only waiting to be carried home by their attendant priests. Before the assembly disperses, Jehovah must vindicate his claims; and therefore he calls into the witness box his chosen people, that they may tell men what they know, and testify to what they have seen.

It is a remarkable appeal. In chapter 42:19 they are blamed for being blind and deaf; but for all that, they are addressed as capable of giving evidence. Though they had misused their opportunities and had made less progress than they might have done in the knowledge of God, yet they knew more of him than any other nation upon the face of the earth and could tell secrets which the profoundest thinkers had missed. "Ye are my witnesses, and my servant whom I have chosen."

See, they come into court and take their stand face to face with monarchies that had ruthlessly despoiled and ravaged them, to speak for him whose character had been so often maligned and misrepresented by their sins. At the period in which they were summoned to give evidence they were actually in captivity, diminished in numbers, brought low through affliction and oppression; and yet, such is the power of witness to truth, their testimony was to silence all other voices, to bear down all rival claims, and to establish Jehovah as the one and only God. They might be vanquished and broken in the realm of physical force, but they were supreme and imperial in the realm of truth. Thus, in later days, the Lord Jesus stood bound before the representative of mighty Rome, bearing witness to a kingdom which did not emanate from this world but before which that of Rome was to pass into the land of shadows.

See, then, the Jews enter the arena, carrying with them their venerable sacred books. The test, as we have seen, was whether Jehovah had uttered predictions which had been fulfilled.

"Has your God foretold the future?"

"Certainly!" they reply.

"Give some instances."

"In our oldest record, centuries before it took place, Jehovah told our ancestor and progenitor Abraham that his descendants would spend a protracted period in Egyptian bondage; and that afterwards they would come forth amid great judgments, to inhabit the land in which he was a stranger. This was precisely fulfilled.

"Again, Jehovah foretold that Hagar's son, Ishmael,

would be as a wild ass, at odds with all his neighbors. This, too, has been realized in the history of the Arabs.

"Again, through his prophet Isaiah, on the fatal day when our great king Hezekiah showed the ambassadors of the king of Babylon his treasures, Jehovah foretold that we would be captives in this land, and our princes chamberlains in the palace of our conqueror—as it is this day."

The Jews have maintained this witness through the ages. Think of Babylon today, wrapped in the sand drifts in the desert. No Arab pitches his tent there, neither do shepherds fold their flocks. It is the haunt of wild beasts, a possession for the bittern, and a dwelling place for dragons. Think of Tyre, on whose site a few fisher-folk get a scanty livelihood, drying their nets on its ruins; while the noble harbor in which, when Nahum wrote, the wealth of the world proudly floated, is choked up with sand. Think of Edom, from whose rock-hewn houses, situated in vast solitudes and seldom visited by man, arise vast flocks of birds, which almost darken the air at the approach of a stranger. No unprejudiced mind could compare the condition of these sites with the predictions of the Old Testament without being impressed with their strong evidence to the truth of Scripture.

The very existence of the Jewish people scattered throughout the world, and yet preserved from absorption amid the populations that surround them—that they have no rest for the sole of their foot; that they have a trembling heart, and failing of eyes, and pining of soul; that they fear night and day, and have no assurance of life; that they are evidently being kept for their land, as their land is being kept for them—all this is in exact conformity to the words of Moses in the Book of Deuteronomy.

The special function of witness-bearing for God is not, however, confined to the Jewish people, but by the express words of the Lord it is shared by the Church. The Church and the Holy Spirit together bear joint witness to the death, resurrection, and eternal life of the Divine Man. "Ye shall be my witnesses both in Jerusalem, and in all Judea and Samaria, and unto the uttermost part of the earth." As the King bore witness to the truth, his subjects bear witness to the truth as it is in Jesus. When his matchless life set* from the eye of men behind Calvary, the Church, illumined by fellowship with him across the spaces which no mortal eye can fathom, testified that he lived for evermore. It may be said of her, as the psalmist did of the heavenly bodies: Day unto day she uttereth speech, and night unto night she showeth knowledge. There is no speech or utterance; her voice cannot be heard; but her line is gone out through all the earth, and her words to the end of the world.

This is also the function of the individual believer: not to argue and dispute, not to demonstrate and prove, not to perform the part of the advocate; but to live in direct contact with things which the Holy Spirit reveals to the pure and childlike nature. And then to come forth attesting that these things are so. Just as mathematical axioms have no need to be argued but simply to be stated, and the statement is sufficient to establish them because of the affinity between them and the construction of the human mind, so it is sufficient to *bear witness to truth* amid systems of falsehood and error. And as soon as it is uttered, there is an assent in the conscience illumined by the Holy Spirit which rises up and declares it to be the *very truth of God*.

There are three points on which the Christian soul is called to give witness. They are suggested by the glowing words of which this call for witnesses is the climax; and we need have no hesitation in appropriating such words—addressed primarily to the Jews—to ourselves,

---

* Like the setting sun. *Editor.*

because we are so distinctly told that we are no longer
strangers from the covenant of promise but are part of
the household of God (Eph. 2:11–19). It is also affirmed
by the apostle that those which be of faith are blessed
with faithful Abraham, and that in Christ Jesus the
blessing of Abraham comes upon the Gentiles (Gal. 3:9–
14).

1. LET US WITNESS TO A LOVE THAT NEVER TIRES.
At the close of the previous chapter we have a terrible
picture of Israel as a people robbed and spoiled, snared
in holes, and hid in prison houses (42:22), upon whom
God was pouring the fury of his anger and the violence
of battle. Then most unexpectedly God turns to them
and says, "Fear not! Thou art mine; thou hast been precious in my sight, and honorable and beloved" (43:1, 4).

Thou art mine. The words are very simple. They would
come to a little lost child from a mother's lips as she
again embraced it. Our deepest emotions express themselves in the simplest words. Depth and intensity of feeling select the monosyllables of the mother tongue. It is
much for you, O exiled soul, robbed and spoiled, that
God still calls you his; and he will not stay his hand
until he elicits your response, "Great and good God, thou
art mine!" Neither sin nor sorrow can cut with their accursed shears the knot of union which the divine fingers have tied between your weak soul and the everlasting Lover of men.

Precious. Israel hardly dared to think it; and certainly
no observer unacquainted with the ways of God could
dare suppose that Jehovah counted his people as his
priceless treasure. But, nevertheless, the words stand
out clearly upon the page, "Thou hast been *precious* in
my sight." Yes, soul of man, you are the pearl of great
price, to obtain which the Merchantman in search of
priceless jewels sold all that he had and bought the world
in which you did lie like a common pebble. Precious-
ness is due to hardships undergone, purchase-money

and time expended, or pains of workmanship; and each
of these three conditions has been marvelously exem-
plified in the dealings of your God.

Honorable. Our origin was in the dust. Our father was
an Amorite, our mother a Hittite. In the day of our birth
none pitied; but we were cast out in the open field and
abhorred. It is marvelous to know that God is prepared
to raise such out of the dust and lift them from the dung-
hill; to make them sit with princes, and inherit the throne
of glory. Ah, how little do the titles of the world appear
to those whom God dubs "right honorable"! On them
the loftiest angels are proud to wait. Their nursing fathers are kings. Demean yourself as one whom God delights to honor! It ill becomes princes of the blood-royal
to lie in the gutter.

Beloved. "I have loved thee." These are words which
call for no explanation or elucidation. We must sit down
to muse on them, and let their quiet influence steal over
us like that of a superb painting, a strain of music, a
landscape. But, oh, believe them! And in the darkest
hours of life, when your feet have almost gone from under
you, and no sun or moon or stars appear, never doubt
that God's love is not less tenacious than that which
suggested the epitaph on Kingsley's tomb: "We love; we
have loved; we will love."

To know all this and to bear witness to it; to attest it
in the teeth of adverse circumstances, of bitter taunts,
and of utter desolation; to persist in the affirmation amid
the cross-questioning of a cynical age; never to falter,
never to listen to the suggestion of doubt rising like a
cold mist to enwrap the soul; never to allow the expression of the face to suggest that God is hard in his dealings—*this* is the mission of the believer.

2. LET US WITNESS TO A PURPOSE THAT NEVER
FALTERS. God does not say, "Think of what was done
yesterday"; he refers back to the purposes of eternity,
the deeds of Bethlehem and Calvary, the everlasting

covenant, the whole trend of his dealings with us. He says, "Read the whole book. Step back and consider the perspective. Get a glimpse of the mighty roots that moor the slight tree of your life." "Fear not, for I have redeemed thee; I have called thee by thy name; I have created thee for my glory; I have formed thee; yea, I have made thee" (vs. 1, 7).

Is it likely that a purpose reaching back into the blue azure of the past will be lightly dropped? The love of yesterday may pass, as the dew from the earth; the hastily formed purpose may be as hastily abandoned. The gourd of the night perishes in the night, but your election is the outworking of an ideal which filled the mind of God before ever the sun began to glimmer, or seraph's voice to strike across the depths of the infinite.

This, too, demands our witness. Men misjudge God, because they look at his work in fragments and criticize half-finished designs. Short-sighted, premature, hasty, the adverse criticism of man must be corrected by the mature, calm judgment which shall view the finished scheme of creation and of the moral government of the universe. It is our duty to appeal for this judgment, and bear our witness to the far reach of a purpose that moves in a slowly ascending spiral to its end.

3. LET US WITNESS TO A DELIVERANCE THAT NEVER DISAPPOINTS. God does not keep his children from the waters and the fire (v. 2). We might have expected the verse would run, "Thou shalt *never* pass through the waters or through the river; thou shalt *never* have to walk through the fire!" But so far from this, it seems taken as a matter of course that there will be the waters and the fire, the overflowing floods of sorrow, the biting flame of sarcasm and hate. God's people are not saved *from* trial but *in* it. Fire and water are cleansing agents that cannot be dispensed with. The gold and silver, the brass, iron and tin, everything that can abide the fire must go through the fire, that it may be clean;

and that which cannot abide the fire must go through the water (Num. 31:22–23).

Sometimes the world wonders at seeing God's people in trouble as other men—not knowing that the King himself has passed through flood and flame; not knowing also that there are fords for the floods and paths through the fire. God does not take us to the city that hath foundations by a way which will mock our faltering footsteps. We must bear our testimony to this also—that we may clear the character of God from the aspersions of the ungodly. He will not break the silence to speak for himself, but we must bear witness *for* him.

The witness box is the home, the place of business, the society salon, anywhere and everywhere where the right is being travestied and misunderstood. There, in the power of the witnessing Spirit, we are called to be *witnesses* for the Lord our God.

THE ALTERING OF GOD'S PURPOSE

(Isaiah 43:21–24)

"To the spirit select there is no choice;
He cannot say, This will I do, or that.

.   .   .   .   .

A hand is stretched to him from out the dark,
Which grasping without question, he is led
Where there is work that he must do for God."
Lowell

THIS passage refers primarily to Israel. It is the theme of the Book of Deuteronomy, that God chose the seed of Abraham to be a peculiar nation unto himself, above all peoples on the face of the earth. It was for this he brought them out from Egypt, the house of bondage, and separated them amid the highlands of Canaan. They were to be his own inheritance. Those two words, *people* and *inheritance,* are perpetually linked together in the Bible. "The Lord hath taken you, and brought you forth out of the iron furnace, out of Egypt, to be unto him a people of inheritance, as at this day." It was as though he viewed his people as a plot of land which after careful tendance would yield to him crop after crop of delight (Deut. 4:20; 7:6).

In his swan song, the great lawgiver went so far as to say that when the Most High gave the nations their inheritance, he apportioned their lot and fixed their bounds with reference to the nation which was as the apple of his eye. Thus will a market-gardener separate a few choice plants and concentrate on them his most eager attention—not for their sakes alone, but that he may procure seed and slips to sow and plant over all the acres that belong to him. "The Lord's portion is his people; Jacob is the lot of his inheritance" (Deut. 32:8–9).

Jehovah's design is clearly declared in the significant passage that heads this portion of the chapter: "They shall show forth my praise." By a long process of careful training, it was his intention so to form the people that their history should turn men's thoughts to the glory and beauty of his own nature, and elicit perpetual adoration and praise. They were to go forth throughout the world teaching men the love and goodness of him who had found them in the waste howling wilderness, a race of untutored slaves, and had made them a nation of priests, of sweet psalmists, and of seers proclaiming the transcendant beauty of the only God. By repeated failure, however, the Jews set themselves against the accomplishment of the divine plan. On three separate occasions they thwarted Jehovah. They came nigh unto cursing instead of praising. They gave men false conceptions of his character. And on three separate occasions they had to experience the temporary suspension and postponement of his purpose.

First, in the wilderness they murmured against him, and were sent back to wander in the waste for forty years (Num. 14:34). Next, after nineteen kings had ruled from David's throne, they were exiled to Babylon for seventy years. And lastly, since the rejection of the Beloved Son, they have been driven into all the world, to be a byword and a proverb. For eighteen hundred years God's purpose has been detained. It shall, no doubt, be ultimately fulfilled. The chosen people shall yet be for a name, for a praise, and for a glory (Jer. 13:11); but in the meanwhile the Gentiles have been called in to take their place—temporarily indeed—but with blessed results for them, until the branches which were broken off are again grafted into their olive tree, and all Israel shall be saved (Rom. 11:23–26).

This change of purpose on the part of God has been the opening of the door for us, and the words which were originally addressed to Israel are now applicable to ourselves. Twice at least in the epistles, and by the lips of the apostles Paul and Peter, we are told that Jesus gave himself for us to redeem us and to purify us unto himself, a people for his own possession; so that we are an elect race, a royal priesthood, a holy nation, a people for God's own possession—that we may show forth the praises of him who called us out of darkness into his marvelous light. We are what we are that we may show forth God's praise; but if we fail to realize his ideal, for us too there will be the inevitable postponement of his purpose. Instead of being realized easily and blessedly, it will be brought about, as has repeatedly been the case with Israel, through tears and blood (Titus 2:14; 1 Peter 2:9).

1. THE PURPOSE OF GOD. "That they should show forth my praise." It has been said that the word translated *praise* is from the same root as *Hallel* in "Hallelujah"; and that it means, first, a clear and shining light; next, a sweet flute-like sound. From this we learn that the people of God are to reflect his glory until it shines from their lives, attracting others to it, and that they are to speak his praise in resonant and harmonious sounds that shall arrest and attract the listening ear. "How fair he must be whose service has filled these souls with such delight! Come, let us seek him, that he may do as much for us."

We may promote God's praise as much by suffering as by active service. To lie still day after day, without complaining—satisfied with what pleases him, and reso-

lute to suffer according to the will of God, though no
word fall from our lips—may be more provocative of
praise than to write psalms which stir successive generations to praise and bless him whose mercy endureth
forever.

In every life there are three regions: that of the light,
where duty is clearly defined; that of the dark, where
wrong is no less clearly marked; and a great borderland
of twilight where there is no certainty, where dividing
lines are not distinct, and where each man must be fully
persuaded for himself. It is here, however, that the temper of the soul is tested. Here the decisions are come to
that make us weak or strong. Here it is that we may
drift into the dark or start a path of upward climbing
that will conduct to the tablelands where the light never
wanes. In threading a difficult way through these devi-
ous tracks there is no clue so helpful or certain as to
ask what will be conducive to the praise of God. All that
would hinder this must be avoided; all that would promote and enhance it must be followed at any cost.

We must also *shine*—and there is more in that expression than simply to do right—that men who see our
good works may glorify our Father and give him praise.
It is through the Church that the principalities and powers of the heavenly realms learn the manifold wisdom of
God (Eph. 3:10). We are disposed to dwell too exclu-
sively on what God is *to us*—and indeed we can never
make too much of the fact that the entire resources of
his being, which the Apostle Paul calls his fullness, are
at our disposal. But let us not forget the other side of
this great truth, and go on to know the riches of the
glory of his inheritance *in us* his saints. Let us not forget to so yield him every acre of our inner life, and every
fragment of our time, that from these the great Husbandman may get for himself crop after crop of praise—
bringing all under cultivation, till the wheatfields of the
lowlands, the pomegranates of the orchards, the vine-

yards of the terraced heights, yield each in its measure their portion of adoration.

2. THE POSSIBLE THWARTING OF HIS PURPOSE. "Ye shall know the revoking of my promise" (Num. 14:34, R.V., margin). There is nothing more terrible in the history of a soul than to frustrate the divine ideal manifested in its creation and redemption, and to prevent God deriving from us that for which he saved us. Such may be your lot, O fig tree, standing straight in the pathway of the Son of Man, to which he comes, hungry for fruit: therefore, beware, and learn from this paragraph the symptoms of Israel's declension. Be warned by these, lest for you also there come the suspension of the divine purpose.

(a) *Prayerlessness.* "Thou hast not called upon me, O Jacob; but thou hast been weary of me, O Israel" (v. 22). Nothing is a surer gauge of our spiritual state than our prayers. There may be a weariness of the brain which is the reaction of overstrain, and against which it is not wise to struggle. When mind and heart are so overpowered by the fatigues of the body that an inevitable drowsiness closes the eye and restrains the flow of thought, it is best to say with the great Bengel, as we yield ourselves to sleep, "O Lord, we are on the same terms as yesterday." But this is very different from the perfunctory and hurried devotions which arise from the preoccupation of the mind in things of time and sense, or the alienation of the heart from God by sin. If this lethargy is stealing over you, beware!

(b) *Neglect of little things.* "Thou hast not brought me the small cattle of thy burnt offerings" (v. 23). The emphasis is on the word *small.* The people were probably careful of the larger matters of Jewish ritual, but neglectful of the smaller details. None of us goes wrong at first in the breach of the great obligations of the law. It is the little rift in the lute, the tiny speck in the fruit, the small gap in the bank, where deterioration begins. Nothing is really small that concerns God or the soul. Let us be careful about slight inaccuracies; about small deviations from the strict integrity of a holy character; about tampering with the gentler admonitions of conscience. Insensibility and carelessness in little things in a child are immediately corrected by the wise parent, who knows to what they may lead.

(c) *Lack of sweetness.* "Thou hast bought me no sweet cane" (v. 24). It is possible to do right things from a hard sense of legalism in which the sweetness and lovableness of true religion are painfully lacking. How often we do things because we must, or because we choose, and not because we are led by the silken chains of love to our dear Lord! This is what the apostle calls being "married to the law" instead of being united to the Man who was raised from the dead, and whose love should be the supreme constraint. His service is perfect freedom; his yoke is easy and his burden is light.

Many are the instances of this change of purpose. God substituted David for Saul; Solomon for Adonijah; the Church for the Hebrew people; Western for Eastern Christianity; the Moravians and Lollards for the established churches of their time. An instance was narrated recently of a church in the United States, which, by an immense majority, refused to receive colored people into its communion. A few years later it had so utterly declined that its building was for sale, and it was purchased by the colored congregation which had gathered around the members it had driven forth. So God takes away his kingdom from those who prove themselves unworthy of it, and gives it to such as will fulfill his purpose and set forth his praise. "Be not highminded, but fear; for if God spared not the natural branches, neither will he spare thee" (Rom. 11:20–21, R.V.).

3. THE FULFILLMENT OF GOD'S PURPOSE THROUGH OUR PAIN. "They *shall* show forth my praise" (v. 21). God's purpose cannot be ultimately set aside. It

may be brought to a halt by some mountain of prejudice or unbelief, but it will be found pursuing its chosen path on the other side—having tunneled, or climbed, or gone around it. So it shall be with Israel and with each of us. But the cost—how enormous!

In the case of mankind, God's purpose to give Adam and his race dominion over the works of his hands was exposed to the terrific interruption of sin—which has cost six thousand years of untold anguish, besides the bloody sweat of Gethsemane and the broken heart of Calvary. But, though suspended for six millenniums, the divine thought in our creation shall yet take effect. The righteous shall have dominion in the morning. All enemies shall be put under our feet. The seed of the woman shall bruise the serpent's head. But, ah, the cost to God, to man, and to the travailing creation!

So in the case of Israel. She shall yet shine as a star and sing God's praise like an angel chorister. But again the cost has been excessive. Sorrow such as this world has never seen has been the purifying furnace through which she has been purged from her dross, and poured into the mold which from the first days of her history was waiting to give her the predestined shape.

So with each child in the family of God. The thoughts of God's heart must stand; his ideal shall be realized; his purposes finally achieve their aim. This may be through the willing obedience and acquiescence of the soul; then there need be no great strain, or pressure, or anguish. Strength will be proportionate for every task; the back suited for every burden; the gradient adapted to the engine that has to climb its steep ascent. But if there is obstinacy, rebellion, murmuring complaint, like that which so often filled the camp of Israel, there will be suffering: exile, the wilderness with its desolation and monotony, the long waiting. And only after years of such discipline shall the soul come back again to stand at the gate of Canaan and enter upon its inheritance, and give to the great Husbandman that praise and glory for which it was originally made.

Has this been your history up till now? Then turn and repent. God declares that he will not remember the past with all its bitter disappointment and misappropriation of opportunity; that he will outdo the wonders of the bygone times by the mercies he will bestow; and that he will make a way through the wilderness, with flowing streams and waving verdure. What though you have brought yourself into the waste!—he will find a way forth into Canaan again. He will give you your vineyards from thence, and change the valley of Achor* into a door of hope . . . and you shall sing as in the days of your youth! Formed for himself, *you shall yet show forth his praise!* Yield to him, that he may win from you all on which he has set his heart, at once and easily. It shall be the best for you.

* The name "Achor" means "troubled." See Joshua 7:24–26. *Editor.*

8

A PERVERTED APPETITE

(ISAIAH 44:6–20)

"All partial beauty was a pledge
Of beauty in its plenitude:
But since the pledge sufficed thy mood
Retain it! Plenitude be theirs
Who looked above!"
                    E. B. Browning

TWO lessons were learned by Israel in captivity—the all-sufficiency of God and the absurdity of idols. Each of these themes is dealt with in the glowing sentences of the paragraph which begins at the sixth verse of this chapter and ends with the twentieth verse.

The all-sufficiency of God is the subject of verses 6, 7, and 8.

The absurdity of idols, verses 9 to 20.

It is on the latter of these that we are now to dwell. We are conducted into the idol factories of the day. As we begin our exploration we are forewarned that we shall find the manufacturers are nothing, and their choicest creations worthless; and that though the whole assembly of them stand together in solid phalanx, they shall be put to utter confusion and shame.

With this caution we enter the workshop where a molten image is being made from glowing metal, beneath the heavy blows of the hammer wielded by the

strong arm of a swarthy smith. Surely the product of
such strength should be strong to help. But see, the
smith himself is tired and thirsty after a few hours of
work; how evidently, then, is he unable to produce that
which can help other men in the extremity of their need!
The effect cannot be greater than its cause. An idol cannot give perennial strength when its manufacturer is so
easily exhausted (v. 12).

Next, we are led into a factory of wooden idols where
a carpenter is at work, stretching out a line of measure-
ment, drawing a pattern with red ochre on the block of
timber and shaping the figure of a man. The floor is
littered with crisp shavings, the furniture is heavy with
sawdust, and the idol that is to fill its votaries with such
awful dread is being very unceremoniously handled in
its process of manufacture (v. 13).

Lastly, we follow some private individual into the forest. He levels cedar or oak; or an ash tree, planted long
before because its durable wood, when grown, would
well suit his purpose. Part of the tree is sawn into logs
and stacked for firing, and the remainder is fashioned
into an idol before which he prostrates himself. How
graphically are these contrasts portrayed. We can hear
the chuckle of delight as the man warms his hands or
roasts his food by the crackling logs; and immediately
after we can see him in prayer, pleading with the remainder of the trunk to deliver him—as his god!

Why do men act thus, with such inconceivable folly?
How is it that they do not realize the incongruity of their
actions? The prophet knows nothing of the modern
theory that men do not worship the stone or wood but
merely accept the effigy as a help to fixedness of thought
and prayer. He would affirm that with the mass of men
this is a fiction, and that the worship of the devotee
stops short with what he can see and touch. The cause
of idolatry lies very deep: "He feedeth on ashes; a deceived heart hath turned him aside, that he cannot de-

liver his soul, nor say, Is there not a lie in my right hand?" (v. 20).

1. THERE IS A HUNGER FOR THE DIVINE IN MAN.

(a) *It is universal.* All men are made on the same plan, whether physically or morally. As the body needs food, so does the mind demand truth, and the spirit God. This is true of every age and clime. Always and everywhere these appetites demand satisfaction. Hence, beside the homes of men you will always find the cornfield, the mango field, or the breadfruit tree; and within a stone's throw a church, or chapel, or temple, the path to which is trodden hard by repeated steps.

(b) *It is significant.* We can tell something of the composition of the human body by the materials which it needs for its sustenance. Similarly the true dignity of man reveals itself in the hunger which perpetually preys upon him. The cattle, when they have taken their full meal, repose contentedly on the grass; but man is not satisfied to have eaten his roast or warmed at his fire. He must needs go forth in search of the beautiful, the sublime, the harmony of sweet colors and sounds, the discovery of truth, the presence of God. Does not this disprove the materialistic philosophy in vogue in some quarters? If man is only matter, if thought is only the movement of the gray matter of the brain, if there is no spirit and no beyond, how is it that the material world cannot supply the supreme good?—and that when, as in the case of Solomon, life is filled with all that wealth and power can yield, man turns from it all as a vain and empty bubble, the mirage of the desert, the apples of Sodom, the chaff which cannot appease hunger? Does not this show that there are component parts of man's nature which are more noble—which, because they cannot be appeased by the contents of the time-sphere, are above time and belong to the eternal and unseen? Must not there be something divine in man if he hungers for the Divine; something spiritual and eternal, since the spiritual and eternal alone can meet his need?

(c) *It is inevitable.* The functions which food performs in our system are threefold. It is needed to replace the perpetual waste which is always wearing down the natural tissues; to maintain the temperature at some 98°; and to provide materials for growth. And each of these has a spiritual analogy. We need God for the same three reasons as the body needs food.

(1) We need God to replace the perpetual waste of our spiritual forces. Each time we act or speak we expend some portion of our physical nature: we break off, so to speak, some tiny fragment of nerve or muscle; we wear thinner some string or wheel in the complex corporeal machine. This needs to be renewed and replaced. Hence life is a perpetual struggle against the forces of disintegration and decay at work within us. Thus it is in the spiritual sphere also: each unselfish act; each remonstrance against wrong or effort on the behalf of purity, peace or righteouness; all right thinking, living, and working; all visits to the sick, discourses, acts of moral heroism—all expend our spiritual forces. We are subject to a perpetual wearing down and consumption of spiritual energy. And therefore there must be hours of quiet fellowship with God in which to restore ourselves and regain our spent vigor.

(2) We need God for warmth and heat. In cold the body requires a good supply of carbon; it must be well fueled. At every point of the immense system of blood circulation there must be fires kept burning, to consume the waste products that choke the veins and to maintain animal heat. Similarly, we need the comfort of the Comforter—the renewal of love and faith and hope, the blessed glow of those coals of juniper of which the Spouse speaks. And this, again, can only be met within fellowship with God.

(3) We need God for growth. As the young child must have milk that it may grow thereby, and as the raven-

ous appetite of the growing lad or girl betrays the immense demand that nature is making for materials out of which to build up her temple—so our spiritual growth depends on how much of God we can take into our being. For want of this divine food, some never get beyond the babe stage to become strong men and women in Christ. That which builds up the inner life is deep and intimate fellowship with God; and the more direct it is the better.

2. THIS APPETITE MAY BE PERVERTED. "He feedeth on ashes." An appetite may be perfectly healthy in itself, but it may be supplied with unsuitable materials. In times of scarcity the Chinese use a kind of edible earth as a substitute for food. Negroes on the west coast of Africa have been known to sustain life on a yellowish earth, used with coarse flour to make it go further; while the natives of Java are said to knead clay into balls for eating, as a luxury. In these ways men tamper with their natural appetite. They literally spend money for that which is not bread, and labor for that which satisfieth not.

But there is a close similarity in their treatment with that wonderful yearning after the unseen and eternal which is part of the very constitution of our being—a hunger after the ideal Food, the ideal Beauty, the ideal Truth, which may be resisted and ignored but still demands satisfaction; and if it does not get it in God, it will seek it in the ashes of idolatry.

Men worship idols yet. The sensualist worships in the old Temple of Venus, though he has never heard the murmur of the blue Aegean around the island dedicated to the grossest impurity under the name of religion. He tries to satisfy his hunger for divine love with the ashes of physical gratification. The man of the world worships money, rank, high office; he is prepared to sacrifice everything to win them. Morning, noon and night, he is expending his choicest gifts at the shrine of the god of this world, invoking his help, propitiating his wrath, endeavoring to win his smile. The golden calf is still the center of worship, decorated by garlands, encircled by the merry crowds. Costly sacrifices smoke before it, though in the solemn heights of Sinai the cloud pavilion glows with the Shekinah.

The child of fashion worships in the temple of human opinion, and feeds with the ashes of human applause an appetite which was meant to satisfy itself on the "Well done!" of the Almighty.

The student who questions or denies the being of God worships in the temple of learning; and feeds with the ashes of human opinion an appetite which was intended to be nourished by eternal truth.

The soldier, in whom the love of adventurous deeds is strong, is apt to worship in the Temple of Mars, and to feed with the ashes of military excitement an appetite which was intended to lead to great exploits on behalf of the oppressed and wronged.

In one shape or another, idolatry is as rife among us as ever, though material emblems are but rarely used. And in every case, these substitutes for God with which men try to satisfy themselves are as incapable of satisfying the heart as are ashes of supporting the physical life.

3. THE TRUE BREAD.

It is the gift of God. "My Father giveth the true bread from heaven." God who made you hunger for bread made bread to grow for its appeasement. There is, of course, the human side in the cultivation and preparation of food; but it is a small thing compared with the divine. "Thou providest them corn, for so preparest thou the earth" (Ps. 65:9, R.V., margin). In every land there is the grain indigenous to the soil. Each type of vegetation has its special habitat. The olive will not grow in Labrador, and the fir does not flourish on the banks of the Amazon. But the True Grain will make its home in every land, and grow on every soil.

He has also provided Beauty for our taste, Truth for our thought, Love for our heart; and has gathered all these and much more into his one gift, Jesus Christ our Lord—who contains within himself all that is required for our inner life, as grain contains all that is needful for the nourishment of the body.

Nature yields her provision to man through death. The armies of standing wheat or barley are mowed down by the sickle. The tender plants yield up their stores through the edge of steel, the grind of millstones, the scorch of fire, to minister to man. The cattle fall beneath the staggering blow, or the gash of the knife. For the wild things of the forest there are the rifle and swift death. So it is through death that Jesus has become the Food of men. The Lord's Supper perpetually reminds us of this. The bread and wine that nourish us there are the emblems of the flesh and the blood of One who has died and is risen again. At that holy feast we commemorate the death of One who lives forever; and show forth that the life which nourishes our spirits has passed through the sharpness of death, that it might nourish within our spirits the eternal life. Our Lord's repeated reference to flesh and blood, which are so significant of death, enforces and accentuates this truth—that it is only through his death, and through our participation with him in death, that he can become the true meat and the true drink (John 6:53–57).

Let it never be forgotten that it is not by the words, nor example, nor deeds of Jesus Christ alone and apart from his death, that we can grow into the stature of perfect men; but by fellowship with him in death, and by the passage of all these qualities through death, and by the careful pondering of his own words, "I was dead, and behold, I am alive for evermore." It is through death and resurrection that the Lord Jesus has become the foodstuff of the spiritual nature of man.

We must assimilate our food. It is not enough that the Lord Jesus should be set forth evidently crucified for us. We must feed on him by faith. We must meditate on all that he is, and all that he has done. We must receive him into our hearts by an act of spiritual apprehension. We must reckon that we have received and do possess. We must especially appropriate him in respect of those special requirements which may have revealed themselves in moments of temptation and failure.

So shall we become strong and glad. Life in full measure will be meted out to us. We shall eat of the Tree of Life, which is in the midst of the Paradise of God. We shall know even as we are known.

9

THE GIRDINGS OF JEHOVAH

(ISAIAH 45:1–6)

"Ere suns and moons could wax and wane,
Ere stars were thunder girt, or piled
The heavens, God thought on me his child,
Ordained a life for me, arranged
Its circumstances every one
To the minutest; aye, God said,
This head this hand shouldest rest upon
Thus, ere he fashioned star or sun."
E. B. Browning

CYRUS, who is named here for the first time in Scripture, is one of the noblest figures in ancient history. Herodotus and Xenophon both praise him. A century after his death, as the latter traveled through Asia Minor, the impression of his noble personal character and wise statesmanship was fresh and clearly defined. Cyrus must, indeed, have been a good and great man, whose character became a model for the Greek youth, in strength, simplicity, humanity, purity and self-restraint. Such was God's chosen instrument for the great work of emancipating the chosen people and reinstating them in their own land.

We have seen that Jehovah assured the people graciously of their return from captivity at the end of the seventy years. Jerusalem would be built, and the cities

of Judah inhabited (44:26). And they probably expected
that the return would be signalized by miracles as stupendous as those which opened the door to freedom
from the bondage of Egypt. Again the waters would start
back, and the river divide; the floor of the desert would
be strewn with manna, and rocks would gush with
watersprings. But their deliverance was not to be on
this wise. The miracle was to be wrought in the world of
mind, not of matter. By a series of unexpected
providences the divine purpose was to be realized
through a heathen monarch, who did not know him by
whom his strength was girded and his path prepared.

At the beginning of his career, Cyrus was chieftain of
an obscure Persian tribe. His first success was in ob-
taining, either by diplomacy or force, the leadership of
two tribes of hardy mountaineers, at that time unknown
beyond the narrow confines of their native hills. With
these he began a course of conquest which swept from
the frontier of India to the blue waters of the Aegean,
subjugating even Croesus, king of Lydia, whose wealth
has passed into a proverb. Doors of opportunity opened
before him quite marvelously; rough difficulties were
leveled; hidden treasures fell into his hands, and the
brazen doors stood open before his triumphant progress.
All this time, though religious according to his light,
and punctilious in acknowledging the gods of his people,
he did not know Jehovah, by whom he was being girded
and used.

At last, after years of unbroken victory, he stood
knocking at the gates of Babylon, demanding from the
son and grandson of Nebuchadnezzar the recognition
of his supremacy. How little did he or they realize that
this summons was the result of a divine purpose, bent
on securing the emancipation of the captive Jews and
their return to their sacred city to become the religious
leaders of the world—the stock from which the true Servant and Anointed of the Lord was to proceed!

For weary months Babylon withstood the siege and laughed to scorn the attempt of barbarous tribes to scale her massive walls or force her mighty gates. But one night when, in fancied security, Belshazzar made a feast to a thousand of his lords, and the vigilance of the guards was relaxed, the mystic hand on the walls of the royal banqueting hall traced the decree that the kingdom was at an end, and had passed into the hands of the Medes and Persians. That night Cyrus diverted the mighty river that traversed the lordly city into a vast reservoir, arranged for the storage of water; and as it left its ancient course, his troops marched along the oozy channel and burst into the city with loud cries that startled the revelers at their cups, and the sleepers in their dreams, inaugurating days of slaughter, rapine and pillage.

Daniel, venerable with age, was beyond controversy the greatest subject of the realm. On the night of the capture he had rebuked Belshazzar for his sins and announced the conclusion of the siege. He held in his hand the keys to the policy of the empire, and was therefore at once sought after by Cyrus and his uncle Darius (Dan. 6:2; 10:1). He had come to see that the period of seventy years was now nearly ended (Dan. 9:2); and he appears to have taken an early opportunity, at least so Josephus says, of acquainting Cyrus with the history of his people—and with those wonderful predictions that had stood so long on the pages of their sacred books, minutely predicting the king's career, and even his name. They also gave forecast of what he was next to do. Notwithstanding the predictions of Chaldean astrologers, God had brought him to the throne of Babylon; and, in spite of all apparent unlikeliness, he would perform the counsel of inspired messengers, saying of Jerusalem, "She shall be inhabited," and of the cities of Judah, "They shall be built" (Isa. 44:26). How startling it must have been when the aged prophet brought to the notice of the young conqueror such words as these: "I have raised

him up in righteousness, and I will make straight all his
ways: he shall build my city, and he shall let my exiles
go free, not for price nor reward, saith the Lord of hosts"
(45:13, R.V.).

It is therefore not to be wondered at that in the first
year of his reign he made a proclamation throughout all
his kingdom, and put it also in writing, saying, "Thus
saith Cyrus, king of Persia: All the kingdoms of the earth
hath the Lord, the God of heaven, given me; and he
hath charged me to build him an house in Jerusalem,
which is in Judah. Whosoever there is among you of all
his people, his God be with him, and let him go up to
Jerusalem, which is in Judah, and build the house of
the Lord, the God of Israel . . ." (Ezra 1:1–4, R.V.).

What a vast conception is here unfolded to us of the
Providence that shapes man's ends, "rough-hew them
as he will"! There is a plan which underlies the apparent chaos of worldly affairs, and is slowly achieving its
ends—though the agents through which it is being executed are largely unaware of what is afoot. In the words
of Nebuchadnezzar, the greatest monarch of his time,
whom Jehovah likened to a head of gold, and who had
ample opportunity of verifying his conclusions, God does
as he will among the inhabitants of the earth, and none
can stay his hand or say, What doest thou? (Dan. 4:35).

1. GOD'S PLAN, AS IT AFFECTS SOCIETY.

(a) *It is comprehensive*, sweeping from age to age,
threading millenniums, building its structure from the
dust of earth's earliest age to the emergence of the new
heavens and earth at the close of time.

But it is minute and particular. No great general can
carry through a successful campaign who is not patient
enough to attend to details. Wellington rode over to see
Blucher the night before Waterloo, to know for himself
when the Prussian legion would come through the forest of Soignies. God ordained the succession of William
of Orange to the throne of England, in the place of the

Stuarts; and it was his hand that made the wind veer from west to east at one critical moment in the night of his landing, or he had missed Torbay and been carried into the heart of the English fleet. Nothing is small with God. The sparrow does not fall to the ground without him; and the tiniest events are woven into the scheme of his all-embracing providence. He makes even the sin and wrath of man to subserve his purpose.

(b) *He works through individuals.* The story of man is for the most part told in the biographies of men. It is through human instruments that God executes his beneficent purposes, his righteous judgments. Through Columbus, he draws aside the veil from the coastline of America. Through a Watt and a Stevenson, he endows men with the cooperation of steam; through a Galvani and an Edison, with the ministry of electricity. Through a de Lesseps he unites the waters of the eastern and western seas, and brings the Orient and Occident together. Through a Napoleon he shatters the temporal power of the Pope, and by a Wilberforce strikes the fetters from the slave. Men do not know the purpose of God in what they are doing. They arise and move onward in a course of unbroken success. They become accustomed to the opening of barred gates, the unclosing of closed doors. They expect and win the highest positions, honors, and prizes of the world. They credit themselves with what they achieve; and their fellows eagerly analyze their make-up and methods to ascertain the secret of their great strength. They know not that they are really instruments in the divine hand, surnamed and girded by One whom they know not.

(c) *God's use of them does not interfere with their free action.* This is clearly taught in more than one significant passage in Scripture. Joseph's brethren acted from the promptings of their malicious hearts, and meant only evil; but God, all the while, was meaning and achieving good to Joseph, to themselves, and to the land of

Egypt. Herod, Pilate, and the religious leaders of the
Jews were swept before a cyclone of passion and jealousy, and it was with wicked hands that they crucified
and slew the Lord of Glory: but they were accomplish-
ing the determinate counsel of God, and doing whatsoever his hand and his counsel foreordained to come to
pass. We cannot understand this mystery, nor reconcile the movements of the far distant planets of this great
system. This arises from the limitation of our faculties
in this our nursery life. But we must accept it as true. It
is incontestably the teaching of Scripture that a man
like Cyrus might be engaged in the pursuance of his
own schemes and ambitions, while, all the time, he was
being girded and used by One whom he did not know.

All these principles should be carefully studied and
prayerfully pondered. They underpin the life of society
and of individuals also.

2. GOD'S PLAN, AS IT AFFECTS INDIVIDUALS. We
are all conscious of an element in life that we cannot
account for. Other men have started life under better
auspices, and with larger advantages than we, but somehow they have dropped behind in the race and are nowhere to be seen. Our health has never been robust,
but we have had more working days in our lives than
those who were the athletes of our school. We have been
in perpetual peril, traveling incessantly, and never were
involved in a single accident, while others were shattered in their first journey from their doorstep. Why have
we escaped when so many have fallen? Why have we
climbed to positions of usefulness and influence which
so many more capable ones have missed? Why has our
reputation been maintained when better men than ourselves have lost their footing and fallen beyond recov-
ery?

There is not one of us who cannot see points in the
past where we had almost gone, and our footsteps had
well-nigh slipped: precipices, along the brink of which

we went at nightfall, horrified in the morning to see how near our footprints had been to the edge. Repeatedly we have been within a hair-breadth of taking some fatal step, yielding to some impetuous temptation, striking a Faust-like bargain with the devil. How nearly we were caught in that eddy! How strangely we were plucked out of that companionship. How marvelously we were saved from that marriage, from that investment, from embarking in that ship, traveling by that train, taking shares in that company!

There is something to be explained in the lives of men which they cannot account for. They describe their consciousness of this anonymous element, as it has been called, by the words "luck," "fortune," "chance"; but these are mere subterfuges, sops thrown to silence the appeals of their common sense. We know better. It is God who has girded us, though we did not know him.

It was God who opened those doors of opportunity; who smoothed those rough places, so that not a pebble remained at which to stumble; who gave treasures where all had been dark; who unlocked gates of brass which had threatened to bar the way. This is one of the luxuries of our mature years, to see all the way by which he has led us. And it will be a cause of adoring gratitude as we review our life course from the heights of heaven. As we stand there with God, he will show us how often our girdings to great tasks were due to his strong hands being placed around and upon us. He ever girds for tasks to which he calls. God cannot desert what has cost him so much. He will finish what he has begun. He will lead you o'er crag and torrent till the night is gone. He will not let one good thing fail. And, like the dying patriarch, standing on the verge of another world, you will see the Angel who has redeemed you from all evil.

When Peter stood with Jesus by the shores of the lake of Galilee, the Lord contrasted the independence of his disciple's earliest days, when he girded himself and walked whither he would, with the dependence of those later days when he would stretch forth his hands and another would gird and carry him. With these words our Lord signified the manner of death in which he would glorify God. What was true of the helplessness of Peter's old age and martyrdom should be true of each of us in the intention and choice of the soul. Let us give up girding ourselves in the assertion of our own strength, and stretch forth our hands, asking our Lord to gird us and carry us whither he will, even to death, if thereby we may the better glorify God.

10

ASKING AND COMMANDING

(Isaiah 45:11)

"Say what is Prayer, when it is Prayer indeed?
The mighty utterance of a mighty need.
The man is praying, who doth press with might
Out of his darkness into God's own light."

Trench

"ASK" and "command." It behooves us to thoughtfully consider these two distinct concepts.

At the beginning of the paragraph of which these words form part stands an exquisite word picture: "Drop down, ye heavens, from above, and let the skies pour down righteousness; let the earth open, and let them bring forth salvation . . ." (v.8). To the eye of the seer the earth lies open to heaven as a wide meadow over which the clouds of heaven hang, the air breathes, and the sun sheds sheets of light. Those clouds are big with righteousness, the special term used throughout this book for the faithfulness of Jehovah. At the call of prayer the skies pour down their precious treasure, and the earth opens every pore to receive the plentiful rain; presently, every acre brings forth salvation, and righteousness springs up in the hearts of men as their answer to the descent of the righteousness of God. It is the wedding of heaven and earth, a fulfillment of the prediction of the psalm: "Truth shall spring out of the earth; and righteousness shall look down from heaven" (Ps. 85:11).

The imagery is one of surpassing beauty. The brooding of heaven; the response of earth. Deep calling unto deep. The nature of God originating and inspiring; the nature of man responding. And when the descending grace of God is thus received by the believing, yearning heart of man, the result is *salvation*. As the margin of the Revised Version reads: "Let the skies be fruitful in salvation, and let the earth cause righteousness to spring up together" (v. 8). The whole paragraph to the close of the chapter rings with *salvation* as its keynote. Does God hide himself? He is the God of Israel, the Savior. Are the makers of idols ashamed and confounded? Yet Israel is saved with an everlasting salvation. Are graven images held up to contempt? It is because they are gods that cannot save. Does God assert his unrivaled deity? It is because he is a just God, and a Savior. Are men bidden to look to him, though they be far removed as the ends of the earth? It is that they may be saved.

Primarily, no doubt, this salvation concerns the emancipation of the chosen people from the thralldom of Babylon, and their restoration to Jerusalem. "He shall build my city, and he shall let my exiles go free, not for price nor reward, saith the LORD of hosts" (v. 13). This deliverance, which is a type of the greater deliverance from the guilt and power of sin, was, in the fixed purpose of God, sure as the creation of the earth and man— guaranteed by the hands that stretched out the heavens and by the word that commanded all their host. As certainly as God was God, he would bring his people again to the land which he gave to their fathers to inherit.

But now, side by side with this avowal of Jehovah's determination, this strange command breaks in: "Ask me of things to come concerning my sons, and concerning the work of my hands command ye me." And its importance is accentuated by the threefold description of the speaker. Observe the opening of verse 11: "The LORD"—that is, God in his everlasting redemptive purpose; "the Holy One of Israel"—that is, the moral perfections of Israel's God, as contrasted with the abominations perpetrated with the sanction of heathen religions; "his Maker"—suggesting there was a purpose for which the clay, gathered in Abraham's time from the highlands of Mesopotamia, was being fashioned into a fair vessel for his use. This threefold description of God introduces the august command which bade the people seek by prayer the fulfillment of the purpose on which the divine heart was set.

In launching an ironclad, the pressure of a baby's finger is not infrequently required to put in operation the ponderous machinery by which the iron leviathan glides evenly and majestically down to the ocean wave. So, if we may dare to say it, all the purposes of God, and the providential machinery by which they were to be executed, stood in suspense until the chosen people had asked for the things which he had promised, and had even commanded him concerning the work on which his heart was set. The victorious career of Cyrus; the dissatisfaction of the priestly caste with the king of Babylon; the evident signs of the disruption of the mighty empire; the near completion of the seventy years, foretold by Jeremiah—all were in vain, unless, like Daniel, the people set their face unto the Lord God, to seek the fulfillment of his word by prayer and supplications, with fasting, and sackcloth and ashes (Dan. 9:3).

1. PRAYER IS A NECESSARY LINK IN THIS PERFORMANCE OF THE DIVINE PROMISES. "Ask me of things to come." God is always saying, "Ask, seek, knock." Even to the Son, Jehovah says, "Ask of me, and I will give thee the nations for thine inheritance, and the uttermost parts of the earth for thy possession" (Ps. 2:8, R.V.). And to the chosen people, at the end of a paragraph jeweled with "I wills," and unfolding the work which he

is prepared to do—not for their sakes, but for his own—he says, "For this, moreover, will I be inquired of by the house of Israel, to do it for them" (Ezek. 36:37). Our Lord is unremitting in the stress he lays on prayer, and pledges himself to do only whatsoever is asked in his name (John 14:13). The Apostle James insists that one reason why we have not is that we ask not (Jas. 4:2).

The declaration of our text is therefore supported by a wealth of Scripture testimony for the necessity of prayer as a link in the accomplishment of the divine purpose.

(a) Prayer is part of the system of cooperation between God and man which pervades nature and life. No crop waves over the autumn field, no loaf stands on our breakfast table, no metal performs its useful service, no jewel sparkles on the brow of beauty, no coal burns in hearth or furnace which does not witness to this dual workmanship of God and man. So in the spiritual world there must be cooperation, though on the part of man it is often limited to prayers which may seem faint and feeble but which touch the secret springs of Deity—as the last pick of the miner may break open a fountain of oil or a cavern set with dazzling jewels.

(b) Prayer, when genuine, indicates the presence of a disposition to which God can entrust his best gifts without injury to the recipient. To bless some men apart from humility, and submission, and weanedness of soul from creature aid, would only injure. And so, in his dear love, God withholds his choicest gifts until the heart is sore broken and cries to him. That cry is the blessed symptom of soul-health. It is like the sneeze of the child on which the prophet stretched himself, which indicated returning life. And such a temper of heart may receive, without danger, blessings whose height was never reached by the majestic flight of an eagle, and whose depths are beyond the fathoming line of the profoundest thought.

(c) Prayer is also in its essence when it is inspired by

faith, an openness towards God, a receptiveness, a faculty of apprehending with open hand what he would impart. Standing upon God's promises, the suppliant cries to the heavens to drop down their blessings—while heart and hands and mouth are open wide to be filled with good. Therefore, let us pray.

Let us pray *unitedly*. God loves the gates of Zion where the *throngs* gather more than the dwellings of Jacob where single families join in prayer. He would be inquired of by the *house* of Israel. If, when a petition is being prepared by a community to the sovereign, only two or three put their hands to it, it is set aside as undeserving of attention. And what does *God* think of the earnestness of his people for the realization of his promises when only two or three gather in the place of prayer?

Let us pray *sympathetically*. The gathering for prayer must not be of bodies only but of *souls*. When one prays audibly, all should pray silently. A prayer offered in the presence of others should receive their endorsement. Soliloquy, disputation, enforcement of some special view of truth—these are out of place in the offerer of prayer. And listlessness, wandering thought, and the mere *attitude* of attention are out of place in those who, with bowed forms and covered faces, assume the posture of devotion.

Let us pray *earnestly*. Prayer is measured not by length but by strength. The divine gauge of the worth of prayer is its pressure on the heart of God. The lock of prayer sometimes turns hard, and calls for strength of purpose. The kingdom of heaven has to be taken by force. There is such a thing as laboring and striving in prayer. Thus Jesus prayed in the garden; and Daniel in Babylon; and Epaphras in Paul's hired house. Such were the prayers offered of old in the catacombs as the torchlight flickered; in Alpine caves where Waldenses cowered; on hillsides where the Covenanters sheltered under the cliffs. Let us pray so that our prayers may reverberate

with repeated blows on the gates of God's presence-
chamber—"Praying always with all prayer and supplication in the Spirit, and watching thereunto with all
perseverance and supplication for all saints" (Eph. 6:18).
Let us pray remembering that everything depends on
the gracious promise of God, but as if the answer de-
pended on the strength and tenacity of our entreaty.

Let us pray *in the name of Jesus*. It is possible to be
so absorbed in the cause of our Lord, to be so eaten up
with the zeal of his house, so one with him, that his
interests and ours become identical. Then, when we pray,
it is almost as though the Son were addressing the Father through our lips, and pouring forth a stream of
intercession and petition by us. This is what Jesus meant
when he repeatedly insisted on our praying in his name.
The filial spirit, that looks into the face of God and says
"Father"; the unselfish spirit, which is quite prepared to
renounce all if only God is exalted; the loving spirit, which
has its center in the interests of its Lord—all this is
comprehended in the prayer we offer in the name of
Jesus. And when we pray thus, we secure the accomplishment of the things to come which God has promised.

2. THE IMPERATIVE ACCENT IN FAITH. "Concerning my sons, and concerning the work of my hands,
command ye me." Our Lord spoke in this tone when he
said, "Father, I will." Joshua used it when, in the supreme moment of triumph, he lifted up his spear towards the setting sun and cried, "Sun, stand thou still!"
Elijah used it when he shut the heaven for three years
and six months, and again opened it. Luther used it
when, kneeling by the dying Melanchthon, he forbade
death to take its prey.

It is a marvelous relationship into which God bids us
enter. We are accustomed to obey him. We are familiar
with words like those which follow in this paragraph: "I,
even my hands have stretched out the heavens, and all

their host have I commanded" (v. 12). But that God should invite us to command *him!* This is a change in relationship which is altogether startling. But there is no doubt as to the literal force of these words. With the single limitation that our biddings must concern his sons, and the work of his hands, and must be included in his word of promise, Jehovah says to us, his redeemed children in Jesus Christ, "Command ye me!"

What a difference there is between this attitude and the hesitating, halting, unbelieving prayers to which we are accustomed, and which by their perpetual repetition lose edge and point! We do not expect that God will answer them now and here . . . but some day, on the far horizon of time, we imagine that they may perhaps achieve something—as waters, by continual lapping, wear a channel through the rocks. How pathetic our attitude.

How often during his earthly life did Jesus put men into a position to command him! When entering Jericho, he stood still, and said to the blind beggars, "What will ye that I should do unto you?" It was as though he said, "I am yours to command." And can we ever forget how he yielded to the Syro-phoenician woman the key to his resources and told her to help herself even as she would? Long familiarity with him even affected the speech of the apostles, for in their Spirit-inspired prayers we can detect this same tone of command: "And now, Lord, look upon their threatenings; and grant unto thy servants to speak thy word with all boldness" (Acts 4:29).

What mortal mind can realize the full magnificence of the position to which our God lovingly raises his little children? He seems to set them beside himself on his throne, and says, while the fire of his Spirit is searching and ridding them of sordid and selfish desire, "All my resources are at your command, to accomplish anything which you have set your hearts upon. Whatsoever ye shall ask, that will I do."

The world is full of mighty forces which are laboring for our benefit. Light, that draws our pictures for us; magnetism, that carries our messages; heat, that labors in our locomotives and foundries; nitrogen, that blasts the rocks—these and many more. So much is this the age of machinery and contrivance that the physical faculties of civilized races are deteriorating through disuse. Man is becoming increasingly proficient in the art of controlling the mighty forces of the universe and yoking them to the triumphal car of his progress. Thus his old supremacy over the world is being in a measure restored to him.

How is it that these great natural forces—which are manifestations of the power of God—so absolutely obey man? Is it not because, since the days of Bacon, man has so diligently studied, and so absolutely obeyed, the conditions under which they work? "Obey the law of force and the force will obey you" is almost an axiom in physics. If you will study, for instance, the laws of electricity and carefully obey them, laying down the level track along which its energy may proceed, you can lead the stream whither you choose and make it do whatever you appoint. All that is required from you is exact compliance with the requirements of its nature.

Correspondingly, God gives the Holy Spirit to them that obey him. All the resources of God dwell bodily in the risen and glorified Lord. They are imparted to us through the communion of the Holy Spirit who goes between the unsearchable riches of Christ and our poverty, bringing the one to the other as the ocean brings the wealth of the world up to the wharves of London or New York. We have then to deal with the Holy Spirit, to study the methods of his operation—what hinders or helps, what accelerates or retards. Obey him, and he pours such mighty energy into and through one's spirit that men are amazed at the prodigality of its supply; resist or thwart him, and he retires from one's spirit, leaving it to struggle as best it may with its difficulties and trials.

Yield yourself to God, O soul of man! Whatsoever he saith unto you, do it. Be careful, even to punctiliousness, in your obedience. Let God have his way with you. In proportion as you will yield to God, you shall have power with God. The more absolutely you are a man under authority to the Commander-in-Chief, the more you shall be able to say to this and the other of his resources, "Go," or "Come," or "Do this." God will be able to trust you and give you his key, bidding you help yourself. You will be admitted to terms of such intimacy with God that you shall hear him bidding you command him. And, while never forgetting the reverence that becomes a subject and the attitude that befits a saved sinner, you shall speak with him concerning his sons and concerning the work of his hands.

But after our greatest deeds of prayer and faith, we shall ever lie low before God—as Elijah did, who, after calling fire from heaven, prostrated himself on the ground, with his face between his knees. The mightiest angels of God's presence-chamber bend the lowest; the holiest souls present perpetually the sacrifice of the broken and contrite spirit. The power to move the arm that moves the world is wielded by those who can most humbly adopt the confession, "I am a worm, and no man."

11

GOD OUR BURDEN BEARER

(ISAIAH 46:1–4)

"Faint not! There is who rules the storm—whose hand
Feeds the young ravens, nor permits blind chance
To close one sparrow, flagging wing in death.
Trust in the Rock of Ages. Now, even now
He speaks and all is calm."

Gisborne

THIS wonderful picture and promise grows out of an incident during the fall of Babylon. Cyrus has broken in, and the mighty city lies open to the Persian army, exasperated by long waiting at her gates. The blood of Babylon's nobles has flowed freely over the marble floors of her palaces; most of her defenders are slain. Women and children are cowering in the inmost recesses of their homes, or filling the streets with screams of terror and appeals for help as they fly from the brutal soldiery. The final and most sanguinary conflicts have taken place within the precincts of the idol temples; but all is still now. The priests have fallen around the altars which they served, their blood mingling with that of their victims, and their splendid vestments have become their winding sheets. And now, down the marble staircases trodden in happier days by the feet of myriads of votaries, lo, the soldiers are carrying the helpless idols. The stern monotheism of Persia would have no pity for the many gods of Babylon; there are no idol shrines in the land of the sun worshipers where they could find a niche, but they are borne away as trophies of the completeness of the victory.

There is Bel, whose name suggested that of the capital itself! How ignominiously it is handed down from its pedestal! And Nebo follows. The hideous images lavishly inset with jewels, and richly caparisoned, are borne down the stately steps, their bearers laughing and jeering as they come. The gods get little respect from their rude hands, which are only eager to despoil them of a jewel. And now at the foot of the stairs they are loaded up on the backs of elephants, or pitched into the ox-wagons. In more prosperous days they were carried with excessive pomp through the streets of Babylon whenever there was plague or sickness. Then the air had been full of the clang of cymbals and trumpets, and the streets thronged with worshiping crowds. But all that is altered. "The things that ye carried about are made a load, a burden to the weary beast. They stoop, they bow down together; they could not deliver the burden, but themselves are gone into captivity" (46:1–2, R.V.). So much for the gods of Babylon being borne off into captivity.

Close on this graphic picture of the discomfiture of the gods of Babylon, we are invited to consider a description of Jehovah in which the opposite to each of these items stands out in clear relief. He speaks to the house of Jacob, and to all the remnant of the house of Israel, as children whom he had borne from birth and carried from earliest childhood. Their God needed not to be borne, he bore; needed no carriage, since his everlasting arms made cradle and carriage both. Such as he had been, he would be. He would not change. He would sustain them, even to the time of gray hairs. He had made and he would bear; yes, he would carry, and deliver.

This contrast is a perpetual one. Some people carry

their religion; other people are carried by it. Some are burdened by the prescribed creeds, ritual, observances, exactions, to which they believe themselves to be committed. Others have neither thought nor care for these things. They have yielded themselves to God and are persuaded that he will bear them and carry them, even as a man bears his son, in all the way that they go— until they come to the place of which God has spoken to them (Deut. 1:31; Isa. 63:9).

1. THE BURDENS FOR WHICH GOD MAKES HIMSELF RESPONSIBLE. The lives of most of us are heavily weighted. We began our race unencumbered, but the years as they have passed have added burdens and responsibilities. We run heavily; we walk with difficulty; we carry weights as well as sins.

Foremost there is the burden of *existence*. We must live. We were not asked if we would live; we are. We had no option than to live, and we have none today. The physical phenomenon which men call death may insert a comma, or draw a line—but life continues yonder if not here, somehow if not thus, and forever. Because the spark on our heart-altars has been kindled at the eternal fires of the divine nature, it will exist when the moon is withered with age and the stars have burned out in night.

There is the burden of *sin*. The word used of bearing is the same as Isaiah uses of the Sin-bearer, who bore our sins in his own body on the tree (53:4). Though the atmosphere presses upon us at the rate of several pounds for every square inch of bodily surface, we are yet unconscious of its weight. So, till Jesus came, man hardly realized the burden of sin, and groaned not beneath its intolerable weight. But as the Redeemer's pure image has passed from land to land, from age to age, it has convinced men of the awful burden of sin. This is shown to be the reason why they are weary and heavy laden; why their spirits lack joy and elasticity; why the step tires so soon, and the day of life drags so wearily to a close. And as the reason is given, we know it is so, and assent to Peter's cry, "I am a sinful man, O Lord."

There is the burden of *responsibility for others*. Our life is so closely entwined with that of others that we cannot live long without becoming weighted with care for them. The son must care for mother and sisters. The young man is linked in imperishable bonds to the twin-soul who is dearer than himself, and whose sorrows and anxieties mean more to him than his own. Then the sweet children who come into our lives, with their guile-less trust; the charge of others bequeathed with dying breath; the care of employee, lonely ones, tempted and persecuted ones. Ah, it is impossible for you or me to move so quickly as we did years ago!

There is also the burden of *our life work*. That we have been sent to do what no one else can do; that we have talents entrusted of which we must give an account; that we are called to cultivate one patch in the vine-yard, to build one bit in the wall, to utilize one talent of the Master's capital—this makes us sensible of the im-portance and urgency of life. It is not possible to realize what our life may mean of blessing or sorrow to others and not feel the solemn weight of responsibility imping-ing on us.

In all these things we are doomed to be solitary. It cannot be otherwise. Each man and woman in our circle is similarly weighted. All have as much hill-climbing, burden-bearing and fighting as they can manage. None can share aught of his oil, or strength, or courage. We can give sympathy, but that is all. Each human soul must bear his own burden of existence, sin, responsi-bility, and work. But it is just here that Jehovah steps in. He does not distinguish between our burdens and ourselves, but takes us *and* them up in his almighty arms and bears us with no sense of fatigue, no fear of failure. We are a dead weight; but it matters naught to him. He has borne us all the days of old: he *daily* beareth our burdens. He *will* bear us and carry us till he sets us down in the land where no burdens can enter, in the city through whose gates they are never borne, in the world where the heavy-laden leap as an hart and the weary are at rest.

2. THE REASON WHY GOD ASSUMES THIS RESPONSIBILITY. "I have made, and I will bear." When a parent sees his own evil nature reappearing in his child—the same temper, the same passions, the same peculiarities—so far from casting that child aside, and quoting its faults as reasons for disowning it, he draws nearer to it, filled with a great pity, and murmurs, "I have made, and I will bear."

When a man has elicited in another a love which will never be at rest till it has nestled to his heart, even though considerations arise which make it questionable whether he has been wise, yet, as he considers the greatness of the love which he has evoked, he says to himself, "I have made, and I will bear."

When a Christian minister has gathered around him a large congregation, and many have been converted from the world—as he looks around on those who count him captain or father, he says to himself, when voices summon him elsewhere, unless some overmastering consideration is pressed upon him, "I have made, and I will bear."

Now let us ascend by the help of these reflections to the nature of the Divine, which is not above similar considerations. God has made and fashioned us; he has implanted within us appetites that only he can satisfy; he has placed us amid circumstances of unusual difficulty and entrusted to us work of uncommon importance. He has committed to us the post of duty which taxes us to the uttermost: and because he has done all this, he is responsible for all that is needed for the accomplishment of his purposes. Since all things are of him, we may rest assured that they will be through him and to him forever. He has made, and he will bear. He has incurred the responsibility of making us what we are and placing us where we are; then he must perfect that which concerns us, since his mercy endures forever and he cannot forsake the work of his own hands.

There are several corroborations of this thought in the Bible. There is that word of our Lord in which he tells us that our heavenly Father is bound to give food and clothes for the body which he has given (Matt. 6:25–26). There is the statement that what God has fashioned us for, and given the down payment of, he must complete. There is the golden chain of Romans 8, each link in which postulates the next, and that the next: predestination involves calling, and this justification, and this again glory. When God thinks of building a character he first considers whether he can complete it; and if he begin, it is a positive assurance that he will carry out his plan. What he makes, he will bear.

It was so with Israel. He made the chosen people by his election and grace. From an obscure tribe of nomads, he made them his peculiar people, his own inheritance, his messengers to the world. Notwithstanding their many wanderings and provocations, he has never put away the people whom he foreknew; through all these weary centuries he has been deeply solicitous for them, and he will yet bring them on eagles' wings to their city and land.

It is so with our world. He made it. It was the nurseling of his love and power, and bore the early imprint of his benediction. Through the depths of space he has never ceased to bear it, although it has been dark with sin and red with crime. He bore its insult and shame when they cast him forth with contempt to the cross. He bore its sin in the agony of Calvary. And the end is sure. He bears it on his heart, and will never put it away until its evil is overcome with his good, and it shines again in its early beauty and sings in unison with its sister spheres.

3. THE CONSOLATION WHICH ARISES FROM THESE CONSIDERATIONS.

(a) *There is consolation in hours of anguish for recent sin.* The sin is our own. In no sense can the sinner lay it on God. "I have sinned," he cries, "and perverted that which was right, and it did not profit me. The sin is mine." And yet from the depth of sin-consciousness there is an appeal to God. He created—permitted us to be born as members of a sinful race. He knew all we would be before he set his heart upon us and made us his own. May we not ask him to bear with us whom he made, redeemed, and took to be his children by adoption and grace? And will he not answer, "I have made, and I will bear"?

(b) *There is consolation in moments of great anxiety.* When burdened with care for ourselves or others, let us fall at the foot of the altar steps that slope through darkness to God. When our circumstances are beyond measure perplexing, and the knots refuse to be untied; when we have no idea what to do, or how to act for the best—is there not every reason to look into the face of God and say, "You have permitted me to come hither; you alone know what I should do. You have made me. Will you not bear me through this swelling tide and bring me on to firm standing-ground?" And will he not again answer, "I have made, and I will bear"?

(c) *There is consolation in days of anxious foreboding.* Sometimes, as we have climbed to an Alpine summit, the gaunt black rocks have risen around us from an ocean surface of fleecy clouds which have, so to speak, washed up against them, filling the whole intermediate valley. The hamlet where we were to spend the night, and the road to it, were alike hidden. So is the future hidden from our view; and with the fear born of ignorance we dread what may be awaiting us. The veil is slight, but impenetrable. What may it not conceal? Then again, let us turn to the ineffable God. He knows all that we can bear, for he made us. It is not likely that he will imperil that on which he has spent time and thought. He cannot fail or forsake. We may freely cast on him the responsibility.

O our Maker!—bear us, as a mother her infant; as a father his tired boy; as a guide the fainting woman turned dizzy at the vision of sheer depth beneath. You have made; will you not bear? Again the answer returns, "Even to old age I am he, and even to hoary hairs will I carry you: I have made, and I will bear; yea, I will carry, and will deliver."

12

SUMMONED TO AN EXODUS

(ISAIAH 48:17–21)

"Think not of rest, though dreams be sweet;
Start up, and ply your heavenward feet!
Is not God's oath upon your head?
Ne'er to sink back on slothful bed,
Never again your loins untie
Nor let your torches waste and die."
Keble

WE now reach the close of the first part of these wonderful prophecies. It really concludes at the end of the forty-eighth chapter, with a summons to the house of Jacob, called by the name of Israel, which had come forth from the loins of Judah (v. 1), to arise and go forth from Babylon.

There has never been an era in which God's people have not been face to face with a great principle of evil, embodied in a city, confederation, or conspiracy of darkness. Always the same spirit under differing forms: always the deification of the human against the divine; always the pride and vainglory of intellect against moral worth; always the effort of man's prowess and scheming to build a fabric without the divine keystone which alone can give solidity and permanence.

This great system is as strong today as when the massive walls of Babylon enclosed their thousands and

proudly dominated the world. Some have identified the
Babylon system with the Church of Rome, or the spirit
of ecclesiastical assumption. But it is better to consider
it as that element which is ever working through human society, which is spoken of as "the world," and of
which the apostle said, "It is without hope and without
God." We are therefore warranted in applying to present
surroundings every item in the description given of this
olden foe of Israel, and of heeding the summons to go
forth from it.

1. SENT TO BABYLON. God's ideal for the chosen
people is set forth under a beautiful similitude. We find
this in verse 18: "Oh that thou hadst hearkened to my
commandments! Then had thy peace been as a river,
and thy righteousness as the waves of the sea."

Their peace might have been as a river. Not as the
brook, as it gushes rapturously forth, breaking musi-
cally on the stones and flashing in the glee of its early
life; not as a streamlet hardly filling its wide bed, and
scarcely affording water enough for the fish to pass to
its higher reaches—but like a river far down its course,
sweeping along with majestic current, deep and placid,
able to bear navies on its broad expanse, to collect and
carry with it the refuse of towns upon its banks without
contamination, and approaching the sea with the harmony begotten of similarity in depth and volume and
service to mankind. Oh, rivers that minister perpetually to man—not swept by storm nor drained by drought,
not anxious about continuance, always mirroring the
blue of the azure sky or the stars of night and yet content to stay for every daisy that sends its tiny root for
nourishment—in your growth from less to more, your
perennial fullness, your beneficent ministry, your volume, your calm, you were meant to preach to man, with
perpetual melody, of the infinite peace that was to rise
and grow and unfold with every stage of his experience!
Such at least was God's ideal for Israel, and for all who

swear by his name and make mention of Jehovah as God.

Their righteousness might have been as the waves of the sea. Walk along the coastline when the tide has ebbed. Mark the wastes of sand, the muddy ooze, the black, unsightly rocks. Not thus did God intend that any of his children should be. It was never his will that their righteousness should ebb, that there should be wastes and gaps in their experience, that there should be the fatal lack of strength and purity and virtue. The divine ideal of the inner life is mid-ocean, where the waves reach to the horizon on every side and there are miles of sea water beneath. No one can look upon the majestic roll of the Atlantic breakers, in purple glory, crowned with the white crest of foam, chasing one another as in a leviathan game, without realizing the magnificence of the divine intention that all who have learned to call God "Father" should be possessed of a moral nature as fresh, as multitudinous, as free in its motion and as pure in its character as those waves which, far out to sea, lift up their voice and proclaim the wealth of the power of God.

What a contrast this is to the troubled sea to which the wicked are compared—sighing, chafing, moaning along the shore, and casting up mire and dirt (57:20). Give me a thousand times rather mid-ocean, where the breezes blow fresh over miles of sea, than the melancholy break of the waves on a low and sandy shore. The one is as the righteous man in the strength and glory of his regenerate and justified manhood; the other as the wicked—always churning, fretting, bringing forth that which will profit him nothing.

This ideal is within the reach of everyone who will hearken to God's commandments. There is a short and easy method by which that peace may begin to flow for you and me, and the waves of that righteousness sweep in jubilant measure over our souls. Hearken and do.

Have his commandments and keep them. Level your
life to your light. But if we refuse, and turn aside and
follow the devices and desires of our evil hearts, we shall
miss inevitably and utterly the realization of that purpose which otherwise would make music in our hearts
and melody to our God. Obedience to the least wish of
the Lord, however and wherever expressed, is the golden
secret by the practice of which we may attain to this
peace and this righteousness.

But if we refuse, we may have to pass, as Israel did,
into the furnace of suffering in the Babylon of the world.
God cannot be thwarted in the realization of his purpose. If we are obstinate, and our neck an iron sinew
and our brow brass (v. 4); if we trust in our idol and
graven image (v. 5); if we will not hear, nor know, nor
open our ear (v. 8)—then we must go by a more circui-
tous and painful route, *via Babylon* with its bitter anguish, where, as in a furnace for silver, the dross and
alloy will be purged away. How many of God's people
are at this moment in the furnace, which would not
have been required if they had been willing and obedient! Not that the furnace always indicates unfaithful-
ness; but if we *are* unfaithful, we must expect the furnace.

2. LIFE IN BABYLON. The mighty city was called the
Lady of Kingdoms. We must think of her with massive
walls, broad spaces, colossal bulls guarding the en-
trances to vast temples with flights of stairs and terraces; with pyramids, towers and hanging gardens; her
wharves receiving the freights of the Indian Ocean; her
marts thronged with the merchants of the world; her
streets teeming with tributary populations. But right
across her splendor ran the fatal bars of cruelty, luxury,
wickedness and devil worship.

Cruelty. When God gave his people into her hand, she
showed them no mercy but laid her yoke very heavily
upon the aged who staggered beneath their loads or

fainted in the horrors of the march to Babylon, while multitudes of the young lay dead beneath the smoking remnants of their cities (47:6).

Luxury. She was given to pleasures and felt very secure (47:8). Her citizens were arrayed in fine linen and purple and scarlet, and decked with gold, precious stones, and pearls. Her merchandise was of gold, silver, precious stones, pearls, fine linen, purple, silk and scarlet, ivory and brass, cinnamon and spice.

Wickedness. In this she trusted: in violence and oppression, in drunkenness and excess, in the impurities of nature worship—so that she made all the nations drunk with the wine of her abominations (47:10).

Devil worship. She labored with her enchantments and with the multitudes of her sorceries (47:12).

Amid such scenes the Jews spent the weary years of their captivity. Very bitter was their lot. They were for a prey or a spoil. Bills of slave sales which have been recently deciphered contain Jewish names. The majority of them were probably employed in exacting toils, in building up the material strength and prosperity of Babylon as their fathers had done for Egypt centuries before.

But through this awful discipline there was slowly emerging a nobler, loftier ideal, which was fostered by the ancient words that foretold their destiny. It was not possible that they should be long held by their captors. Were they not the elect people of God, destined to bless the world? Were they not called to bear the Ark of God in the march of the race? Was not the Covenant, made of old with Abraham, still vital in all its provisions? Yes, they might be in Babylon like many another captive people, but they had a great hope at their heart. And in the light of that hope, under the searching fires of their anguish, they forever abandoned their love for idolatry; they turned from the outward rites of worship to cultivate a strong moral and religious life; and they gave themselves up to the study of their inspired Scriptures with an ardor which, from that moment, made the synagogue and the scribe an indispensable adjunct of their national life. Never again was the Jew an idolater. Always after, conscience was quick and sensitive. Without exception, the Jewish Scriptures, kept with the most exact and scrupulous care, and the Jewish synagogue, accompanied the movements of the scattered race. In addition, there was a breadth of view—enlarged conceptions of the dealings of God with man, an expansion of interests—which prepared the way for the further revelations of the gospel as to the catholicity of the love of God and the brotherhood of man. As a river in its flow over various soils becomes impregnated with their products, so did the Jewish people receive lasting benefits from their painful sojourn in Babylon, with whose waters they so often mingled their tears.

Some who read these words now are in their Babylon. They look back to a sunny past, which might have continued had they not stepped out of the narrow path of obedience. Their peace was then as a river, their righteousness as the waves of the sea; but, alas, all this is but a memory! They involved themselves in coils of difficulty and suffering from which deliverance appears hopeless. The weary years seem destined to run out their slow and painful course without remedy. Yet let such still hope in God; they shall still praise him! Let them repent of their sins and put them away; let them learn the deep lessons which God's Spirit is endeavoring to teach; let them dare to praise God for the discipline of pain. In these dark hours light is being sown for the righteous, and gladness for the upright in heart. Presently the clarion call of the exodus will ring out: "Arise and depart, for this is not your rest. Cry unto her, that her warfare is accomplished, that her iniquity is pardoned. Go ye forth of Babylon, flee ye from the Chaldeans" (Micah 2:10; Isa. 40:2; 48:20).

3. EXODUS FROM BABYLON. The old order was changing and giving place to the new. In a magnificent apostrophe, the virgin daughter of Babylon had been summoned to come down from her imperial throne and sit on the ground. She was no more to be called tender and delicate. She must step down to the level of the common household drudge, who grinds the meal and carries the burden of the house. Loss of children and widowhood were to come to her in a moment—in one day; and neither the enchantments of magicians nor the efforts of those who had traded with her would avail to avert her calamities (47:1–9).

From the ruins of the fallen Babylonian kingdom the Jews are bidden to go forth. "Go ye forth of Babylon, flee ye from the Chaldeans." The edict of Cyrus was only the countersigning of the divine edict which had already gone forth. And it is very remarkable that while Babylon has vanished, leaving no trace except in the records of the past, the people whom they held for seventy years in captivity are not only in existence still but have control of the secret springs of the world and are destined to play a great part in its future history. Amid the removing of those things which could be shaken, because they were made by the wisdom or power of man, they have received a kingdom that could not be shaken—the kingdom of moral force, of character, of spiritual power.

This summons for an exodus rings out to the Church of the living God from the heavenly watchers. "I heard another voice from heaven," says the seer, "saying, Come out of her, my people, that ye be not partakers of her sins, and that ye receive not of her plagues" (Rev. 18:4). And in the words that follow there is an evident reference to the overthrow of Babylon, with an application to the godless system of human society which confronts the Church in every age. In the early centuries it was represented by the Roman Empire; now it is present in the spirit of the world. The race of Babel-builders is not

extinct. By his intellect and energy man is still endeavoring to rear a structure, independently of God, to make
himself a name—to defy the waters of time's deluge from
sweeping away his work. All human imaginings,
strivings, energizings—man's ceaseless activities, the
outcome of human life apart from the Spirit of God—
constitute a fabric as real as that of Babel or Babylon
the Great, though no material fabric arises as its visible
memorial.

From all this we are bidden to "come out and be separate." "Love not the world, neither the things that are in
the world." "Touch no unclean thing." Let the spirit of a
divine love burn out the spirit of worldliness and
selfhood. Come out—out from all fellowship with iniquity; out from all communion with darkness; out from
all concord with Belial; out from partnership with un-
believers!

Beyond Babylon lies the desert which must be traversed ere Jerusalem is reached, and we dread the privations through which we may be called to pass. The
fear of these withheld large numbers of the Jews from
obeying the edict of Cyrus. They remained in the land of
their captivity till they lost their autonomy, and became
the people of the Dispersion. Let no such fear withhold
you, O Christian soul! It may seem as though the desert
were to be traversed by you, without break or intermis-
sion for many a weary year. But take heart! He will lead
you through the deserts; he will cause waters to flow
from the rocks; he will cleave the rock, and the waters
shall gush out (v. 21). Supplies of which you have no
conception shall surprise you with their fitness and
abundance. Your track shall be marked with flowers and
trees, glades where now are wastes, wells where now
are the dunes of the desert. The time is fulfilled. Your
discipline is complete. The year of your redemption is
come. Go forth from the captivity which has so long held
you, to a freer, nobler, diviner life.

13

A POLISHED SHAFT

(ISAIAH 49:1–8)

"The best men, doing their best,
Know peradventure least of what they do:
Men usefullest in the world are simply used;
The nail that holds the wood must pierce it first,
And he alone who wields the hammer sees
The work advanced by the earliest blow. Take heart!"
E. B. Browning

O ISLES of Greece, famed as the home of verse and song, you were never summoned to listen to a voice so sweet as that which speaks in these words! Not Sappho, nor Homer himself, so well deserved your heed. And you, you people of the world, though the speech be that of one of your obscurest tribes, an alien in a land of strangers and itself falling into disuse, yet it contains words which, once heard, shall be absorbed into all your many tongues and recited in every dialect and language the world over: "Listen, O Isles, unto me; and hearken, ye peoples from far!" (v. 1).

And who is this that speaks in the Hebrew tongue and presumes to address the world as his audience? We had thought the Jew's speech too exclusive, too conservative, too intolerant of strangers to care to make itself heard beyond the limits of Judaism. "The Jews have no dealings with the Samaritans." To the Jewish

mind, Gentiles are dogs beneath the table. Whence these
worldwide sympathies? Whence this sudden interest in
the great family of man? Ah! these are the words of the
Messiah, the *ideal* Jew! He is speaking in the name of
the elect race and representing its genius—not as warped
by human prejudice but as God intended it to be! "*He*
said unto me, Thou art my servant; Israel, in whom I
will be glorified" (v. 3).

There can be no doubt that this is the true way of
considering these noble words. This servant is clearly
called "a light to the Gentiles, . . . my salvation unto the
end of the earth" (v. 6). And this was expressly referred
to Jesus Christ by his greatest apostle on one of the
most memorable occasions in his career. The little synagogue at Antioch was crowded to its doors. All the city
was eager to hear the stranger who had dropped down,
so to speak, "from the snows of the Taurus." But this
seriously affected the Jews, with their proud suscepti-
bilities, and galled their pride. "They were filled with
jealousy, contradicted the things which were spoken by
Paul and Barnabas, and blasphemed." After a while the
preacher realized that the terms of his commission did
not require him to expend his words on those who at
every syllable refused them, so he suddenly changed
his note. He had made an offer of eternal life, which had
been rejected with disdain; there was nothing left but to
turn to the Gentiles, and he quoted the climax words of
this paragraph in defense of the course he thereupon
adopted: "For so hath the Lord commanded us, saying,
I have set thee for a light of the Gentiles, that thou
shouldest be for salvation unto the uttermost part of
the earth" (Acts 13:47, R.V.).

But, it may be asked, how can words so evidently
addressed to Israel be appropriated with equal truth to
Jesus Christ? To reply to this in full would take us too
far afield. It is sufficient here to say that he was the
epitome and personification of all that was noblest and

divinest in Judaism. When, in spite of all that they had suffered in their exile, they for a second time failed to realize or fulfill their great mission to the world; when under the reign of Pharisee and scribe they settled down into a nation of legalists, casuists, and hair-splitting ritualists—*he* assumed the responsibilities which they had evaded and fulfilled them by the message he spoke and the Church he formed. In the mission of Jesus, the heart of Judaism unfolded itself. What he was and did, the whole nation ought to have been and done. As the white flower on the stalk, he revealed the essential nature of the root. The very life of Jesus had a striking similarity to the history of the chosen people; and, therefore, Matthew with perfect propriety applies to him a text which Hosea wrote to the entire nation: "Joseph arose and took the young child and his mother by night, and departed into Egypt; and was there until the death of Herod: that it might be fulfilled which was spoken by the Lord through the prophet, saying, Out of Egypt did I call my Son" (Hos. 11:1; Matt. 2:14–15, R.V.).

We are justified, therefore, in referring this paragraph to the Lord Jesus as the ideal servant of God. And we may get some useful teaching as to the conditions of the loftiest and best service which, by following his steps, we may render to his Father and our Father, to his God and ours.

1. THE QUALIFICATIONS OF THE IDEAL SERVANT.

(a) *A holy motherhood.* "The Lord hath called me from the womb" (v. 1). The greatest and best of men have confessed their indebtedness to their mothers; and not a few have, without doubt, enshrined in their character and developed in their life inspirations which had thrilled their mothers' natures from early girlhood. It is from their mothers that men get their souls. Many an obscure woman has ruled the world through the child in which her noblest self has been reproduced in masculine deeds and words. Rachel in Joseph; Jochebed in

Moses; Hannah in Samuel; Elizabeth in John the Baptist; Monica in Augustine; the mother of the Wesleys in her illustrious sons. With all reverence we say it, Mary of Nazareth has attained an influence which the Church of Rome could never give her, through her Son who rules the ages. We know that in him the male and female blend in perfect symmetry; and yet sometimes we think, in the human side of this wondrous nature, we trace the Virgin Mother—her delicate and quick sympathy; her keen appreciation of beauty; her reverent and accurate knowledge of the Old Testament scriptures.

To make a man, God begins with his mother. How necessary it is, then, that young girls should be carefully trained to lofty thoughts and pure imaginings, that shall afterwards reappear in the strongest, fairest characters. And how important it is that young women should carefully watch their hearts, restraining what is vain and evil, and reaching out after whatsoever things are true, just, pure, lovely, and of good report, not only in outward appearance but in the inner chambers of the heart—for there the formative influences are ever brooding and maturing.

Few of us realize the immense importance attaching to the education of girls. Those who bear the children make our times. She that rocks the cradle rules the world. The zenanas of India must be taken for Christ before that great continent will yield to the gospel. Anyone, therefore, who can influence women by speech or pen, by education or example, has an almost unrivaled power over the destinies of our race. It is only a shallow and superficial critic who will sneer at a congregation of servant girls. The tendency of the present day notwithstanding, the highest function of woman is to give noble children to the world; in this she gives herself, and for this all education and environment should prepare her.

(b) *Incisive speech.* "He hath made my mouth like a sharp sword" (v. 2). Speech is the most Godlike faculty in man. Christ did not scruple to be called the Word or Speech of God. "The tongue of man," says Carlyle, "is a sacred organ. Man himself is definable in philosophy as an incarnate word; the word not there, you have no man there either, but a phantasm instead." At the bidding of the human voice conceptions of beauty and thought emerge, darkness is dispelled, truth is unfolded, resolutions are born, inspirations conceived, crusades set on foot. Before the voice of man the lower creation trembles; and with his voice man joins in the ascriptions of adoration and praise which are ever arising around the eternal throne.

This regal faculty is God's chosen organ for announcing and establishing his kingdom over the earth. He uses silence, the uncomplaining passivity of the downtrodden and oppressed; he uses deeds, erecting vast structures as their monument; he uses books, the seed-baskets of thought—but he especially uses words. When John was cast into prison, Jesus came preaching. He opened his mouth and taught; he bade his disciples go into all the world and preach his gospel to every creature. By the foolishness of preaching it is God's pleasure to save them that believe. And so long as the pulpit is willing to be the mouthpiece of the living Spirit, it cannot be superseded by the press.

Our mouth must be surrendered to God, that he may implant there the sharp two-edged sword that proceeds from his own lips (Rev. 1:16). We must see to it that we do not speak our own words, nor think our own thoughts, but must open our mouths wide that he may fill them with the Word of God, which is quick and powerful, and sharper than any two-edged sword (Heb. 4:12). "He hath made"—precious words, denoting on the one hand the submissive attitude which yields itself to receive; and on the other, the touch of the living God, who promises to be with the mouth and teach what we should say. Who does not want to speak as Peter did, when, on

the day of Pentecost, many were pricked in their heart?—
or as Stephen did, when, in the Sanhedrin, we are told
that his opponents were cut to the heart by his incisive
speech? We do not want to give mere swordplay to delight the eyes of our hearers, but we must pierce to the
dividing asunder of soul and spirit, so that those who
are unbelieving may be convicted and judged, and the
secrets of their hearts revealed.

(c) *Seclusion.* "In the shadow" (v. 2). We must all go
there sometimes. The glare of the daylight is too brilliant; our eyes become injured, and unable to discern
the delicate shades of color or appreciate neutral tints.
Perhaps you are in the shadowed chamber of sickness,
the shadowed house of mourning, the shadowed life from
which the sunlight has gone. But, fear not!—it is the
shadow of God's hand. He is leading you. There are lessons that can only be learned there. The photograph of
his face can only be fixed in the dark chamber. Do not
suppose that he has cast you aside. You are still in his
quiver; he has not flung you away as a worthless thing.
He is only keeping you close till the moment comes when
he can send you most swiftly and surely on some errand in which he will be glorified. Oh, shadowed solitary ones, remember how closely the quiver is bound to
the warrior, within easy reach of the hand, and guarded
jealously!

(d) *Freed from rust.* "A polished shaft" (v. 2). Weapons
of war soon deteriorate. A breath of damp leaves its cor-
roding mark; and the rust shows where the metal is
slowly being eaten away. In archery, a rusted arrow-
point will fail to penetrate and will glance away from the
target. And so in war: a sword or spear corroded by rust
cannot cleave its way through helmet or shield.

Rust can best be removed by sandpaper or the file.
Similarly *we* must be kept bright and clean. There must
be no rust on our hearts resulting from inconsistency
or permitted sin. To keep us from thus deteriorating is

God's perpetual aim; and for this purpose he uses the fret of daily life, the chafe of small annoyances, the wear and tear of irritating tempers and vexing circumstances. Nothing great or crushing, but many things that gall and vex—these are the sandpaper and the file that God perpetually employs to guard against whatever would blunt the edge or diminish the effect of our work.

2. APPARENT FAILURE. "But I said, I have labored in vain; I have spent my strength for naught and vanity" (v. 4). This heartbreak seems inevitable to God's most gifted and useful servants. It is in part the result of nervous overstrain: as, after the great day of Carmel, Elijah threw himself down beneath the juniper tree and asked that he might die. But in part it results from the expanding compassion of the soul, becoming aware how little one man can do to mitigate the anguish of the world.

We are so long in learning how to work: we have to unlearn so much, we have to return from so many paths that lead nowhere. It is already afternoon when we start to use the experience we have gotten and pursue the right tracks that we have at last discovered; then, after an hour or two of bright labor, our strength begins to wane, the sun of our brief day nears the western hills, and all is over. The night has come, in which no man can work. How often we thought our mothers hard when in childhood they said that we must come in and go to bed. And the most strenuous workers will feel like that when God calls them home—unless they are very tired and lonely because so many of their companions have left them. *Then* they will perhaps be glad.

The heart is capable of infinite yearnings and compassion, while the physical strength is limited and finite. Evil is so hydra-headed and Protean. The bias to evil in each generation is so strong and inveterate. The restless sea of which the prophet spoke is so constantly sweeping away the embankments and walls reared against its incursions. It seems so impossible to reach the root, the secret spring, the heart. The circle of light only makes the surrounding darkness more pitch-black. What can one weak man effect against such overwhelming odds!

There are three sources of consolation. First, that failure will not forfeit the bright smile of the Master's welcome nor the reward of his judgment seat. He judges righteously—and rewards not according to results but according to faithfulness. "Yet, *surely*, my judgment is with the Lord, and my recompense with my God" (v. 4). Secondly, the soul leans more heavily upon God: "My God is become my strength" (v. 5). Thirdly, we turn to prayer. How sweetly God refers to this, saying, "In an acceptable time have I answered thee, and in a day of salvation have I helped thee" (v. 8).

Thus God deals with us all. He is compelled to take us to the backside of the desert, where we sit face to face with the wreck of our fairest hopes. There he teaches us as only he can, weaning us from creature confidence and taking pride from our hearts. Then from the stump of the tree, hewn almost to the ground, comes the scion of a new life, which fulfills the promise that seemed forever annulled.

3. ULTIMATE SUCCESS. When Jesus died, *failure* seemed written across his life work. A timid handful of disciples was all that remained of the crowds that had thronged his pathway, and they seemed disposed to go back to their fishing boats. Man despised him; the nation abhorred him; and the rulers set him at naught. But that very cross which man deemed his supreme disgrace and dethronement has become the stepping stone of universal dominion. Israel shall yet be gathered, and the Gentile Church become as the sand of the sea.

Thus it may be with some who peruse this page. They are passing through times of barrenness, and disappointment, and suffering. But let them remember that the Lord is faithful (v. 7). He will not allow one word to fail, one seed to be lost, one effort to prove abortive, one life to be wasted. And *because* of this, they shall be preserved; lands which they have discovered and cultivated shall teem with men; measures that they have inaugurated shall effect the liberation of the blind and the enslaved; trees they have planted shall become forests, and beneficially affect the climate of the world. Yea, these shall be light things, to be succeeded by greater and yet greater as the circle of their influence widens through the universe and the throb of their life reacts on coming ages.

While Christ from the throne of his glory sees the travail of his soul, he is assuredly satisfied; and when, from the hills of glory, as from another Pisgah, we behold the results of our lifework—the way by which God led us, and answered our prayers, and blessed our feeble attempts to serve him—we shall forget the pain and disappointment amid the gladness of the overwhelming and transporting spectacle.

14

THE LOVE THAT WILL NOT LET US GO

(ISAIAH 49:9–50:1)

"My God, thou art all Love!
Not one poor minute 'scapes thy breast
But brings a favor from above—
And in this Love—I rest."
　　　　　　　　　Herbert

THIS chapter is strewn with assurances to the chosen people on the eve of their return from Babylon. They were timid, and reluctant to quit the familiar scenes of their captivity. They dreaded the dangers and privations of the journey back, and questioned whether the great empire of their captors would ever let them go or permit their city to arise from her ruins. Therefore Jehovah's voice takes on a tone of unusual tenderness, and speaks as he only can. Let us heed his successive assurances of comfort and compassion, "for the Lord hath comforted his people, and will have compassion upon his afflicted" (v. 13).

1. HE WILL LEAD WITH A SHEPHERD'S CARE. The prevailing characteristic of the early Hebrews was pastoral: "Jacob kept sheep." The patriarchs of the nation were "the stateliest shepherds of all time." Its ideal king and its earliest prophet were taken from tending the flocks. The imagery of the flock, therefore, deeply dyed the national speech and enriched it with striking analo-

gies. The king, and every true leader, and above all, Jehovah, was called the Shepherd of his people. "We are
the sheep of his pasture." This is the concept that underlies these tender assurances: "They shall not hunger
nor thirst; neither shall the heat nor sun smite them:
for he that hath mercy on them shall lead them, even by
the springs of water shall he guide them" (v. 10).

The life of the Eastern shepherd is very different from
anything we are accustomed to in these northern climes.
He occupies some rocky coign of vantage, whence he
looks out on his sheep thinly scattered over the moorland. Or he leads them down to the valleys with their
strips of green pasture and waters of rest; or conducts
them through gloomy gorges where wild beasts have their
lairs—they huddling close to his heels. He is wakeful,
far-sighted, weather-beaten, armed with club and staff,
always thoughtful for the defenseless, helpless creatures
of his charge. You detect the accent of the true shepherd in Jacob's excuse for not accompanying the rapid
march of Esau and his warriors. "The flocks and herds
with me give suck, and if they overdrive them one day,
all the flocks will die. I will lead on softly, according to
the pace of the cattle that is before me" (Gen. 33:13–
14).

All this, and much more, is summed up in the exceedingly beautiful words, "He that hath mercy on them
shall lead them." What comfort is here! He knows our
frame. He is touched with the feeling of our infirmities;
he will not overdrive us. He will go before and lead us,
but he will suit his pace to ours. The longest day's march
shall be adjusted to our capacities. The severest strain
shall not overtax our powers. However rough and difficult the path, ever remember that you are being led by
him who has mercy on you. Hunger and thirst will be
impossible for those who abide in his care and fellowship. Are you enveloped in shadow? It is only lest heat
or sun smite you. Is the descent swift and precipitous?

It is only that he may bring you shortly to the springs of the water of life (Rev. 7:17).

Do not murmur, Christian soul, but ever repeat to yourself, like a sweet, soft refrain, "He that hath mercy on me is leading me; even to springs of water is he guiding me. Sing, O heavens; oh, be joyful, O earth; and break forth into singing, O mountains!"

2. HE WILL MAKE OBSTACLES SERVE HIS PURPOSE. "I will make all my mountains a way"(v.11). Mountains are prohibitory. The student of the geography of Palestine cannot fail to be impressed with the strong barricade of mountains with which God fenced in the Land of Promise on its southern frontier. "South of Beersheba, before the level desert is reached, and the region of roads from Arabia to Egypt and Philistia, there lie sixty miles of mountainous country, mostly disposed in steep ridges running east and west. The vegetation even after rain is very meager, and in summer totally disappears. No great route leads, or ever has led, through this district. Its steep and haggard ridges are utterly inaccessible."

Similarly, the mountains of Switzerland have sheltered liberty, and those of Afghanistan have made conquest difficult—to impossibility. There were great mountains between Israel and home, yet God does not say that he would remove them; rather, that they would form a pathway, as though contributing to the ease and speed of the return. "I will make all my mountains a way."

We all have mountains in our lives. There are people and things that threaten to bar our progress in the divine life. That trying temperament; that large family; those heavy claims; that uncongenial occupation; that thorn in the flesh; that daily cross. We think that if only these were removed, we might live purer, tenderer, holier lives; and often we pray for their removal. O fools and slow of heart! These are the very conditions of achievement; they have been put into our life as the

means to the very graces and virtues for which we have
been so long praying.

You have prayed for patience through long years, but
there is something that tries you beyond endurance;
you have fled from it, evaded it, accounted it an
unsurmountable obstacle to the desired attainment, and
supposed that its removal would secure your immediate deliverance and victory. Not so! You would only gain
the cessation of *temptations* to impatience. But this
would not be patience. Patience can only be acquired
through just such trials as now seem unbearable. Go
back, and submit yourself. Claim to be a partaker in
the patience of Jesus. Meet your trials in him. Thus
shall the mountains that stand between you and your
promised land become your way to it.

Note the comprehensiveness of this promise. "I will
make *all* my mountains a way." There is nothing in life
which harasses and annoys that may not become sub-
servient to the highest ends. No exception can prevail
against this great though small word, *all.* Consider also
that possessive pronoun. They are *his* mountains. He
put them there.

But do not forget that the promise is in the future tense.
"I *will* make." We do not espy the pathway from afar, but
in the distance see only a tumbled mass of rocks. The
keenest sight cannot discern the point at which the
threading path shall intersect them. But why anticipate?
We know that God will not fail his promise. "He
understandeth the way thereof and knoweth the place
thereof; for he looketh to the ends of the earth, and seeth
under the whole heaven" (Job 28:23–24). And when we
come to the foot of the mountains, we shall find the
way.

3. GOD'S LOVE IS DEEPER THAN THAT OF MOTH-
ERHOOD. Many devout but misguided souls have
placed the Virgin Mother on a level with God, and worship her, because they think that woman is more ten-

der, more patient, more forgiving than man. "The love of woman" was David's high-water mark of love. And of woman's love, none is so pure, so unselfish, so full of patient, brooding pity, as a mother's. Oh, heart of woman, it is in the first ecstasy of motherhood that you are ensnared. Bending over the laughing babe, returning your kisses and sallies, in an ecstasy of delight; soothing the suffering and wakeful one with snatches of lullabies and broken bits of baby talk; watching beside the little flickering taper that will soon go out, leaving you cold and dark; giving nights and days without a murmur or regret; prepared to surrender sleep, food, life, for your child—that is what motherhood means. And that love follows us through life. Often repelled and unrequited, it lingers near us in prayers and tears and holy yearnings. At the first symptom of illness or summons of distress, it hurries to our side; it schemes and plans; it will stand by the felon in the dock, and hunt for a girl through Sodom. It sheds over our graves tears no less scalding than those of husband or wife.

Such love is God's. Indeed it is a ray from his heart. If a mother's love is but the ray, what must *his* heart be! But there is sometimes a failure in motherhood. "They may forget" (v. 15). Maddened with frenzy, soddened with drink, flushed with unholy passion, infatuated with the giddy round of gaiety, a woman has been known to forget her sucking child. Indeed, as is recorded of the siege of Samaria, there have been times when women have stayed their hunger with the flesh of their children. But God can never so forget.

We may fall into such dishonor that our dearest will disown us; but he will not forget. We may become scarred and sin-pocked so as to be almost unrecognizable; but he will not forget. We may be away in the far country so long that the candle will cease to burn at night in the window of the most faithful friend; but he will not forget. The fires on all human altars may have burned to white ash; but his love will be what it was when first we knew him.

4. GOD TREASURES THE THOUGHT OF HIS OWN. The orientals have a custom of tattooing the name of beloved friends on the hand. That is the reference here (v. 16); but notice the emphasis. Not the name of Zion merely, but Zion herself—the city where David dwelt, and Solomon built his temple. This was engraved on the divine hand. Yes, child of God, you are imprinted where God must ever behold you, on his hands—on his heart. You are never for a moment out of his thought, nor hidden from his eye.

Not on one hand only, but on both. It is the plural in each case: "On the palms of my hands."

Not tattooed or photographed—the marks of which might be obliterated and obscured—but graven. The graving tool was the spear, the nail, the cross. "Don't write there," said an urchin to a young exquisite scratching with a diamond on the window of a waiting room. "Why not?" was the startled inquiry. "Because you can't rub it out," was the instant retort. Glass will not give up its inscriptions, nor the onyx stone its seal, nor the cameo its profile; but sooner might they renounce their trust than the hands of Christ. "In the midst of the throne a Lamb as it had been slain." "He showed unto them his hands and his side."

Not Zion's ruins; but her walls as they were before Nebuchadnezzar broke them down—as they were meant to be. For fifty or sixty years those walls had been in ruins. Nehemiah tells us that the *debris* forbade the beast he rode to pass, when he made by moonlight his first sad tour of inspection. Sanballat mocked about the heaps of rubbish. But God did not keep those ruins in mind, associated as they were with Israel's follies and sins. Zion's *walls* were ever before him (v. 16). Our ideal self; what we are in Jesus; what we long to be in our best moments; what we will be when grace has perfected its work and we are comely in the comeliness he shall put upon us—this is the ineffaceable conception of us that is ever before God.

What a contrast between Zion's wail about being forsaken and forgotten (v. 14), and God's tender regard! So the believer, considering the desolations of his soul and the ruins of past joys, is apt to think himself a castaway. But it is not so. At the time of his deepest despair, God is thinking of him, as a mother of her first-born babe; and his need is ever before him.

5. GOD'S LOVE IS STRONG ENOUGH TO CARRY OUT ITS PURPOSE. "Shall the prey be taken from the mighty, or the lawful captive delivered?" (v. 24). Such is the question of despondency, asked by Israel, from the heart of the mighty empire in which she was a helpless captive.

But Jehovah had well calculated his resources. Let but his hand be uplifted and his people would be restored, brought back to their land by the solicitude of kings and queens. Do not consider the difficulties of your deliverance, nor brood over past failure and mighty foes; look away from these to him. *He* will become your Great-heart, your Champion; *he* will espouse your cause and carry it through; *he* will show himself strong on your behalf. "Thus saith the Lord, Even the captives of the mighty shall be taken away, and the prey of the terrible shall be delivered; for I will contend with him that contendeth with thee, and I will save thy children" (v. 25).

6. GOD'S LOVE WILL NOT PUT AWAY. When the Jew put away his wife, he gave her a bill of divorcement (Mark 10:4). Without this piece of writing the divorce was not complete, and the husband could take his wife again without blame. Israel, away in the land of exile, thinks herself a divorced wife. She does not say as much—but she thinks, she fears it. Jehovah answers those unspoken questionings by reminding her that she cannot produce a certificate of divorce. "Thus saith the Lord, Where

is the bill of your mother's divorcement, wherewith I have put her away?" (50:1, R.V.). He may well ask where it is: he knows that it cannot be found, for he has never given it.

God cannot divorce those whom he has once taken into covenant with himself. Backsliding, rebellious, and faithless they may be; but they are his still. Though the universe be ransacked, the bill of divorce cannot be produced. The devil himself cannot confront us with it. And the love of God will yet win back the souls on which it has set itself. In a little wrath he hid his face for a moment; but with everlasting kindness will he forgive and gather and have mercy (54:7–8).

15

WORDS IN SEASON FOR THE WEARY

(ISAIAH 50:4–11)

"Thou knowest, not alone as God, all-knowing;
As Man, our mortal weakness thou hast proved:
On earth, with purest sympathies o'erflowing,
O Savior, thou hast wept, and thou hast loved:
And love and sorrow still to thee may come,
And find a hiding place, a rest, a home."

H.L.L.

EVER since the world began, men have been weary.
"Weary" denotes a class to which a multitude belong that no man can number, of every nation, kindred,
tribe and people. *Physical* weariness—of the slave on
the march; of the toiler in the sweating mill; of the seamstress working far into the night; of the mother worn
out from watching her sick child. *Mental* weariness—
when the imagination can no longer create images of
beauty and the intellect refuses to follow another argument, master another page, or produce another column.
Heart weariness—waiting in vain for the word so long
expected but unspoken; for the returning step of the
prodigal; for the long-delayed letter. The weariness
caused by the *inner conflict* of daily striving against the
selfishness and waywardness of the soul. The weariness common to the *Christian worker,* worn down by
the perpetual chafe of human sorrow, sin and need.

If only we could make one brilliant assault on the powers of evil which would forever crush their might, so that they would retreat, leaving the field to us—who would not accept this as the most blessed gift of God? But instead of this, we are engaged in a conflict which is tedious, incessant, and terribly wearing. If we defeat our enemy today, he seems ready to meet us tomorrow with equal force. If we conquer him in one thing, he straightway disguises himself in another. Beneath this long ordeal our heart and flesh fail, and we sigh for the refuge over whose gate Christ has written, "Come unto me, all ye that labor and are heavy laden, and I will give you rest" (Matt. 11:28).

Thus, in one way or another, all souls at some part of their life get weary. There is nothing novel in this; but the novelty, the great novelty, consists in the infinite care that God takes of the weary. There is nothing like it outside the Bible and the literature to which it has given birth. Man hears with apathy that scores of weary ones have fallen out of the march of human life and lie stretched on the scorching sand, doomed to expire of fatigue and thirst. God, on the other hand—the High and Holy One inhabiting eternity—stoops to the need of the weakling; expends his care on the lame, halt, maimed and blind; adopts into his family those who had been rejected for their deformities and ugliness; gathers up the broken fragments; ransacks the highways and byways for the waifs and strays whom no one invites to his table; and is perpetually engaged in brooding over each weary heart with its wounds, its tears, its yearnings, its despair. This God is *our* God forever and ever, unrivaled in his tender pity—the God of the fatherless and the widow!

But the deep tenderness of God for every tired atom of humanity would have been hidden from our knowledge had it not been for the Good Servant who speaks in these paragraphs, and who combines in himself the form of a servant and equality with Jehovah. No one ever comforted the weary as he did. He could not look upon a great multitude, distressed and scattered as sheep not having a shepherd, without being moved with compassion towards them and speaking as only he could. How many weary souls did he sustain with his words (v. 4, R.V.); to how many did he speak a word in season (v. 4, K.J.V.)! Ask him, if you wish, from what source he derived this matchless power, and he will answer, "The Lord God gave it to me. Because of his great love for weary souls everywhere, he raised me up to be their Shepherd. Through days and nights he taught me, wakening me morning by morning for some new lesson of sympathy and mercy, comforting me amid the assaults of my foes and the darkness of dark hours, so that I might be able to comfort others with the comfort wherewith I myself had been comforted by my Father."

We are brought, then, to consider the education, resolution, vindication, and entreaty of the true Servant of Jehovah—*himself* God over all!

1. THE EDUCATION OF THE DIVINE SERVANT. We must notice the difference between the Authorized Version [K.J.V.] and the Revised. In the first, "The Lord God hath given me the tongue of the learned, that I should know how to speak a word in season to him that is weary." In the other, ". . . hath given me the tongue of them that are taught"—or, as the margin reads, "of disciples." The thought here is that the Lord Jesus in his human life was a pupil in the school of human pain, under the tutelage of his Father. He said, "I do nothing of myself, but as the Father taught me, I speak these things"; "I am a man that hath told you the truth, which I heard from God" (John 8:28,40). This is in keeping also with that marvelous word in the Epistle to the Hebrews: "Though he was a Son, yet learned he obedience by the things which he suffered; and, having been made perfect, he became unto all them that obey him the au

thor of eternal salvation" (5:8). Yes, *his education was by God himself.* "The Lord God hath given me. . . . Morning by morning he wakeneth mine ear. . . . The Lord God hath opened mine ear" (vs. 4–5).

It was various. He passed through each class in the school of weariness. Being wearied with his journey, he sat by Sychar's well; they took him, even as he was, in the ship; he looked up to heaven and sighed, because of the pressure of human pain and the obstinacy of unbelief; he suffered being tempted; he once cried in the bitterness of his soul, "How long shall I be with you, and suffer you?" He was glad when the hour came that he should go home to his Father. The waves of human sorrow broke over his tender heart, and though possessed of an inexhaustible patience there was an incessant waste of his physical tissues, so that at last he fainted on the way to Calvary.

It was constant. "Morning by morning" the Father woke him. After his brief snatch of sleep amid the thyme of the hillside, or in the fishing smack, or on the couch that the sisters' love had spread for him at Bethany, the Spirit touched and summoned him to the new lesson of the fresh young day. Morning by morning he was awakened to learn, by the ever-changing circumstances of daily providence, some deeper phase of the world's suffering and its medicine. Would that we were quicker to detect that same awakening touch, and to learn the lessons taught by the circumstances of our lot as to the treatment of the weary and suffering.

It dealt with the season for administering comfort. "That I should know how to speak a word in season" (v. 4). It is not enough to speak the right word. You must speak it at the right moment, or it will be in vain. Many a word spoken out of season has fallen like a seed on the wayside to be devoured by birds; while the same word, uttered at the right time by a voice with less quality of tone, has been God's balm.

It is not easy to know just when to speak to the weary. There are times when the nervous system is so over-strained that it cannot bear even the softest words. It is best then to be silent. A caress, a touch, or the stillness that breathes an atmosphere of calm, will then most quickly soothe and heal. This delicacy of perception can only be acquired in the school of suffering. Our Master knows when to speak and when to be still, because he has graduated there.

It embraced the method. "That I should know *how.*" The manner is as important as the season. A message of goodwill may be uttered with so little sympathy and in tones so gruff and grating that it will repel. The psalm-ist (141:5, R.V.) speaks of words so soft that the head will not refuse it. The touch of the comforter must be that of the nurse on the fractured bone, of the mother with the frightened child. God knows how delicately strung our system is, and how it demands the gentle tread across the floor; movements like the fall of rose petals on the grass; methods of perfect sympathy. All these *he* has provided, who made the snow descend in noiseless flakes and the ocean break in silvery ripple on the sand. Your King has been trained to this: lo, he comes, meek and lowly, sitting on the ambling foal. He will not break the bruised reed, nor quench the smok-ing flax.

It seems to me as if the education of our High Priest has not ceased with his transference from this world of sorrow to the realm where weariness is never felt. His ministry to weary hearts through succeeding ages has made his eye more quick, his touch more delicate.

O weary soul, I have seen him coming to your help! The voice of the Shepherd lifts itself, calling your name. He is searching for you in crag and thicket and torrent bed. He knows just how to extract you. He will lay you on his shoulders rejoicing, and so bring you home.

2. HIS RESOLUTION. From the first, Jesus knew that

he must die. The Lord God poured the full story into his
opened ear. With all other men, death is the close of
their life; with Christ it was the object. We die because
we were born; Christ was born that he might die. From
his birth the shadow of the cross fell athwart his soul,
as the young pigeons shed their blood for him in the
temple courts. To Nicodemus he said, "The Son of Man
must be lifted up." The scenes in the halls of Caiaphas,
Herod and Pilate were as present to his prevision as the
scenes of the past are to our memory! Frequently he
took his disciples aside and told them that the Son of
Man would be delivered into the hands of men who would
handle him shamefully—mock, spit upon, scourge and
kill him (Mark 10:34). But though he anticipated all, yet
he was "not rebellious, neither turned away back" (v. 5).

On one occasion towards the close of his earthly career, when the fingers of the dial were pointing to the
near fulfillment of the time, we are told he set his face
steadfastly to go to Jerusalem. What heroism was here!
Men sometimes speak of Christ as if he were effeminate
and weak, deficient in manly courage, and remarkable
only for passive virtues. But such conceptions are re-
futed by the indomitable resolution which sets its face
like a flint and knows that it will not be ashamed.

Note the voluntariness of Christ's surrender. The
martyr dies because he cannot help it; Christ died because he chose. He laid down his life of himself; no one
took it from him. He might have been rebellious and
turned away backward, or called for twelve legions of
angels, or even pinned his captors to the ground by the
out-flashing of his inherent Godship. But he forbore.
Listen to his words as he treads the winepress alone!
"Thy will, not mine, be done." It is this which throws his
resolution into such clear relief. It is this that stirs our
hearts with admiration and devotion, as we see him
deliberately giving his back to the smiters and his cheeks
to them that pluck off the hair (v. 6), and exposing to

shame and spitting the face that angels gaze on with
unceasing reverence—and from which, some day, heaven
and earth will flee away.

It is said that the "opened ear" (v. 5) refers to something more than the pushing back of Jesus' flowing locks
in order to relay the secret of coming sorrow. Presum-
ably it has some reference to the ancient Jewish custom of boring the ear lobe of the slave to the doorpost of
the master's house. Under this metaphor it is held that
our Lord chose with keen sympathy the service of the
Father and elected all that it might involve, because he
loved him and would not go out free. I can accept this
interpretation—part way. The images may be combined.
Be it only remembered that he knew and chose all that
would come upon him, and that the fetters which bound
him to the cross were those of undying love to us and of
burning passion for the Father's glory.

3. HIS VINDICATION. "He is near that justifieth me"
(v. 8). These are words upon which Jesus may have sustained himself through those long hours of trial. The
Father who had sent him was with him. Not for a moment did he leave him alone. God was near. The triumph with which Paul quotes these words—when applying them to the justification in which the soul which
has made Jesus its refuge is privileged to robe itself—is
but the sigh of an aeolian harp contrasted with the peal
of an organ in comparison with the exultation that filled
the heart of the Son of Man as *he* contemplated his vindication by his Father before all worlds.

"Who is he that condemneth me?" we hear him say;
"It is God that justifieth!"—justification being used here
in the sense of vindication, not, as with us, of the impu-
tation of righteousness.

Scoffers said that he was the friend of publicans and
sinners. God has justified him by showing that if he
associates with such, it is to make them martyrs and
saints.

They said that he was mad. God has justified him by making his teaching the illumination of the noblest and wisest of the race.

They said he had a devil. But God has justified him by giving him power to cast out the devil and bind him with a mighty chain.

They said that he blasphemed when he called himself the Son of God. But God has justified him by raising him to the right hand of power, so that he will come in the clouds of heaven with power and great glory.

They said he would destroy the temple and the commonwealth of Israel. God has justified him in shedding the influence of the Hebrew people through all the nations of the world, and making their literature, their history, their conceptions, dominant.

Where are those who in past centuries have condemned the Lord Jesus? Their books rot on the top shelves of libraries in undisturbed dust. Their names are only remembered as quoted in the apologetics of the defenders of the Christian faith. Their memory has not survived moth-eating time. Behold, they have all waxed old as doth a garment! The moth has eaten them up (v. 9). They have passed away as an ill dream—while the exalted Savior is enthroned daily in more hearts, with more enthusiasm, and with growing appreciation. His throne is established forever and ever!

Oh, do not be afraid of the wrath of man, thou child of the King!—for "the moth shall eat them up as a garment, and the worm shall eat them like wool" (51:8). The fate that has overtaken the adversaries of your King shall overtake *yours*. Only be still, as he was. Set your face as a flint; commit your cause to God; count not on your protestations but upon his vindications—and "he shall bring forth thy righteousness as the light, and thy judgment as the noonday" (Ps. 37:6). He will help you; fear not, you shall not be confounded (v. 7).

4. HIS APPEAL. To obey the Lord's Servant is equiva-

lent to fearing the Lord. He who does the one must do
the other. What is this but to proclaim his deity? Those
who are thus designated—who, because they fear God,
brave the wrath of man; who dare to obey the voice of
the Servant as the voice of his Father—are often called
to walk through darkness, where there is no light. It
may be the valley of the shadow of death, or the garden
of Gethsemane, or the midday-midnight of Calvary. But
from the depth of his own experience the Divine Servant counsels such that they should trust where they
cannot see and rely upon God (v. 10).

Do not stand still or sit down or go back; do not despair but keep right onward, believing that the growing
light on the fringe of the darkness heralds the advent of
the morning. God *will* help you! You shall not be
ashamed. Set your face as a flint. Let your feet hold to
the appointed track.

The temptation at such an hour is to kindle a fire and
surround oneself with firebrands (v. 11, R.V.); but these
die out after a brief sparkle, leaving the darkness more
intense. Then with dazzled eye, the self-sufficient soul
stumbles in the thicket and falls headlong into the pit
of destruction. "This shall ye have of mine hand; ye shall
lie down in sorrow" (v. 11). How awful such a lot must
be!—to lie down in the dying moment with sorrow for a
wasted life behind and a dark eternity before. Oh, abandon your fire with its sparks, and avail yourselves of the
light of the Word of God—as a lamp to your feet and a
light to your path, until the day dawns and the Daystar
rises in your hearts!

16

THE THRICE "HEARKEN"

(ISAIAH 51:1–8)

"Be still, sad soul! lift thou no passionate cry,
But spread the desert of thy being bare
To the full searching of the All-seeing eye;
Wait!—and through dark misgiving, blank despair,
God will come down in pity, and fill the dry
Dead place with light, and life, and vernal air."
J. C. Shairp

THESE paragraphs are exceedingly dramatic. We become conscious that we are approaching a revelation of unparalleled sublimity which shall be in Scripture what heart or brain or eye is in the human body.
The encasing of each of these in strong protecting walls
should convince even the most superficial reader of the
priceless value of the treasure they are formed to guard.
And as we consider the thrice "Hearken" of this paragraph and the thrice "Awake" of the succeeding one, we
realize that we are entering the presence-chamber of
the profoundest mysteries of love and redemption.

Travelers who have visited the ruined temples of Egypt
tell of the splendor of their approaches: long corridors,
guarded by the imperturbable and stupendous statues
of defunct deities; avenues of pillars; and the shadow of
imposing facades and porticoes—everything that human
art could devise prepared the mind for the magnificence

135

of the inner shrine. Similarly, as we read these several chapters, our mind becomes educated, our eye focused and adjusted, our sense of perspective trained, so that with hushed and awful dread we may pass into worship before the dying Man of Calvary.

The people, notwithstanding the promises of deliverance from exile and the summons to depart, seemed unable to believe that they were destined to become again a great nation, or that Zion's wastes would be repaired! Already the Servant of Jehovah had sought to answer their anxious questionings, and to reassure them by announcing a love that would not let them go. And in these words he betakes himself to the same strain. He prefaces his words by the thrice repeated "Hearken," addressed to those who "follow after righteousness" in the first verse; and to those who "know righteousness" in the seventh. These are always the stages in the development of character: those who follow presently possess.

1. THE LESSONS OF RETROSPECT. It is wholesome for the pillar, with its fluted column and decorated coronal, to look down at the quarry whence it came; and for us all to look back at the lowliness and obscurity of our origin. Such considerations deepen our humility, and augment our thankfulness for the grace of God which has made us what we are.

Remember, O man, the rock of the first Adam, with its pit of selfhood, passion, murder—out of which you were taken (v. 1). She who plucked the tempting fruit in violation of her Maker's word was your mother; and he who cast the blame on her and preferred the indulgence of the flesh to the regimen of the spirit was your father. For your brother you must take Cain, and for your sister Rahab. You know the strong affinities by which you are bound to each of these. You cannot rid yourself of the features of the family likeness, nor wholly escape the betraying accent of the family speech! What has brought you from such an origin and made you a pillar in the temple of God but the grace which had no reason except itself, no measure other than infinity? Boast not thyself. There is nothing in you to account for such transformation. Render your homage where it belongs, and reason that if God has done so much, he can easily perfect it. If you were excavated, surely you can be shaped! If you were hewn, surely you can be polished! If you were justified, surely you can be sanctified! If, when an enemy, you were reconciled by the death of his Son, how much more, being reconciled, shall you be saved by his life!

It was for her encouragement that Israel was primarily directed to this retrospect. The nation was greatly reduced in numbers, and the godly were but a handful. It seemed preposterous to suppose that they would ever attain to such prolific numbers as to rival the sands on the shore or the stars of space. The tree had been so mercilessly cut down, and pruned, that they despaired of again beholding its spreading branches laden with fruit. In answer to such forebodings the voice of inspiration cries, "Look back! Consider Abraham and Sarah. There was a time when they were the sole representatives of the Hebrew race; yet from them and from the one son of their old age sprang countless myriads. What little cause, then, is there for fear! Though you were reduced to a single aged pair, these might become the origin of a mighty nation! How much more is there reason for hope now that you may still be counted by your thousands!" "Look unto Abraham your father, and unto Sarah that bare you; for when he was but one I called him, and I blessed him, and made him many" (v. 2, R.V.).

Let us recount the steps of Abraham's pruning, on which God lays stress in saying, "When he was but one, I called him."

He stood alone. First, Terah died, after having started with him for the Land of Promise—emblem of those who

in old age start on the pilgrimage of faith and hope, not
too much tied by the conservatism of nature or the tra-
ditions of the past. Then Lot dropped away, and went
down to Sodom; and it must have been difficult for
Abraham, as he saw the retreating forms of his camp
followers, to be wholly unmoved. Then Sarah's scheme
miscarried, and Hagar was thrust from his tents with
her child. Lastly, his Isaac was laid upon the altar. By
successive strokes the shadows grew deeper and darker;
and he stood alone, face to face with God and his purpose. But the fire that burned in his heart rose higher,
shone brighter, and has ignited myriads with its flame.
You only need a spark to light a conflagration. Chicago
was burned down by the upsetting of a tiny lamp. If
there be heroic faith in one lonely heart, it shall spread
to untold millions.

His faith was sorely tried. First by the long delay; then
by the growing unlikelihood that he should have a child,
since natural force was spent; then by the summons to
offer Isaac on Mount Moriah: every test was applied to
his power of endurance. To the end of his life he was a
stranger and pilgrim, only seeing the promises from afar,
and dying with an unfulfilled hope. He little realized the
perfect work his patience was producing. He may not
have understood how utterly God must reduce and cut
us down before he can graft upon us his rarest fruit. He
did not see that our proud flesh will glory, even though
it be of a strand, a smoking flax, a broken reed. To him
the necessity for knife and fire was not so patent as to
us. As we look back upon it all, we see that it could not
have been otherwise. If the seed was to be a divine gift
to his faith, then nature herself must forfeit vitality and
hope so that God might be all in all.

From Abraham I turn to you, much-suffering believer,
cut to the quick and to the roots, brought into the dust
of death, stripped of reputation, wealth, prestige, the
gifts and graces of oratory, faculty to command. Yet be

of good cheer!—Abraham passed this way before you. It is all part of a necessary process. Nothing has happened to hinder, but all to help you to become the parent of a great spiritual progeny. Because of the destruction of nature, you may reckon on the prolific abundance of grace.

His history is the type of God's dealings with men. Not just once nor twice in the record of the Church has the cause of truth been entrusted to a tiny handful of defenders who have deemed it forlorn or lost. The prophet has stood alone, lamenting that he only was left. The dens and caves have sheltered the loyal but diminished few. Ragged, tattered, harried, exiled, these have gathered around the banner and followed it. Few of the mighty, noble or learned have been called, and not many of the poor. But suddenly God has called out from some unlikely quarter one man, and it has seemed as though the dust were suddenly transformed into warriors, and truth sprang up from the dust as luxuriantly as grass after spring rains. Sir Walter Scott's picture of the apparently empty glens suddenly teeming with armed men at the sign of the chieftain has often had its counterpart in the great army which has arisen from the life, or words, or witness, of a single man.

It was so in the days of the Arian heresy, when Athanasius stood alone against the world for the deity of Christ. It was so at the Reformation, when Europe lay asleep under the soporific of the Papacy. It was so when first the abolition of slavery began to be agitated. God has repeatedly shown that he has no taste for strong battalions: he chooses a Gideon, a Judas Maccabaeus, a Luther, a Wilberforce. The history of the Church is largely a story of the lives of individuals. It is through a Livingstone, a Judson, a Carey, that whole nations have been brought to the feet of Jesus, to sit clothed and in their right mind.

If, therefore, some lone and single-handed Christian

worker should read these words, there is no reason for
despair. Are you a cypher? But you may have God in
front of you! Are you but a narrow strait! Yet the whole
ocean of Godhead is waiting to pour through you! The
question is not what you can or cannot do, but what
you are willing for God to do. When God makes use of
one man, he becomes the father of a vast multitude as
Abraham did of Israel. The only condition is the presence of God in us, with us, through us. Open your whole
being to God, for he is about to comfort the waste places
of Zion. He will make her wilderness like Eden, and her
desert like the garden of the Lord; joy and gladness shall
be found therein, thanksgiving and the voice of melody
(v. 3).

   2. THE IMPERISHABLENESS OF SPIRITUAL QUAL-
ITY. In the following verses there is a marvelous contrast between the material and the immaterial, the temporal and the eternal. The gaze of the people is directed
to the heavens above and the earth beneath (v. 6). Those
heavens seem stable enough, far removed from the convulsions and shocks of time. To them surely no change
can come. Yet they shall vanish like a puff of smoke
borne down the wind. And as for the earth, it shall wax
old. Nature has often been described as God's vesture,
the veil under which he hides. But the day shall come
when it shall be laid aside. There shall be new heavens
and a new earth, for the first heavens and the first earth
shall pass away. But amid the general wreck, spiritual
qualities will remain imperishably the same. "My salvation shall be forever, and my righteousness shall not be
abolished" (v. 6).

   This shall be forever true of God. We cannot discern
what awaits us in the near future. This world is destined to see—and perhaps soon—the sudden unveiling
of the divine plan to which God has been working
through the ages: vast natural convulsions; nature in
the throes of travail; the advent of the King; the setting

up of the Judgment; the Resurrection. But though such things take place around us, we need not doubt that God will remain the same—his love and faithfulness, his covenant and promise, his purpose and choice. Our friend's heart is the same when he appears in a new attire; and God will be the same in his feelings and dealings towards us amid the crash of matter and the wreck of worlds as he is today. We shall still be his adopted children, still accepted in the Beloved, still included in his everlasting covenant, still one with his Son, as members of his Body and his Bride.

The Jews took great comfort in the thought of God's unchangeableness. Had he not said that his righteousness was near and his salvation gone forth?—that his arms would judge the people, and the isles wait for him? (v. 5). Then Babylon might fall beneath the assault of Cyrus and the whole world be in confusion; floods of anarchy might burst on the nation—yet God's word would be fulfilled; he could not recede from his purpose or alter it. They could possess their souls in the sure confidence that, as he had promised, so he would perform. Some such assurance may well steal into our hearts as we anticipate the changes that are always coming over ourselves, our homes, our churches, and our time. Everything else alters—the most stable foundations of our trust give way—but God is unchangeably the same; the qualities of his character are as permanent as his throne.

This shall be forever true of man. When we partake of God's righteousness and assimilate it, we acquire a permanence which defies time and change. The love we derive from the heart of God and have for each other abides forever. The peace we receive deepens in its perennial flow. The patience, courage, strength of character, which we acquire here with so much pain, are not to go out as a candle nor vanish as a puff of smoke. If it were so, what would become of God's infinite painstaking? No! Our schoolhouse may be in ruins, and not a vestige of it left; the primers from which we read, the hard desks at which we sat, may vanish—but the characters we acquired shall outlive the world of matter. These shall be forever, and shall not be abolished. Oh, let us not murmur at the slow progress of our education and at the care that God takes for us thoroughly to master each lesson—turning it back, making us review it again and again. He is working for eternity.

What a lesson is given in these words of the relative value of things! To the man of the world, the *having* is all-important; to the man of faith, the *being*. The child of sense sacrifices all for what is but a puff of smoke, or a moth-eaten garment at the best. But the child of eternity looks for a kingdom that has foundations, whose Builder and Maker is God—where the moth does not eat, nor rust corrupt, nor fire consume, nor change intrude. A man's life consists not in the abundance of the things that he possesses, but in meekness, faith, fidelity, devotion, love.

3. THE IMPOTENCE OF MAN. These exiled Jews hardly dared to hope they would be able to break away from their foes. The air was laden with their reproaches and revilings. What mercy could they hope for from those who refused to restrain their bitter words? When their oppressors passed from malignant threats to action, there would be little shrift or quarter. We have all known something of this fear of men who seemed waiting to destroy. But to us, as to the exiles in Babylon, the divine word comes, "Fear ye not the reproach of men, neither be ye dismayed" (v. 7, R.V.).

The paragraph closes with an application of the word used by the great Servant as to his situation. "The moth shall eat them up," we heard him saying of his accusers; "they shall all wax old as a garment" (50:9). But now we are bidden to apply those same expressions to our tormenters: "The moth shall eat them up like a garment, and the worm shall eat them like wool" (51:8). With these assurances behind us, we may face a world in arms. Men may try to wear out the saints, but they must fail—because our souls are fed from the perennial springs of the divine nature, and because God has imparted to us both patience and courage which are eternal in their nature. He *will* take care of his own.

17

"AWAKE, AWAKE!"

(Isaiah 51:9–52:2)

"Oh, quickly come, dread Judge of all!
For, awful though thine advent be,
    All shadows from the truth will fall
And falsehood die, in sight of thee.
    Oh quickly come! for doubt and fear
    Like clouds dissolve when thou art near."

Tuttiet

THE thrice-occurring "Hearken" of the preceding paragraphs is followed by the thrice-cried "Awake" of
these. The first (51:9) is addressed to the arm of Jehovah, which, with rich poetic license, is imaged as being
asleep; the other two (51:17, 52:1) to Jerusalem, either
to the ruined city or to her sons then dwelling by "the
waters of Babylon."

Let us take the central paragraph first (51:17–23).
There Jerusalem is addressed as being stupefied by some
intoxicating potion. She has drained it to its dregs, and
lies as one asleep. But her drunkenness is not caused
by wine, nor by strong drink (v. 21); she has drunk at
the hand of the Lord "the cup of his fury." Such imagery
is often used by the prophets, picturing the cup of God's
wrath as drunk by those on whom it descends and in-
flicting on them the insensibility and stupefaction with
which we are but too familiar as the effect of excessive
drinking.

The whole city has succumbed under the spell. Her
sons have fainted and lie strewn in all the streets, like
antelopes snared in the hunters' nets, from which their
struggles have failed to extricate them (v. 20). Amid such
circumstances, the Servant of Jehovah is introduced,
crying, "Awake, awake! Stand up, O Jerusalem, which
hast drunk at the hand of the Lord the cup of his fury"
(v. 17).

As the tremor of light in the eastern sky stirs the life
of the sleeping city; as the warm breath of the south
wind dissipates the snow and frost of winter; as the
whisper, "Talitha cumi," aroused the sleeping maiden
in the house of Jairus—so did that call awake the stupefied city of Zion, and suddenly the pulse of life began
to throb. Arousing herself, she thought God had been
asleep, and called on him to awake. She had to learn
that it was not so. It was *she* that had been sleeping!
And therefore the appeal was flashed back from God to
her, "Awake, awake! Put on thy strength, O Zion; put on
thy beautiful garments, O Jerusalem, the holy city"
(52:1).

There are soporifics in addition to the wrath of God:
the air of the enchanted ground; the laudanum of evil
companionship; the drugs of worldly pleasure, of absorption in business, of financial security. By these we
are all liable to be thrown into a deep sleep. The army of
the Lord is too apt to put off the armor of light and
resign itself to heavy slumbers till the clarion voice warns
that it is high time to awake. Not once nor twice in the
life of the disciples did they become heavy with sleep.
And we, too, lose the ardor of our zeal, the warmth of
our love, the certainty of our faith, the enthusiasm of
our service, and become benumbed and insensitive. Mer-
ciful Awakener of souls, we adore thee for so often standing beside us, and saying, "Awake, awake!" Often we
have started from slumber, thinking that thou had been
asleep, whereas it was ourselves!

1. ZION'S APPEAL TO GOD. "Awake, awake! Put on strength, O arm of the Lord. Awake!" (51:9).

The first symptom of awaking is a cry. It is so with a child. Wherever the mother may be engaged about the house, she is on the alert for the first sounds of her babe's awakening. She says, "Did you hear the child cry?" It is so with the soul. When Saul of Tarsus was converted, the heavenly watchers said, "Behold, he prayeth." It is so with the Church. The outpouring of the spirit of prayer is the first symptom of renewal and revival, just as the murmur of the streams in the valleys shows that the snows are melting on the upper Alps.

The cry in this case was founded on a mistake. The prayer refers to what is familiar to us all in the divine life: there are ebbs and flows, the winter and summer, the Transfiguration height and the valley with its demoniac child. Sometimes God seems alert, alive, and energetic: the pulse of his energy stirs in us; his voice summons us to new and heroic tasks. At other times a heavy lethargy hangs over the landscape of earth and intercepts our view of heaven. But our mistake is to attribute the cause to God instead of finding it in ourselves. If there are variations in our inner life, it is because our rate of reception differs from time to time. It is not God who sleeps, but we. It is not for God to awake, but for us. It is not necessary for the divine arm to gird on strength, but for the human to take that which is within its easy reach.

The cry is short and earnest. Thrice the suppliant cries "Awake!" When we are suddenly startled from sleep, conscious that something is wrong and needs mending, we cry vigorously to God. This is well, even though we shall learn presently that we are ourselves to blame because there has been a pause, a break in our receptivity. Still, earnestness is good, even though at first it may be in a wrong direction.

The best basis for our cry is memory of the past. "Art

thou not it that cut Rahab [i.e., Egypt] in pieces, that pierced the dragon [i.e., of the Nile]?" (v. 9). It is well to quote past experiences as arguments for faith. Our past life will have missed its aim if it has not revealed God to us. Each incident is intended to show us some new trait in his character for us to treasure for all coming time. Not that we expect God to repeat himself, but so that we learn to say, "If he did all this, he is resourceful, tender-hearted, wise and strong. There is no emergency with which he cannot grapple, no need he cannot fulfill. He gave manna—he surely can provide water. He delivered from Egypt—he can certainly emancipate from Babylon. He dried up the waters of the great deep, and made the depths of the sea a way for his ransomed (v. 10)—then surely he can make the wilderness a pool of water and all the mountains a way."

The arm of God is strong. It stretched forth the heavens and laid the foundation of the earth (v. 13). The same divine energy has left a lasting monument of its might in the works of nature. Surely, child of God, it is able to defend you—to be your bulwark and defense, your fortress against your mightiest foes. The fury of the oppressor may seem ready to destroy, but it shall break in vain on the arm of God—even as the sea breaks on the long harbor wall which is built out into the angry breakers, and behind which the smallest craft may shelter.

The arm of God is far-reaching. It reaches down into the pit (v. 14). There is no depth so profound to which it will not stoop. The psalmist said: "If I make my bed in hell, thou art there." Like Jonah, we may go down to the base of the mountains, compassed with the waters and wrapped about with weeds; yet from that place shall God deliver us. "Nor height nor depth . . . can separate us from the love of God which is in Christ Jesus our Lord" (Rom. 8:39). However low we sink, underneath are the everlasting arms. They are always underneath.

The arm of God is tender. It comforts us (v. 12). It is what the arm of the mother is to the sick and tired child; what the arm of love is to the beloved, who leans on it with a sense of happy security! Those arms were stretched out on the cross, spread wide to encompass the world. They welcome to the tenderest bosom that heaves anywhere in the universe. John found it a soft place at the Last Supper. Let us not hesitate to lean back in that embrace and near that heart, to be comforted when our heart is sick and the flesh faints. None can pluck us thence.

> *"Safe in the arms of Jesus,*
> *Safe on his loving breast,*
> *There by his love o'er-shaded*
> *Sweetly my soul shall rest."*

We are too apt to forget all this, to forget the Lord our Maker and Redeemer (v. 13). We think more of the earth than of the over-arching heavens; more of the fading grass than of the tree of life; more of man than of God. The near has obscured the distant; the flaring gas lamps have dimmed the shine of the stars; the human has eclipsed the divine. Oh, think of him who sits at the right hand of God, the seat of his resistless and unceasing energy, and believe that he is between you and all adverse circumstances, though they be ready to destroy. To fear continually all the day because of the fury of the oppressor is impossible for those who dwell all day between the shoulders of Emmanuel and are hidden in the shadow of his hand (v. 16).

2. THE APPEAL TO ZION. When we become thoroughly awake, and have time for reflection, we discover that the fault and blame lie entirely with ourselves. It is not God who has been lethargic; he can neither slumber nor sleep. We have slept.

It is blessed to be awakened out of sleep—life is pass-

ing by so rapidly. The radiant glory of the Savior may be
missed unless we are on the alert, for we may fail to give
him the sympathetic ear he needs and an angel will be
summoned to do our work. Besides, the world needs
the help of men who give no sleep to their eyes nor slumber to their eyelids, but are always eager to help it in its
need. Being awake, we shall discover two sets of attire
awaiting us. The first is strength, the other beauty; and
each has its counterpart in the New Testament—the one
in Ephesians 6, the other in Colossians 3. "Put on the
whole armor of God." "Put on the Lord Jesus Christ"—
his temper, spirit, and character.

We must put on our beautiful garments. There should
be a bloom and beauty about us. Not only garments,
but *beautiful* garments. The emblem of the life to which
we are called is the bridegroom decked with a garland,
or the bride with her jewels, or the garden filled with
blossoms (61:10–11). We must not only do right things,
we must do them beautifully; not only speak the truth,
but speak it in love; not only give to the poor, but do it
unobtrusively, without the appearance of patronage or
ostentation. The beauty of the Lord our God must be
upon us. The apostle's enumeration of the clothing of
the redeemed soul is largely occupied with its temper
and disposition, what might be called its bloom—"compassion, kindness, humility, meekness, patience."

We cannot weave these qualities. We are not able to
spin such a cocoon out of our own nature, nor are we
required to do so. They are all prepared for us in Jesus;
we have only to put them on, by putting *him* on. Assume the meekness, gentleness, and purity of Jesus.
Be a partaker of the kingdom and patience which are in
Jesus (Rev. 1:9). Or, to state the same truth in a different way, take Jesus to be what God has made him—
"wisdom, righteousness, sanctification, and redemption."

This can only be done when the heart is at leisure.
There must be deep recollection of soul in the Master's

presence; then the reverent and glad attiring of the soul with the qualities of his glorious nature, and the reckoning that they are assumed in response to the act of faith. The beautiful garments await the poorest, weakest, unlikeliest. None of God's own need go in rags; none need be arrayed in anything else than the light with which God is said to cover himself. "Thou coverest thyself with light, as with a garment." "Let us put off the works of darkness, and put on the armor of light."

We must put on strength. "Put on thy strength, O Zion" (52:1). God provides strength for every possible emergency or demand in life. Whatever call is made upon us, there is always a sufficiency of grace by which it may be met. Undoubtedly, temptation and trial are permitted to come so that we may be compelled to appropriate supplies which lie within our reach, but of which we would not have availed ourselves unless hard pressed and put to it. Always the danger is that even under such circumstances we will fail to put on the strength which is stored for us in Jesus Christ our Lord.

We are not bidden to purchase strength, or to generate it by our resolutions, prayers and agonizings—*but to put it on*. It is already prepared, and only awaits appropriation. Put on your strength, O tempted one! Before passing from the quiet morning hour into the arena which has so often witnessed failure and defeat, put on the might of the risen Savior. Do not simply pray to be kept, or to be helped, but arm yourself with the whole armor of God; take hold of his strength and be at peace; wrap yourself about with the mail of him who is stronger than the strong man armed. Reckon that it is yours! Dare to believe that you are more than a match for your worst foes. Say with David, "I will not be afraid of ten thousands of people who set themselves round about. The Lord is my light and my salvation; whom shall I fear? The Lord is the strength of my life; of whom shall I be afraid?" (Ps. 3:6, 27:1).

We must expect to be delivered from the dominion of sin. Babylon had been bidden to descend from her throne and sit in the dust; Jerusalem is now commanded to arise from the dust and sit on her throne (52:2). The chains on her neck were to be unloosed; her gates were never again to be entered by the uncircumcised and the unclean. So entire was to be her deliverance by Jehovah that she was henceforth to be "the holy city," set apart for the exclusive service of God.

These words have an application for us. The inner citadel of the heart is intended to be God's alone. He purchased the site; he built and reared its walls; he claims it as the seat of the royal residence. The heart is the Holy See. And if we are thoroughly yielded to him as our Judge, our Lawgiver and our King, he will save us. The walls shall be salvation, and the gates praise. There shall not enter the abominable, the unclean, nor the lying thought. Diabolus shall be driven from Mansoul, and Emmanuel shall be enthroned in his glory and beauty. Then the bells shall ring, and the streets shall be filled with chorister-bands, and white-robed priests, and shining ones with harps and vials full of odors.

18

"DEPART YE, DEPART YE!"

(Isaiah 52:7–12)

"Break up the heavens, O Lord! and far
Thro' all yon starlight keen,
Draw me, thy bride—a glittering star
In raiment white and clean!"
                                    Tennyson

A T last the climax of the long prophetic stairway is
gained. The prophet had anticipated it in a previous passage (49:20), but had been diverted by the objections urged against the possibility of such a conclusion to the long captivity. It could not be, Israel argued. It was unheard of that a strong nation like Babylon should let one of its captive peoples go free without fee or reward. The archives of all nations might be searched in vain for such a precedent. One by one, the servant of God had met and answered these objections; had declared his own unalterable resolve; had startled their lethargy with the thrice "Hearken!" and the thrice "Awake!" And now again he puts the trumpet to his lips, and announces the exodus—"Depart ye, depart ye! Go ye out from thence; touch no unclean thing" (v. 11).

From the glowing sentences of this paragraph we can reconstruct the picture of the return from exile as it presented itself to the seer. It was notably the return of

153

the Lord to Zion (v. 8, R.V.). The stately procession moves slowly and fearlessly. It is not the escape of a band of fugitive slaves, dreading pursuit and recapture: "Ye shall not go out in haste, neither shall ye go by flight" (v. 12). Before it speed the messengers, appearing on the sky-line of the mountains of Zion with good tidings of good, publishing peace and proclaiming salvation (v. 7).

The main body is composed of white-robed priests, bearing with reverent care the holy vessels—which Nebuchadnezzar had carried from the temple, which Belshazzar had introduced with mockery into his feast, but which Cyrus restored. Their number and weight are carefully specified, 5,400 in all (Ezra 1:7–11).

As the procession emerges from its four months of wilderness march onto the mountains which were about Jerusalem, her watchmen, who had long waited for the happy moment, lift up their voice; with the voice to-gether do they sing. They see eye to eye. And the waste places of Jerusalem, with their charred wood and scorched stones, break forth into joy and sing together. The valleys and hills become vocal, constituting an or-chestra of praise; and the nations of the world are de-picted as coming to behold and acknowledge that the Lord has made bare his holy arm. But they do not see—it is hidden from all but anointed eyes—that the Lord goes before his people and comes behind as their rear guard, so that their difficulties are surmounted by him before they reach them and no foe can attack them from behind.

The literal fulfillment of this splendid prevision is de-scribed in the Book of Ezra. There we find the story of the return of a little band of Jews, 1,700 only in num-ber. They halted at the river Ahava, the last station be-fore they entered the desert, for three days, to put them-selves with fasting and prayer into God's hand. They had no experience in desert marching. Their caravan was rendered unwieldly by the number of women and children in it. They had to thread a district infested by wild bands of robbers. But they scorned to ask for an escort of soldiers and horsemen to protect them, so sure were they that their God went before them to open up the way and came behind to defend against attack. In the midst of the march were priests and Levites, with their sacred charge of which Ezra had said, "Watch and keep them, until ye weigh them . . . in the chambers of the house of the Lord" (8:29).

We do not read in Ezra of any songs by the pilgrim host, as here foreshadowed. Even so, they may have risen morning and evening on the desert air, enlivening the monotony of the march. There are many psalms which date from this period, and these may have been favorites with the pilgrim host as they passed over the dunes of the desert or sat around the campfires. In several respects there seems a falling short between the radiant expectation of the prophet and the actual accomplishment in the story of Ezra; but we must remember that it is the business of the historian to record the facts rather than the emotions that colored them, as the warm colors of the sun color the hard gray rocks. And is it not always so, that through our lack of faith and obedience we come short of the fullness of blessing which our God has prepared for us?

We may learn here some of those qualities which should characterize us in our march through this desert world to the city of God.

1. THERE SHOULD BE PERPETUAL EXODUS. The Jews had become habituated to Babylon. Custom makes most things endurable. In the days of Ezra, few were left who remembered the anguish of the inception of the captivity. The people who were born in the land of their conquerors had conformed their methods of life to the conditions of that great civilization—which was destined to exert an influence upon them in all after-days. Some of them probably longed for the expiry of the allotted

years of captivity; but the majority were settled in comfortable—and in some cases opulent—circumstances,
and not at all anxious to exchange Babylon for the ruins of Zion. The result was that they became dispersed
throughout the East, building synagogues, enjoying
material prosperity—but becoming lost as a river in the
sand.

In all lives there are Babylons, which have no claim
on the redeemed of Jehovah. We may have entered them
not without qualms of conscience; but, as time has
passed, our reluctance has been overcome. A comrade-
ship has grown up between us and one from whose language and ways we once shrank in horror. An amuse-
ment now fascinates us, one which we earlier regarded
with suspicion and conscientious scruple. A habit of
life dominates us from which we once shrank as from
infection. A method of winning money now engrosses
us; but we can well remember how difficult it was to
coax conscience to engage in it. These are Babylons
which cast their fatal spell over the soul, and against
which the voice of God urgently protests. "Depart ye,
depart ye! Go ye out from thence."

When stepping out from Babylon to an unaccustomed
freedom, we naturally shrink back before the desert
march, the sandy wastes, the ruined remnants of happier days. Those who remembered the first temple wept
when the foundations of the second were laid; and
Nehemiah could not restrain his tears at the sight of
heaps of rubbish. But we shall receive more than we
renounce. Forsaking the outward and temporal, we shall
find ourselves possessed of the inner and eternal. In
the desert we see the eternal constellations burning
above us; we feel the breath of God upon our faces; we
have a reward which could compensate for a hundred
such renunciations: "I will receive you, and be a Father
unto you."

2. IT SHOULD BE WITHOUT HASTE. "Ye shall not go

out in haste." There are many English proverbs which
sum up the observation of former days and tell how
foolish it is to be in a hurry. But, outside of God, there
is small chance of obeying these wise maxims. The age
is so feverish. Men haste to be rich; they rush from pleasure to pleasure; they make the tour of the world in six
months; they do Rome in a week. We cram children's
minds with undigested knowledge. And this feverish,
unresting spirit has invaded our religious life, our clos-
ets, our musings, our worship. It is impossible to give
ourselves thoroughly to anything, because our watch is
always in our hand lest we miss our train.

No great picture was ever painted in a hurry. No great
book was ever written against a tight deadline. No great
discovery was ever granted to the student who could
not watch in Nature's antechamber for the gentle opening of her door. The greatest naturalist of our time devoted eight whole years almost entirely to barnacles.
Well might John Foster long for the power of touching
mankind with the spell of "*Be quiet, be quiet.*"

In this our Lord is our best exemplar. He moved slowly
and deliberately through his crowded years. He had leisure for every appeal, for the touch of each wan hand.
There was no trace of feverishness or unrest. Men were
always urging him onward; but he answered, "Your time
is always ready; mine is not yet." His secret, using our
human phrase, lay in his simple faith. He believed, and
therefore did not make haste. Every incident in his life
had been arranged by his Father's unfailing care. There
was time for everything, and everything must be fitted
to its time. If there was work to be done, he was secure
against arrest till it was finished. Herod could not kill
him till he was perfected.

This hastelessness was possible to Israel so long as
the people believed that God was ordering, preceding,
and followed their march. Why should they go by flight,
as though the foe were about to fall on the hindmost,

when God was their rear guard! Why rush forward to
gain some advantage if God went in front to seek out
their resting place! When we really believe in God, his
providence and his arrangement of our lives, to us too
there will come this blessed calm; and whenever we are
tempted to get feverish and fretful, we shall compel ourselves to go out beneath the arch of God's eternal years,
saying, "Return, my soul, unto thy rest. God is behind,
intercepting pursuit from past failure and sin."

3. WE MUST BE AT PEACE ABOUT THE WAY. In
early life our path seems clearly defined. We must follow the steps of others, depend on their maxims, act on
their advice—till suddenly we find ourselves at the head
of the march, no footprints before us on the expanse of
moorland or of sand. It is only when the years grow
upon us that this sense of *waylessness*, as it has been
termed, oppresses us. So the exiles must have felt when
they left Ahava and started on the desert march.

At such times the lips of Christ answer, "I am the
Way." Throughout the Acts of the Apostles, we find that
the almost invariable term by which the gospel was
known was "the Way"; as if those first believers were
intoxicated with the rapture of feeling that at last they
had discovered the track of the blessed life, the pathway which would thread the perplexities of earth and
bring them to the city of God. And if we had asked any
one of them to give an equivalent for the term they so
constantly employed, they would have answered, without a moment's hesitation, JESUS. Probably there is no
better way of ascertaining the true method of life than
by asking ourselves how Jesus would have acted under
similar circumstances. His temper, his way of looking
at things, his declared will—these resolve all perplexities.

All this was set forth in the figure before us. "The
Lord will go before you." When the people came out of
Egypt, Jehovah preceded the march in the Shekinah

cloud that moved softly above the ark. When it advanced, they struck their tents and followed; when it brooded, they halted and fixed the camp. It was the one visible and unerring guide through those trackless wastes. There was nothing of this sort when Ezra led the first detachment of exiles to Zion; but, though unseen, the Divine Leader was equally in the forefront of the march. Thus it is also in daily experience. When the way forks, when the track dies in the grass, when the expanse of desert lies in front without a beaten pathway—stand still; take an observation; hush all voices in the presence of Christ. Ask what he would have done; ask what he would wish you to do. Remember that the Good Shepherd, when he puts forth his sheep, goes before them, and they follow him. Jesus is ever going before us in every call to duty, every prompting to self-sacrifice, every summons, to comfort, help and save. With God behind as rear guard, and God in front as leader, and God encompassing us with songs of deliverance, there can be no doubt that we shall at last reach that Zion in which there are no waste places, and whose walls have never reeled before the shock of armed men.

4. WE MUST BE PURE. "Touch no unclean thing. Be ye clean, ye that bear the vessels of the Lord" (v. 11). Those vessels, as we have seen, were very precious. The enumeration is made with minute accuracy (Ezra 8:25–27). But they were above all things holy unto the Lord. For generations they had been employed in temple service. Those that bore them were no common men but Levites, specially summoned to the work, and possessed at least of a ceremonial cleanliness. Thus they passed across the desert, holy men bearing the holy vessels.

Through this world, unseen by mortal eye, a procession is passing, threading its way across continents of time. It bears holy vessels. The forms of expression in which divine truth is enshrined may be compared to the vessels of the old dispensation, set apart to serve the purposes of the sanctuary. Testimony to God's truth, the affirmation of things unseen and eternal, the announcement of the facts of redemption—such are our sacred charge. We must contend earnestly for the faith once delivered to the saints. Take heed to thyself, *and to the doctrine.* The greatest service the Church can give to the world is its perpetual witness to the truth of God's being and will—to the facts of redemption, of judgment, and of the world to come. Concerning all these, the olden charge is given us, "Watch ye and keep them, until ye weigh them before the chiefs of the priests and of the Levites, in the chambers of the house of the Lord."

What manner of persons ought not we to be, to whom so high a ministry is entrusted! How careful that our holy trust should not be forfeited because of our unholy life! How eager lest the glistening glory of our charge be blurred or dimmed by our thumbmarks! How watchful that the testimony of a doctrine be not contradicted by the life of those that profess it! Men estimate the worth of the truths to which we bear witness by the worth of our personal character. Let us commend the gospel by the holiness and elevation of our lives.

Before that procession, we are told, waste places would break forth into song. It is a picturesque concept, as though their feet changed the aspect of the territories through which they passed. What was desert when they came to it was paradise as they left it! What were ruins became walls! Where there had been hostility, suspicion and misunderstanding, there came concord and peace, the watchmen seeing eye to eye.

This is a true portraiture of the influence of the religion of Jesus over the hearts and lives of men. Creation herself, which now groans and travails, shall presently burst into hallelujahs like those with which the Psalter closes. God give us grace to join in that procession, and with beautiful array pass onward without haste, under divine convoy, till the glowing predictions of prophecy and psalm be realized in an emancipated universe!

But let us never forget the importance of prayer, as a necessary link in the achieving of these marvels. In the former chapter there had been one eager and intense petition, "Awake, awake, put on strength, O arm of the Lord. Awake as in the ancient days!" (v. 9). That prayer had entered into the ear of the Lord God of Sabaoth, and here we are told that "the Lord hath made bare his holy arm in the eyes of all the nations" (v. 10). Pray on, O child of God! Your breath is not misspent; your tears are not wasted: "Behold, the Lord God will come as a mighty one, and his arm shall rule for him" (40:10, R.V.).

19

THE VINDICATION OF CHRIST

(ISAIAH 52:13–53:12)

"It is the Day;
No more sad watchings by the midnight sea,
No twilight gray,
But, crowned with light and immortality,
He stands from henceforth, triumphing alway
In God's own Day."
B. M.

HERE is the "funeral song" of the suffering Servant.
There is only one brow which this crown of thorns
will fit. As the eunuch sat in his chariot and read this
wonderful lyric of sorrow even unto death, which in its
rhythm and diction stands alone among these marvelous chapters, he questioned of whom the writer spoke.
"I pray thee," he said to Philip, "of whom speaketh the
prophet this? of himself, or of some other?" (Acts 8:34).
The evangelist, in reply, commenced to preach from this
same scripture, Jesus.

Jesus is the Key which the whole New Testament, in
many allusions, puts into our hands to unlock these
mysteries in which heaven and earth, the eternal and
the temporal, the love of God and the weakness of man
blend with no apparent horizon line. But even apart from
the precise testimony of the Holy Spirit, we could have
found none worthy to take this scroll and open it seal

by seal other than the Lamb in the midst of the throne, the Lion of the tribe of Judah, the Son of God himself.

Efforts have been made to apply this or the other line and fragment of this prophecy to one and another of the great sufferers of history: to Jeremiah, to Ezekiel, to some unknown martyr in the days of the captivity! And it is quite likely, since sorrow and pain are the heritage of all, that in some particulars this vision was realized by lesser men than the Son of Man. A child's hand may strike notes on the Freyburg organ! But who of woman born except the Christ could take these words in their entirety and say, "I claim that all this was realized in myself; this portraiture is mine. There is neither line nor lineament here which has not its correspondence in me"? Should any of the sons of men put in such a claim, he would encounter at once the full force of a world's ridicule and contempt. But when the Man of Nazareth approaches and claims to have fulfilled this dark and bitter record; when he opens his heart and shows its scars; when he enumerates his unknown sufferings, and asks if there were ever grief like his—no one dares to challenge his right to claim and annex this empire as his own. Nay, deep down in the heart there is a tacit confession that probably he touched yet profounder depths and drank more bitter draughts than even these words record.

This elegy of sorrow is unfortunately divided by the arbitrary arrangement of the chapters in our Bibles. Really, it begins at 52:13, with the word which so often arrests attention in this book: "Behold." It consists of five stanzas of three verses each, the closing paragraphs being somewhat longer. No English translation can give a conception of the cadence and sad minor tones which sob through its chords.

The theme is the sufferings of the Servant of God; the wrong conclusions which his fellows formed of them; and the triumphant vindication which he has received.

1. A STORY OF SORROW AND PAIN. Three *mysteries* meet here—as clouds brood darkly over the mountains when a thunderstorm is imminent.

The mystery of humiliation. The tender plant; the sucker painfully pushing its way through the crust of the caked ground; the absence of natural attractiveness. Such imagery awaits and receives its full interpretation from the New Testament, with its story of Christ's peasant parentage, his manger bed and lowly circumstances—fisherfolk his choice disciples; poverty his constant lot; the common people his devoted admirers; thieves and malefactors on either side of his cross; the lowly and poor the constituents of his Church. This surely is humiliation! Even so, these irregularities of human lot are scarcely distinguishable when viewed from the heights whence he came.

The profoundest stoop of his humility was that he became man at all. He was infinite in his unstinted blessedness; rich with the wealth that has flowered out into the universe; radiant in the dazzling beauty of perfect moral excellence. What agony, therefore, must have been his to breathe our tainted air, to live in daily contact with sinners, and to be perpetually surrounded by the most miserable and plague-stricken of the race! And that he should die! That the Life-Giver should pass under the dark portal of the grave! That the Son of God should become obedient to a death of ignominy and shame at the hands of men! This is a mystery of humiliation indeed.

The mystery of sorrow. You can see its ineffaceable mint mark on that marred face. We need no further proof that he was a Man of Sorrows and acquainted with grief. But what is sorrow? Each of us knows by experience what it is; but who can define it, or say in a sentence of what it consists? It is that emotion which results when love meets with dark shadows threatening its beloved. There is doubtless a selfish kind of sorrow which re-

pines at losses that can be counted in gold, and bewails
the curtailing of sensual gratification. But this may not
be mentioned here, where we are within the precincts of
the sorrow of the world's Redeemer. We are treating sorrow as it might exist in his peerless heart, and in those
who are being molded in his image.

Such are capable of a divine love; and by the very
measure of that capacity they are liable to supreme sorrow. When love beholds its objects eluding its embrace—
their love turning cold, their souls poisoned by misunderstanding and misrepresentation, their lives engulfed
by eddies from which it would save them if it could, but
they refuse its aid—then there is sorrow. This is as certain as rain meeting a blast of frosty air will turn to
snow and fall in white flakes.

We need go no further for the reason why Jesus sor-
rowed as he did. It could not have been otherwise. Men
could not be loved by him without causing him infinite
pain. Have you not wounded him, crucified him, wrung
his heart, just because you were not able to appreciate
the delicacy and sensitiveness of the heart which was
pouring out its stores for you with prodigal lavishness?
Throughout the ages he has come to his own and they
have barred the door to his entrance. He has desired to
gather them as a hen her chicks, but they have refused
him. He has come into his garden to gather the precious fruit and spices that would refresh his soul, but
he has found the wall in ruins and the choice stores
rifled—slights, where there should have been tenderness; rebuffs, where he looked for a welcome; put to
open shame, instead of reception in the inner shrine of
esteem and love. Surely this will account for this mystery of sorrow.

The mystery of pain. Wounded, bruised, chastised; the
spittle of the soldiery on his face; the scourge plowing
red seams in his flesh; the bloody sweat beading his
brow; the cry "Forsaken!" There is suffering here! Well

might Pilate cry, as though to move the pity of the crowd
with such a spectacle of misery, "Behold the Man!"

A suggestion of the anguish which our blessed Lord
endured, and which the liturgy of the Greek church refers to as "his unknown sufferings," is given in those
remarkable words of the Epistle to the Hebrews which
tell us that after pouring out his prayers and supplications with strong crying and tears unto him who was
able to save him from death, he was heard in that he
feared. In every age Christian men have pondered those
words, asking what they meant. Is it not at least possible for Jesus to have meant that he was so wrung with
anguish that he thought he must die in the garden before ever he reached his cross? The pressure of pain
was almost unendurable; and there was every fear that
his nature would collapse ere the expiatory sacrifice
could be offered. If this is the right rendering of the passage, what a marvelous panorama is afforded of the sea
billows of suffering which surged up and rolled over the
human nature of the Redeemer! If the anticipation of
Calvary so wrung his heart, what must not the endurance have been! Such was the mystery of pain.

O King of suffering and sorrow! Monarch of the marred
face, none has ever approached thee in the extremity of
thy grief. We bow the knee, and bid thee "All Hail!" We
are conquered by thy tears and woes. Our hearts are
enthralled; our souls inspired; our lives surrendered to
thy disposal for the execution of purposes which cost
thee so dear.

2. WRONG SUPERFICIAL CONCLUSIONS. Every age
has connected misery with guilt, anguish with iniquity,
suffering with sin. Special pain has been regarded as
the indication of special wrongdoing. It was in vain that
Job protested his innocence; his friends insisted that
the reason for his awful sufferings must be sought in
evils, which, though he had screened them from the
gaze of men, were doubtless well known to himself and

God. The awful absence of sight which the blind man had suffered from his birth made the disciples speculate as to whether he or his parents had perpetrated some terrible crime, of which that privation was the evidence and the result. And when, on the storm-swept shore of Malta, the apostle's hand was suddenly encircled by the viper, creeping out of the heat, the natives concluded that he was a murderer, who, though he had escaped the sea, could not escape the penalty which justice demanded. So the verdict which the thoughtless crowd might be disposed to pass on the unique sufferings of Christ would be that they were, without doubt, richly merited. This, in point of fact, is the explanation put into the mouth of his own people by the prophet: "We did esteem him stricken, smitten of God, and afflicted."

Perhaps the members of the Pharisee party who consented to his death—swept on against their better judgment by the virulence of Caiaphas and Annas—may have comforted themselves, as the shadows of that memorable day fell on the empty crosses, that such sufferings could not have been permitted by God to overtake the Nazarene had he not been guilty of the blasphemy for which he was adjudged worthy of death.

But all this while Jesus opened not his mouth! Silent before Caiaphas, except when his refusal to speak might appear to compromise his claims to death; silent before Herod, as one to whom speech was vain; silent before Pilate, except when the Roman governor seemed really eager to know the truth—"He was led as a lamb to the slaughter, and as a sheep, dumb before her shearers, so he opened not his mouth."

Why this speechlessness? In part it was due to the Savior's clear apprehension of the futility of arguing with those who were bent on crucifying him. It was also due to the quiet rest of his soul on God, as he committed himself to him that judgeth righteously and anticipated the hour when the Father would arise to give him a complete vindication. But it was due also to his consciousness of carrying in his breast a golden secret, another explanation of his sufferings than men were aware of—a divine solution of the mystery of human guilt.

We give our highest eulogy to those who suffer for others without a murmur of complaint; who carry silently a load of pain and grief which these have caused them—misunderstood and maligned, but keeping their lips fast sealed lest the true reason should escape, until the best moment had come for its revelation—for such strength of purpose we reserve our highest praise. With what reverence then should we not regard the Lord's reticence. He knew the secret that underlay the Levitical dispensation and that gave all its meaning to his own approaching death—the great law of the transference of suffering. He realized that he was God's Lamb, on whom the sin of the world was lying; the scapegoat carrying guilt into a land of forgetfulness; the antitype of bull, and calf, and dove. His soul was quieted under the conviction of these sublime constructs, and he could afford to be dumb until he had put away sin by the sacrifice of himself. What though men judged him falsely—God the Father knew all that was in his heart. Time would vindicate him presently. What he carried as a secret in his heart would be proclaimed from the housetops of the world.

We all need to learn this lesson. We are so quick to pour the story of our wrongs into the ears of men, complaining of every injury and slight. We are prone to rush into speech or print, justifying our conduct, rebutting false accusations and demanding justice. All this is unworthy of those who know that God is waiting in the shadow, "keeping watch upon his own," and sure to bring their righteousness to the light, their judgment to the noonday. For the sake of the wrongdoer we should endeavor to arrest the commission of wrong—as Jesus did

when he remonstrated with the high priest for his fla-
grant violation of the principles of Jewish jurisprudence.
But where high-handed evil rushes forward, as a wild
beast crashes through the slight resistance of reed-beds
to reach his prey, then our wisest and most Christlike
attitude is not to revile again, nor threaten, but to lift
up our eyes to the hills from whence our help comes.

3. THE SUFFERER'S VINDICATION. It may tarry, but
it surely comes at length. It came, and is always coming, to Christ. Each age has only established more completely his absolute moral beauty, the dignity and majesty of his bearing under the sufferings of his last hour,
and the infinite value of his cross and passion.

Vindicated by the growing convictions of men. We, the
prophet says, speaking of men generally—*we* esteemed
him not, because we thought that God was punishing
him for his sin, but now we have discovered that he
bore *our* griefs and carried *our* sorrows; that he was
wounded for *our* transgressions, bruised for *our* iniquities, chastened for *our* peace. In other words, the great
truth of substitution is looming ever clearer on the conscience and heart of man. As never before, light is breaking on the heights of the doctrine of vicarious suffering,
bringing into distinctness that wondrous line of virgin
peaks which no human foot but One has ever scaled.
Not that we can fully measure or define what Jesus did
for us on the cross, but that we are coming to understand that his sufferings there have secured redemption for mankind and laid the foundation of a temple
whose walls are salvation and its gates praise. The growing conviction of this fact is, in part, Christ's vindication.

Vindicated by the trust of each individual soul. Each
time one comes to him and finds healing, peace and
salvation in his wounds, cleansing in his precious blood,
shelter beneath the outspread arms of his cross, he sees
his seed—he sees the result of the travail of his soul

and is satisfied. He is vindicated and recompensed for all his pain.

Vindicated by his exaltation to the right hand of power. "Ye denied the Holy and Righteous One, and killed the Prince of Life, whom God raised from the dead" (Acts 3:14–15, R.V.). That is his vindication—that he is seated on his Father's throne, entrusted with all authority and able to save to the uttermost all who come. Every cry of angel or seraph that he is worthy; every note of adoration and tribute from orders of being to us unknown; every crown cast at his feet, or palm waved in his train; every accession of honor and glory as the ages roll—not to mention his resurrecting of all the dead; his session on the great white throne; his eternal reign—attests the vindication of his Father. "He shall divide a portion with the great, and a spoil with the strong."

"Heaven is comforted—
For that strange warfare is accomplished now,
Her King returned with joy."

20

FAITH AS A SWITCH

(Isaiah 53:1; John 11:40)

"If thou couldst trust, poor soul,
In him who rules the whole,
Thou wouldst find peace and rest.
Wisdom and sight are well; but Trust is best."
A. Procter

A LAWYER whom I know took me the other day to see the fireproof strongroom in which he keeps valuable deeds and securities. It is excavated under the street, and a passage leads far into the interior, lined on either side with receptacles for the precious documents. On entering, he took up what appeared to be a candle, with a cord attached to it; the other end he deftly fastened to a switch at the entrance, by means of which the electricity which was waiting there poured up the wire hidden in the cord, glowed at the wick of the glass candle—and we were able to pass to the end of the passage, uncoiling cord and wire as we went. That candle when *un*lighted resembles the Christian worker *apart* from the power of the Holy Spirit. *Faith* may be compared to the *switch,* by means of which the saving might of God pours into our life and ministry.

It cannot be too strongly insisted on, that our faith is the absolute condition and measure of the exertion of God's saving might. No faith, no blessing; little faith, little blessing; great faith, great blessing. According to our faith, so it is always done to us. The saving might of God's glorious arm may be waiting close against us, but it is inoperative unless we are united to it by faith.

The negative and positive sides of this great and important truth are presented in the texts before us: one of which complains that the arm of God is not revealed, because men have not believed the inspired report; the other, from the lips of the Master, affirms that those who believe shall see the glory of God. Between them, the texts will help us to understand why some who are best equipped for service fail, while others, with very indifferent equipment, achieve great and lasting success.

1. THE ARM OF GOD. This expression is often used in the older parts of Scripture and everywhere signifies the active, saving energy of the Most High. We first meet with it in his own address to Moses: "I will redeem them with a stretched-out arm." Then, in the triumphal shout that broke from two million glad voices beside the Red Sea—and frequently in the book of Deuteronomy—we read of the outstretched arm of Jehovah. It is a favorite phrase with the poets and prophets of Israel—the arm that redeems; the holy arm; the glorious arm; the bared arm of God. We have already noticed how it is bidden to awake and put on strength (51:9). This metaphor in Isaiah 53 is somewhat different. The conception is that, owing to the unbelief of Israel, the Lord's arm lies inoperative, hidden under the heavy folds of Middle Eastern drapery, whereas it might be revealed, raising itself aloft in vigorous and effective effort.

All that concerns us now is the relation between faith and the forth-putting of God's saving might. God's arm was revealed at the Red Sea, making a path through its depths by which his ransomed might pass over. Then Moses' faith was in eager and triumphant exercise, and the people believed the report which he had given of the

words of Jehovah. But it sank into repose during the
long forty years of wandering, because Israel believed
not his word.

God's arm was revealed at the Jordan, and through
the remarkable career of Joshua: it cleft the river at
flood, overthrew the walls of Jericho, chased in flight
the armies of the aliens, restrained the deepening shadows of the night, and gave the Land of Promise to the
chosen race—and this because Joshua never wavered
in his strong, heroic confidence. But again it sank paralyzed and powerless to rest when, in the days of the
judges, the people ceased to exercise the faith to which
nothing was impossible. Whenever the fire gleamed up
from the dull, white ash, as in the days of Gideon, Barak,
Jephthah and Samson, instantly the arm of the Lord
was made bare.

The arm of the Lord was revealed in the days when
David's faith realized that the living Lord was still among
his people, well able to save without armor or spear or
sword. What a springtide was that! The birds of holy
song warbled sweetly under a clear heaven of love; the
flowerets of nobility, righteousness and truth jeweled
the soil; the light was that of a morning without clouds.
There was no standing against the onset of the soldiers,
who in the cave of Adullam had acquired lessons of heroic faith as well as those of knightly chivalry. But again
the arm of God relapsed into quiescence and allowed
the foes of his people to work their will even to their
captivity—because Israel's faith had become like the
Temple of Solomon, a desecrated and ruined shrine.

So we are taught in the Epistle to the Hebrews, that
all the great exploits and episodes of Hebrew story were
due to the faith which believed that God is *a present
force in history*, and *a rewarder* of those who diligently
seek him.

2. THE LIFE OF THE SON OF MAN. As this chapter
of Isaiah suggests, Christ's life seemed, from many points

of view, a failure. The arm of the Lord was in him, though hidden from all save the handful who believed. Probably our Lord never wrought a miracle unless faith was in exercise on the part either of the recipients or spectators of his saving help. The centurion, though a Gentile; the Syrophoenician woman, though accounted a dog; the leper, though an outcast pariah—these drew from him virtue that healed and saved. But the bulk of the nation, and especially the companions of his early life, missed the benediction which had come so nigh them, because they wrapped themselves in proud indifference. Through unbelief the branches were deprived of the richness of the Root of David. And the condition of Israel in the world today is due to persistent unbelief, which has cut them off from the help of the right arm of the Lord.

3. A SPECIMEN CASE. For two days Christ had lingered beyond the Jordan, though urgently needed in Bethany, where life was ebbing fast—and tears were flowing which were not wholly due to the sickness and death of him whom Jesus loved. A sense of forlornness—an inability to account for the delayed appearance of the dearest Friend, who neither came nor sent word—made those tears more bitter. The Master, however, was keenly sensitive to all that was taking place. He knew that sickness had become death, and said presently, "Our friend Lazarus sleepeth." That interval of silence and absence seems to have been filled with prayer—to which he referred in the words he spoke aloud at the grave (John 11:41–42), so that the people might be led to attribute all the glory to his Father and to appreciate the love and beauty of his character. Before our Lord left his hiding place, he knew that the Father had granted him, in his human nature, the life of his friend. "I go," said he, "to awake him out of sleep. I am glad that I was not there to stay the fall of life's ebbing tide; because, in raising him from the dead, such a proof will be furnished of my oneness with the Father as to compel your faith, and be a

comfort and inspiration in all days to come."

But even though our Lord went to Bethany with the
assurance that the arm of the Lord would certainly be
made bare, yet he must of necessity have the cooperation and sympathy of someone's faith.

Such faith he discovered in Martha. This is startling,
and helpful. We would not have been surprised to learn
that it was found in Mary, because her still and spiritual nature was so closely akin to his own. She had
drunk so deeply into his words; she was capable of such
a white-heat of love, consecration and self-forgetting
devotion. But we would not have expected *Martha* to
manifest faith—to connect the stored life of Jesus with
the tomb where Lazarus lay, four days dead. Yet so it
befell. She met Jesus with the assurance that he possessed power enough to have averted death, had he only
been in time; she declared her belief that his prayer could
secure its will from God, and confessed that for long, in
her secret soul, she had believed that Jesus was the
Messiah, the Son of God, the long-expected Redeemer.
These admissions on her part showed that faith was
already within her soul, as a grain of mustard seed awaiting the summertide of God's presence, the education of
his grace.

There are many earnest Christians whose energies
are taxed to the uttermost by their ministry to others.
Philanthropists, housewives, workers in every depart-
ment of Christian service—such are their engagements
that they have no time to sit quietly at the feet of Christ
or to undertake great schemes of loving sympathy with
his plans as Mary did when she prepared her anointing
oil for her Lord's burial. And yet they are capable of a
great faith. Beneath the bustle and rush of life, the im-
pulses of the Divine are being responded to. Their faith
in the living Savior is ripening to a golden harvest; forces
are being generated which will surprise themselves and
others. Christ will one day detect, reveal, and educate

that faith for great exploits.

He put a promise before her. "Thy brother shall rise again." Faith feeds on promises, as the spark that trembles on the hearth grows by the fuel heaped on and around it. If we consider circumstances, we stagger and faint. But if we look away to the strong clear words of God, and through them to the Promiser, we become, like Abraham, strong in faith and sure that what God has promised he is able also to perform. Make much of God's Word: faith cometh by hearing. Listen to the report—it will induce belief; and this will secure the revelation of the Almighty's arm.

He showed that its fulfillment might be expected here and now. Martha was quite prepared to believe that Lazarus would rise again at the last day; but she had no faith in the immediate vivification of the body that lay in its niche behind the stone. Jesus said, "I AM the Resurrection and the Life. Here and now is the power which, on that day of which you speak, shall awaken the dead; do but believe, and you shall see that resurrection anticipated."

Ponder the force of this I AM. It is the present tense of the Eternal. At the burning bush, it was the first lesson that Moses had to learn. God is the I AM. He is; he is here; he is able and willing to do now all that he ever will do in the days that are yet to be. Man is so apt to postpone the miraculous and divine till some dim horizon line has been attained and passed. God *has* blessed, and he *will* bless. God did marvels at the First Advent, and he will repeat them at the Second. But the present is the period of Divine *absenteeism*—so we think. Oh to believe that Jesus is waiting to be all that he has ever been to souls or will be! Oh to hear him say, "I am Resurrection to the dead. I am also the more abundant Life to all who live and believe in me"!

He aroused her expectancy. For what other reason did he ask that the stone might be rolled away? It is certain that it would have been perfectly easy for his voice to reach the ear of the dead through the stony doorway; and had he willed it, Lazarus could have emerged from the grave even though the stone still sealed its mouth. Almost certainly the direction to remove the stone was intended to awaken Martha's expectation and hope that the arm of the Lord would presently be revealed. And it had the desired result. Despite her immediate objection to his mandate, when the Lord persisted and reminded her that this was the opportunity for her faith, her soul leaped up to receive with ardor the blessing he was there to give. She believed, and she beheld the glory of God in the face of Jesus Christ.

The one aim for each of us should be to bring Christ and the dead Lazarus together. Death can no more exist when he is present than can night when the sun is rising. Corruption, impurity and sin flee before him to whom the Father gave to have life in himself, and who came that we might have life and have it more abundantly. Let your faith make an inlet for the Life-giver into your circle of society, your church, your class, your home. Nothing will suffice if this is lacking. Eloquence, learning, position, these will fail. But *faith*, though it be of the weakest, simplest nature, will link the Savior, who is alive for evermore and has the keys of death and Hades, with those who have been in the graves of sin so long that corruption has asserted its foul dominion over every part of their nature.

Let us ask Christ, our Savior, to work such faith in us; to develop it by every method of education and discipline; to mature it by his nurturing Spirit, until the arm of God is revealed in us and through us and the glory of God is manifested before the gaze of men.

At the same time, it is not well to concentrate our thought *too much* on faith, lest we hinder its growth. Look away from faith to the *object* of faith, and faith will spring of itself. It is the bloom of the soul's health. See to it that your soul is nourished and at rest: then faith will be as natural as scent to a flower, or bloom to a peach. Do not ask if your faith is of the right sort; all faith is right which is directed towards him whom God has set forth to receive the loving devotion of all human hearts.

21

HIS SOUL AN OFFERING FOR SIN

(ISAIAH 53:10)

"To the cross he nails thine enemies—
The law that is against thee, and the sins
Of all mankind, with him there crucified—
Never to hurt them more, who rightly trust
In this his satisfaction."

Milton

IT is strange, but it is true, that the saddest, darkest day that ever broke upon our world is destined to cure the sadness and dissipate the darkness for evermore. It is to the passion of the Redeemer that loving hearts turn in their saddest, darkest, most sin-conscious hours to find solace, light and help. It is for this reason, doubtless, that Scripture lays such stress on the wondrous cross, and that prophets and evangelists proceed with such deliberation to tell the story of that death—which is the death of death for all who understand its inner meaning.

With what elaborate care the meaning of the cross is set forth in the chapter under our consideration! As though to eliminate the possibility of mistaking its meaning, we are reminded again, and yet again, that the death of the Divine Servant was no ordinary episode but was distinguished from all other deaths, from all martyrdoms and sacrifices, in its unique and lonely grandeur—

the one perfect and sufficient sacrifice and oblation for
the sins of the whole world. Every form of expression is
used to accentuate the thought that its excessive agony
was not the symptom of special sin on the part of the
Sufferer—as the superficial spectator might be disposed
to think—but that he was wounded for our transgressions, bruised for our iniquities, stricken with our
stripes, and involved in the penalty which we deserved.

The prophet's thought will become apparent if we
notice, first, the common lot of man; then, the one point
in which the experience of Jesus was unique; and, lastly,
if we apply the sentiment of the text to our own experience.

1. THE COMMON LOT OF MAN. It may be summed
up in three words—suffering, sin, death.

(a) *Suffering.* Nature is beautiful, but her gladdest
scenes cover the suffering that pervades ocean and land.
In the woodland glade, where spring has scattered her
first wild flowers, you may detect the scream of the rab-
bit captured by the stoat. From the blue summer sky
the eagle swoops down on the pasture lands. The placid
surface of the lake is ruffled by the struggles of the min-
now to escape the pike. Nature groans and travails in
pain; much more so, human life.

The boys and girls with their merry laugh and frolic
today will tomorrow be bending over the cradle where
the wee babe is dying; or presently bearing the stern
discipline which seems an inevitable part of human destiny. You cannot traverse a street without hearing an
infant's wail, or visit a home on which there is no shadow.
Sooner or later each man has to say, Either I must master or be mastered, either I must vanquish or succumb
in this bitter conflict with the mysterious, all-pervasive,
impalpable, yet deadly antagonist: suffering . . . pain
. . . sorrow unto death. "Man is born to sorrow, as the
sparks fly upward." That was the reflection of the wise,
pensive East centuries before the wear and tear of mod-

ern life began.

(b) *Sin.* We all know this also—the sense of sin, of discord, of distance and alienation from God. Behind all our suffering we feel there is a secret which some-how explains and accounts for it. We have scorned and perverted that which was right. We have done things we ought not, or left undone things we ought to have done. Men try to evade this consciousness of sin. They plunge into affairs, travel from land to land, go far afield in search of adventure and ceaseless change, give them-selves up to gaiety and dissipation. In fact, they are ever eluding the fixed, sad gaze of conscience, and adopting any subterfuge which promises a moment's cover. But it comes back again and again. The prophet-voice ar-raigns us; the inerrant sleuth-hound runs us down. "Thou art the man!"

This sense of sin has covered the world with altars, temples and churches. Wherever men are found, some religious rite betrays the heavy sense of sin. Men are prepared to give rivers of oil or flocks of sheep, yea the very fruit of the body, to stay the gnawings of the heart.

(c) *Death.* The conscience of man connects sin and death by an inevitable sequence. Prior to the writing of the Epistle to the Romans, the older scripture of human experience and observation asserted also that death had passed upon all men because all had sinned. For this reason we can never get reconciled to death. Call it by euphemistic titles; talk of it lightly as a transition, a passage, an exodus; speak of the victory which Jesus Christ achieved when he abolished death and brought life and immortality to light—still we can never dissoci-ate from death the idea of sin, without which it need not have been: "In the day that thou eatest thereof, thou shalt surely die."

These three are inevitable factors in human life.

2. THE NOTABLE EXCEPTION SET FORTH IN THIS CHAPTER. The Divine Servant presents a noble excep-

tion to the lot of man—not in his sufferings, for he was
"a man of sorrows, and acquainted with grief"; nor in
his death, for he died many deaths in one (v. 9, R.V.,
margin); but in his perfect innocence and goodness. "He
had done no violence, neither was any deceit in his
mouth." Let us consider this and the conclusion to be
derived from it. There is sorrow in this chapter, as in all
the world. The marred face tells a true tale; for the tur-
bid streams of unknown sorrows have poured into the
Sufferer's heart until it has brimmed to high-water mark.
Despised and rejected, wounded and bruised, led to the
slaughter and cut off from the land of the living amid
degradation and cruelty, the Divine Servant has passed
through every painful experience, has drunk to its dregs
every cup, has studied deeply every black-lettered volume in the library of pain.

In Jesus' case, man's hastily formed conclusions are
falsified. Generally we pass from singular suffering to
discover its cause in some hidden or remote transgression. "Who did sin, this man or his parents, that he was
born blind?" Untold anguish has been inflicted through
the indiscriminate application of this method. Myriads,
like Job, have winced as the probing knife, wielded by
unsympathizing hands, has searched the most secret
passages of life to attempt to discover where the wrong
lay that was being avenged. And the sufferer has been
made to fear lest he had been unwittingly guilty of an
offence against the infinite God which could only be
expiated by the infliction of excessive chastisement.

In the case of Jesus Christ, however, this explanation
of his unique sufferings is altogether erroneous. His life
was searched with microscopic care to discover, if possible, a single flaw to justify his condemnation. The most
secret passages of his dealings with his disciples and
friends were ransacked by the keen eye of the traitor,
with the object of discovering an excuse for his dark
deed. But all was in vain. Pilate and Herod asserted his

absolute faultlessness. Finally, he, who of all men was most humble and meek, bared his life to the world with the challenge he knew could never be taken up, "Which of you convicteth me of sin?" (John 8:46, R.V.). Another explanation must therefore be forthcoming to account for the sufferings of the innocent and spotless Savior.

This explanation lay hid, like a secret concealed in a hieroglyph, in the vast system of Levitical sacrifice which foreshadowed the "offering of the body of Jesus Christ once for all." Year by year, myriads of innocent and spotless animals surrendered their lives prematurely, their lifeblood flowing freely for no fault of theirs but on account of the sins of those who brought them to the altar of God. To the most casual observer, and altogether apart from the disclosures of the Epistle to the Hebrews, it was clear that the sufferings of these victims were altogether due to sins not their own. This was a light on the one act of Calvary (Rom. 5:8).

Does not a father suffer for his son when he strips himself to penury to pay his offspring's profligate debts? Does not a physician suffer for the sins of others should he be stricken down in his effort to rescue another from the incidence of disease caused by violating the elementary laws of health? Have not thousands perished in rescuing others from fire and flood? Such actions as these illustrate, though very imperfectly, that of the sinless Savior pouring out his soul unto death.

So, under divine guidance, men were led from the conclusions of verse 4 to those of verse 5. Instead of accounting Christ as smitten and afflicted by *God,* they came to see that he had borne *their* griefs, carried *their* sorrows, and died for *their* sins; that he was the *Lamb* of God, taking away the sins of the world: that his death was the voluntary substitution of himself for a *world of transgressors.* These conclusions, expressed here as the verdict of the human conscience after scanning the facts in the light of history, are confirmed and clenched by the unanimous voice of the New Testament: "He was made sin for us, though he knew no sin." "Through his one act of righteousness, the free gift came unto all men to justification of life."

This is the great exception which has cast a new light on the mystery of pain and sorrow. It may be that there is other suffering which, in a lower sense and in a smaller measure, is also "redemptive," fulfilling divine purposes in the lives of others—but no sufferer is free from sin as Christ was, and none has ever been able to expiate sin. However saintly, none can ransom his brother's soul.

3. THE PERSONAL APPLICATION OF THESE TRUTHS. "Thou must make his soul a guilt-offering" (v. 10, R.V., margin). This term, "guilt-offering," occurs in the Book of Leviticus. If a man committed a trespass in the holy things of the Lord, he was directed to select and bring from his flock a ram without blemish. This was his *guilt-offering*—the word used here. He was to make a money restitution for his offence; but the atonement was made through the ram. "The priest shall make atonement for him with the ram of the guilt-offering, and he shall be forgiven" (Lev. 5:15–16).

Similarly, if a man sinned against his neighbor, either in oppressing him or withholding his dues, or neglecting to restore property which had been entrusted to him, he was not only to make restitution but to bring his guilt-offering to the Lord—a ram without blemish out of the flock—and the priest made an atonement before the Lord, and he was forgiven concerning whatsoever he had done to be made guilty thereby (Lev. 6:1–7).

Is there one of us who has not committed a trespass and sinned in the holy things of the Lord? Failures in fulfilling his sacred commissions; in yielding time and thought to the cultivation of his holy friendship; in maintaining inviolate the temple of the soul—these come to mind and stop our mouths, so that we stand guilty before God.

Is there one who has not failed in his obligations to neighbor and friend? Even if we have not failed in those specific instances named in the old law; even if our conscience does not accuse us of oppression, or withholding dues, or neglecting to restore—still there may have been serious departures from the standard of perfect love. It is so easy to say some contemptuous word which robs another of his garb of honor; or to be silent when we ought to speak in defense and vindication of those who are wrongfully accused. Moses taught that this was sin not against man only but against God. Restitution was to be made to the one; but an atonement had also to be made to Jehovah. Did not this lead David to cry to God, when his sin had robbed Uriah's home of its choice jewel, "Against thee, thee only, have I sinned, and done this evil in thy sight"?

How certainly we need to present the guilt-offering! If in his dimmer light the Jew felt his need, how much more we, who know that every sin is not only a mistake but a crime, violating the eternal law of righteousness and bringing an inevitable penalty unless it be intercepted and averted by the interposition of another. Explain it how we may, it is a fundamental fact in our inner consciousness that the sense of sin points to the bar of eternal justice, summons us there, and threatens that we shall not go till we have paid the uttermost farthing. Then we look around for a daysman, a mediator, for one who will not only plead our cause before that high tribunal but who will interpose to avert the deserved penalty by receiving it into his own bosom.

When the weight of remembered sin presses you to the earth; when awful sorrow calls to remembrance the almost forgotten sins of early years; when the searchlight of God's truth shines clear into the dark cave of the soul, revealing the evils that lurk there as slimy things under the covert of thick darkness; when some terrible fall has mastered you; when perpetual failure makes you think that forgiveness is impossible—fear not to seek it from the One whom God has "exalted with his right hand, to be a Prince and a Savior . . . to give forgiveness of sins" (Acts 5:31).

There is no mention made of the necessity of summoning priestly aid. This is the more remarkable when we consider the strict Levitical system in which Israel was cradled. It would seem that in the great crisis of its need, the soul of man reverts to an earlier cultus and goes back beyond the elaborate system of the temple to the practice of the patriarchal tent, where each man acted as his own priest and offered the guilt-offering with his own hand. No third person is needed in your transactions with God. Jesus is Priest as well as Sacrifice. There is no restriction to your approach; no barrier against your intrusion; no veil to be passed by the initiated few. The way into the holiest is made manifest, and with boldness you may "enter in by the blood of Jesus" (Heb. 10:19).

To do so is to secure peace. The proof of the truth of the gospel is to be found in the absolute rest which overspreads the soul which avails itself of its provisions and adjusts itself on its strong and steadfast principles. Let a man believe in Jesus Christ—not *about* him, but *in* him; not in his death, but in *him* who died and rose again—and he will be instantly conscious of a peace that passes understanding, arising from the depths of his nature and overspreading it like an evening calm. The peace of the world is from without and superficial; the peace of God is from within and is all-pervading.

In that peace much else is included. Sorrow is not banished from the life, but it becomes radiant with light; suffering is borne with a new resignation and fortitude; pain is welcomed with the blessed conviction that it may have a redemptive quality which shall operate somehow, somewhere; and death is contemplated without alarm. Thus from the darkest day that ever dawned upon our world have come rays of hope and joy which are ushering in the world in which there is no night—neither sorrow, nor crying, nor pain, nor death; and where God shall wipe the tears from all faces.

And that darkest day in the experience of our blessed Lord has won for him a revenue of gladness which can never be exhausted—as the blessed harvest of his tears and blood is reaped by individuals and worlds. He sees his spiritual seed, he finds a multiplication of his life, he realizes that the scheme of redemption, which is also the pleasure of his Father, is prospering in his hands.

22

THE SATISFACTION OF THE MESSIAH

(ISAIAH 53:11)

"He shall reign from pole to pole
With illimitable sway;
He shall reign, when like a scroll
Yonder heavens have passed away.
Then the end; beneath his rod
Man's last enemy shall fall.
Hallelujah! Christ in God,
God in Christ, is all in all."
Montgomery

SATISFIED! Very few can say that word on this side of heaven. The alpine climber cannot, so long as inaccessible summits rear themselves beyond his reach. The conqueror who has overrun the world cannot; he weeps because there are no more worlds to conquer. The philosopher cannot, though he has discovered the hidden harmonies of nature and unveiled her ancient order, for his circle of light only extends the circumference of the dark unknown. Even the Christian cannot say it, since he has not yet attained, neither is already perfect. But Christ shall be satisfied, and is already drinking deep draughts of the joy set before him when he endured the cross, despising its shame.

There is no satisfaction for those who are self-centered; and we say reverently that God himself could not

have known perfect blessedness unless he had been able
to pour himself forth in blessing upon others. We are
therefore conscious of a fitness in meeting this allusion
to the satisfaction of Christ amidst these words that
speak of his sacrifice unto death. Whatever may be the
character of that joy which he had with the Father before the worlds were made, it surely will pale in intrinsic
value before that joy which for evermore will accrue to
him as the interest upon his expenditure at Calvary.

We might put the truth into four sentences. There is
no satisfaction apart from love. There cannot be love for
sinning, suffering souls without travail. There cannot
be travail without compensating joy. In proportion to
the travail, with its pangs and bitterness, will be the
resulting blessedness.

1. THE TRAVAIL OF CHRIST'S SOUL. He suffered
because of his quick sympathy with the anguish that
sin had brought to man. He probably saw, as we cannot, the timid oppressed by the strong; the helpless vic-
tim pursued by rapacity and passion; mothers weeping
over the children that had been torn from their forlorn
and desolate hearts. He heard the wail of the world's
sorrow in which cries of little children, the shriek or
moan of womanhood, and the deep base of strong men
wrestling with the encircling serpent-folds mingle in one
terrible medley. He sighed over the deaf and dumb, had
compassion on the leper, wept at the grave. As the
thornbrake to bare feet, so must this world have been
to his compassionate heart.

He must also have suffered keenly by the rejection of
those whom he would have gathered as a hen gathers
her chickens under her wing, but they would not. Was
there a contemptuous name they did not hurl at him;
an insult that did not alight upon his head; an avenue
along which man's hate can reach the heart of his fel-
low-man which was not trodden bare by those who re-
paid his love with a hate which had the venom of hell in

it—even though his love had the fragrance of Paradise?

But these elements of pain are not to be compared with that more awful sorrow which he experienced as the substitute and sacrifice of human guilt. In a following verse we are told that "he poured out his soul unto death." It was a voluntary act to which he was nerved by the infinite love that dared to make his soul an offering for sin. What did Jesus suffer on the cross? The physical pain that wracked his body was probably hardly perceptible to him amid the pressure of those stripes with which we are healed. He was wounded, not in his tender flesh only, but in his holy, loving heart. He was bruised between the millstones of God's justice and unswerving fidelity to truth. He was stricken because he received into his soul the penalty of human guilt. He stood before the universe charged with the sins of the race and their consequence. He tasted death for every man. He was so identified with sin, its shame, suffering and penalty, that he deemed himself forsaken by God. In that one act of the cross he put away sin, exhausted the penalty, wiped out the guilt, and laid the foundation of a redemption which includes the whole family of man.

It could not be otherwise. He could not have loved us perfectly without becoming one with us in the dark heritage of our first parent. Son of Man as he was, though himself sinless, he could not but be involved in the entail of condemnation which was the lot of the human family. With us, and for us, he must suffer. With us, and for us, he must die. With us, and for us, he must meet the demands of a broken law and satisfy them eternally.

Do you love Christ? The first duty he will lay on you will be love to others. He will tell you there is no true love for himself which does not go out for those whom he has loved. Whatever sentiment of the human heart there be with an aspect towards him, it has at the same time an aspect towards all. So if you truly love, you too shall find your need of soul-travail. You too will have to go outside the camp, bearing his reproach. You cannot love men into life without suffering with them and for them—not to the same extent that Christ suffered, but in your measure. Think it not strange when that fiery trial comes; but rejoice that you are called to be a partaker of the sufferings of Christ, that at the revelation of his glory you may rejoice with exceeding joy.

2. THE CERTAINTY OF INFINITE COMPENSATION. "He *shall* see." It is impossible to suffer voluntarily for others and not in some way benefit them. Of course there is pain in the world which is punitive, deadly—the pain which is the result of pride, that frets and chafes against the rule of the Almighty like the sea churning itself in yeasty rage at the foot of the cliffs; the pain of those that fling themselves on the serried ranks of God's order and law—like the French cuirassiers on the English squares on the field of Waterloo; the pain of those that suffer for the pain they have themselves inflicted. But there is other pain which is remedial and life giving. The pain of the mother bringing forth her first-born. The pain of the woman's nature that clings to a prodigal—husband, brother or son—sharing his shame; agonizing in his repeated outbreaks; and by tears, prayers and sacrifice, winning him for God. The pain of nature, groaning and travailing with the genesis of the new heavens and earth. The pain of the Savior, giving life and salvation to myriads born again into the kingdom. The pain of the Spirit, groaning within the saints, and ushering in the Church of the first-born. The pain of the children of God who groan within themselves, waiting for the adoption as sons, the redemption of our bodies.

The earth is full of each kind of pain; but the first is characteristic of the first Adam; the last, of the Second. The first belongs to an order which is destined to vanish away; the last to an age, the dawn of which, as sighted from the highest peaks of saintliness, is fairer than any light which has ever broken on the eyes or hearts of man. Woe be to you, O son of man, if you know nothing of this blessed travail; if you have never known what it is to be in anguish for the souls of others; if your bosom has never been rent with strong cryings and tears; if you have never known the wish to be accursed from God, so that you might win your brethren according to the flesh! Blessed are you if you *do* know such pain! Your pain may sometimes seem abortive—the mighty throes that rend you for the souls of others appear in vain; but it is not really so. Drop by drop your tears shall presently turn the scale. Patience shall have her perfect work. The laws of the harvest in this sphere are as certain in their operation as in that of nature. God guarantees the results. He is *faithful.* You shall come again, bringing your sheaves with you: they that sow in tears shall reap in joy. In the golden future, if not before, you shall meet again each tear and sigh, and pang and prayer, transfigured in the result.

3. THE NATURE OF CHRIST'S COMPENSATION. It will come:

(a) *In the glory that shall accrue to the Father.* It has been the one aim of the Second Person in the Holy Trinity to reveal the character and glory of the First, that all intelligent and holy beings may love him. He has done this in creation; also in the government of the worlds; but, above all, in his cross. There we behold righteousness and peace kissing each other; the wisdom that invented a way of salvation consistent with the claim of moral law; the faithfulness which, in the fullness of the times, fulfilled the earliest promise; and, above all, God's love. To Calvary shall wend the intelligences of every sphere, to acquire new and enlarged conceptions of the divine character. And as, age after age, increased powers of vision reveal fresh wonders on the cross, Christ shall see the growing results of the travail of his soul.

(b) *In the redemption of untold myriads.* Great as the

harvest of sin has been, we believe that the saved shall vastly outnumber the lost. Nothing less will satisfy Christ. Remember that in the first age, before mention is made of the latter triumphs of the gospel, John beheld in heaven a multitude which no man could number. This was but the first-fruit sheaf; let who will compute the full measure of the harvest! The martyr throng; the Christians who were recognized by no fellow-believer and numbered in no church; the babes caught to his bosom; the godly souls in every nation, like Cornelius, who have been saved by virtue of a death of which they never heard; the myriads that shall be gathered in during the Millennial age—*these* are streamlets that shall swell the river of the ransomed to overflowing. In them shall Christ see the fruit of the travail of his soul and be satisfied.

(c) *In the character of the redeemed.* He shall present them to himself without spot or wrinkle, or any such thing. He shall present them to his Father with exceeding joy—the devil's handmark obliterated from their character; the Father's image complete. Think you when Jesus takes to himself his peerless Bride, purchased by his blood, sanctified by his Spirit, adorned in her marriage array—that he will not see the purpose of the travail of his soul and be satisfied?

(d) *In the destruction of the devil's work.* What is involved in the majestic promise that Christ will destroy the works of the devil is not yet made manifest. In due time we shall see it all. The mists that now veil the landscape, the scaffolding which hides the building, will be removed. We shall see what God means. The curse gone from nature. Grace abounding much more where sin and death had reigned. Man lifted nearer God than he could have been had he dwelt forever in an unsullied paradise. The kingdoms of the world, and of all other worlds, become the kingdoms of our God and of his Christ. Then, as the hallelujah chorus breaks from millions—like the triumphant shout from the lips of the emancipated Israel; as the waves of harmony break around the sapphire throne in tumultuous melody; as the forms of monster evils lie strewn around the shores of the crystal sea mingled with fire—Christ shall see the goal of the travail of his soul, and be satisfied.

4. THE GREATNESS OF THOSE RESULTS.

(a) *They must be proportionate to the glory of his nature.* It is not difficult to satisfy, at least temporarily, a little child. Imperfect knowledge will hush its curiosity, trifling toys please its fancy. But as its nature develops, it becomes increasingly hard to content it.

But surely there is a far greater difference between the capacity of an angel and that of a man than between the capacities of a man and a babe. If a man requires for his satisfaction more than a child, how much must not the capacious bosom of an angel need! The power for which humans contend is child's play to those who control the rush of winds and regulate the motion of worlds! The knowledge that men esteem as marvelous, to an angel is but the prattling of a babe. How much would have to be accumulated before an angel could say, "It is enough, I am satisfied"! But, great as an angel is, his capacity is limited and finite. What then must be the measure of that blessedness, of that harvest of souls, of that result of his travail, which can content the Divine Redeemer? His nature is so vast that nothing short of a redeemed seed like the stars of the sky or the sand on the shore can satisfy.

The immeasureableness of the results of redemption can only be estimated by those who consider the immeasureableness of the divine nature of the Redeemer.

(b) *They must be proportionate to the intensity of his suffering.* The results of God's work are always commensurate to the force he puts forth. You cannot imagine the Divine Being going to an immense expenditure without a sure prescience that he would be recouped.

When he puts his hands to a work it is because he knows that he can carry it through, and that the golden gain will be satisfactory remuneration. When, therefore, we behold the Son of Man emptying himself, stooping to the humiliation of Bethlehem, the anguish of Gethsemane, the death of Calvary, we know that the spoils which will fall to his share, when he divides them with the strong, will not be unworthy or inadequate.

Satisfied! We shall hear his sigh of deep content and see the triumph on his face. We shall witness the sublime transference of the kingdom to God, even the Father. We shall see the satisfactory termination of the mystery of evil. And if Christ is satisfied, *we* shall be. On this let us rest. And when our hearts misgive us because of the waste and havoc, the tears of blood, the awful suffering that sin has brought into the universe of God, let us assure ourselves that all will yet be well; and that we shall drink deep draughts of the satisfaction of our Lord when we too see all the results of the travail of his soul, and are satisfied.

23

THE GREATNESS OF THE SIN-BEARER

(ISAIAH 53:12)

"We must not stand to gaze too long,
Though on unfolding Heaven our gaze we bend,
Where lost behind the bright angelic throng,
We see Christ's entering triumph slow ascend.

"No fear but we shall soon behold,
Faster than now it fades, that gleam revive,
When issuing from his cloud of fiery gold
Our wasted frames feel the true Sun, and live."
Keble

IT is impossible to mistake the majestic personality speaking through the pronoun "I." It is the voice of God himself; and it is befitting that, as he introduced his Servant in the opening verses of this marvelous portraiture, so, in these closing words of Isaiah 53, he should pronounce his verdict on his Servant's career. We have watched, as the chapter has unfolded, how the opinion of the speaker and others, represented repeatedly by *we* in the first six verses, passed through many phases— hostility, criticism, pity—before it settled to penitence and faith. In this respect it is a true delineation of the attitude of the world generally towards Jesus of Nazareth, who realized this unique ideal; and surely, the words on which we are now to dwell anticipate the verdict of the Eternal when the mystery of sin and suffering is over forever.

In this verse two things are clearly predicated of the Sin-bearer. First, that he would be great; and secondly, that he would attain his commanding position not as the founder of a new school of thought, nor as the leader of a social reformation, nor as someone possessed of exceptional saintliness—but as a sufferer.

This should be clearly noted. It is because "he poured out his soul unto death"—a phrase which calls attention to the voluntary and oral aspects of his sufferings; because he allowed himself to be numbered among the transgressors, as sympathetically one with them; because he interceded for them, as standing beside them and identified in their interests—that the Almighty Father gives him a portion with the great and causes him to divide the spoil with the strong.

We are not dealing here with the glory he had with the Father before the worlds were made. Of that he emptied himself when he came to earth to live and die as man. This greatness, which he obtained through death, is entirely distinct from that.

1. THE GREATNESS WAS GIVEN BY THE FATHER AS THE REWARD FOR CHRIST'S OBEDIENCE TO DEATH. It was fitting that such a reward should be bestowed, for the sake of those who would afterwards follow in the footsteps of their Divine Master. Here was one who never swerved from the narrow track of obedience, whose course glorified and magnified the character of God. If it could be shown that such unparalleled devotion was fruitless and unrecognized, that it was treated with complete indifference—the faithful Servant being permitted to lie in an unknown and dishonored grave—would it not deter other ardent souls bent on following his example, forcing them to feel that the interests of God were antagonistic to those of man? None

could ever deserve more or better than Christ; and if he were without recognition or reward, might it not be thought that Heaven had no prize to give for faithful service? Surely he must have a reward, or the very order of the universe might be deemed at fault!

But what reward should he have? What could compensate him for having laid aside the exercise of his divine prerogative; for having assumed our nature; for having passed through the ordeal of temptation, sorrow and pain; for having become obedient to death, even the death of the cross? All worlds were already his by native right; all holy beings owned his sway as Creator and God; all provinces of thought, emotion and power sent him their choicest tribute. What reward could he be given?

The answer may be suggested by recalling our own pleasure in conferring pleasure, our joy in giving joy. To bless, to save, to help another, will fill our bosom with the most unalloyed blessedness of which the heart of man is capable. But our power and capacity are limited; we cannot do as we would. Let, however, the limitations imposed by our mortality or circumstances be removed; let us be able to realize to the full the yearnings and promptings of our noblest hours—and probably we would at once drink deep draughts of blessedness like God's.

This is the blessedness of Christ, and the reward which the Father has given him: all *power* is given him in heaven and on earth, because he is the Son of Man and can use it for the unmixed benefit of those whom he has, in such wonderful condescension, made his brothers! He is raised to the right hand of the Father—that he may requite with coals of fire the nation that rejected and crucified him? No—by giving repentance and remission of sins! And God has given him a *name*—the name Jesus, Savior, which is above every name—so that in it and through it every knee should bow and every tongue confess that he is Lord, to the glory of the Father. All that come to him may now be *saved*, even to the uttermost! All that yield to him are delivered from the power of darkness and translated into the kingdom of God's love! To the furthest limit of its meaning, Jesus is able to realize his own prayer: that the essential oneness and blessedness of the divine nature should be realized in those who believe.

God himself could not give, nor the Savior ask for, a greater reward than this. And, in its magnificence, it appeals to all who would tread in his steps. The closer we approach him in his self-sacrifice, the more fully we shall attain to his recompense. The deeper we drink of his cup and are baptized with his baptism, the more we shall be able, in our measure, to assist him in his redemptive purpose. This is what he meant when he spoke of us sitting with him on his throne and ruling the cities of men in the interests of purity, righteousness and peace (Rev. 3:21).

Ask Paul why he was so eager to discipline his body, in his zeal making it black and blue with blows; why he denied himself legitimate gratification; why he was so abstemious and self-denying—and he will confess that it arises from his supreme desire, lest, having proclaimed as a herald the rules of the contest for others, he might miss the prize. And if you inquire further of what that prize consisted, he will modestly tell you that its charm and value to him lie in the greater power that it will confer for saving others (1 Cor. 9:20–27).

This is Heaven's supreme reward: that all who pour out their souls to death shall obtain enlarged opportunities and possibilities for service. It is clear that they will not abuse them to their own hurt. It is equally certain that the exercise of such prerogatives will ensure the richest and most unalloyed blessedness for those by whom they are exerted.

2. OBSERVE THE GREATNESS THAT CHRIST'S DEATH HAS SECURED HIM AMONG MEN. He is worthy to take the mysterious scroll of destiny and break its seals because of the light he has cast on the great mysteries by which our lot is shadowed.

(a) *Pain.* As we have sadly learned, it is ubiquitous. Sooner or later it finds us out. And when it enwraps us in its fiery baptism, we are apt either to *accuse ourselves* or to *doubt God.* "Have you come, O sting of fire, to bring my sin to remembrance, and avenge the sins of my youth?"—such is our cry under the first of these impressions. "God is unjust or careless, otherwise he would never let one of his innocent children suffer thus. There is no righteousness in his government of the world. I will curse him and die"—such is our cry under the second.

But Jesus has taught us that there is yet a third way of regarding pain. *He* had not sinned, yet he suffered as none of woman born ever did. Evidently, then, pain is not always symptomatic of special sin. He was once so submerged in anguish that for a time he lost the sense of his Father's love: but he never suggested that there was failure or obliquity in the moral government of the world. The death of Jesus has therefore robbed death of these two implications, and has taught us that it is often sent, and must be borne, with the view of benefiting others. It is because God loves our race and desires to save and enrich it that he calls some—yea, many—apart from its ranks and causes them to drink the cup of pain so that inestimable benefits may accrue to all.

Whenever, therefore, we are called to suffer—especially if unconscious of special sinnership—let us not charge God foolishly, but consider that somehow and somewhere our patient and heroic endurance of anguish, whether physical or mental, will certainly conduce to the furtherance of those redemptive purposes which fill the heart of Jesus—purposes in the sacred partnership of which he has called us to take a share.

What a priceless service was this—to transform pain; to persuade sufferers that by their travail of soul they were enriching the whole world of men; to show the persecuted, the victims of human passion and lust, the paralyzed, cancer-eaten and bedridden that they had an opportunity of cooperating with the Prince of sufferers in the overthrow of the dark tyranny which has been fraught with such unutterable agony for them and for myriads! For this we count Christ great: that through his death he has transfigured pain.

(b) *Death.* Men dread it. It is the inevitable shadow which creeps over the warmest sunshine and silences the gladdest joy. But he, by his dying, has abolished death and brought life and immortality to light. He spoke of going to his Father; of reunion with his own on the other side of death, in paradise; of coming again to receive his own to himself. He showed that there was a track threading the drear valley which he could walk and rewalk until all his sheep were safely folded. He had no fear himself, and taught us to have none. It was the way *home,* that was all.

Before Jesus came, men had hoped and dreamed that this was so. But no one knew. Their prognostications were like those of Columbus before he turned his prow westward and plowed the first furrow across the Atlantic. But when Jesus *rose,* death and resurrection were no longer matters for reasoning or speculation; that *fact* spoke to all ages as the guesses of philosophers never could have done. Life and immortality were brought to light! For this, therefore, we count him great: that through death he undid death.

(c) *Sin.* When Jesus died on the cross, he was numbered with transgressors; but he stood over against all transgressors, distinct from them and bearing their sin. The sin of the race was imputed to him. The guilt and penalty accruing to us *all,* in consequence of our connection with Adam's fallen family, were borne by him. As God's Lamb he bore the sin of the world. As man's scapegoat he bore it into a land of forgetfulness, whence it could never again be recovered.

Nay, more, he bore *our sins* in his own body on the tree. Not *sin* alone, as the common heritage of the race, but *sins* also—yours and mine: so that if we as believers confess them with humility and penitence, we may receive immediate and abundant pardon—a pardon which does not violate but is guaranteed by the faithfulness and justice of God. God must be faithful to his promises, and just to his Son. The natural and secondary consequences remain, although transfigured; but the penal ones are forever gone, having been exhausted when Christ gave himself a ransom and sacrifice for us all. This surely constitutes an overmastering claim for us to count Christ great! In his death he finished transgression; made an end of sins; purged away iniquity; and brought in everlasting righteousness. Thou art worthy, O Lamb of God; for thou wast slain, and hast redeemed us to God by thy blood.

3. BEHOLD THE GREATNESS WHICH CHRIST'S DEATH WILL WIN FOR HIM IN THE ESTIMATION OF OTHER RACES OF BEING. Not to the Mount of Beatitudes but to the cross will distant worlds send their deputations in all coming ages—to learn the manifold lessons which it alone can teach. There they will learn to know the very heart of God: his hatred against sin, his love for the sinner, his fidelity to covenant engagements, his righteousness, his truth. The cross is the heavenly prism that enables us to distinguish the constituents of the divine nature. There they will be amazed to discover the devotion of divine love which could stoop to such humiliation and suffering to win its Bride. There they will gladly recognize the victory of the Son of God over all the malice and power of the enemy.

The volcano of hell has, perhaps for ages, belched out

its fury on the universe, to its great detriment and misery. But since Jesus died and rose, it has been made manifest that its power is broken—its empire at an end. What a relief to the whole moral universe! For what Jesus did on his cross pertains not to men only but to all races and orders of beings—to whom it proclaims peace! And having made peace through the blood of his cross he shall finally reconcile *all* things to himself—whether things upon the earth or things in the heavens (Col. 1:20)!

24

"SING, O BARREN!"

(Isaiah 54:1–10)

"Howbeit, all is not lost
The warm noon ends in frost . . .
Yet through the silence shall
Pierce the Death Angel's call,
And 'Come up hither,' recover all.
Heart, wilt thou go?—'I go:
Broken hearts triumph so!'"

E. B. Browning

IN the previous chapters we have heard the exiles summoned to leave Babylon, and have beheld the Divine Servant becoming the Sin-bearer for them and for the world. Here our attention is startlingly recalled to the desolate city of Jerusalem. "Barren"; "Forsaken"; "Desolate"—such are the terms applied to her by one who cannot err. And they are corroborated by the testimony of a contemporary. "Then said I unto them," is the faithful record of Nehemiah, "Ye see the evil case that we are in, how Jerusalem lieth waste, and the gates thereof are burned with fire" (Neh. 1:3; 2:3, 13–17).

But how is this? Have we not learned that the Mediator has put away sin at the cost to himself of wounds and bruises, stripes and death? How then does this city lie as an open sore on the face of the earth? Cannot God's forgiveness which has triumphed over sin also

triumph over the wreck and ruin that sin has caused?
Is that redemption complete which fails to grapple with
all the results and consequences of wrongdoing?

This opens up a great subject, and one that touches
us all. We are conscious that though our sin is forgiven,
yet certain consequences remain, of which that ruined
city is a type. We cannot undo the past; God himself
cannot undo it. It can never be as though it had never
been. The seventy years of captivity, the shame, the sorrow, the anguish to God, the forfeited opportunities, the
thistledown so thoughtlessly scattered! Ah me! God can
forgive; but these things cannot be altered now. But what
is meant by that word *Redeemer?* What is the meaning
of the passage which asserts that where sin reigned unto
death, *there* grace would reign unto eternal life? What
is meant by the promise of fir trees instead of thorns, of
myrtles instead of briars? These questions are often
asked in spirit, if not in so many words; and it is well to
attempt an answer. They open up the great subject of
the natural consequences of sin and how God deals with
them.

1. THE NATURAL CONSEQUENCES OF SIN.

(a) *We must distinguish between them and the punitive or penal.* Suppose that a man is taken into custody
for being drunk and disorderly. There are two results of
that outbreak of uncontrolled passion. On the one hand
he has broken the law of his country, for which a penalty of imprisonment or fine must be inflicted. But on
the other, and in addition, he has brought on himself
the racking headache, the depression of spirits, the awful
nervous reaction which is the natural and inevitable
result. These will pursue and scourge him as with the
whip of the furies even when his standing is adjusted
with his country's laws.

So, when we sin against God, two consequences accrue. Our sin cries against us, as Abel's blood against
Cain; its voice goes up to high heaven, and can only be

stilled and hushed by the pleading of the blood of Jesus. It is only as we take that precious blood in hand and bear it with us into the holiest, presenting it as our propitiation, that we find peace and rest, and deliverance both from the guilt and the penalty that could otherwise accrue to us. But when this has been effected, and we are forgiven, accepted and blessed, there are yet other results to be faced. The drunkard may be forgiven, but his health is undermined, his fortune impaired; he can never be what he would have been had he lived soberly.

Take the case of a man who, in his devotion to politics or society, has sinned against the laws of the home. Night after night he has been away from his young children, till they regard him as a stranger. There is none of that wholesome companionship, that trust, which are such sacred ties and make the man the father of the household. The mother cannot supply the firmness and strength which the young life needs. Almost insensibly the family grows away from him; and after a few years, when disappointment drives him back, he finds, to his infinite regret, that the love of the children has gone beyond recall. The boys are now men, and seek their pleasures outside the home; the girls think it irksome to while away his weary hours by their company. Now he sees his mistake, and tries to remedy it; but it is too late. He is forgiven by his God, and his wife—who never ceased to cling to him; but he cannot get back that forfeited love. This is his ruined Jerusalem.

(b) *This distinction is scriptural.* One illustration will be sufficient. When, in response to Nathan's parable, David broke the long silence and cried, "I have sinned!" the prophet immediately answered, "The Lord hath put away thy sin"; but he added, "The sword shall never depart out of thy house." So far as the sin lay between God and David's soul, it was removed immediately on his confession; but, so far as the natural consequences were concerned, they followed him for many a long year.

The death of Bathsheba's babe, the murder of Amnon, the revolt of Absalom, the rending of the kingdom, were the harvest of which that sin was the autumn sowing.

We need not reiterate the many lessons of this chapter but only recall the assurance of the fortieth chapter, that Jerusalem's iniquity has been pardoned, and contrast it with the allusions of this chapter to its desolate ruins and waste. It is clear then that we may, through penitence and faith, realize the perfect pardon of our Savior and yet there may be the hideous waste, the scar, the lost years, of which this ruined city was so significant.

(c) *These natural consequences are bitter to bear.* The enumeration, as given here, reminds us of Marah before the tree—true emblem of the cross—had, by divine direction, been cast into the waters. To bear no children; to work without result; to have little sense of the presence of God; to suffer in mind or nerve, or circumstance, or, worse than all, in the lives of others—these are among the natural consequences of sin and are fraught with anguish sometimes through long years. Let us remember the inevitableness and bitterness of these results when tempted to the indulgence of passion. It is quite true that one look of confession and faith will secure reinstatement in the favor of God; but it is also true that what a man sows, he must reap. And though he be a Christian, accepted and forgiven, if he sows seeds of the flesh, he must reap.

2. HOW GOD OVERRULES SIN'S NATURAL CONSEQUENCES. Jehovah says, *"Sing."* "Sing, O barren; break forth into singing, and cry aloud!" (v. 1).

"How can I sing?" says Israel. "My city is in ruins; my temple burned with fire; my precious things laid waste. How can I sing?"

"Nevertheless," is the divine reply, "the time for singing has come. Sing, not because of what you have but of what I have promised to give. Enlarge the place of your tent; lengthen your cords; strengthen your stakes; make room for the incoming of a great host that shall own you as mother."

"But the results of our backslidings remain. You cannot undo them, though you may forgive. You cannot give us back the seventy years of exile. You cannot obliterate the scar of bruise and wound and sore. You cannot intercept the inevitable recoil of our sins."

Yet Jehovah answers, "O barren one, you must sing as you did when you came from Egypt! Not with the same exuberant joy, but with a deeper insight into that grace which, in addition to its abundant pardon, can transform the irreparable past, transmuting its briars into myrtles and its thorns into fig trees, bringing good out of evil; transforming 'Benonis,' sons of sorrow, into 'Benjamins,' sons of the right hand."

So God our Father is able to make men and women in middle life sing again, as in the days of their youth—with a joy chastened by their memory of the failures and transgressions which yet have yielded honey like the carcass of Samson's lion. As, in the great world, Adam's sin has been overruled to the great enrichment of the race, so in the small world of our individual experience we rise by our falls, triumph in our defeats, and through the experience of the wilderness enter into the land of rest.

Let us illustrate this in the history of the exile. Terrible as was the immediate loss inflicted by the national backsliding, demanding the penalty of the captivity, yet in three respects that captivity was overruled to enrich the religious life of the chosen people, and ultimately of the world.

(a) *They conceived new and enlarged ideas of God.* Before that time, they had thought of him as a local and national deity, like the gods of the nations around; now they learned that the Holy One of Israel should be called the God of the whole earth (v. 5).

(b) *They understood better the nature of true religion.*
Before the captivity, in the estimation of the majority of
the Jewish people, it consisted in rites and ceremonies
and outward observances; but when there was no
temple, altar or priest, and still the prophets exhorted
them to godliness, it became apparent to even the least
thoughtful that true and undefiled religion was independent of the material and sensuous, and demanded
only God and the soul. In the captivity we first meet
with the institution of the synagogue, where devout souls
could worship God in simplicity and spirituality.

(c) *They realized their world-wide mission.* In the thinking of the chosen people rose the dawn of a new conception of the purposes of God in their calling and discipline: they were to be as the dew of the Lord on the
earth, disseminating everywhere those blessed truths
of which they were the divinely chosen custodians, and
enlarging their tent (v. 2) to include the Gentiles (Gal.
4:27). There was a sense, therefore, in which their casting away was the reconciling of the world.

Such were the results of their exile. God's grace
touched the darkness and blackness of their righteously
deserved afflictions and transmuted them to gold. So it
is still. The forgiven drunkard can never undo the rav-
age to health or fortune, but he is made humble, thoughtful, intent on saving those who are under the same spell
as he was. The violator of the laws of the homelife becomes more tender, more unselfish, more refined and
sensitive in the love he gives than he would have been
had not disappointment and heart hunger done their
perfect work. In those who have suffered from the results of their sins, there is a humility, tenderness, softness in speech, delicacy in understanding the temptations and failures of others—the soul of the prophet,
the intercession of the priest—which are beyond price.
The pardoned prodigal can talk of his Father's love in a
way that the older son could never do; and as we hear

him speak, we know that he is enriching us with spoils gathered by his experiences in the far country.

While we mourn our sins and bitterly lament their cost and pain, yet we can see how God is at work taking up the very waste of our lives and making it up again into the fairest fabrics—as rich dyes are made from the produce of gas retorts, and white paper from old and disused rags. In our exile we get new thoughts of God, of religion, and of our mission among men. Probably we would have reached them in some other way had we never wandered, but we may have learned them under conditions which will forever give a special flavor and tone to our affirmation of these mighty truths.

3. WORDS OF HELP TO ANY WHO MAY BE SUFFERING FROM THE RESULTS OF PAST WRONGDOING. The past cannot be altered, but it is a comfort to know that it can be forgiven and the soul made white and clean. These great blessings should not be lost sight of amid the outbursts of an infinite regret.

There is a world of difference also between punishment and chastisement. The one is for the Savior, who bore the guilt and penalty for man on the cross; the other only is for us who are one with him by a living faith. Let us not say we are being punished when the recoil of past transgression strikes us with mailed hand, but that we are being chastened so as to escape condemnation with the world. The same circumstances that are punitive to the ungodly are disciplinary to the child of God. Our Father chastens us for our profit, using as his rod the natural consequences of our sins.

At such times God calls us back to himself as a wife forsaken and grieved in spirit. He knows the disappointment and shame of the downcast soul (v. 6). He waits to *gather* with great mercies, and to show mercy with everlasting kindness (vs. 7–8). Let us heed his call and return to him, not allowing the sorrows and sufferings we endure to alienate us but counting them as opportunities for claiming more of his aid.

We must also believe in his inalienable love. He is our Husband still, and cannot put us away from him; the kindness with which he has had mercy on us is everlasting. He has even sworn that the waters of death and destruction shall not forever separate us from him. He has entered into a covenant of peace with us which shall outlast the mountains and the hills. We may grow apathetic and careless, bringing to ourselves pain and woe— grieving and dishonoring him, and hindering the development of his purposes. But he cannot cease to love. His tender pity will still embrace us—grieving to see our self-inflicted sorrows, but using them as a furnace, the fervent heat of which will consume our bonds while it leaves our skin unscorched and the hairs of our head unsinged.

If I ascend into heaven, O God, your love is there; but if I make my bed in hell, it is there also. If I take the wings of the morning, and dwell in the uttermost part of the sea—placing it as a great gulf of separation between yourself and me—even there shall your hand lead me and your right hand uphold me. If I say, "Surely the darkness shall cover me," even the night shall be light around me—and through it you will follow my every step, leading me back to yourself. And through my very wanderings you shall accomplish the loftiest purposes for my purity and holiness. Such love is too wonderful for me, I cannot attain unto it; but I will lie down and rest in its everlasting arms.

25

THE CITY OF GOD

(ISAIAH 54:11–17)

"Far o'er yon horizon
Rise the city towers,
Where our God abideth;
That fair home is ours!
Flash the streets with jasper,
Shine the gates with gold,
Flows the gladdening river;
Shedding joys untold."
Dean Alford

THE reference is still to Jerusalem. In the former paragraph she was addressed as a barren wife; here she is destined to arise from her encumbering ruins and become the joy of the whole earth. Of course, the primary reference is to that actual rebuilding which took place under the direction of the good Nehemiah. But there is a further and more spiritual meaning. These words must refer to that city of God which is ever arising amid the ruins of all other structures—watched by the ever attentive eye of the great Architect, wrought by unseen hands, tested by the constant application of the line of truth and the plummet of righteousness, and emerging slowly from heaps of rubbish into strength and beauty.

A description is given of the pricelessness of the structure (vs. 11–12), the privileges of the inhabitants (vs. 13–14), and the safety which is assured by the Word of God (vs. 15–17); and let us not hesitate to appropriate this blessed vision. It is put clearly within our reach by the assurance with which the chapter closes, that this is the heritage of all the servants of the Lord.

1. THE PRICELESSNESS OF THE STRUCTURE. What an enumeration of precious stones! The sapphire, the agate (the R.V. reads "ruby") and the carbuncle vie with each other and flash with varied but resplendent color. Now, let us consider what jewels are. They are by nature only lumps of dull and inert matter; the sapphire is clay, the diamond is carbon. But why the difference between their appearance and that of the ordinary soil? The answer is not easy to give, but this exquisite effect is probably due to crystallization, conducted under exceptional circumstances of convulsion, pressure and fire. A jewel is a bit of ordinary earth which has passed through an extraordinary experience. Thus there is a special fitness in this address to the afflicted people of God: theirs are the convulsions; theirs the awful pressure; theirs the fiery baptism. They count it hard—they cannot understand why they are treated thus. But they will see it all one day, when they learn that God was making agates for windows, carbuncles for gates, and sapphires for foundations.

Foundations of sapphires. The sapphire is one of the fairest of jewels. It is born in the darkness; but it hides the secret of the rarest beauty at its heart. The blue of the sapphire perpetuates in unfading hues the loveliness of the gentian, the violet, and the forget-me-not; of the summer sky and the summer sea; and that of the glacier depth where perhaps the deepest blue is to be seen in the walls of ice rock. It is frequently mentioned in Scripture. The elders saw a pavement of sapphire under the feet of the God of Israel. It was fifth among the precious stones in the breastplate, and second

among the foundations of the New Jerusalem. Blue is
the most prevalent color in nature, forming the back-
ground of sea and sky and distance; it also predomi-
nated in the tabernacle and temple, where it was always coupled with gold in the description of the sacred
furniture. As the gold was emblematic of the glory and
majesty of God, so was blue of his love and grace in
Jesus.

It is very suggestive to be told that the foundations of
the divine structure are laid with sapphires.

(a) *They are full of love.* The sapphire is the emblem of
love; and underneath our lives, underpinning the history of the world of men, the one ultimate fact for us all
is the love of God. Go down as deep and as far as you
will, you must come at last to the bedrock of God's love
in Christ.

(b) *They are stable.* Jewels are the most lasting of all
earthly objects, as imperishable as they are beautiful.
Such is the basis of Christian hope—not a dream of the
fancy; not a structure of clouds, which a puff of wind
may hurl into red ruin; nor a pictured reflection of giant
mountain forms on the bosom of the lake, which may
be destroyed by the fitful breeze. Christian hope is as
enduring and eternal as the very throne of God.

(c) *They are fair.* The loveliness of God's world is not
only in what meets the eye but reaches into the unseen.
Not only does he lavish beauty on flowers and wood-
lands and outspread landscapes, but on the massive
foundations of the earth where lie the pure white quartz,
the granite and porphyry with their rich veins and colors. But how fair are the foundations of our religion!—
the covenant made in the council chamber of eternity;
the blood of the atonement; the identification of the Redeemer with the lost; the eternal purpose which from
all ages God has purposed in himself, that grace shall
conquer sin.

Windows of agates. Agates are varieties of quartz, and

bear evidently in their texture the mark of fire. Indeed, they are always found in the igneous rocks, from which they drop out when such rocks decompose under the action of water and air. The agate is partially transparent. Not opaque, as flint; not transparent, as rock-crystal—it admits light, tempering it as it passes.

God makes windows of agates. That may be interpreted to mean that he takes our sorrows and makes them windows through which we may gaze into the unseen. We shall not in this world see eye to eye, or know as we are known; the medium of our seeing will always be partially obscured. But let us be very grateful that we can see at all. In sorrow we see the unsatisfying nature of the world and the reality of the unseen; we learn to appreciate the tenderness and delicacy of human love; we have insight into the meaning of God's providences; we behold the value and truth of Scripture. Windows of agates, but still windows. O soul tossed with tempest and not comforted, you will yet surely praise your God that you were passed through the fire—if only that you might see!

Gates of carbuncles. There is a good deal of uncertainty as to the precise stone indicated by the Hebrew word rendered "carbuncle." It seems better, therefore, to take the suggestion of the duplicate vision in the Apocalypse and to think of *Gates of pearl.* The pearl is said to result from the infliction of a wound in the oyster, which leads it to throw out the precious fluid that congeals into a pearl. If so, every pearl on the neck of beauty is the lasting memento of a stab of pain. At any rate, each pearl commemorates the hazard of human life in the diver's descent into the ocean depths. Think of gates brought from the heart of the sea, each due to the action of suffering and at the risk of precious life. It is true of life: all our outgoings into wider ministry, nobler life, greater responsibility of blessedness, are due to the precious action of sorrow, self-sacrifice and pain.

There is no gate into the life which is life indeed, which
has not cost us dear. God makes our pearls into gates,
and our gates of pearls.

When next you are overwhelmed in sorrow and pain,
or tossed with tempest and not comforted, dare to look
to the outcome of your stern discipline. It is not for the
present joyous, but grievous; nevertheless *afterward.* . . .
Our light affliction, which is for the moment, is like a
millshaft which you find difficult to turn—it strains your
every nerve; but on the other side of the wall it is grinding golden grain, the quality and weight of which will
more than compensate you. Learn, then, to look on God
as making pleasant stones for the borders of your life—
for the walls of salvation and the gates of praise. Is it
not a blessed thing to realize that God is making jewels
out of very common materials through the fire of trial
and pain?

2. THE PRIVILEGES OF THE CITY'S INHABITANTS.
All thy children shall be taught of the LORD. Our blessed
Lord quoted this promise in one of his greatest utter-
ances. "It is written in the prophets," he said, "And they
shall be all taught of God. Every man therefore that hath
heard, and hath learned of the Father, cometh unto me"
(John 6:45). It is a deep and helpful thought that God
has opened a school in this dark world and has himself
undertaken to act as Schoolmaster. He delegates to no
inferior hand the sublime work of educating the human
soul. But fear not!—it is as a *Father* that he teaches. He
knows our frame, and remembers that we are dust. Alas,
that so many hear and do *not* learn! There is a great
contrast between these two.

How often, when we were at school, in the long sum-
mer-like days—far away now, when days were long—
and the door stood open into the garden, our eyes would
stray from the book and follow after the butterflies hov-
ering over the flowers and the big bees droning lazily
past; or were attracted by the rabbits running across

the path and the birds flitting to and fro! We have heard, but not learned; and the lesson has been missed. Oh, the irksomeness of those required lessons, when all nature awaited us outside! Similarly we evade those divine lessons given on the pages of Scripture, or by conscience, or through experiences of human life, and inculcated by the divinest tenderness. If we truly learned from the Father, we would inevitably get to the feet of Jesus. When men say that they believe in God but not in Jesus Christ whom he has sent, they consciously or unconsciously depart from the truth. The sincere deist, when Christ is presented, must come to him.

To be taught by God, to be led by his own hand into a perfect knowledge of the mysteries of redemption, to sit at the footstep of his throne, to be a pupil in his school, to be his disciple, to have all that the psalmist so repeatedly asked when he cried, "Teach me thy statutes; lead me in thy way and teach me"—this is the first of the blessed privileges of the children of the city of God.

Great shall be the peace of thy children (v. 13). We have first peace *with* God, through faith in the blood and righteousness of Christ; then the peace *of* God, which here is called "great," and elsewhere "that passeth understanding." Some parts of the ocean laugh the sounding line to scorn. You may let out 1,000, 2,000, even 6,000 fathoms, and still the plumb falls clear. So it is when God's peace, driven from all the world, comes to fold its wings of rest in the heart. It is better than joy, which falters and fluctuates; better than the ecstasy which may have its reactions. Deep, sweet, still, all-pervading—eye has not seen, nor ear heard, nor heart conceived its like.

And these two rest on each other. The more you know God, the more peace you have—because you find him more worthy of your trust. We humans have peace with each other when we know that each is worthy of all our confidence. Peace grows from less to more; from a con-

dition which is largely experimental to one which is fixed
and everlasting—and always in proportion to the extended areas of our acquaintance with God. Acquaint
then yourself with him, and be at peace; for much good
shall come to you. Great peace have they that love his
law, and nothing shall offend them.

3. THEIR SAFETY. Even something which destroys
fulfills a useful function: a knife that cuts away dead
wood; fire that purges out the alloy; the winnowing fan
that rids the wheat of the chaff; the east wind tearing
through the forest; the frost crumbling up the soil; the
vast army of animals that devour and destroy. "I have
created the waster to destroy" (v. 16). This is the strong
Hebrew way of saying that God permits, and overrules,
and brings out good by means of the evil that had seemed
destructive of all good.

Think it not strange concerning the fiery trial which
is to try you. Be not afraid when you see the smith blowing up the fire in his forge and bringing forth a weapon,
the teeth of which might send a shudder through a
stouter heart than yours. Your God created *and can control* him. Nothing which God has made can do more than
he permits. Your Father is over all, and he has said,
without hesitation or reserve, that no weapon formed
against his own shall prosper, and that his children shall
condemn all tongues raised against them in judgment
(v. 17).

It is impossible to escape the ordeal. It would not be
good for us if we could. "They shall surely gather against
thee." "In the world," said the Master, "ye shall have
tribulation. If they have hated and persecuted me, they
will hate and persecute you." But they cannot really hurt.
Keep on doing what is right in his sight, with a single
eye for his glory and a simple resolve to do his will. The
fire may burn around you, but only to consume your
bonds; the storm may arise against you, but the billows
which break in thunder on the beach shall not break

one splinter from the cliffs. Do not seek to vindicate or avenge yourself. Be still and know that your God reigns! He will interpose at the exact hour of need. He will vindicate: he will turn the edge of the weapons of your foes against themselves, and silence every accusing, whispering, slandering voice. This is your heritage. If you are his servant, your honor is in God's keeping.

This is the City of God, and we walk its streets day by day. We have come to Mount Zion, the city of the living God, the heavenly Jerusalem; its breeze constantly fans our faces, its music fills our ears, its bright and holy inhabitants touch us in the streets. Its interests and employments even now engage our hands. The New Jerusalem, for us at least, *has* come down from God out of heaven, and is *here*.

26

OUR GLORIFIED LEADER

(ISAIAH 55:1–5)

"He is gone—and we remain
In this world of sin and pain;
In the void which he has left,
On this earth of him bereft.
We have still his work to do;
We can still his path pursue;
Seek him both in friend and foe,
In ourselves his image show."

Stanley

THERE are things which money cannot buy. They are hinted at in the opening verses of this chapter. It would be absurd to bring gold or silver, or any such equivalent for them, for they are without price. They therefore elude the rich, who have acquired the habit of supposing that money is the only medium of exchange and who find it hard to think of wealth other than that which passes current in the market. Yet they are within the reach of those who have no money but are sorely athirst. What these things are will appear presently. Suffice it only to say that they are contained in a Person, and that it is impossible to have them unless we enter into living union with him.

It was highly necessary that God should call the attention of the Jewish people to these unpurchasable

possessions, for their life in Babylon had become so luxu-
rious. They had so suddenly acquired wealth and they
had so easily bartered for mercenary consideration their
spiritual prerogative as the priests of men that there
was every danger of their losing sight of the great facts
of the spiritual world. It was needful, therefore, for them
to be reminded that the immortal thirst of the soul cannot be quenched by waters whose source is in the depths
of the earth, though the wells be deep as Sychar's; and
that its hunger cannot be satisfied with the provision
beneath which the tables of a Dives groan. True satisfaction—that which is really bread, the fatness that delights the soul—can only be obtained where the cur-
rency of this world has no value—in fellowship with him
whose voice is ever speaking in the halls of commerce,
saying, "Ho, everyone that thirsteth, come ye! Hearken
unto me; buy wine and milk! Eat ye that which is good!"

These gifts of the spiritual world by which the soul
lives are given in covenant, and each man must enter
for himself into covenant relationship with God. Yet, in
the deepest sense, the covenant has been already made
on the behalf of all faithful souls by their Representative, who here looms out amid the mists of the far past
in the unmistakable glory of the Son of Man.

Thus we have three clear issues before us: The Prince
of Life; the Everlasting Covenant; the Abundant Provision which is ours in him.

1. THE PRINCE OF LIFE. "Behold, I have given him
for . . . a Leader and Commander to the people" (v. 4).

(a) *He was typified in David.* This shepherd boy was
God's gift to Israel to save his people from the anarchy
into which Saul's willfulness had plunged them, to deliver the land from the incursions of the Philistines, and
to lead Israel like a flock. God entered into a covenant
with him to make him a house and declared that his
son would sit upon his throne, assured of the living presence of Jehovah and of the certainty of an established

throne forever. These were the "sure mercies" (v. 3) promised to David when God appointed him prince over his
people (2 Sam. 7:8–17).

In each of these respects the Almighty entered into
covenant with great David's greater Son. He has been
constituted Prince. His name is made great. His throne
shall be forever. His kingdom shall be made sure. For a
great while to come his house shall stand. His name
shall be continued as long as the sun, and men shall be
blessed in him. All nations shall call him happy (Psalm
72). Yes, the type was spoiled by David's infidelity and
sin. The pattern of things in the heavens always bears
the soil, the fret, and the tarnish of this world. But even
though this was so, on God's side there was no vacilla-
tion, no swerving from his purpose. His mercies were
sure. Much more in the case of Jesus Christ, the eternal purpose cannot miscarry. There can be no failure
upon his part to perform the conditions of the covenant;
and God will not run back from his word. He has made
with his Son a covenant which is orderly in all things
and sure. It would be easier to break the procession of
day and night than that one item of its provisions should
be invalidated.

(b) *This title is applied to Christ after his resurrection.*
Four times only in the New Testament is Christ called
Leader or Prince, and always in resurrection. In his ser-
mon in the temple, Peter accuses the Jews of having
killed "the Prince of Life," and immediately adds, "whom
God raised from the dead" (Acts 3:14–15). Again, before
the Sanhedrin, he affirms that "God exalted him with
his right hand to be a Prince and a Savior"—that exaltation evidently referring to his ascension from the depths
of the grave to the right hand of power (Acts 5:31). In
the Epistle to the Hebrews we are told that God has
made "the Leader of our salvation perfect through sufferings, and has crowned him with glory and honor"
(Heb. 2:9–10). And again in the same Epistle we are told

to look to Jesus, who has sat down at the right hand of
the throne of God, as "the Author of faith" (Heb. 12:2).
However translated, whether as *Author, Prince, Captain*
or *Leader,* it is the same Greek word—*Archegos*—and is
applied to Christ in his risen state.

(c) *The original meaning of the word is very interesting.* Etymologically, it means the first of a file of men,
and therefore their leader and commanding officer. This
concept therefore is presented to our mind: that our
Lord is the first of a long procession of souls whom he is
leading up from the grave with its darkness and corruption, through the steeps of air, past principalities
and powers, to the very throne of God! He is the First-
born from the dead, and therefore Ruler of the kings of
the earth. And in this capacity he also has obtained the
right to proclaim light to the Gentiles.

If this thought of Christ being the first of a long procession is carried out, in respect to the passages mentioned above, it yields grand results.

He leads the dead out of death into life. There is a
close analogy between the life and work of Joshua and
of Jesus. After the death of Moses, God gave Joshua to
be a witness to the people of truth and righteousness—
to be their leader and commander. To make the analogy
perfect, we may well suppose that Joshua first passed
across the dried bed of the Jordan, hard by the little
group of priests standing there with ark on shoulder,
and that the long procession of Israel trod in his steps.
Whether that was so or not, it is impossible to say. But
this, at least, is true, that Christ has preceded us through
the waters of Jordan which always stand for death; and
that he will hold them back until every one of the ransomed has passed "clean over Jordan."

*He leads the vanquished into the victory of the
heavenlies.* In his exaltation as Man to the right hand of
the throne, he opened a path to be trodden in after ages
by a company which no man can number. Where he is,

they are to be; as he has overcome, they are to overcome; as he reigns over principality and power, they are to sit on his throne till their enemies are made the footstool of their feet.

He leads sufferers through suffering into perfection — which is only possible as grievous pain is sanctified through the grace of the Holy Spirit. Son though he was, he learned obedience by the things that he suffered; and he transformed suffering, showing that it was an alembic, a purifying furnace, a means of discipline, strength and ennoblement—all of which have become the heritage of the suffering people of God. All who suffer meekly according to the will of God are following in the long procession which he headed.

He leads also the ranks of believers. In the eleventh chapter of the marvelous treatise already quoted, we have a roll call of the heroes of faith. But the writer is careful to tell us that not Abel, though he was the first in time, not Abraham, though first as progenitor, not Moses, though first in the marvels wrought, but *Jesus* is the true file-leader of faith.

(d) *These conclusions suggested by the New Testament are substantiated and confirmed by the expression used here.* "Thou shalt call a nation that thou knowest not" (v. 5). To whom can this refer, save to the Gentiles, who were once far off? "Nations that knew not thee shall run unto thee." Of whom can this be true, save of that vast ingathering suggested to our Lord by the Greeks who came to him before he died and concerning whom he said, "I, if I be lifted up, will draw all men unto me"? These words in Isaiah are a direct statement by the people of God to their directly given Leader. Full of thanks, they remind him that the Holy One of Israel has glorified him. And when did our Lord receive honor and glory except when, for his obedience unto death, he received a name which is above every name, and at which every knee shall bow and every tongue confess!

O Glorious Leader of faithful souls, who has conducted so great an exodus from the grave and the dark domain of selfishness and sin, and from the realm of the transient and material to the unseen and eternal—the sinless and sorrowless world—we who follow you pray that nations who have not known you may run to you, that there may be a great gathering of the peoples around your banner, and that many who are wasting their energy for waters that cannot quench their thirst and for bread that cannot satisfy their hunger may follow you to the river of the water of life and to the tree of life which is in the midst of the Paradise of God!

God has given—will you accept his gift? He gave his only begotten Son, and with him will freely give all things. Draw near and take; and let him be for your comfort, sustenance and salvation, world without end.

2. THE EVERLASTING COVENANT. Towards the close of David's life, he sang one brief strain concerning which he was very sure that the Spirit of the Lord was speaking by him, and that his word was upon his tongue. He seems to have had a glimpse of the lost opportunities of his life. He says sadly that one who rules over men righteously would be like sunrise, as a cloudless dawn, as the tender grass, the joint product of rain and sun. That was what his reign might have been, but the fair ideal had never been realized. He had not always ruled in the fear of God. He had committed iniquity, for which he had been chastened by the rod of men and with the stripes of the children of men (2 Sam. 7:14–15, 23:3–5).

He had been forgiven; but the natural consequences had remained. His house had not been faultless before God. Incest, murder, hatred, had rent it; and his last words make mention of the ungodly who could not be taken unless the hand were armed with sword and spear. Adonijah, Joab, Shimei and others were as thorns in the side of the aged king. But in spite of all, he knew that God's covenant with him was sure. God had said,

"My mercy shall not depart, as I took it from Saul whom I put away before thee." In David's own words, the "covenant was ordered in all things and sure."

A similar covenant has been enacted between the Father and the Son as the Representative of the redeemed. God will never be unfaithful to its provisions. The work of the cross has been definitely accepted on our behalf. The precious blood has been accounted a sufficient atonement. The obedience and death of Jesus Christ are enough. Those who believe in him shall never perish. God's mercies to us in Christ are sure. But we *must* definitely enter into that covenant for ourselves! Note the emphasis. Listen! come! hear! and—I will make an everlasting covenant with *you*.

Men talk much in the present day of the solidarity of the race and are accustomed to group men in one great family, to the obscuring of the equally true doctrine of individualism. We must not allow these two to collide. Each is necessary to the true development of the soul. It is true that all who repent and believe are included in the provisions of the eternal covenant—entered into in the council chamber of eternity; but it is equally true that there is a personal transaction between God and each soul by virtue of which it enters into that blessed relationship, which neither life nor death, things present nor things to come, can violate or interrupt.

3. THE ABUNDANT PROVISION. It is described under several terms—waters, wine, milk, satisfying bread, the good, fatness. We are invited to come for water, and lo! we find a feast prepared at which we sit to eat. All this reminds us of words in the Epistles, the wealth of which surpasses thought: "Blest with all spiritual blessings in the heavenlies in Christ." "All things are yours." "His divine power hath given to us all things that pertain to life and godliness."

It is too much our habit to pray as though by our entreaty we should obtain for ourselves what we need for life or service. We cry, "No, no! I will pray day and night for this or the other grace; I will buy this power by tears and sighs and many prayers." Oh that we could realize that the table is spread, that there is enough for us, that our name lies between the knife and fork, that the doors stand open, and that we have only to take! Everything that the apostles had is ours. All that God can give is given. All that the soul wants is ready at hand. We have not to ascend into heaven to bring down the grace of God; or to descend into any depth to bring it up. It is nigh, it is here. Eat, O beloved, eat and drink abundantly; there can be no stint for those whom God calls as his guests to sit at the table of his Son. We talk as though the feast were at the end of this dispensation; but the oxen and fatlings are already killed, and all things are now ready. Come ye!

Without money, and without price. And is it really so? Is there indeed nothing to pay? Men are not accustomed to this. However, we buy by confessions of our need; by revealing our emptiness and destitution; by being willing to be pensioners drawing on the bounty of God. To give up yourself, to renounce all faith in prayers and tears and entreaties, to be willing to take as a little child from the open hand of God—this is the purchase money for the priceless wealth of heaven.

Let it never be forgotten that the rich provisions of God's grace can only be enjoyed by those who follow their Leader, Christ, and obey his commands. This Captain of ours demands absolute obedience. If he says, "Come!" we must come, whatever we leave. If he says, "Go!" we must go, into whatever difficulty we plunge, or whatever peril we incur. If he says, "Do this!" there is no appeal. Run to him, abide in him, sit with him in the heavenlies, obey him! Take him as God's best gift; give him the glory of your homage as the Father has given him the glory of his own bright home. So shall you drink wine and milk, and eat bread that satisfies, and delight yourself in the fatness of his holy temple.

Thus earth may partake somewhat of the blessedness of that eternal world where it is said that "they follow the Lamb whithersoever he goeth; and they hunger no more, neither thirst any more, neither does the sun strike upon them, nor any heat." In fact, the whole Church drinks from the same refreshing river, and upon the same conditions. In each world the flock must follow the lead of Christ. In each world they find satisfaction as they drink of the river of the water of life proceeding from the throne of God and the Lamb—the one group near its source, the other in the lowlands of this world.

27

THE NEAR AND HEAVENLY HORIZONS

(ISAIAH 55:6–11)

"Mine is an unchanging love,
Higher than the heights above,
Deeper than the depths beneath,
Free and faithful, strong as death."
Cowper

THE *thoughts of God!* We can form some conception of them through the works of his hand, whether in nature, providence or redemption. The psalmist describes them as permanent in their endurance; as surpassing the reckoning of human arithmetic; and as being a fathomless deep. It is told of Kepler that one night, after hours spent in observing the motions of the heavenly bodies, he exclaimed, "I have been thinking over again the earliest thoughts of God." But there are earlier thoughts than those impressed on nature. The love that led to the choice of man in Christ, and that will culminate in Glory, is older far. Let us think more often of these thoughts of God, until we cry, "How precious are thy thoughts unto me, O God! How great is the sum of them!"

The ways of God. He made them known unto Moses; as though he could communicate a more intimate knowledge of his dealings to his favored servant than was possible to the children of Israel, who were only made cognizant of his acts. God's way is in the sea of mystery; his path lies through the great waters of sorrow. It was the cry of the psalmist that he should be taught God's ways; it was the divine complaint against Israel that they had not known them.

It is of these thoughts and ways that we are told that they are as much above ours as the heavens are above the earth. First, the heavens are so far above the earth, and *therefore so pure.* Second, they are so far, and *therefore so abundant.* Third, they are so far, and *therefore so beneficent.* And in each of these respects they are emblems of the nature and the mercy of God.

1. SO FAR, AND THEREFORE SO PURE. In the firmament of heaven there enters nothing that works abomination or defiles. The miasma with its poison, the smoke belched from the chimney with its dark stain, are powerless to sully the purity of the azure. A fitting emblem this of the purity of God, whose name is Holy and who dwells in the high and holy place. The contrast between heaven and earth in this respect is the contrast between God's thoughts and ways and man's. Such is evidently the teaching of this passage: "Let the wicked forsake his *way,* and the unrighteous man his *thoughts.* . . . For *my thoughts* are not your thoughts, neither are your ways *my ways,* saith the Lord. For as the heavens," etc.

Of course man could never emulate the thoughts and ways of God in their measure and movement, their infinitude or their incomprehensible extent. This is not required; nor is it accounted a sin that we should fall short in the measure and quantity. But since we are made in the image of God, it is evidently possible that we should manifest a strong likeness to his thoughts and ways, so far at least as their *quality* and *essential nature* are concerned.

The calculations of astronomers prove that there is an identity between the divine and human mind in arith-

metic and mathematics. The transcription of the work
of God by the artist or sculptor proves that there is an
identity in the appreciation of beauty. The perpetual
tendency on the part of man to produce, whether it be a
poem or a cathedral, proves an identity in the creative
faculty. Similarly, there must be an identity in the moral
and spiritual. What is true to God is so to us. Love,
purity, compassion, humility, are the same in the divine and in the human. It is by the spectroscope of our
own hearts that we are able to determine the elements
that compose the being of God. The original creation of
man in God's image, and the incarnation which showed
that it was possible for God to think and act through
our nature, establish beyond controversy that man can
and should think God's thoughts and tread God's ways.
Though his home is on the earth, he is not the child of
earth but of heaven; and he is called to seek, not the
things below but those above, the things of God and
eternity.

The entrance of sin into our world has altered all this.
Earth's attraction has proved too strong. The transient
and visible, with their appeal to the senses, have rup-
tured the harmony which the Creator intended to sub-
sist between the divine and the human, like noble words
married to celestial music. It is but too evident that the
imagination of the thoughts of man's heart is only evil
continually, and his ways corrupt. By nature, the trend
of our thinkings and activities is downward, earthly,
sensual, devilish. Hence the awful disparity between the
ways and thoughts of God and ours.

It is impossible, therefore, for the natural man to understand God. We humans can know one another only
through the spirit of man which is in us. Our quick
human intuition reveals instantly, and with a flash, what
no words could tell. But we must be like-minded before
we can read each other. It is equally so as between ourselves and God. The natural man, whose tastes and ways

are foreign to God's, can no more receive the things of the Spirit of God than can a savage understand the thoughts and ways of a highly cultured, refined and spiritual man among ourselves. "They are foolishness unto him, neither can he know them; because they are spiritually discerned."

It is impossible, also, for the natural man to please God. God's thoughts are holiness, his ways purity; but those of the unregenerate are unholy and impure. God's thoughts are love, his ways tenderness; but those of the unregenerate are self-centered and injurious. God's thoughts are truth, his ways faithful; while those of the unregenerate are insincere and deceptive. How impossible it is, therefore, for those who are in the flesh to please God! They are not subject to the law of God, neither indeed can be.

It is impossible, also, for the natural man to live with God forever, unless the wicked forsakes his ways and the unrighteous man his thoughts. Whatever the sufferings of the outer darkness may be, those of the inner chamber, to the evil and profane, would be incomparably worse. To the diseased eye, nothing is so excruciatingly painful as the floods of summer sunshine in which age and youth rejoice. And to the unholy soul, no suffering would be more awful than to be compelled to live forever amid the blaze of God's presence with which it was in perpetual opposition and contrariness. If it were possible for such a one to enter the city of God with its light above the brightness of the sun, its music, its festal crowds, its holy exercise, the olden cry would be heard exclaiming, "What have I to do with thee, the Holy One? Thy presence torments me."

It is imperative, then, that the ways and thoughts of the wicked and unrighteous should be forsaken. They must return from Bypath Meadow and reverse the current of their thinking. The eyes that had been fixed on worthless things must be lifted toward the track of the ascending Lord; the feet that had almost gone over the precipice to perdition must run in the way of God's commandments; and the will must be so put in the line of God's will that God may work in it that which is well pleasing in his sight, for the glory of his Holy Name. The ascension gives us the direction, Holy Spirit the power by which the new and better life shall henceforth be lived (Col. 3:1–4). Thus the pure life of the heavens may be brought down to our earth, even as it was in the life of our Lord who during his earthly sojourn did not hesitate to speak of himself as being yet in heaven (John 3:13).

2. SO FAR, AND THEREFORE SO ABUNDANT. Measure the height of the heavens above the earth; attach yourself to some angel-aeronaut, and let him pilot you through their ample spaces to the boundaries of our system, where Pluto and Neptune shine with brilliant glory; then across the dark, silent gulf which intervenes between them and the nearest fixed star—a space so great that, supposing our sun were represented by a two-foot globe, it would be equivalent to the distance between our shores and Australia. From that distant point you might pass on to worlds so inconceivably distant that, though their light has been traveling towards us for millenniums, it has never yet reached our world. Thence you might pass to the margin of the ocean of space, where the waves of ether break in music on their shores. Such are the heavens. In truth, they are higher than the earth; and in precisely the same proportion is the abundance of God's pardon beyond the furthest reach of our imaginings. "He will *abundantly* pardon. *For* my thoughts are not your thoughts, neither are your ways my ways, saith the Lord. For as the heavens are higher," etc.

This is the thought which the Apostle Paul expands in one of the most glowing passages on the page of revelation (Rom. 5:12–21). His point is that whatever was done by sin, and through sin, must be paralleled and outdone by the grace of God. If death came to all men through the trespass of a sinner, of course grace must come to them all through the person and work of the one glorious and unfallen Man, Jesus Christ. If it was possible for death to get such a foothold through one act of selfishness as to reign, it must be equally possible for eternal life to reign through the matchless act of self-denial which shines from the cross. If sin reigned in death, much more must grace reign through righteousness unto eternal life. He goes so far as to say that God gave the law that the full virulence and violence of sin might be discovered. It was as though he gave *carte blanche* to sin to do its worst. At the cross, where the dispensation of law culminated, there was an apocalypse, an unveiling, of the exceeding sinfulness of sin. Only God before that had known what sin really was in its essence and possibilities; from that moment the dark secret was revealed to the universe. But if sin, like the dark waters of the Deluge, covered earth's highest mountains, grace in its abundant provisions was as much above it as the heavens were above the floods when they were at their worst.

There is no parallel between our forgiveness and God's. We must not measure his by ours. We say we would forgive if there were more adequate contrition, more complete confession; or we would forgive if the sin were not so willful and unprovoked; or we will forgive, but we cannot forget. Our forgiveness is not prompt, and we are often cautious and chilly towards those who have offended us but to whom we have become reconciled. With such memories as these, is it surprising that we cannot realize the completeness of God's forgiveness, nor the full meaning of his assurance that he will remember our sins no more? Leave your miserable standards behind, whether of your own forgiveness or that of others; they positively will not help you here. Your fathoming lines are utterly useless, your estimates futile. Measure the height of yonder heavens above the earth—and then begin to compute the abundance of God's pardon to those who return to him with words of confession on their lips and true penitence in their hearts.

The prodigal thinks at the very most that he can only expect a stinted pardon and a servant's fare. That is because his notions of forgiveness range no higher. But the father runs, falls on his neck, kisses him, clothes him with the most sumptuous dress, and seats him at the table with the most royal provision. That is the difference between man's notions of pardon and Christ's.

When God forgives, he ceases to remember; he blots out iniquities as a cloud, and sins as a thick cloud. He does not treat us simply as pardoned criminals, but takes us to his heart as beloved sons. He imputes to us a perfect righteousness; he treats us as though we were credited with the perfect loveliness of the Best-Beloved. He transforms the sad consequences of our sins into blessings, so that as we return from the far country the mountains break forth into song, the trees of the wood clap their hands; instead of the thorn, up comes the fir tree, and instead of the briar the myrtle tree—and these transformations become everlasting memorials of what God's love can do for the repentant sinner. This surely is as much above man's notions of forgiveness as the heavens are high above the earth.

3. SO FAR, AND THEREFORE SO BENEFICENT. Because the heavens are so far above the earth, they are able to collect in their ample bosom the moisture of the earth. The clouds, like barges, bear their precious cargo of rain and snow over the parched earth, to drop the one in fertilizing streams and the other as a warm mantle on the upturned furrows. Thus, because the heavens are higher than the earth, the rain comes down, and the snow from heaven, and waters the earth and makes

it bring forth and bud, that it may give seed to the sower
and bread to the eater.

The very greatness of God is an obligation. Just because he dwells in the ample pavilion of heaven, he is
under a moral indebtedness to help us in our low and
fallen state. The possession of power among all right-
minded men constitutes an irresistible argument for the
relief of sorrow and distress; how much more with the
Infinite One who is Love! If Paul held himself as debtor
to all men, how much more God!

And how graciously and generously he has met the
demand! His word distills as the tender dew, and is pure
and warmth-giving as the snow. Who can tell the number, pricelessness, or glory of his gifts in Jesus Christ?

> *Streams of mercy, never ceasing,*
> *Call for songs of loudest praise.*

The one question for us all to answer is our response
to these descending influences from the heart of God.
We read that land which has drunk the rain that comes
oft upon it and bears thorns and thistles is nigh unto a
curse, and its end is to be burned (Heb. 6:7–8). Have *we*
thus recompensed the grace of God which has fallen on
our souls? Alas for us, if we have! Yet even now they
may be changed to bear myrtles and fir trees. Happy
are they who bring forth flora meet for him for whose
sake they have been tilled. Who can this be, save Jesus
Christ our Lord—whose inheritance we are, and who
has expended on us the bloody sweat of his brow, the
labor and patience of long years.

"Seek ye the Lord while he may be found; call ye upon
him while he is near."

28

THE TRANSFORMATIONS OF GOD'S GRACE

(Isaiah 55:12–13)

"Now—the spirit conflict-riven,
Wounded heart, unequal strife!
Afterward—the triumph given,
And the Victor's crown of Life!
Now—the training, strange and lowly,
Unexplained and tedious now!
Afterward—the Service holy,
And the Master's 'Enter thou!'"
F. R. Havergal

THE wealth of God's abundant pardon is here set forth in metaphors which the least imaginative can understand. Not only were the exiles forgiven, their warfare accomplished, their iniquity pardoned, but they would be restored to the land of their fathers—"Ye shall go out . . . ye shall be led forth . . ." Not only were they to be restored, but their return was to be one long triumphal march. Nature herself would celebrate it with joyful demonstration; mountains and hills would break forth into singing, and all the trees of the field would clap their hands.

But even this was not all. One of the necessary results of the depopulation of the land of Israel was the deterioration of the soil. Vast tracts had passed out of

cultivation. The terraces, reared on the slopes of the
hills with so much care, had become heaps of stones.
Where grain had waved in the rustling breeze, or lus-
cious fruits had ripened in the autumn sunshine, there
was the sad fulfillment of the prediction, "They shall
smite upon their breasts for the pleasant fields, for the
fruitful vine. Upon the land of my people shall come up
thorns and briers" (32:12–13, R.V.). But this, too, was
to be reversed. Literally and metaphorically, there was
to be a complete reversal of the results of former sins
and backslidings. Instead of the thorn would come up
the fir tree, and instead of the briar would come up the
myrtle tree; and it would be to the Lord for a name, for
an everlasting sign, that would not be cut off. An everlasting sign! That surely indicates that sacred lessons
are hidden under this prediction, lessons which are of
permanent interest and importance. Let us seek them
in the light of other passages of Scripture.

"Unto Adam he said, Cursed is the ground for thy
sake; in sorrow shalt thou eat of it all the days of thy
life; thorns also and thistles shall it bring forth unto
thee" (Gen. 3:17–18).

"And the soldiers plaited a crown of thorns, and put
it on his head" (John 19:2).

"There was given me a thorn in the flesh. . . . Concerning this thing I besought the Lord thrice, that it
might depart from me. And he said unto me, My grace
is sufficient for thee" (2 Cor. 12:7–9, R.V.).

Our thought naturally divides itself thus: The Thorns
and Briars of Life; The Royalty of Suffering Them; The
Transformations of Grace.

1. THE THORNS AND BRIARS OF LIFE. In many cases
we reap what others have sown, but some of the times
we sow for ourselves. In yet other instances we suffer
because of neglect: we have failed to use our opportunities, and therefore crops of rank growth cover the debts
of the past and thistledown hovers in clouds, threaten-

ing the future.

Ill health is surely one crop. Many of us, through God's goodness, have known but few days of sickness in our lives; others have known very few of complete health. Disease which fastened on them in early life has sapped their strength and is slowly working its way to the citadel of life. For some, the excesses of their ancestors—for others, their own—have sown the furrow with the seeds of bitter harvests which they have no alternative but to reap. Dyspepsia, cancer, the slow progress of paralysis along the spinal cord, nervous weakness and depression—these are some of the many ills to which our flesh is heir; and they are thorns indeed. Paul's thorn was probably ophthalmia.

Bad children are another. Did David not mean this when he said that his house was not so with God; and that the ungodly, like thorns, must be thrust away with the armed hand?

Was he not thinking of Absalom, Adonijah, and others in his home circle? He was certainly describing the experience of many a parent whose life has been embittered by stubborn, dissolute and extravagant children. When the daughters make unfortunate marriages and sons spread their sails to every gale of passion, there are thorns and briars enough to make misery in the best appointed and most richly furnished homes.

Strong predispositions and tendencies towards evil may be classed among the thorns. To be of a jealous or envious temperament; to have an inordinate love for praise and flattery; to be cursed with the clinging habit of impurity, intemperance, or greediness; to be of an irascible or phlegmatic disposition; and to be so liable to doubts that all the affirmations of fellow disciples fall on dull and irresponsive ears—this is to be beset with thorns and briars. It is like all the goodness of a field going to waste in weeds.

Compulsory association with uncongenial companions in the workplace or the home. When day and night we are obliged to bear the galling yoke of fellowship with those who have no love for God, no care for man, we know something of these cruel thorns. The old punishment of the men of Succoth at the hands of Gideon has its counterpart still: "And he took the elders of the city, and thorns of the wilderness and briars, and with them he thrashed the men of Succoth" (Judg. 8:16).

Difficulties that bar our progress, like hedges of prickly thorns in some tangled forest, may be included in this enumeration. Competition in commercial life makes thorny the path of many a man of business. Perplexities and worries, annoyances and vexations, fret us almost beyond endurance; the tender flesh is pitilessly torn, the heart bleeds secretly, hope dies in the soul; we question the wisdom and goodness of God in having made or permitted such a world where such things were possible. Each life has experiences like these. Messengers of Satan come to buffet us all, making us ask the Lord—not once nor twice, but often—if the stake may not be taken out of the flesh and the soul set free to serve him. Surely, we argue, we could live nobler and more useful lives if only we were free. "Not so," says the Lord. "I cannot take away the thorn—it is the only means of royalty for you. But I will give you my all-sufficient grace."

2. ROYALTY THROUGH THORNS. It is very remarkable that the sign of the curse became, on the brow of Christ, the insignia of royalty. The lesson is obvious— that he has transformed the curse into a blessing; that he has discovered the secret of compelling it to yield *royalty.*

There was some dim hint of this in the words of the primeval curse on the ground, "Cursed is the ground *for thy sake;* thorns also and thistles it shall bring forth unto thee." What can this mean—unless there was an ulterior design in this infliction on the material world? It is not very clear what is implied in this sentence on the ground. Almost certainly there were thorns and thistles before Adam's sin brought a blight on God's fair world; but probably from that moment they became more prolific or the conditions that had been unfavorable to their growth became more favorable, or malign hands were permitted to scatter their seeds afar. But, however it befell, there can be no doubt that God's purpose was wholly benevolent. Cursed is the ground *for thy sake;* that is, out of the obduracy of the soil and its tendency to breed thorns and thistles will come to you the best and highest blessing.

Surely this has been verified. Where has man attained his noblest development? In lands where kindly nature has been most prodigal of her good gifts?—where the soil has only needed scratching to yield a bountiful return? Where life has been free from care, as that of bees among the limes? No, not there. By her profusion—the bountiful provision of all that her children needed for their sustenance and comfort—nature has enervated them; men have become inert and sensual, ease-loving and muscleless. But where the soil has been unkindly, the climate inhospitable, the struggle for existence hard, the presence of the thorn ever menacing the cultivated patch and threatening to invade garden or field—where every endeavor has been required to wring subsistence from the unwilling ground—there man has arisen to his full height and put forth all his glorious strength of brain and sinew. It is through nature's churlishness and stinginess, through man's long wrestle with her in the dark, through the bearing of travail and sorrow of toil, that the supple, crafty, characterless Jacobs have come forth as Israels, crowned princes with God.

Probably this is what is meant in the thorn-crown on the brow of Christ. It teaches that man can only attain his true royalty by meeting, enduring, and overcoming these elements in life which forbode only disaster and loss. The purpose of God is wholly benevolent in the stern discipline to which he is subjecting you. He has set you down among those thorns to give you an opportunity of changing the wilderness into a paradise; and in the act of transformation you will suddenly find yourself ennobled and transfigured. Around your brow the thorns—borne, mastered, subdued—shall weave themselves into a crown, and you shall glory in your infirmities.

What a magnificent picture this gives of the possibilities of sorrow! Too many estimable people fret against God's ordering of their lives, and his permission of the evils which afflict them. Like Paul, they are always praying to be delivered. But God is too good to answer these blind requests. The thorns remain; they must grapple with them, as did the old monks when they chose some tangled swamp as the site of a new monastery. No alternative is afforded. And in proportion as we patiently submit ourselves to our Father's appointment, we come to see the reasonableness and beneficence of his design, and find ourselves adopting the thistle as our badge. We discover that it has been the means of unfolding and perfecting our character, of giving royalty and dignity to our demeanor, and making us kings by right of conquest as well as by right of birth.

3. THE TRANSFORMATIONS OF GRACE. "Instead of the thorn shall come up the fir tree; and instead of the briar, the myrtle tree." "My grace is sufficient for thee; my strength is made perfect in weakness." "I will therefore glory in my infirmities."

(a) God gives us new views of dark things. What we thought was punishment turns out to be the chastening of a Father's love. The knife is not that of the destroyer but that of the surgeon. What seemed to be unto death is shown to be achieving a fuller life. The fire that had threatened to consume only shrivels our bonds so that we walk freely over the glowing embers. We are permitted to stand beside God on the Mount while he passes by and proclaims his name, and gives his reasons, and takes us behind his providences. That illness was sent to rid the system of a poisonous infection that had otherwise proved fatal. That child was permitted to be deformed by a terrible accident because in no other way could she have been saved from a dark temptation, to which she must have yielded. That commercial disaster befell because the young children of the household would have been enervated by too much luxury. The thorns change to myrtles when God shows his reasons.

(b) God makes our sorrow and losses occasions for giving more grace. There are two ways of helping the soul bent double under some crushing load. The burden may be removed; or additional strength, equal to its weight, may be inbreathed. The latter is God's choice way of dealing with his children. And if we were wise, we would not pray for the extraction of the thorn but claim the greater grace. Oh, how precious the trial is then! How many a sufferer has had to bless God for pain! To how many the rack has seemed like a bed of down, and the torture chamber the vestibule of heaven! Thorns, under such emotions, are changed to fir trees, and briars to myrtles.

(c) The grace of God actually transforms awkward and evil dispositions, both in ourselves and others. Softness becomes meekness; cowardice gentleness; impulsiveness enthusiasm; meanness thrift; niggardliness generosity; cruelty consideration for others; irritability and vehemence patience and longsuffering. God did not destroy the Roman Catholic pulpits at the time of the Reformation—he did better, he filled them with gospel preachers. Similarly, he does not destroy any of our natural characteristics when he brings us to himself; he only eliminates the evil and develops the good. The evil tenant leaves, making room for the new and holy spirit.

Where sin had reigned unto death, grace now reigns unto eternal life. The thorns of passion and temper are replaced by fir trees, and the briars by myrtles. He takes the heart of stone out of our flesh and gives us a heart of flesh. "In the habitation of jackals, where they lay, is grass with reeds and rushes" (35:7, R.V.).

(d) How glad is the wife, when, instead of the brute-like cruelty which reigned in her husband's life, there is gentleness and consideration. How rejoiced is the mother Monica when her Augustine is no longer the slave of passion, but clothed, subdued, restored to his right mind, is seated at the feet of Jesus! How indicative of the power of Christ it is to see a nation of savages so transformed that the arts of civilization and the practices of Christianity flourish where once the cannibal dance and demon worship held undisputed possession.

(e) When the discipline has done its work, it is removed. The Great Husbandman knows well the delicacy of the grain, and he will not always be threshing. You have had your full experience of thorns and briars, and have borne and not fainted; but now, since the lesson has been learned with lowly submission, the discipline will be removed. Your Joseph lives, and you shall see him again and clasp him to your arms. You shall embrace a Samuel, whose prattle will make you forget the smarts of the adversary. You shall receive seven times as much as was swept away from you so suddenly. You shall come again out of the land of the enemy. Instead of the thorn, the fir; instead of the briar, the myrtle— because they have accomplished the purpose for which they were sent.

These glowing predictions were partially fulfilled in the restoration of Israel under Ezra and Nehemiah; and no doubt they would have been more fully realized if there had been more perfect faith in the divine promises.

These glowing words, however, shall be perfectly fulfilled in those coming days when Israel shall return to the land from all lands whither her people have been scattered. Their conversion, the apostle tells us, shall inaugurate the times of refreshing, of which the prophets have spoken from the beginning of the world. Then will creation be delivered from the bondage of corruption into the glorious liberty of the children of God. Then shall mountains be orchestras of songs, and the trees vocal with melody. Then shall the ancient curse be removed from off the earth, and the malignant influence of the great enemy of God's work be forever at an end. Then shall earth smile and sing, as in the day of her creation. It shall be to the Lord for a name, for an everlasting sign that shall not be cut off. And the story shall be recited throughout the universe, for evermore, of the sufficiency of God's love to cope with and overcome every manifestation of evil and self-will that may rear itself against its sway.